Conquest of Persia

By Alexander Geiger

Prime Directive (2013)
Flood Tide (2019)
Conquest of Persia (2019)
Immortal Alexandros (2020)
Funeral Games (2021)

Book Three of the Ptolemaios Saga

Conquest of Persia

*An Epic Novel of the Triumph of
Alexander the Great*

Alexander Geiger

Requests for permission to make copies of any part of the work may be sent to:

Permissions Department
Ptolemaios Publishing & Entertainment, LLC
668 Stony Hill Road, Suite 150
Yardley, PA 19067

www.PtolemaiosPublishing.com

ISBN-13: 978-0-9892584-6-3 (pbk)
ISBN-13: 978-0-9892584-7-0 (ebook)

Library of Congress Control Number: 2019937858

Cover Design: Scott Schmeer, Prometheus Training, LLC

The author of this work is available to speak at live events. For further information, please contact the author at Alex@AlexanderGeiger.com

First Edition

Manufactured in the United States of America

To the memory of Alice Geiger,
who taught me the meaning of unconditional love.

Table of Contents

". . . courage is the knowledge of the grounds of fear and hope . . ."

Plato, Laches, 196[1]

---

[1] From *The Dialogues of Plato,* translated by B. Jowett (3rd ed., Oxford University Press, 1892)

Maps and Animated Battle Depictions[2]

---

[2] In lieu of black-and-white maps and static battle depictions in this book, color maps and animated depictions of battles are available at AlexanderGeiger.com.

Conquest of Persia

List of Principal Characters[3]

Alexandros Aniketos (356-323) – King of Macedonia (336-323)

Antigone (unk-unk) – Philotas's mistress

Antigonos Monophthalmos (c. 382-301) – Military commander under both Philippos and Alexandros; appointed satrap of Phrygia by Alexandros

Antipatros (397-319) – Macedonian nobleman; served as regent under both Philippos and   Alexandros

Aristandros of Telmessos (c. 380-331) – Alexandros's seer

---

[3] Each of the following characters is an actual historical figure. The numbers in parentheses refer to the year of birth and death of that figure, to the extent these dates are known. All years are B.C.E. In some cases, the actual dates are either uncertain or in dispute. In those cases, the year in question is preceded by a c. In a few cases, the actual dates are simply lost to the shifting sands of time.

It is important to remember, however, that this is a work of fiction. The author has taken some liberties with a few of his characters. For example, the date of Kleitos's birth is uncertain but he was probably several years older than depicted in this book. The reader should not draw any conclusions from the dates of death listed here about the lifespan, fate, date of death, or manner of demise of any character. To find the answers to all those questions, the reader should read the book. Simply looking at a List of Principal Characters would be just too easy.

Aristoteles (384-322) – Alexandros's teacher in Mieza

Arrhidaios (358-317) – Alexandros's half-wit half-brother

Artabazos (c.387-c.328) – Persian nobleman; father of Barsine and Artakama, among others

Artakama (347-unk) – Artabazos's daughter; Barsine's sister

Barsine (355-309) – Alexandros's mistress

Bessos (unk-329) – Satrap of Baktria

Dareios (c.380-330) – Persian Emperor (336-330)

Hephaistion (356-324) – Alexandros's closest friend

Kallisthenes (c.368-327) – Aristoteles great nephew; accompanied Alexandros as campaign historian

Kassandros (358-297) – Antipatros's son

Kleitos Melas (c.357-327) – A commander in Alexandros's army

Kleopatra (354-308) – Daughter of Philippos and Olympias; Alexandros's sister

Krateros (365-320) – A commander in Alexandros's army

Lysimachos (360-282) – A commander in Alexandros's army

Mazaios (380-328) – Persian nobleman; satrap of

Conquest of Persia

Babylonia and Mesopotamia

Nikanoros (358-331) – A commander in Alexandros's army; Parmenion's son

Olympias (a/k/a Myrtale) (377-314) – Philippos's 4th wife; mother of Alexandros Aniketos

Parmenion (400-330) – Leading Macedonian general; served both Philippos and Alexandros

Perdikkas (359-321) – A commander in Alexandros's army

Philippos Amyntou Makedonios (382-336) – King of Macedonia (359-336); father of Alexandros

Philippos of Akarnia (unk-unk) – Alexandros's physician

Philotas (360-330) – A commander in Alexandros's army; Parmenion's son

Ptolemaios Metoikos (c.364-282) – One of Alexandros's bodyguards

Seleukos (358-281) – A commander in Alexandros's army

Sisygambis (unk-323) – Dareios's mother

Stateira (c.365-331) – Dareios's 1st wife

Thais (unk-unk) – Famous Athenian hetaira

Alexander Geiger

Chapter 1 – Fruits of Victory

As she applied aromatic oils to her face and body, Barsine tried to imagine how Alexandros prepared for battle. The last time they had played together, she had been eleven and he twelve. She remembered him as a bright, self-assured, determined kid, who laughed a great deal. She suspected that his life experiences during the intervening eleven years might have leavened his sense of humor, assuming he had any sense of humor left. She looked at herself in the large mirror standing in the corner of her luxurious tent, hefting her breasts and twisting from side to side. Even after four children, her arsenal was as formidable as ever.

She tried to recall the last time she had enjoyed a genuine, heart-felt, spontaneous laugh but all that came to mind were the many instances when she pretended to be amused by the jokes of the men who controlled her life. And she was determined to laugh at the least provocation in the presence of the latest man to take possession of her. Having outlined her eyelids with kohl, she crinkled her eyes in mock merriment as she checked her handiwork in the mirror. It was important, she knew, that her entire face, including her eyes, be in on the joke.

She dressed in reverse order, donning the items she expected to remain on her the longest first. She started with the ankle bracelets, thin strands of gold bearing tiny bells that tinkled tantalizingly every time she moved her legs. Next came the gold bands that circled up her wrists, emphasizing the slender elegance of her arms. The necklace, with the long, agate pendant nestled provocatively in her cleavage, completed her jewelry ensemble. She chose to dispense with undergarments, putting on nothing more than a light linen chiton, the color of blushing peach, fastening it at each shoulder with matching gold clasps, and letting the fabric drape in a graceful arc far down her bosom. She then ingathered the dress beneath her breasts, belted it at the waist, and carefully arranged the pleats, seeing to it that they were even and straight, all the way down to the floor. Finally, she put up her luxuriant black hair in an artful bun, making sure it would cascade down her shoulders at the pull of a pin.

She had done this many times before but never quite so deliberately. Let others bewail their fate as captives. She had a job to do, children to protect. Finding herself in Alexandros's custody was a stroke of luck and she was not about to let it pass her by. She fought the butterflies fluttering in her stomach. She wondered whether he felt any jitters going into battle. Finally ready for Alexandros's visit, she positioned herself demurely on the only chair in the tent, facing the entrance flap, hands folded in her lap, and waited.

She had no idea how long she had waited, having fallen asleep at some point. She was awakened by the touch of a man's hand on her bare shoulder.

"You haven't changed a bit." The man laughed. He was clearly drunk but evidently in a good humor.

She offered him more wine. "I can't say the same about you, sire. Last time I saw you, you were a boy. And now you're the ruler of half the world."

"Flattery will get me every time, Barsine, but you needn't call me 'sire.' I'm still the same boy you remember from Pella."

She smiled warmly, letting her dimples crease her cheeks and the tips of her perfect teeth peek out through parted lips. "I don't think so. I don't remember those muscles rippling beneath your tunic the last time I saw you."

"Let me take a closer look at you." Alexandros put down his wine cup and retrieved an oil lamp from its shelf. He inspected her in silence. "They told me you were beautiful but they have no idea what they're talking about. To call you beautiful is like calling a rose red. Doesn't quite get the idea across."

She blushed on cue, illustrating his point.

"I hope you understand why I decided to keep you as my guest," he continued. "I thought you'd be safer this way than if I'd let you go."

"I'm honored to be your guest, sire. And there's no place else I'd rather be."

"Tell me what's happened to you since last I saw you."

She provided an edited version of her history. She mentioned her two arranged marriages but emphasized their involuntary nature. Understandably she neglected to mention any resultant issue. And then she quickly switched the subject to his military adventures. Alexandros spoke for a long time while she listened, transported by every detail.

"What's that?" she suddenly cried, noticing the bandage on his thigh when the bottom of his tunic rode up.

"Oh, that's nothing." He laughed. "Just a scratch I received the other day."

"You must let me take care of it," she insisted. "I have all kinds of unguents here for the treatment of wounds."

"No, that's fine. My physician already did that. And really, it's no big deal."

But she persisted, removing the bandage and admiring the rapidly healing dagger wound by the light of the oil lamp. "I can do a better job than your physician," she told him confidently.

She proceeded to apply a cooling ointment, carefully rubbing it all around the wound. It was clearly making her patient feel better, so she applied a little more, covering a slightly greater area.

Alexandros would have been more than human had he withstood her ministrations. Soon, the proceedings were far beyond his control. The hair pin came out, the shoulder clasps were unfastened, the belt untied, and the blushing peach chiton fluttered to the floor. He was not interested in removing her jewelry ensemble, finding the synchronized tintinnabulation of her ankle bracelets strangely arousing.

By the time he awoke in her bed the next morning, the effects of the wine had worn off but he was still completely besotted.

****

Dareios, accompanied by a handful of bodyguards, rode all night, never slackening his pace. When his horse could go no farther, he switched mounts with one of his bodyguards and pressed ahead, leaving the poor man behind to fend for himself. When daylight arrived, he discarded his royal purple cloak, took off his armor, removed all imperial insignia, handed it all to another bodyguard, and told him to stay where he was and await further instructions. When his diminishing group reached the Euphrates River after a punishing day of riding, he didn't pause to rest. He swam across, pulling his horse behind him, jumped back aboard, dripping wet, and continued to ride through a second night.

Dareios couldn't stop, even for a brief nap, not only because he was sure Alexandros and his army were right on his heels but also because, every time he closed his eyes, he could still see Alexandros's face, as the Macedonian slashed his way toward Dareios's chariot. He knew that he shouldn't have abandoned the battlefield, that he should have stood his ground and, if necessary, died in hand-to-hand combat with his adversary. As he replayed the scene in his mind, hour after tiring hour, he was unable to understand what exactly had caused him to flee. He had participated in many battles – had been a great soldier, in fact. He was not afraid of death, which was inevitable for all mortals. What mattered was the manner of one's departure. His army was not losing at that critical juncture. From all the reports he had received until that moment, they were well on their way to a famous victory. For all he knew, the Persian army did in fact prevail in the end, notwithstanding his premature departure. Well, actually he knew to a moral certainty that they had lost but only because their commander had fled the battlefield.

Why? What had caused him, in an instant of madness, to throw away a lifetime of training, belief, and achievement? His hasty flight could well cost him his very life because the generals, the courtiers, the nobility, the rank-and-file soldiers, the lowly attendants, the bodyguards charged with protecting him, none of them would stand for an emperor who was a coward. He wanted to rage against the gods who had abandoned him but he was not a particularly superstitious man and he knew he couldn't lay the fault at the doorstep of Ahura Mazda or any of the other, lesser spirits. He accepted the authorship of his own demise and sought merely an explanation. It had to be that visage.

There was nothing remarkable about Alexandros's face as Dareios recalled it during his long nocturnal ride. The Macedonian king's eyes were alert, focused, and burning with joy. His countenance was clear, composed, concentrated, and confident. There was no doubt he was enjoying his work but what had shaken Dareios was the realization that Alexandros knew he would win. It wasn't that the gods had abandoned Dareios; it was more that they had switched sides and were fighting on Alexandros's behalf and Alexandros knew it. At least that was how it seemed to Dareios, in that split second when their eyes had locked and Dareios had found himself running away.

Midmorning, on the second day after the Battle of Issos, Dareios and his three remaining bodyguards were overtaken by a small dust storm and completely lost their way. Stumbling onto an irrigation canal, they followed it upstream and found themselves in a small farming village on the left bank of the Euphrates. They hadn't eaten in two days. They were dressed in dirty, smelly, torn tunics, although they still had their swords and daggers. Their faces were streaked with dust, sweat, and desperation.

Dareios alighted at the first hut they reached and poked his head through the entrance hole, eliciting a frightened shriek. "Don't be scared." He kept his tone level and soothing. "We're wayfarers, on our way to Marduk's shrine. We mean you no harm." There was no response. "Can you give us something to eat and drink?" Still nothing. "We can pay," Dareios cajoled.

Finally, a young girl, perhaps twelve years old, emerged from the gloom at the back of the hut and approached gingerly, reaching out a hand to touch his face, as though unsure whether she was dealing with a man or a specter. "I won't bite, I promise," Dareios said. "Now, where is your mother?" The young girl brushed wordlessly past him and ran away, leaving behind one crestfallen emperor and three forlorn bodyguards.

There was no one else in the hut but they did find some freshly-baked bread, which they promptly devoured. They also took a chance on a pitcher of seemingly clean water. Then they resumed their desperate journey. In their rush, they neglected to leave behind any coins for the bread they had consumed.

Dareios didn't halt his headlong flight until he had reached the walls of Babylon, eight days later. Arriving after dusk, he snuck into his own palace under cover of darkness. The only thing that saved him from being killed on the spot was the fact that the emperor was away and the guards had relaxed their vigilance in his absence. When Dareios was finally recognized by his chamberlain, he bathed, ate, donned his regalia, and suppressed his trepidation long enough to issue a few orders. He had the guards who had permitted him to penetrate the palace summarily executed; he exiled the chamberlain and his assistants, who had witnessed his humiliation, to the farthest reaches of Sogdiana; he ordered all eight gates of Babylon sealed and regular patrols mounted on the walls, in anticipation of the arrival of Alexandros's army, which he was sure was in hot pursuit; and he summoned his court scribe, telling him to bring plenty of writing materials and to come alone.

****

Contrary to Dareios's expectations, the pan-Hellenic army was going nowhere fast. Alexandros had wanted to give chase the moment he saw the Persian emperor take to his heels but, at that point, the outcome of the battle still hung in the balance. Alexandros chose to assist his beleaguered troops and secure victory, even at the cost of breaking off his pursuit of Dareios. By the time the fighting was finished, the opportunity to capture the opposing commander had slipped from his grasp. Rather than mounting a pointless goose chase, Alexandros decided to give his soldiers a much-needed rest.

He did dispatch his second-in-command, Parmenion, with a battalion of infantry and a couple squadrons of cavalry, to the dusty little town of Damaskos, where Dareios had maintained his temporary headquarters prior to the Battle of Issos. Parmenion's instructions were to take the city and capture the rest of Dareios's treasury, harem, and baggage train. But, with the exception of Parmenion's small force, Alexandros, his commanders, and the rank-and-file soldiers all paused to enjoy the fruits of their victory and to contemplate their rosy prospects. They participated in thanksgiving rites, athletic games, musical contests, and endless banquets. Alexandros conferred decorations for conspicuous bravery, made generous distributions of booty, and, unfortunately, delivered many heart-felt funeral speeches.

The troops were in a happy mood. And yet, there was a subtle shift in their celebrations, as compared to the euphoria following their victory at Granikos. That triumph had been a welcome surprise. Certainly, the troops had always had faith in Alexandros and had always been hopeful of victory because people who fight for a living must be optimists by nature but, deep down, they hadn't known what outcome to expect. On the one hand, they considered Persian soldiers unskilled, effeminate, and cowardly (and, mostly, they were wrong on all three counts); on the other hand, whether they admitted it to themselves or not, the Persian Empire itself carried a formidable mystique. Backward and fragmented Greece simply couldn't defeat the unified might of the greatest empire the world had ever seen. When they emerged victorious after a set piece battle against a Persian army, fighting on its home soil, they were understandably overjoyed.

By the time the Battle at Issos rolled around, the pan-Hellenic army had become used to winning. Led by the invincible Alexandros, they fully expected to win against Dareios's hordes. Ironically, they had come very close to losing, notwithstanding their confidence going into the battle. Afterward, having snatched victory from the jaws of defeat, they considered the outcome nothing more than their just due. They were exhilarated after the hard fight, to be sure, happy to have survived, proud of their part in overcoming the enemy, and pleased with whatever plunder they might have gained, but they weren't euphoric. Instead, they were ready to go home.

Alexandros had other ideas. The objectives of the invasion, at least in his own mind, had shifted. The point was no longer the liberation of the Ionian Greeks and the unification of all Greek-speaking people around the Aegean Sea in one great Hellenic League. Even while the Macedonians were busy beating the Persians in Anatolia, the ingrates on the Greek mainland were doing their best to undermine Macedonian leadership of the League. As long as Dareios was around, fomenting rebellion in Greece, and as long as naval forces subservient to Persia controlled the Aegean, the triumph of the pan-Hellenic expeditionary force was bound to be transitory. Alexandros wanted to leave something permanent behind. And besides, he enjoyed waging war and winning battles.

While making plans and preparing to break the news to the troops that their return home would be somewhat delayed, Alexandros permitted everyone to enjoy a few days of rest and relaxation. The men did their best to sate their appetites. It helped that there was, in the camp, a sudden influx of women engaged, whether voluntarily or under duress, in the booming business of prostitution.

Their commanders, of course, indulged themselves as well but they were able, if they chose, to enjoy the exclusive attentions of captive women, rather than having to share them with others. Fast Philotas, for example, gave a new twist to his old nickname, falling at first sight head over heels for a captured Greek hetaira named Antigone. He managed to consummate his conquest in less time than it took his thirsty comrades to finish a cup of wine. Thereafter, he spent his nights gorging his libido in her arms, while Antigone, confined to Philotas's tent, spent her days plotting her revenge against her new, voracious proprietor.

After five days of athletic and artistic contests, solemn rituals, and hedonistic celebrations, Alexandros scheduled one last banquet. At the height of the postprandial revelry, he rose to his feet, called for silence, and made public his plans. There was some groaning, a few catcalls, but no overt resistance. Alexandros laughed off any objections. "Are you telling me," he asked, his voice tinged with incredulity, "that you're prepared to stand up and leave the banquet before the dessert is even served?" A few of the men shook their heads. "That you're prepared to stand up and walk away while a beautiful woman, ready to be ravished, lies there waiting for you?" A chorus of no's rang out. "That with a string of defenseless cities begging to be stripped of their treasure you're ready to turn around and go home?"

"We're with you, Aniketos[4]," the men roared as one.

_____

[4] "Aniketos" was Alexandros's nickname. It meant "invincible."

"Alright then. We'll start our march down the coast to Phoenicia in a couple of days. But first, let's finish the wine and then slake our thirst with our favorite ladies of the night."

Alexandros took his own advice, sending word to Barsine that he intended to pay her a visit after the banquet.

****

Parmenion fretted all the way to Damaskos. A battalion of allied infantry and a couple squadrons of Thessalian cavalry was a puny force to assault a walled city defended by a strong garrison. He needn't have worried, assuming the old soldier was capable of ever being free of concern.

Word of Alexandros's victory, and of Dareios's flight, had traveled to Damaskos faster than Parmenion's troops could march. When they were still two days out and in the process of making camp for the night, trying to stay warm in the bitter cold and driving snow, a messenger arrived, carrying a letter from the satrap of Lowland Assyria.[5] As the man in charge of the Damaskos garrison and the man ultimately responsible for the protection of Dareios's baggage train, traveling treasury,

---

[5] The Assyrian Empire had long since fallen to the combined assault of the Babylonians, Medes, and Persians. It was eventually absorbed into the Persian Empire. Two Persian satrapies, however, continued to use the name.

most of the harem, and many other distinguished guests, the satrap didn't wish to betray the emperor who had elevated him to his high position. He thought of himself as a man of honor and principle. However, he was also a practical man and he didn't believe that either the crumbling walls of Damaskos or his small group of Persian fighters could resist a siege by the invincible Macedonians.

Accordingly, the satrap determined that the most responsible course of action open to him was to evacuate all the people and goods entrusted to his care. At the same time, he also thought it prudent to stay on the right side of the Macedonians, just in case they ended up in charge of things. Hence, the letter brought by the messenger. It advised Parmenion of the exact day and hour of the planned evacuation from Damaskos. And, incidentally, the letter also made it clear that, upon evacuation, the city would be stripped bare of any armed defenders, the gates to the city would be left open, and the column of refugees would be rendered vulnerable to attack.

Parmenion and his small force arrived at the outskirts of Damaskos on the appointed day and "surprised" the long caravan of evacuees. The garrison troops charged with the responsibility of protecting the column of dignitaries and concubines ran away at the first sight of the Thessalian cavalry. The porters carrying the precious goods of the refugees dropped their cargo and followed suit. The teamsters driving the emperor's treasure-laden wagons unhitched their animals and rode away. And the fancy ladies and honored guests were left sitting in the slushy snow.

Parmenion's troops spent the rest of the day taking possession of all the goods, treasure, and captives. The old general insisted that all the spoils be carefully sorted and catalogued. According to the final inventory, his troops amassed 2,600 talents of assorted coins; two tons of gold and silver plate, cups, and ornaments; two dozen of Dareios's purple robes; a score of jeweled swords, staffs, bridles, and chamber pots; and four ornamented parade chariots. They also captured forty-eight high-ranking Persians, numbering among them members of several noble families; a dozen ambassadors, including interestingly enough ambassadors from Athens, Thebes, and Sparta; the wives and children of Dareios's commanders; Dareios's entire household staff, among whom were 277 cooks, caterers, and wine stewards; and the inmates of Dareios's harem, including 69 concubines.[6]

After all the loot was sorted, catalogued, and stored, and after all the fugitives securely locked up, Parmenion took possession of Damaskos, settling his troops in the houses abandoned by the escaping garrison,

---

[6] Dareios had taken his favorite wives, including his number one wife, Stateira, and their three children, as well as his mother, Sisygambis, on campaign with him. As a result, they had all been captured previously at Issos.

and sent a detailed report to Alexandros, appending to it the list of captured goods and prisoners.

Chapter 2 – Marching Down the Coast

Parmenion's messenger reached Alexandros's tent two days later. Alexandros admitted the messenger, read Parmenion's report, and then passed it around among the assembled officers. "We've rested long enough," was his only comment. "Get your men ready for the march down the coast. We're off first thing tomorrow."

People were still milling about in the command tent when Hephaistion, Alexandros's best friend and most devoted sycophant, announced the arrival of two ambassadors from Dareios.

Alexandros arched an eyebrow. "What do they want?"

"They bring a letter from the Persian emperor."

"Henceforth, he is to be referred to as the Persian coward," Alexandros informed him, without a trace of a smile. "Go get the letter and bring it in."

Conquest of Persia

After a momentary delay, Hephaistion returned with word that the ambassadors wished to make an oral presentation before handing the letter over. Alexandros exploded. "Since when do Persian ambassadors tell me what to do? Bring that letter right now! You can kill them if that's what it takes." The letter materialized within a minute or two.

Alexandros read the letter, while absent-mindedly dismissing everybody in the tent with a wave of his hand. "Not you, Ptolemaios," he said to me, without looking up.

After Alexandros read the letter twice, and after making sure we were alone in the tent, he handed it over. "What do you think?"

I read Dareios's letter:

His Majesty, Dareios, King of Kings, to King Alexandros: Greetings.

Your father, King Philippos of Macedon, and my predecessor, King Artaxerxes of Persia, were on terms of friendship and alliance but, upon the accession of Artaxerxes's son Arses, your father launched an unprovoked invasion of the Persian lands. Since you and I both became rulers of our respective lands, you have not sent any representatives to my court to confirm the former friendship that had existed between our countries. On the contrary, you have crossed into Asia with your armed forces and have caused much damage to the Persian lands. It was for this reason that I took the field in defense of my country and of my ancestral throne. The outcome of the battle was as some god willed it; however, if a state of war persists between our countries, the one certainty is that both of our countries will suffer.

I seek to reinstate the friendship and alliance that had once existed between Philippos and Artaxerxes, to the mutual benefit of both of our countries. To that end, I am prepared to cede to Macedonia all the Persian lands to the west of the Halys River, including all of Phrygia, Hellespontine Phrygia, Kilikia, Karia, Lydia, Ionia, and all the Aegean islands off the coast of Anatolia. This is far more land than you have conquered by force of arms and certainly far more land than you can possibly hold. I make this offer because I seek peace and not war. If we continue to war, your kingdom will be destroyed and mine damaged. If we resume the alliance that had heretofore existed between our countries, our peoples will be able to live in peace and prosperity because there is no army on the face of this Earth that can withstand our combined might.

In addition, you have captured my mother, my wives, and my children. If you will restore them to me, I will immediately deliver to you a payment of 10,000 talents of gold.[7]

---

[7] This was an unimaginable sum of money. Athens, at the height of its empire, collected less than 1,000 talents of gold a year from all of its allies and that tribute was sufficient not only to finance the Peloponnesian War but also the building programs of Perikles, which transformed Athens into the architectural wonder of the ancient world.

I urge you to dispatch your own representatives to accompany my ambassadors back to my court, so that all the terms of a treaty can be negotiated and finalized, proper oaths and guaranties exchanged, and peace concluded between our countries.

"Well, what do you think?" Alexandros asked when I had finished reading.

Why is he asking me, of all people? For some obscure reason, Alexandros had chosen to confide in me from time to time. Being the king's confidant was the last thing I wished to become, not only because such a position was rife with potential Prime Directive[8] violations but also because I knew it was a short step from being a trusted confidant to becoming a dangerous former aide who knows too much. "Perhaps others would be in a better position to advise you, sire."

"I'm going to ask plenty of other people, Ptolemaios, don't worry. But right now, I want to know what you think."

I shrugged. "I think, sire, that congratulations are in order." I looked up, trying to determine Alexandros's reaction but his face was inscrutable. "You have

---

[8] The Prime Directive was the paramount commandment drummed into the heads of all time travelers, to do nothing that might influence, interfere with, or change the future course of events.

accomplished everything that you, and your father before you, have strived to achieve. Not only does the Persian coward cede to Macedonia all of the Greek-speaking cities and islands of Ionia but also a good portion of the rest of Anatolia. The age-old dream of the Aegean Sea as a Greek lake will be at hand. And the ransom payment is a nice bonus. If you were to distribute that money among the troops, it would be enough to make each man rich for life."

"Your math is off," Alexandros interrupted. "At best, that's enough to cover four years' wages for the troops. Hardly enough to make them rich for life."

I chose not to argue, although it seemed to me that four years' wages, in a lump sum bonus, would be a nice stake for each man to take back home.

"And so is your strategic acumen," Alexandros continued. "Weren't you the one who told me to march down the coast to deprive the Persian navy of its bases of operations? How is the Aegean going to become a Greek lake if the Persians control the seas? And what makes you think we could trust any oath or guaranty undertaken by that jellyfish?"

"Well, even if you don't accept it, it's still a good offer. Perhaps it could serve as a basis of further negotiations."

Alexandros shook his head. "If you think it's a good offer, imagine what the others are going to think."

"They'll think whatever you wish them to think, sire."

Alexandros laughed mirthlessly. "Go get Kallisthenes," he ordered. "Tell him to bring plenty of writing materials and make sure nobody sees the two of you coming in here."

When we returned, Alexandros turned directly to the scribe. "I'm going to ask you to write a letter for me."

Kallisthenes switched immediately into his attentive mode. "Yes, your highness."

"What you're going to write is confidential. Is that understood? No one is to know what I'm about to ask you to do."

"Anything you tell me, sire, I'll take to the grave with me, if that's your wish."

Alexandros looked at me. He didn't need to say a word. I could see the question in his eyes and I nodded my assent.

"Here, take a look at this." Alexandros handed Dareios's letter to Kallisthenes. "I want you to make a copy. Can you do that?"

"Certainly, sire."

"It needs to look exactly like the original, so someone looking at it would have no doubt it came from the Persian coward. Do you think you can manage that?"

"It's not a problem, your highness."

"Alright then, let's get to it." Kallisthenes set to work. "But there are a couple of minor changes I need you to make in the copy." Kallisthenes nodded. "In the salutation, take out the word king, so it reads 'His Majesty, Dareios, King of Kings, to Alexandros: Greetings.'" Kallisthenes started to write. His ability to mimic the writing style of his Persian counterpart was uncanny. "The first paragraph is fine as it is, except for the very ending. Go ahead a copy it but stop when you get to 'one certainty'."

By the time Kallisthenes finished copying Dareios's letter, with Alexandros's slight emendations, the letter read as follows:

His Majesty, Dareios, King of Kings, to Alexandros: Greetings.

Your father, King Philippos of Macedon, and my predecessor, King Artaxerxes of Persia, were on terms of friendship and alliance but, upon the accession of Artaxerxes's son Arses, your father launched an unprovoked invasion of the Persian lands. Since and I both became rulers of our respective lands, you have not sent any

24

representatives to my court to confirm the former friendship that had existed between our countries. On the contrary, you have crossed into Asia with your armed forces and have caused much damage to the Persian lands. It was for this reason that I took the field in defense of my country and of my ancestral throne. The outcome of the battle was as some god willed it; however, if a state of war persists between our countries, the one certainty is that your army will be utterly destroyed and all your cities will be become Persian vassals.

I seek to terminate the hostilities between us. To that end, I am prepared to permit your army to depart our shores without interference. This is a far better outcome than you can achieve through the force of arms.

In addition, you have captured my mother, my wives, and my children. If you will restore them to me, I will immediately deliver to you a payment of 10,000 talents of gold.

I urge you to dispatch your own representatives to accompany my ambassadors back to my court, so that all the terms of a treaty can be negotiated and finalized, proper oaths and guaranties exchanged, and a temporary truce arranged to permit the withdrawal of your army.

As soon as Kallisthenes finished preparing the new version of Dareios's letter, Alexandros burned the original in a brazier. Then he invited the command staff back "to consider the Persian coward's arrogant and insolent proposal." Predictable outrage followed.

With the advice and consent of the command staff, Alexandros dictated the following reply:

His Majesty, King Alexandros, to Dareios: Greetings.

The Dareios whose name you have wrongfully appropriated inflicted utter destruction upon the Greek inhabitants of the Hellespontine coast, including the citizens of the Greek colonies of Ionia. He then crossed the sea with a mighty army, bringing war against Macedonia and the rest of the Greek mainland. On another occasion, his successor Xerxes invaded again, destroying our cities and burning our fields. In addition, it is well known that my own father Philippos was murdered by an assassin whom your people had suborned with promises of a huge Persian reward.

The wars that you Persians wage are impious and wicked wars. You have weapons and yet you hire assassins to kill enemy leaders, as you yourself recently tried to do, offering a thousand talents of gold to one of my own men if he would kill me. We are not the aggressors in this war. We are acting in self-defense and justifiable retribution for past offenses against us. The justness of our cause is borne out by the fact that our army has conquered most of Asia[9] and I have defeated you personally on

---

[9] The geographic term "Asia" had a somewhat variable meaning back then. To the Greeks, whose knowledge of Asia came principally from Herodotos, it covered a hazy expanse of land stretching eastward from the Aegean Sea but how far it extended, nobody knew. When Alexandros first crossed the

the battlefield. As you yourself observed, the gods, who are always on the side of justice and merit, have chosen the Greek side in our struggle.

You do not deserve any consideration in light of your breach of the rules of war but if you come to me as a supplicant, I will return your mother, your wives, and your children to you without the payment of any ransom. Do not be concerned for your safety, if you decide to come to me. I give you my oath and guaranty that you will not be harmed. And the next time you write, remember to address me as your king.

Alexandros chose Thersippos as his envoy to deliver the reply. He gave Thersippos strict instructions that, under no circumstances, was he to engage in any discussions, explanations, or negotiations at the Persian court. His assignment was to deliver Alexandros's letter and leave, without saying a word.

Thersippos departed with the Persian ambassadors. The next morning the pan-Hellenic army set off for Lowland Assyria and the Phoenician coast beyond.

******

Hellespont "to conquer Asia," what he really meant was conquering the maritime provinces of Anatolia and, in his heart of hearts, he would have been pleased simply to gain control of the Troad and Ionia.

In the wake of Issos, the army marched at a more measured pace, weighted down by tons of booty and dragging a mini-army of camp followers behind. This time around, it took us three days to reach the Phoenician seaport of Myriandros.[10] En route, we picked up Parmenion and his squadrons of Thessalian cavalry, as well as the treasure and the additional hostages they had captured at Damaskos. (Parmenion's battalion of allied infantry stayed behind on garrison duty, along with their own commander, whom Alexandros now named the new satrap of Lowland Assyria.)

After Myriandros, we continued down the Phoenician coast to Gabala, Paltos, and on to Marathos. The inhabitants of each of these ports greeted us as liberators, throwing their city gates open to us, partly because they hated their Persian overlords and partly because news of Issos had preceded us.

Marathos was an important and powerful Phoenician seaport. Its merchants had grown enormously wealthy because their city served as the terminus of the main caravan route from Palmyra and Babylon. It controlled a significant land area, including forested mountainsides and fertile valleys. Its harbor was protected by a fortified island that was impossible to reach by land and virtually unassailable by sea, while the city itself sheltered behind tall, well-constructed walls. It possessed

---

[10] For the location of Myriandros and other places mentioned below, see Map 8 at AlexanderGeiger.com.

a strong navy and employed a decently-sized garrison of mercenaries. Marathos presented a hardened target to any would-be besieger. It reminded me of the difficulties we had encountered during our siege of Halikarnassos. However, it turned out that we would not need to invest and storm Marathos.

Unfortunately for the Marathians, their navy had been conscripted by Dareios, before the Battle of Issos, to assist the Persian naval commander Pharnabazos in his efforts to occupy the islands of the Aegean and make preparations for the Persian invasion of the Greek mainland. The ruler of Marathos, a man named Gerostratos, along with most of the mercenary garrison, had sailed off with the Marathian navy. After Issos, Gerostratos had decided to sail back home but was still at sea when the pan-Hellenic army arrived at the city gates. Gerostratos's young son Straton, who had been left in charge of the city but without the benefit of either a garrison or a navy, looked down from the city walls at the victor of Issos and decided to welcome Alexandros with open arms. He personally led a delegation of city dignitaries through the nearest gate, presented Alexandros with a golden diadem, and surrendered the city to him, together with all its assets, inhabitants, and territories. Alexandros graciously accepted the proffered gifts, took possession of the city, and entertained the young man at a sumptuous banquet, paid for by the Marathians.

After a few days of rest in Marathos, we resumed our march south. By now, our column stretched over many miles. The cavalry squadrons rode on their horses, of course, but almost everyone else had to make his or her way on foot. Our column included hundreds of wagons but they were intended to transport cargo, not people. The only exception were some of the hostages captured at Issos and in Damaskos. For example, Dareios's mother, wives, and children rode in wagons. They were even provided with makeshift tents atop the wagons, which afforded a modicum of privacy. Barsine had her own tent-covered wagon, as did Antigone and a few of the other "special" captives. But all the other noble ladies marched along on foot, together with the less special ladies of the night who had attached themselves to our army, the few eunuchs who had survived the slaughter at Issos and at Damaskos, and the many, many servants, children, and assorted hangers-on who made up our new mini-army of camp followers.

Alexandros was particularly anxious to provide security for the women in the wagons, partly to protect them from harm and partly to prevent their mysterious disappearance en route. He assigned squadrons of Companion Cavalry to ride alongside the captives' wagons, with strict instructions that there was to be no intercourse between the passengers and the outside world. Furthermore, to minimize the risk of fraternization, he rotated the squadrons assigned to this guard duty on a daily basis.

Conquest of Persia

One day, when it was my squadron's turn to guard the hostages, I was riding along with my horsemen. While overtaking one of the tent-covered wagons, I noticed an open flap, through which a graceful hand emerged. The fingers of the hand seemed to be beckoning, whether to me or someone else was impossible to tell. Intrigued, I decided to take a closer look. The owner of the hand proved to be Barsine and she was in fact trying to catch my attention.

Having identified my silent siren, I was inclined to ride on but something caused me to steer my steed over to her wagon. I knew I was in the process of making a mistake, which was unusual in itself because normally I only realize my errors long after it's too late to fix them. And yet, I couldn't resist. I knew I had already done more than I should have, in light of the Prime Directive, when I intervened during the sack of the enemy camp at Issos to protect Barsine and her children. I then compounded my transgression by delivering them to the soldiers guarding the imperial precinct with instructions that they were not to be harmed. I also knew that Alexandros had decided to appropriate Barsine for himself and was displaying overt signs of infatuation. To approach her now or, even worse, to engage in conversation with her, would've been the height of stupidity.

"I trust your ride is comfortable, Barsine," I said.

A dazzling smile illuminated her face. "How did you know my name?"

"Oh, I have my ways," I assured her and dug my heels into Pandaros's ribs, trying to spur him into taking me away from an imminent calamity. My trusty mount, however, chose that moment to disobey orders and continued to trot along tranquilly by the side of Barsine's wagon.

"Well, that doesn't seem fair." Her face blushed. "You never did tell me your name."

Why am I still talking to this woman? I knew I had behaved humanely, if unwisely, in protecting her from rape, slavery, and possibly death in the wake of the battle. Perhaps I had somehow acquired a proprietary interest in her future well-being. And, although I was loath to admit it, her breathtaking beauty was making it harder for me to ignore her. "Metoikos,"[11] I finally managed by mumble after a long pause.

She laughed. "I could tell that much from your accent. What's your real name?"

"They call me Ptolemaios."

"But that's not your real name either, is it?"

---

[11] "Metoikos" was Ptolemaios's nickname. It meant "traveler, alien, stranger, outsider."

"It's as real as it gets."

She didn't persist. "I never had a chance to thank you for your kindness the other day. I don't know what would've happened if you hadn't appeared."

"It was the least I could do." I looked away, trying to put on my most modest expression. "Besides, I'm sure my intervention made no difference in the greater scheme of things." I was talking to myself, as much as to her, trying to assuage my concern that, in rescuing her, I had violated the Prime Directive. There was no way she would know that, of course.

Her smile lit up her eyes. "Other than keeping me and my children alive, I'm sure you're right. But in my selfish, smaller scheme of things, that was an important difference."

I looked around to see who might be listening. My own troopers, who mostly liked me and were mostly not morons, had the tact and good sense to ride beyond the immediate eavesdropping perimeter, leaving an island of privacy around Barsine and me. However, there was no way to tell who might be on the far side of the wagon and certainly anyone with eyes could have seen what was going on, even if they couldn't hear the conversation. If anything, the auricular margin afforded to us by my troopers served to highlight the magnitude of my transgression.

"Well, I'm glad I was there," I finally said.

"I hope one day I can repay your kindness."

I waved her thanks away. "Having a chance to speak with you and to look at you is payment enough." My mind was in full rationalization mode. *If you're going to commit suicide, you might as well do it with flair.*

She surprised me by blushing. "In another time, another place, who knows ...." Her voice trailed off. Then she caught herself. "However, you're taking a chance simply by speaking with me. And frankly, I'm taking a chance by speaking with you."

"Some chances are worth the risk."

"I agree but probably for a different reason than you think. I need to ask you for your help once again. Please don't think me ungrateful. There is no one else I can ask. Do you remember my children?"

"You mean your servants' children?" I corrected her. "Yes, of course I remember them. How could I not remember them?"

When I saved her, she had told me that the father of her children was Memnon of Rhodos, a Greek mercenary commander who had been in Dareios's service and had proven to be a thorn in Alexandros's side. Even though Memnon had died, I was sure Alexandros's enmity against him lived on undiminished. For the sake of the children's welfare, I had suggested to Barsine that she arrange with her serving girls to treat the children as theirs, rather than hers and Memnon's. She had evidently taken my advice.

"Yes, of course, that's exactly what I mean."

Is there some way you could arrange for my children to ride with me?"

"Why don't you ask Alexandros to let the servants' children ride with you?"

"Because it would sound pretty strange, don't you think?"

"Not at all. It wouldn't sound strange at all if you insisted you had to have the services of your servant girls at all times. And naturally they would have to bring their kids along because where else would they put them."

She smiled, causing my heart rate to soar. She had some kind of magical power over me. "I should've thought of that myself," she said. "But I've had very little time with Alexandros and we've been otherwise occupied."

It was my turn to blush. "I'm fairly sure he'll accede to any request you might care to make. And besides, I suspect you'll be able to manage it so he'll think it was his own idea."

She laughed. "Now, how could I ever manage such a thing? Listen, I know we have to stop this conversation but could I ask you one more thing?"

The tinkling sound of her laughter was making it difficult for me to keep my mind on what she was saying. I finally refocused my attention. "Your last request certainly wasn't too taxing," I assured her.

"Well, this one is tougher. Could you find my sister and do what you can to make sure she's safe?"

I was unable to conceal my delight. "You have a sister?"

"I have many sisters but only one of them is part of this refugee train. She was captured in Damaskos, along with some of the other Persian women. I'm pretty sure she's marching somewhere behind us but I'm worried about her."

"I'll go find her right now. Does she look like you? I'm only asking so I can identify her."

Barsine laughed. "Oh no, she is much prettier than me."

"Well, in that case, it's been nice chatting with you." I pretended to ride away. "What's her name, by the way?"

"Artakama," Barsine said when I pulled back up to the open flap. "But you should know she's only fourteen. And her Greek is almost as bad as yours." She winked and let the tent flap fall shut again.

I floated toward the back of the column of marchers, vaguely looking for a girl named Artakama, unable to chase Barsine's visage from my mind. And that preoccupation is perhaps as good an explanation as any for my failure even to consider the possible consequences of my reckless conduct.

****

Dareios was stunned. He'd spent the last two weeks trying to figure out how to disclose his peace overture to his own barons, courtiers, and commanders without losing his head in the process. The idea that Alexandros could turn down his offer had never crossed his mind. Here he was, the absolute ruler of the most powerful empire the world had ever known, offering to turn over to this jejune interloper from a barbarian backwater a huge chunk of his own territory, an area no invader could've possibly conquered, much less held for long. Even Dareios himself couldn't quite understand why he'd sent that letter.

Furthermore, even if the impulsive youth, in his madness and war lust, was inclined impetuously to turn down an offer that no sane person could reject, surely there were cooler, more prudent, more pragmatic commanders among his advisors who would've never permitted Alexandros to rebuff Dareios's peace overture, much less to compose the insolent reply that he was now holding in his hands. If Alexandros's father had still been alive, he would've accepted the offer without hesitation. It fulfilled every territorial dream and ambition Philippos had ever entertained, not to mention the ten-thousand-talent bounty to boot.

After a long, catatonic afternoon, Dareios finally shuddered back to life, shook his head, hollered to his attendants to assemble the command staff, and started to issue orders. He dispatched Nabarzanes to Anatolia to organize the campaign to cut Alexandros's lines of communication back to Macedonia and to take control of the Hellespont. Nabarzanes left immediately, taking with him the surviving elements of the elite Persian heavy cavalry. These formidable knights were to serve as the core of the Persian assault force, to be augmented by local troops that Nabarzanes would recruit among the bellicose tribes of the Anatolian highlands.

Dareios also ordered Pharnabazos to resume the naval campaign in the Aegean, in preparation for the long-delayed invasion of the Greek mainland. As part of his remit, Pharnabazos was also given overall responsibility for bribing Greek leaders and doing everything possible to foment rebellion against Macedonia and the Hellenic League among the Greek city-states.

In pursuit of this assignment, Pharnabazos arranged to meet with the Spartan King Agis[12] at Siphnos, a small island in the Aegean, located about half way between the Peloponnese and Anatolia. Agis arrived aboard a single trireme and sailed out with ten triremes, thirty talents of gold, and the promise of 8,000 Greek mercenaries, all designed to assist Agis in spearheading an uprising of as many Greek city-states as possible against Macedonia. Agis promised to do all he could and, in this respect at least, he proved to be a man of his word.

Finally, Dareios ordered Mazaios to oversee the mobilization of the massive reserves of men and materiel contained in Persia's endless eastern provinces for the coming showdown with Alexandros. All of Anatolia, after all, comprised less than ten percent of Persia's landmass and there was an unlimited supply of fierce fighters inhabiting the hinterlands of Parthia, Baktria, Sogdiana, and the Hindu Kush, seething to be set loose against the effete European sophisticates.

---

[12] Sparta never became a member of the Hellenic League and its leaders had worked assiduously to undermine the League since the day Macedonia assumed a leading role in the League under King Philippos Deuteros.

And then Dareios settled down, in the hanging gardens of Babylon, to sip wine, enjoy the attentions of what was left of his harem, and plot his revenge.

Chapter 3 – Tyros

Alexandros was enraged. In all the years I had known him, I'd never seen him lose his temper quite so precipitously. Of course, it might have been just an act.

The day had begun normally enough. We broke camp on the road from Sidon to Tyros and resumed our southward march. We reached the outskirts of Old Tyros by midafternoon. We found the gates wide open and the city abandoned.

"Where is our welcome committee?" Alexandros joked. "Let's see if we can find somebody to tell us what's going on."

While search parties fanned out looking for signs of sentient life, Alexandros set up his headquarters in the dusty, deserted agora and waited.

"I liked our arrival at Byblos better," he said after a while. "They didn't run away. They welcomed us; they feasted us; they billeted us; they promised never to revert to Persian rule; and then they walked us out of town, just to make sure we were really gone."

"I thought Sidon was the best," Hephaistion opined.

"You would," Perdikkas laughed. "After all, you got to pick a king."

Sidon was the next big city after Byblos on our route down the coast of Phoenicia. It was a large, prosperous port, ruled by a native king, Abdastart, whose Persian leanings were evidently unpopular with the inhabitants. As soon as the pan-Hellenic army arrived, the citizens expressed their disapproval of the king by executing him and presenting the royal scepter and diadem to Alexandros, inviting the celebrated conqueror to designate a successor to their former ruler.

Alexandros was too busy enjoying the sights, the delicacies, and the local vintages to spend time searching for a successor. Instead, he delegated the task to Hephaistion. The elegant sycophant, given a measure of autonomy, chose to exercise his mordant sense of humor. He plucked out a ragged, sunburnt, wrinkled old caretaker named Abdalonymos, whom he found cultivating some flowerbeds in the late king's garden, and installed him in the royal palace. Afterward, when some of the oligarchs questioned Hephaistion's choice, he explained that Abdalonymos was a long-lost, impoverished scion of the

Sidonian royal house. It pleased Hephaistion thus to illustrate the caprice of the Fates.

Remembering the incident, Alexandros turned to Perdikkas, one of his leading commanders. "Maybe I'll let you pick the new king of Tyros."

Our scouts finally returned. "Sire, there's not a soul left in this town," one of them reported. "They took everything they had, their families, their livestock, their possessions. I think even the mice have left."

"It looks like many of the houses have been abandoned for some time, although a few show signs of hurried departure," another searcher chimed in.

Alexandros shrugged. "Well, let's settle down for the night and we'll attack them tomorrow." He issued some routine orders. "After the entire column is inside the city, bar the gates and post sentries on the walls. Set up the kitchen and mess tents right here in the agora and then distribute everyone in the surrounding houses. We'll have a nice feast tonight, get some rest, and then we'll get to work in the morning."

Nobody bothered to argue. We all knew Alexandros well enough to realize there was no point. Plus, it was always possible he might change his mind after a good night's sleep.

The whereabouts of the Tyrians were no mystery. In fact, we could see some of them, as we walked over to the wharves. They were all in what was known as New Tyros. Centuries earlier, the Tyrians had built a fortress on a large island, about half a mile offshore. As Tyros grew in importance and wealth, they kept enlarging the fort until it covered the entire island. The battlements facing the mainland, where we stood, looked impressive notwithstanding the distance between us and New Tyros. The ramparts were built right at the edge of the water and rose to a height of a hundred and fifty feet. The Tyrians left nary a strip of ground outside the wall on which to land, just a sheer, enormous, manmade cliff. And at the top of this cliff, we could see soldiers strolling insouciantly about.

The fortifications of New Tyros were legendary. They surrounded the entire island and were said to be impenetrable. Of course, in order even to attempt to breach them, a besieger would have to reach them first, which was no easy task, because the half-mile channel between Old and New Tyros was deep, turbulent, beset by strong currents, and prone to sudden storms. It didn't help matters that Tyros possessed the strongest navy in the Mediterranean, manned by the best sailors in the world. We, of course, possessed no navy at all.

Over the years, as New Tyros grew, most Tyrians moved to the island permanently. And when the population exceeded the capacity of the island, Tyros sent out colonists to establish mercantile outposts around the entire

Mediterranean, the largest and most famous of which was Carthage. Perhaps it was the dream of Philippos to make the Aegean Sea a Greek lake but arguably the much larger Mediterranean, of which the Aegean was but a gulf, had been a Phoenician lake for centuries. This was the reason why Old Tyros was empty when we arrived. Most Tyrians had abandoned it years ago and the few inhabitants who had remained were easily evacuated to New Tyros when news of our approach reached them.

The notion that we could somehow storm New Tyros against the will of the Tyrians was clearly fanciful. However, as our leader had decreed, we would feast tonight and figure out what to do tomorrow. We milled around the agora, watching the quartermaster's crew pitching tents and making preparations for the banquet, when a cry rang out from one of the lookouts stationed on the harborside wall: "Ship in the channel, sire."

Those of us with nothing better to do rushed over to the quay and, indeed, we could see a galley laboriously making its way toward us. Soon, it became clear that the small ship was ferrying over a group of distinguished personages, judging by their sumptuous attire. When word of the arriving dignitaries reached Alexandros, his curiosity got the better of him and he walked over to join us on the quay.

Eventually, the ship was lashed to a wharf and the distinguished diplomats disembarked and asked to see King Alexandros.

"You've found him," Alexandros called out and, without standing on ceremony, walked up to the group.

They didn't prostrate themselves, kneel, or so much as bow. Instead, a young man, roughly the same age as Alexandros, stepped forward and extended an open, weaponless hand toward the Macedonian monarch in the traditional gesture of peaceful intentions. "I'm Abdimilkos, son of Azemilkos. My father is the king of Tyros." He spoke passable Greek.

Alexandros ignored the proffered hand. "I've heard the name. So, where is he?"

"My father is sailing with the fleet at the moment but he left me in charge in his absence."

Alexandros cast a sidelong glance at the Tyrian prince. "Would that be the Persian fleet?"

It was now Abdimilkos's turn to ignore Alexandros. "The men with me are the leading citizens of Tyros. It's our pleasure to welcome you to our great city. We have brought food and drink for your men and a few trifling gifts for yourself." He nodded to the sailors standing behind the delegation and they brought forward a heavy chest, placed it at Alexandros's feet, and opened the lid. A treasure-trove of golden plates and chalices, alabaster statuettes, glass perfume bottles, silver kraters, pearl necklaces, silken robes dyed a shimmering Tyrian purple, ivory-handled daggers, aromatic spices, and many other exotic goods spilled out. "A small memento of your visit." Abdimilkos smiled. "Now, if you could assign a few porters, my men will deliver the comestible and potables for your men."

Alexandros ignored the treasure chest. "We have some details to discuss," he informed Abdimilkos. "Please join us, you and the rest of the ambassadors, at our feast tonight." And without a further word, he spun on his heels and left. Once beyond the ambassadors' hearing range, he turned to Hephaistion. "Post a guard on the delegation and the crew. I don't want any harm to come to them but I don't want them wandering about gathering intelligence either. At the banquet, seat Abdimilkos next to me. Keep the rest of the delegation surrounded and at the back. And have the quartermaster's crew pick up whatever fodder and slops they have brought for us. If it's edible, add it to the banquet menu."

The feast was a rousing success. The delectable delicacies brought by the Tyrians were every bit as exotic as their presents for Alexandros had been. "The benefits of our far-flung trade routes and shipping lanes," Abdimilkos modestly observed when Alexandros inquired about some of the dainties.

Their local wines were equally intoxicating. Hephaistion practically smacked his lips while sipping it. "It's like drinking nectar." After a few rounds, tongues began to loosen and the level of ambient noise reached a convivial pitch. An underlying tension remained, however.

The word Alexandros wanted to hear and the Tyrian delegates refused to utter was "surrender." After the capitulation of Myriandros, Gabala, Paltos, Marathos, Byblos, Sidon, and all the small towns and villages in between, Alexandros expected an invitation to place his designee on the Tyrian throne and to bivouac a Macedonian garrison in the fortress of New Tyros. The Tyrians, on the other hand, after centuries of dominating the Mediterranean shipping lanes and in possession of an impregnable fastness, didn't seek a confrontation with Alexandros but had no intention of surrendering their city to him, either. If that meant withstanding a siege, so be it.

After spending the entire banquet pussyfooting around the topic, Alexandros couldn't stand it any longer. "I understand the festival of Melqart is about to begin." Melqart was the leading deity of Tyros and his temple the most magnificent structure on the island of New Tyros. The annual festival in his honor was the foremost event on the Tyrian religious calendar and attracted visitors from the entire Phoenician diaspora. "I think it would be appropriate for me to lead the sacrifices this year." Hearing no response, he forged ahead. "You may not know this but the Phoenician Melqart is the same god as our Greek

Herakles." Abdimilkos nodded. "And of course the Argeads, the royal family to which it's my privilege to belong, is descended from Herakles."

"Yes, your royal highness, we are well aware of your descent from Herakles, as well as the equivalence between the Greek god Herakles and the Phoenicians god Melqart. It would indeed be a special honor if the current head of the royal house of Argead were to offer sacrifices to Melqart this year. And as luck would have it, there is a suitable temple of Melqart right here in Old Tyros."

"That's an old, abandoned temple that no one visits any more, least of all the god himself. No, I meant the actual shrine of the god, in New Tyros, which is where the festival will be celebrated in a couple of days."

"I'm afraid that won't be possible, your royal highness." Abdimilkos smiled pleasantly. "As long as the war between the Greeks and the Persians continues, we in Tyros are determined to maintain our neutrality. We won't permit either Persian troops or your troops to enter New Tyros. Regrettably, that means we can't have you attend the festival of Melqart, any more than we would've welcomed Dareios, had he expressed a wish to participate."

"Bullshit!" Alexandros's tone went from conversational chatter to tent rattling shout in the space of one word. An abrupt silence descended on the entire banquet, pierced only by Alexandros's yelling. "You slimy mollusks, you've been the snot smoothing the Persians' way for decades. Their navy is built, paid for, and manned by your people. And you have the gall to talk about neutrality?"

Abdimilkos was too startled by the sudden outburst to respond.

"Nobody but nobody refuses my offer to preside at a religious festival. When is the next time a descendant of Herakles will pass your way, you despicable snail eaters?"

He called out to the guards surrounding the banqueting tent. "Seize them and get them out of here!" And then, turning back to Abdimilkos, he added ominously. "I won't kill you and your delegation right now because you came to me carrying the immunity of ambassadors but I'm coming for you. Your walls can't protect you against the might of my army. You and every citizen of Tyros will come to regret your foolish decision. We will wipe Tyros from the face of the Earth before we leave." He was beginning to splutter. "The only thing anyone will remember of your crappy little port is that Alexandros once came this way and brushed some noxious pests into the sea. Now begone!"

The Tyrian delegation was hustled out of the tent and onto their ship; Alexandros continued to rage. Hephaistion tried to ply him with drink, while carefully removing his sword, hoping to calm him down, but Alexandros kept on stomping around, yelling and screaming. The other participants at the banquet quickly and quietly dispersed to their quarters.

******

In the cool, dispassionate light of the new day, Alexandros's rage had simmered down to a still red-hot but somewhat rational fury. Instead of ordering an immediate assault against New Tyros, which was totally impractical, he dispatched two ambassadors to resume negotiations. The talks evidently didn't go well. The next time we saw our ambassadors, they were being dragged to the edge of the Tyrian battlements facing us. As we watched in horror, our ambassadors were pushed over the edge and sent tumbling and flailing to their deaths in the rocky foam below.

"Send a ship to get their bodies," Alexandros ordered quietly. "I don't care how many additional men or ships we lose. We don't leave our people behind."

The bodies were retrieved and cremated with full military honors shortly after noon. Before dusk, Alexandros assembled his command staff to inform us of his plans. "We're going to build a causeway to that accursed island and we're going kill each and every one of them." He never raised his voice, which made his forecast all the more chilling.

The idea was utter folly. The channel was half a mile wide, more than twenty feet deep most of the way, scoured by a strong current, and lashed by violent storms.

We all looked to Parmenion but even the old general lacked the courage to voice an objection. "You don't have to say it," Alexandros laughed. "I know what you're all thinking. But it can be done and we will do it. Ptolemaios did it with the King's Castle when I left him to mop up in Halikarnassos."

"Comparing King's Castle to New Tyros is like comparing an ant hill to a mountain," Perdikkas pointed out.

"Exactly," Alexandros agreed. "You can walk up an ant hill and you can walk up a mountain. It just takes a few more steps, that's all."

"Is it really necessary for us to take New Tyros?" Krateros asked. "Couldn't we simply let them stew on their island and continue our march to Egypt?"

Krateros was a new addition to the command staff. Those of us who knew Alexandros stroked our chins to cover our smiles. Alexandros surprised us with unexpected patience. "Our strategy, Krateros, is to systematically deprive the Persian navy of their bases. Bypassing their single most important naval base would tend to defeat our strategy, wouldn't it?"

"Even if we succeed in building a causeway to New Tyros, where will that get us?" Philotas asked. "We will be faced with a hundred-and-fifty-foot-tall escarpment, with a lot of defenders on top."

"Which is why we're going to build a hundred-and-sixty-foot-tall siege engine and roll it over there."

This time nobody laughed. There was some discussion of technical details concerning the required dimensions of the causeway to accommodate the siege engine. (We settled on a sixty-foot-wide causeway, high enough to remain above the waves during high tide and during bad storms, and level enough for the enormous siege engine wheels to roll across smoothly.)

"How long do you think it will take us to build the mole, chief?" Kleitos asked.

"A couple of months." Alexandros's tone was so confident, we were almost willing to believe him. "We'll put every man in the army to work on this project," he continued, "plus we'll draft all able-bodied men in the surrounding communities to help us. We have enough cash to pay them and we have enough muscle to make them see the benefits of cooperation."

"But how will we feed everybody for months on end?" Philotas asked. "There isn't enough food in all of Phoenicia to feed our troops, much less the involuntary laborers we're planning to draft."

"Which is why we're going to dispatch foraging parties far beyond the borders of Phoenicia to ask for supplies. In return, we'll promise not to invade their territories. In fact, Philotas, I'm sending you, with your squadron, to some place called Judea. It's to the southeast of here. Their capital is called Jerusalem. I understand it's quite a fertile land. I'm sure they'll be anxious to cooperate with us, if you ask them nicely."

By the time the briefing was done, half a dozen squadrons were assigned to foraging duty in Phoenicia, Assyria, Samaria, Judea, and as far south as Gaza. Other commanders were told to go out and conduct enlistment drives in the neighboring towns. The rest of us were told to pitch in as necessary on the construction project itself. "We'll start by demolishing Old Tyros's city walls and every house, stable, and privy within. We can use the resulting rocks, blocks, and bricks in building the causeway. But leave the temples alone for now, unless we really need the building materials."

We were starting to disperse when Alexandros, with one more assignment to make, turned to me. "Ptolemaios here will be in charge of building the causeway, since he's done it before."

I didn't bother to argue but Seleukos had one last question. "How are we going to convince the troops?"

"I'll take care of it in the morning," Alexandros assured him. "Just assemble everybody in the agora after the morning meal."

******

54

Conquest of Persia

The morning muster didn't go as well as Alexandros might have hoped. The veterans, who were ready to go home after Issos and were only persuaded to stick around for the march down to Egypt by promises of unlimited loot, especially once we had reached the fabled land of luxury on the Nile, were not eager to pause for several months, while they exchanged their swords and spears for picks and shovels. "We're not construction workers," they yelled. "There's nothing worth getting in New Tyros." "Let's keep marching to Egypt." "Or let's go home instead."

"They killed our ambassadors," Alexandros pleaded. "How can you let their deaths go unavenged?" The soldiers piped down but failed to evince any enthusiasm for the mission.

That was the first time I'd ever witnessed Alexandros fail to establish instant rapport with his troops. Even he seemed shocked by their resistance. "We'll have some athletic contests and musical entertainment this afternoon, followed by another nice feast, and we'll discuss how to proceed tomorrow." He shook his head, as if to banish a bad dream, and ordered the bugler to signal dismissal.

When we assembled again the next morning, we were greeted by an altar, several sacrificial victims, Aristandros the Seer standing by in his whitest finery, with mallet and butcher knife in hand, and Alexandros ready to address the troops.

Seeing Aristandros holding a butcher knife brought unpleasant associations to my mind. The specter of his cutting my throat while I slept had been haunting me for months. And, after recent events conclusively established that my fears were based on objective reality and not simply paranoia, I'd resolved to kill him before he had a chance to do it to me first. But killing someone without detection, especially someone who's expecting an attack, is a complicated business. As a result, there I stood staring daggers at Aristandros while he studiously ignored me.

Our commander-in-chief brought me out of my reverie. He raised a hand to gain our attention. "I had a dream last night." He paused, waiting for the last few murmurs to die down. "In this dream, I saw my forebear Herakles, as clear as I see you now. He was standing atop the parapet yonder, on the other side of the strait, and he was beckoning to me. He was also shouting to me but I couldn't make out the words over the roar of the surf. Then he gave me one more smile, waved, and descended into New Tyros."

The soldiers, who were a superstitious lot, listened respectfully.

"I have no idea what this dream means," Alexandros continued, "which is why I've asked our ablest diviner to come this morning and interpret the dream for us."

Aristandros was in his element. The interpretation of the dream was rather obvious (and its authenticity perhaps somewhat suspect) but what mattered was the performance. A bleating goat was brought forward. Aristandros placed a garland around its horns and communed with the animal for a minute before slamming its forehead with his mallet. When the goat sank to its knees, Aristandros slashed its throat with a theatrical flourish, then lifted its still-attached head and watched all the blood spurt out onto the dirt, doing his best to avoid getting splattered in the process. When the bleeding slowed and the goat collapsed to the ground, he moved on to an emaciated-looking ass and repeated the operation. The final victim was a hinny, looking almost like a small horse. It seemed more intelligent than the other two and shied away when Aristandros approached. But in the end, the charlatan worked his magic and the hinny met its end.

Once all the animals were down, three assistants proceeded to butcher them, reserving the entrails for Aristandros, setting aside generous slices of tenderloin for the gods, and preparing the rest of the carcasses for the roasting spit. Aristandros knelt for a long time, surrounded by bloody offal, alternatively staring at the sky above and the gore below, his lips constantly moving in silent prayer or perhaps malediction. Finally, he rose to his feet, a beatific smile illuminating his face, and bellowed to the assembled ranks. "Rejoice, men! The gods will assist us in taking Tyros." There was restrained cheering. "But it will require some Herculean work," the seer added sagaciously. The cheering subsided. "Now, let us join our leader and, incidentally, Herakles's descendant, in offering our thanks for the assistance we're about to receive."

Alexandros took over. "Alright, men. We start by paying obeisance to the gods, then we feast, then we do some work, then we loot Tyros of all its possessions, and then we march on to even greater treasures." The soldiers had seen and heard all this before but somehow they found Alexandros's appeal irresistible. The prayers, paeans, and other rituals proceeded in the usual fashion and by the end of the day, the soldiers were ready to build a causeway across the River Styx, if that's what Alexandros asked for.

When the first galleys sallied out of Old Tyros and we started pounding cedar trunks into the sandy seafloor and dropping large rocks into the resulting wooden framework, the men standing atop the fortifications of New Tyros laughed and jeered. Their amusement waned, after a week or two, as forty thousand soldiers and another sixty thousand local laborers swarmed over Old Tyros, dismantled it, brick by brick and block by block, and a discernible causeway started to emerge from the turbulent waters of the Tyrian strait.[13]

---

[13] See Map 9 at AlexanderGeiger.com for an outline of Old Tyros, New Tyros, and the causeway in between.

Conquest of Persia

I got caught, as I knew I would be. I had managed to arrange for Barsine's children and the serving girls who acted as their putative mothers to be housed near Alexandros's quarters. Eventually, I even succeeded in locating Artakama (who, at fourteen years of age, gave every promise of surpassing her sister's allure) and moving her in with her nieces and nephew. While visiting our commander-in-chief, I found myself holding a message from Barsine to her children. Eventually, I conveyed their reply to her. Somebody must have seen me sneaking into Barsine's quarters and promptly informed our leader.

"I had another dream last night," Alexandros told me when I responded to his urgent summons. "I was hoping to have you interpret it for me, rather than troubling Aristandros with it."

"I don't do dream interpretations, sire," I objected. "You know that."

"Well, maybe you can help me with this one. See what you think. I dreamt I was visiting Barsine. She was in her bed, her body enticingly silhouetted through the thin fabric of her coverlet. I stripped and rose to the occasion, as I usually do, and slipped under the coverlet with her. But when I reached for her body, my hand landed on a hairy bastard instead. I threw the coverlet off in alarm and what did I see, lying there next to Barsine?"

He paused and looked at me. I played along. "I have no idea, sire."

"It was you! Naked as a jaybird. Trust me, not a pretty sight." He cackled. "Needless to say, I was taken aback, in this dream of mine, to find you in bed with my mistress. I awoke immediately and found myself reaching for my sword. It was all I could do to stop myself from tracking you down and running you through, right there in the middle of the night. That's how vivid the dream was." He looked at me again, no longer laughing. "So, what do you make of this dream?"

I hesitated. The alleged dream seemed to be an even more transparent fabrication than the Herakles dream had been a few days earlier. And its intent no less obvious. However, what my response should be was not as apparent.

"Or should I call in Aristandros to help interpret the dream?" Alexandros seemed to be enjoying my discomfiture.

I raised my hands and waved them back and forth, as if to ward off the evil specter. "No, I don't think that'll be necessary. I think we can manage to figure it out without him."

Alexandros nodded. "Yeah, I think so too." Any trace of humor had vanished from his face. "This is how I see it. That dream is trying to tell me that, if I ever hear you've been sniffing around Barsine again, you're a dead man. What do you think of that interpretation?"

"Sounds about right to me, sire."

On the one hand, I knew I'd been saved from committing another grave transgression. I'd been dancing on the edge of the Prime Directive precipice way too often lately. On the other hand, one can get used to anything, including dancing on the edge. And, even though we had conversed only briefly, I genuinely admired this woman. She struck me as quite possibly the most impressive person I'd met during my involuntary sojourn through this vibrant era and it had nothing to do with her beauty. Or so I told myself.

I resolved to refrain from direct contact with Barsine but that didn't mean I couldn't continue to help her children and sister. One consoling thought cruised through my mind. *He didn't say anything about not seeing the children or Artakama again.*

****

Our work was proceeding nicely. Everybody concluded that the faster we could finish the causeway, the sooner we could move on to more profitable and enjoyable pursuits. We settled down to a regular routine, with fresh supplies of timber arriving daily from the forested hills of Phoenicia and ample building materials piling up on the quay as Old Tyros was systematically reduced to rubble. It also helped that the channel was relatively shallow near the coast. In a matter of a few weeks, the causeway extended a third of the way across the strait. Then the water got deeper and the Tyrians got more worried.

On the off chance that our causeway might reach the base of their battlements, the Tyrians started an energetic artillery building program. Almost every morning, when we arrived for work, we could see the skeleton of another catapult or stone-throwing machine rising on the parapet. We were still too far away but I was not looking forward to the day when our causeway came within range of their weapons. The other thing the Tyrians did was to send ships, with lots of archers aboard, to take potshots at my workers. With thousands of men working in close quarters, they could hardly miss, whether they bothered to aim their arrows or not.

Rather than keep losing dozens of men a day, I had no choice but to divert a portion of my workforce toward building screens to protect the workers. Some of the timber that would have gone into the construction of the causeway ended up supporting stretched canvas and animal hides, behind which the construction could proceed in relative safety. In short, we were building not only a sixty-foot-wide artificial isthmus from Old Tyros to New but creating the only isthmus in the world lined by a continuous, twenty-foot-high curtain wall on either side. And the water kept getting deeper and our progress correspondingly slower.

The walls that we were building were far from impenetrable. The Tyrian ships kept coming and the archers and slingers aboard kept shooting. Although they couldn't see my men behind the screen walls, they could make a shrewd guess concerning their whereabouts, so their arrows and bolts continued to exact a heavy toll. In response, I ordered two towers to be built, one near the current end of the causeway and one about half way to the shore. Once these towers were up, I stationed archers and slingers on top of each, whose job it was to pour missiles down on the heads of the rowers, archers, and slingers aboard the Tyrian ships. Pretty soon, it seemed as though half my manpower was devoted to fighting a running battle to protect the other half.

We were just beginning to reach deep water when disaster struck. I was walking on the causeway, supervising the work as usual, when a shout rang out from one of the men atop the farther tower. "Burning ship bearing down on us! Burning ship! Starboard side! Burning ship!"

I ran to the starboard-side screen and pulled the canvas sheets apart. It took a moment for the significance of the sinister sight to register. There were actually three boats: A plain merchant galley, flanked by two triremes. The galley was in flames. There were no oarsmen on the galley. In fact, I couldn't see anyone aboard. *They must've dived off when their ship caught fire.* On the other hand, every oar on the two triremes was manned and the rowers were pulling for all their worth. The triremes were flying. But so was the galley between them. The three vessels acted almost as three hulls of a trimaran. I realized the galley was tethered to the two triremes. There was something strange about that galley, I thought, besides the fact that it was aflame. *Its cargo must've shifted aft, causing the prow to ride way up, well above the water.* I noticed two poles extending beyond the bow of the galley, with some kind of kettle attached to each. Unbelievably, the trimaran was picking up speed, streaking faster than the speed of flight, aiming straight for the end of our unfinished causeway. And suddenly I understood.

I started hollering. "Everybody off the towers!" I yelled. "Evacuate the causeway! Run!"

The men around me put down their tools, wheelbarrows, or rocks in their hands, straightened up, and looked at me as if I were a madman.

"Run!" I yelled in desperation. "Get going! Move! Get to the shore! Run!" I was windmilling my arms, trying to get my message across. Some of the men started to move. I ran to the nearer of the two towers and shook it. "Get down! Get down! Get off the causeway!" I ran back to the gap in the screen to look at the ships again. I knew exactly what was going to happen. I continued to scream as the inexorable disaster unfolded, almost in slow motion, in front of my eyes. Except it turned out to be much worse than I had imagined.

Conquest of Persia

Just before the trimaran collided with our causeway, a man in each trireme started chopping desperately at the ropes tying the triremes to the galley. As soon as the ropes were severed, the triremes sheered off to either side and started rowing back to New Tyros, while the galley, maintaining it momentum, continued to streak toward the causeway. *The cargo hadn't shifted*, I realized. *They placed it toward the stern precisely to get the prow out of the water.* The conflagration was spreading and growing higher, engulfing almost the entire ship. Even the two poles holding the kettles on either side of the bow were now aflame. And the boat was still flying. And then the prow reached the causeway. It was sufficiently high above water level to easily ride up onto the causeway, tearing through the screen of timber, canvas, and animal pelts as if it were made of dried grass. Almost the entire flaming galley ended up skidding onto the causeway.

I continued screaming the entire time as I watched the galley come aboard the causeway, although I can't remember exactly what I was yelling. By that point, everybody on the causeway was screaming and running. Everybody, that is, except the men on the far tower and the men working at the far end of the causeway, whose escape route was cut off by the burning ship. All they could do was stand and watch as the causeway under their feet ignited. And then the poles holding the kettles burnt through and the contents came crashing down. There must have been gallons and gallons of highly flammable oil in those kettles. When they hit the burning causeway, there was a tremendous explosion and a wall of fire whooshed out in a 360-degree circle, moving much faster than the fastest workers could run.

I was in mid-scream when I was engulfed by the zooming wall of fire. Suddenly, I had no air in my lungs, only a searing vacuum. My clothes were aflame and all the hair on my body singed off. I dove through the gap in the canvas screen and kept swimming until I hit the seafloor. Fortunately, I'd managed to avoid hitting the rocks that formed the base of our causeway. When I looked up, the heavens above me had an eerie orange glow, unlike any sunset I had ever seen. Except it was not the sky I was seeing but the surface of the water, some twenty feet up.

Should I swim back up or should I stay down here? But then involuntary reflex took over and I found myself bursting through the surface, gulping for air. Fortunately, the water itself was not on fire but the entire causeway, including the towers, the screens, the wooden support structures, even some of the filler materials were all ablaze.

I started swimming toward the shore, not even noticing the chill of the waves smashing into my face or the sting of the brine seeping into my burns. I swam parallel to what used to be our causeway, unable to take my eyes off the carnage. The causeway was still glowing, except for those black smudges that used to be people. Charred bodies dotted the entire length of the causeway, hundreds of bodies, jumbled one over the other, some of them still moving, some of them still moaning. Somehow, I kept swimming.

****

After the causeway conflagration, Alexandros didn't exactly remove me from command of the construction project. Instead, he placed Perdikkas and Krateros in charge of the entire Tyrian theater of operations, including the construction of the causeway, and told me I'd be reporting to them when I recovered from my injuries. "The causeway will be built," he told me grimly, "bigger, better, and stronger than it was before the accident. And I want you to get back to work as soon as you can. In the meantime, I have to return to Sidon; some things I need to look after."

The urgent business that recalled Alexandros to Sidon was a meeting he had scheduled with the rulers of the Phoenician cities that had previously submitted to us. Each of these cities had at least a few warships, all of which had been pressed into service with the Persian navy under Pharnabazos. However, after the Persian defeat at Issos, and after receiving word from home that their cities were now under Macedonian control, all of these rulers suddenly discovered that their warships were urgently needed at home. By coincidence, Alexandros realized at the same time that it was simply impossible to take a strongly-defended island fortress without a navy. He went to Sidon to persuade all these rulers that they should contribute their warships, along with crews, to the newly-reconstituted pan-Hellenic navy.

It turned out that Alexandros was entirely successful in his entreaties. He was a persuasive young man and the rising power in the region. It also helped that the audience hall in the Sidon royal palace, where the meeting took place, was surrounded by Macedonian troops in order to assure the safety of the participants, all of whom were required to leave their own soldiers outside the city walls and to enter the royal palace unaccompanied and unarmed. Perhaps the presence of their host, the newly-crowned erstwhile gardener Abdalonymos, conveyed a subliminal message as well.

Interestingly, when word spread of the formation of the new pan-Hellenic navy, other squadrons of warships began to arrive at Sidon. Ten ships sailed in from Rhodos, ten from Lykia, three from Soloi in Kilikia. In a matter of days, the pan-Hellenic navy numbered more than a hundred warships. Then, a few days later, while Alexandros was still in Sidon, more than 120 triremes showed up from Kypros. The new pan-Hellenic navy, although it had almost no Greeks in it, was far more formidable than the old navy, which Alexandros had disbanded at Miletos, had ever been. For one thing, it could now deploy a great many more ships than the Tyrian navy.

Soon after the arrival of the Kypriot contingent, Alexandros decided to return to Tyros with his newly found navy and resume siege operations. Rumors circulated of further defections from Pharnabazos's Persian fleet but Alexandros was too impatient to wait any longer. He simply sent word to all the Macedonian-controlled ports that any defecting ships wishing to join the pan-Hellenic navy should report for duty at Tyros.

Like a child enjoying a new toy, Alexandros couldn't get enough of his navy. He appointed himself commander of the fleet and decided to sail to Tyros aboard one of his ships, rather than making his way back on shore. He also embarked most of the foot soldiers who had accompanied him to Sidon, turning them overnight into marines, without the benefit of any training in the specialized tactics required for boarding enemy ships at sea. "Fighting is fighting," was his response to anyone who implied that different skills might be involved.

When the approach of Alexandros's ships was reported to the Tyrian navarch, he sailed out with his navy to intercept them and presumably destroy them before they could join the siege. There was no doubt in the navarch's mind that any fleet manned by Greeks was no match for the Tyrian sailors and marines. Then the pan-Hellenic armada appeared on the horizon. As the two fleets closed on each other, it became clear to the Tyrian navarch that he was not facing Greek sailors and, more importantly, that the enemy had many more ships than he had at his command.

The Tyrian navarch made the sensible choice and ordered his fleet to turn around and head back home. Alexandros, as soon as he realized there would be no naval engagement that day, saw an opportunity and didn't hesitate to seize it. "They're running away," he yelled. "Let's beat them back to the Northern Harbor!"[14]

Another epic regatta ensued, the fifty Tyrian triremes racing desperately not only to save their own lives but also the lives of their compatriots because, if the pan-Hellenic ships reached the harbor first, there would be very little to stop the marines on board from storming the city itself. It was a close race but the Tyrians reached the Northern Harbor barely ahead of Alexandros's lead ships. Upon reaching the mouth of the harbor, the last three Tyrian triremes turned around and engaged the pursuing ships. It was a hopeless stand. All three triremes were sunk and their crews killed in short order. However, their sacrifice bought enough time for the rest of the Tyrian fleet to reorganize just inside the harbor.

When the pan-Hellenic armada reach the harbor entrance, it found itself confronting an orderly arc of Tyrian triremes, lined up side by side, with their menacing, armored beaks pointing straight at their pursuers. Alexandros had no choice but to call off the attack,

---

[14] New Tyros had two excellent harbors: the Northern Harbor, which faced northeast, and the Egyptian Harbor, which faced southeast. For ships approaching from Sidon, the Northern Harbor was the closer of the two.

contenting himself with bottling up the Tyrian fleet in the Northern Harbor.

The situation in the Egyptian Harbor proved to be similar. The Tyrians had enough naval power to defend the harbor but weren't strong enough to break through a pan-Hellenic blockade. In fact, Alexandros quickly established a cordon around the entire island, cutting off any incoming supplies as well as all avenues of escape. And then he turned to me, telling me to resume building the causeway.

****

The rippling ramifications of our victory at Issos, as well as our subsequent successes down the Phoenician coast, continued to reverberate throughout the Aegean basin, making an impression as far as the lower reaches of the Peloponnesian Peninsula. Kleandros, who had been laboring mightily for almost a year to recruit mercenaries for our cause in the Peloponnese and throughout the Greek mainland, suddenly found himself flooded with volunteers, once word of Alexandros's victory, and his consequent wealth, became the common currency of gossip. After Kleandros had assembled a select crew of 4,000 heavy infantry soldiers, it took him another six months to march up the spine of the Greek mainland, across Macedonia, the entire length of Thrake, across the Hellespont, and back down the western coasts of the Aegean and the Mediterranean, all the way to Old Tyros.

Not only did Kleandros bring with him much needed reinforcements, he also brought other good news besides. He informed us that Pharnabazos's fleet was rapidly melting away and was no longer able to prevent Greek ships from crossing the Hellespont at will. Even more unexpectedly, Nabarzanes, in command of the elite Persian heavy cavalry, reinforced by savage local fighters, had run into a stone wall in his efforts to cut Alexandros's lines of communication back to Macedonia. He had fought three pitched battles against the undermanned forces of Antigonos Monophthalmos, the old Macedonian general whom Alexandros had named satrap of Phrygia. Good old One-Eye, despite having only one Macedonian infantry battalion at his disposal, had beaten Nabarzanes, one of Dareios's leading commanders, every time they met on the battlefield. Finally, Nabarzanes was forced to return to Dareios in Babylon with his tail between his legs.

Hearing all this, Alexandros threw himself into the prosecution of the siege with renewed vigor. He assigned Kypriot and Phoenician engineers, who had arrived with their respective navies and who had highly specialized expertise in the assembly of maritime weaponry, to mount siege engines, artillery pieces, and battering rams aboard barges and transport ships. At the same time, he visited our construction project daily to encourage the enthusiasm of the workforce. The mole was growing much more quickly now because we had passed the deepest part of the channel, because the harassment by Tyrian ships had ceased, and because we were getting more efficient at getting the job done.

By this time, we had been working on the causeway for more than six months. It was the height of summer. The crews worked by torchlight through the night to accelerate our progress but they had to take a couple of hours off in the middle of each day to escape the worst of the heat. Remarkably, through all those months, Dareios never lifted a finger to help the city that had been a faithful Persian ally for two centuries. In response to many urgent appeals, he claimed to be busy making preparations for the coming showdown with Alexandros. In truth, he was still too shaken by his encounter at Issos to hazard a fresh confrontation. The many daughter colonies of Tyros never came to the assistance of their ancestral home either, despite fulsome promises of succor which had undoubtedly contributed to the stiff-necked attitude of the Tyrian ambassadors. Representatives of powerful and wealthy Carthage, the greatest of Tyros's colonies, who had been visiting the island fortress while Abdimilkos was negotiating with Alexandros, quietly slipped away when hostilities broke out and were never heard from again.

Finally, the tip of our causeway approached within shouting distance of the battlements of New Tyros. At that point, I was forced to divert some of my crews because Alexandros needed men for the erection of catapults, mangonels, mechanized slings, and stone throwers of all kinds. When the day arrived on which the end of the mole got within artillery range, while we were preparing to dodge incoming missiles launched from the Tyrian battlements, Alexandros ordered all his newly-assembled equipment to be rolled and rowed into position. And then the bombardment of New Tyros began.

From the machines positioned at the end of the causeway and from the floating artillery pieces lying at anchor all around the city, Alexandros initiated a relentless barrage of stones, bolts, arrows, and assorted other missiles. Some of the heavy boulders battered the building blocks at the base of the battlements. Lighter rocks, but still larger than a man's head, flew over the ramparts and destroyed houses inside the city, killing the inhabitants within. (The men called these rocks "head stones.") Arrows and bolts picked off defenders stationed on the parapet, killing them one by one. When these assorted missiles missed their intended targets, which was most of the time, they landed in the streets and broke through roofs, indiscriminately killing and maiming the civilian population.

The Tyrians fought back as best they could, despite running out of provisions, projectiles, and personnel. They shot flaming arrows into our siege engines and down onto our causeway, starting a few small fires. The fires were quickly extinguished and the causeway continued its implacable advance toward the base of the city walls. The Tyrians erected screens made of wicker, hides, and cloth, trying to catch the incoming missiles, but our stones quickly smashed through the screens.

Conquest of Persia

When the large boulders began to loosen the foundations of some of the battlements, Alexandros ordered the floating battering rams into action, pounding the weakened walls and causing some sections to collapse. The Tyrians worked feverishly to strengthen and rebuild the walls or to erect new screen walls behind any collapsed sections. They also toppled large boulders into the water at the base of the battlements to hinder the approach of our ships.

The bombardment of New Tyros continued for four days and nights. At that point, the causeway reached the escarpment and we rolled our giant siege tower into position. Unfortunately, it was simply impossible to build a rolling tower taller than the Tyrian fortifications. As a result, even with the tower in place, it was still necessary to place ladders on top of the tower in order to enable our soldiers to scale the wall. When they attempted to do just that, the Tyrians were ready. The poured superheated sand and gravel down onto their heads, which worked its way inside their armor, causing horrific burns. The attempt to scale the wall from the siege tower had to be abandoned.

However, while the defenders were busy fighting off the attempted assault from our siege tower, a section of the wall near the Egyptian Harbor collapsed. Two companies of Macedonian marines immediately disembarked near the rupture and tried to clamber over the jumble of fallen building blocks and construction debris. They were driven back with heavy losses but the gap in the fortifications remained. It was only a matter of time and determination until Alexandros found a way to exploit this vulnerability. He gathered all his amphibious assault troops in a special camp on the outskirts of Old Tyros while directing all his commanders to maintain the barrage against New Tyros day and night.

The assault battalion consisted of eight hundred of the very best Macedonian infantry veterans in the army. For two days, they practiced maneuvers under Alexandros's watchful eye, rested, ate, and drank. On the evening of the second day, Alexandros scheduled a service of propitiation and a lavish feast. Aristandros was in attendance, tasked with reading the signs as usual. With his nose in the steaming entrails, he could clearly see that Alexandros was both confident of a breakthrough and impatient. Therefore, he rose to his feet and announced, in his most stentorian and sanguinary tones, that Macedonian troops would be inside the city of New Tyros before the end of the current month. Naturally, loud cheering greeted his oracular pronouncement. There was only one problem: It was the twenty-seventh day of Gorpiaios. The current month would end the next day.

Alexandros seemed unconcerned. "Eat well, men," he told them, "for we'll be eating inside New Tyros tomorrow and I hear they're down to eating grass and earthworms over there." The men took him at his word. They ate well and they slept well, secure in the knowledge that Aristandros was inerrant and Alexandros invincible.

Conquest of Persia

Overnight, the floating catapults concentrated their barrage on the weak point of the wall near the Egyptian Harbor, driving back the Tyrian workers who were trying to effect repairs and enlarging the breach even further. The next morning, before dawn, the amphibious battalion arrived and launched an immediate assault, led by their commander Admetos. At the same time, the Kypriot and Phoenician ships circling the island commenced a sudden attack against the Tyrian ships bottled up in the Egyptian Harbor.

The Tyrians fought back ferociously. Admetos, fighting at the point of the attack, was killed by an axe through his skull. His position was taken over by Alexandros himself. The allied warships in the harbor, advancing despite a hail of arrows, bolts, and random trash, succeeded in ramming, boarding, and sinking one Tyrian vessel after another. The Macedonian veterans fighting in the breach, anxious to keep their king safe, bounded from building block to building block, killing anyone who got in the way. When the allied warships reached the wharf and discharged their complements of marines, the Tyrian defenders found themselves threatened from two sides and retreated from the battered remnants of their wall. They barricaded the streets and fought, alongside their wives and children, on the barricades, on the roofs, in their courtyards, reception halls, bedrooms, and kitchens, in their gymnasia, baths, and temples. But the Macedonians and their allies just kept coming.

When the fighting finally died down, seven thousand men and scores of women and children lay slain in the streets. Thirty thousand men, women, and children survived and were sold into slavery. Fifteen thousand more disappeared, presumably managing to make their way off the island under the merciful cover of the approaching night. The city itself was looted and burnt to the ground, save the great Temple of Melqart, which was preserved on Alexandros's express order.

It was in this magnificent edifice that Alexandros finally presided, while the fires in the city were still burning, over the annual celebration of Melqart's reign, an honor that had been denied to him by the Tyrian ambassadors exactly eight months earlier. He followed the traditional Tyrian liturgy to the letter, omitting only one time-honored aspect of the ceremony. "We have no need of sacrificial victims today," he told Aristandros. "We've had more than enough already."

******

The rest of our march to Egypt was uneventful, with one exception.

Chapter 4 – Gaza

"Will the adulation never stop?" Alexandros cried out in mock frustration. He'd been ready to leave Tyros for the past eight days but a steady stream of envoys, well-wishers, supplicants, and functionaries kept him confined to his sumptuous, spoils-of-war command tent. In the meantime, the fabulous riches of Egypt beckoned. He'd recruited local guides and acquired indispensable intelligence about the remainder of our trek to Egypt; he'd dispatched foraging parties to collect victuals and fodder in Lowland Assyria, Phoenicia, Samaria, and Judea; he'd trained a corps of sappers and engineers to quickly build and then equally quickly dismantle our nightly encampments along the route of our journey; he'd ordered his newly-acquired navy to sail along the coast of the Mediterranean as it turned from Asia to Africa and to establish food, fodder, and fresh water depots at regular intervals along our projected expedition once we'd made our way beyond Gaza and entered the desert guarding the approaches to Egypt; he'd established the order of march and appointed commanders for each segment of our train and each squadron of the screening cavalry. He was ready to go. He wanted to cover the remaining three hundred miles from Tyros, the last major port in Phoenicia, to Pelousion, the principal port on the eastern branch of the Nile delta, in thirty days. There was no particular reason to rush but Alexandros knew no other speed. And still, he couldn't leave.

"His excellency, the mayor of Jaffa," Hephaistion announced. "It's a small port along our projected route," he added under his breath. An old man, in a gleaming white robe, wearing a tall, pointed hat and a long, pointed beard, entered, knelt, and bowed deeply to the king. He said something in a language none of us understood. "Get him to stand up," Alexandros ordered, "and find a translator."

In short order, the mayor conveyed the pleasure of the entire population of his town at the prospect of the forthcoming visit of the valiant Macedonian conqueror and commended his humble hamlet to his care. He mentioned some gifts and the availability of abundant seafood. He asked that, if possible, the army be bivouacked somewhere else. He was dismissed in less than five minutes, with assurances that no harm would come to his town or its people.

Hephaistion cleared his throat. "There is a large delegation from the Hellenic League waiting outside."

"How large?" the king wanted to know.

"Fifteen ambassadors and many more attendants."

"Where are you all from?" Alexandros asked in lieu of greeting when the delegation was admitted. There followed a roll call of all the important member states of the Hellenic League, of which Alexandros was the titular leader. He seemed bemused. "Welcome. Always a pleasure to see ambassadors who can speak Greek."

"Sire, we've been sent," the chief of mission began, orating in a formal voice, "on behalf of all the members of the League, to convey our congratulation for the great victory gained by the pan-Hellenic army at Issos. As a token ..."

"That was nine months ago," Alexandros observed, speaking in a stage whisper to Hephaistion.

The chief ambassador ignored the interruption. "As a token of our appreciation and gratitude ..."

"They were waiting to see whether our victory would stick," Hephaistion replied.

"As a token of our appreciation and gratitude for protecting the freedom and safety of all Greeks ..."

"What do you think was their original mission, when they set sail?"

The ambassador, growing increasingly flustered, paused uncertainly. "Here," he finally said, handing a beautifully wrought, heavy, gold wreath to the king. "From the League, sire."

Alexandros nodded to one of the guards to take possession of the expensive present. Then he addressed the entire delegation. "Thank you. We'll have you join us for our evening meal tonight and you can tell us all about conditions back home then. But now, if you'll forgive me, I've got others waiting."

As the Hellenic League delegation was ushered out, he turned to Hephaistion. "What do you think they would've done with that wreath had our siege of Tyros failed?"

Hephaistion didn't miss a beat. "They would've offered it to the king of Tyros, of course." All the Macedonians in the tent laughed.

The next group of supplicants consisted of about a dozen bearded men, all wearing white pants, fine linen tunics cinched at the waist with colorful belts, and elaborate white woolen turbans. Their leader's outfit was much more extravagant because, in addition to the garments worn by his colleagues, he also wore a beautiful, embroidered, floor-length robe and a wide, fancifully decorated belt. The bottom of his robe was weighted down with lots of little bells and pomegranate ornaments, as a result of which he tinkled brightly with every step he took.

As if all these layers were not enough, he had also put on a sort of apron, except he seemed to be wearing it backward. It covered his entire rear end but left a gap in the middle of his front. On his chest rested a smallish silver breastplate, decorated with twelve large precious stones. The pièce de résistance of his ensemble, however, was his chapeau. His elaborately wound white turban was much larger than those of his fellow delegates and it was embellished by a wide golden diadem, which carried some kind of indecipherable inscription.

He was a tall man, made even taller by his enormous headgear. He stood rigidly erect, perhaps as a reflection of his dignity or maybe to keep his hat from falling off. In his hands was a large golden tablet. He didn't prostrate himself, kneel, or so much as bow his head.

It took Hephaistion a moment to recall who was next on the audience list. Finally, he found his place. "His holiness, the high priest of Jerusalem."

Alexandros was amused by the stiff-necked stance of the old man and beckoned him to approach closer. "What's your name?"

Although the high priest didn't speak Greek either, he'd had the foresight to bring a translator with him. "His name is Jaddua son of Yohanan. He's a holy man, chosen by god," the translator said.

"Which god?" Alexandros was always interested in learning more about the local deities.

"Our god," the shocked translator blurted out, a look of consternation on his face. A rapid, animated dialogue ensued between the translator and the high priest. Finally, the high priest raised the golden tablet in his hand and pointed to it.

Alexandros, assuming that the tablet was meant as a present to him, reached out for it. The priest snatched it back in horror.

"It has the name of god engraved on it," the translator hurriedly explained. "He's trying to show you god's name. But no one except the high priest may touch the tablet."

Alexandros squinted at the tablet. "I can't read it. Say it for me."

The translator frowned. "No one is allowed to say god's name."

Alexandros looked quizzical. Everyone in the tent held his breath. Finally, the king burst out laughing. "This is the queerest bunch we've seen yet."

"You're lucky the king is in a good mood," Hephaistion informed the translator. "Now, what does your man want? And make it quick because the king's patience may be wearing thin."

Jaddua's equanimity didn't waver. Perhaps someone had briefed him concerning Alexandros's interest in local deities or maybe he was guided by his faith. In any event, he discoursed at length, through his translator, about the power of his god. He also shrewdly promised Alexandros military success if the Macedonian king protected the freedom of the Judeans to worship their one true god. To our collective amazement, it appeared that he'd found a receptive audience.

Alexandros told Jaddua that Jerusalem would continue to enjoy the same degree of autonomy as it had under Persian rule and that its taxes and dues wouldn't be increased but merely redirected. He told him that Jerusalem didn't have sufficient strategic importance to warrant a garrison. He politely declined an invitation to visit, explaining that the city wasn't on his planned marching route. He assured the priest that the religious freedom of the Judeans would be protected. Before dismissing the high priest, he reached, apparently on a whim, for the gold wreath left by the Hellenic League delegation and gave it to the old man. "For your temple," he said. "Make a sacrifice and hold a service to your god on my behalf."

The high priest took the wreath, spun on his heels, and left, without saying a word.

"I liked that guy," Alexandros said after the delegation filed out. "Don't ask me why." *Perhaps you're tired of all the adoration*, I guessed. It was an incorrect conjecture, as the course of events would demonstrate soon enough. "Are we done?"

Hephaistion's hands rose in a gesture of apology. "There's one more group. I saved the best for last."

"Who are they?"

"They're Dareios's ambassadors. They have another letter from the emperor for you."

"If I've said it once, I've said it a hundred times. Stop calling him the Persian emperor. He's to be referred to as the Persian coward. Got it?" Suddenly, Alexandros's patience was at an end. "I'll see them tomorrow. But in the meantime, bring me the letter."

****

Dareios's letter was not much different from the previous letter he'd sent after the Battle of Issos. His salutation conformed to Alexandros's demand that he be referred to as King Alexandros. Of course, the first letter had used that salutation as well, before it had been changed in Kallisthenes's forged version, but Alexandros had forgotten that detail. Dareios's tone had softened a bit but, in terms of territorial concessions, he was still offering all the territories west of the Halys River. (Of course, that had been a breathtakingly generous concession in the first place.) In addition, he raised the proposed ransom payment for his family, whom we had captured in the aftermath of the Battle of Issos, to 20,000 talents. Finally, in a new wrinkle, he offered his eldest daughter Stateira in marriage to Alexandros, with the clear implication that, as Dareios's son-in-law, Alexandros would accrue all the benefits due to a member of the Persian royal family. In a concluding paragraph, Dareios pointed out the obvious: Persia was a vast country with limitless resources. It was only a matter of time before it swallowed Alexandros's small army, unless there was a peace agreement.

This time, Alexandros didn't see any need to substitute a forged version before showing the letter to his command staff. And the staff knew better than to argue. After Tyros, and after all the casualties we'd suffered, it was obvious even to Parmenion that Alexandros was not in a compromising mood.

Alexandros handed his reply to Dareios's ambassadors the next morning. His rejection was as subtle as a stroke of lightning. In response to the emperor's new offers, he observed tartly that he didn't need Darcios's permission to marry Stateira, if he was so inclined, since she was already in his possession. As far as the increased ransom payment was concerned, he informed Darcios that he had already seized more treasure than Dareios had offered and he expected to collect a lot more. Finally, he advised Dareios that, if he wanted to keep his empire, he'd better come and fight for it because he, Alexandros, intended to find him and hunt him down. It wasn't a response calculated to lead to an amicable resolution.

****

In Pella, there was a steady stream of visitors as well. They tended to arrive alone, after dark, without the benefit of attendants, bodyguards, or even torchlight. They wore dark, inconspicuous garb. By the time they were ushered into Antipatros's presence, their boots and sandals were frequently steeped in horse manure. That was a small price to pay, at least as far as Antipatros was concerned, for maintaining the secrecy of these surreptitious audiences.

As regent of Macedonia, Antipatros entertained many official visitors, ambassadors, and invited guests from various member states of the Hellenic League, as well as from some of the "friendly" neighboring barbarian tribes. They were all received, with a great deal of pomp, in the newly-refurbished official audience hall of the Pella royal palace, with Antipatros seated on an elevated throne, with lots of officious aides, resplendent servants, and heavily-armed bodyguards in attendance, and with endless speeches, courtesies, and professions of loyalty. Almost invariably, not a single sincere word or item of useful information passed anyone's lips. It was all theater and deceit.

All the utile conversations took place after dark, in the royal stables, attended only by Antipatros, one or two bodyguards, occasionally Antipatros's son Kassandros, and the person being interviewed. One of the visitors was a short, fat, balding man, acutely distressed that the hem of his fancy, expensive robe had become stained as he tried to navigate across the malodorous stalls. "Surely, we could have found a more convivial venue for this meeting," he exclaimed upon spotting Antipatros in a pool of torchlight at the back of the stables.

Antipatros smiled in response. "It is nice to see that you haven't changed a bit, Demades, since the last time we met."

"Last time we met, as I recall, we were reclining comfortably on soft couches, sipping excellent wine, attended by comely young lasses, discussing important matters of state."

"I find these horses more discrete," Antipatros observed drily. "Tell me, how are the conspirators getting on in Athens?"

"Well, first of all, sire, Athens is awash in Persian darics. In all honesty, I could've become a rich man by now, if I weren't held back by my friendship and loyalty to you."

Antipatros burst out in laughter, slapping his thigh and unable to speak for a moment. "That's why you're my favorite diplomat, Demades." He finally caught his breath. "It takes brazen balls to profess poverty while being paid off by all sides. By the way, here's your current installment." He handed over a heavy sack filled with clinking coins.

"Sire, you do me injustice," Demades protested in a hurt tone, while accepting the proffered bounty. "My loyalty to King Philippos and now to you has never wavered."

Antipatros clapped the fastidious, paunchy, pouting short man on the shoulder. "Have a seat, my friend." He pointed to a soiled stool. "Sounds like you have a lot to tell me."

The two men talked late into the night, mostly about the Spartan king Agis and his tireless efforts, funded by Persia, to organize a general uprising of all the Greek city-states against Macedonia. "Athens is in play," Demades warned. "My fellow citizens dream of a return to the glory days of Athenian greatness and chafe at Macedonian primacy."

"Do they think they'd achieve primacy if the Spartans were in charge? Have they forgotten the Peloponnesian War?"

"As you know, sire, the Peloponnesian War ended more than seventy years ago. It's only been six since your victory against us at Chaironeia. There is nobody alive who fought against Sparta but there are plenty of Athenians who fought against Macedon."

"Including you, my friend."

"The funny thing, sire, is that no matter what they say about me, I was born an Athenian citizen and I'll die an Athenian citizen and if my city goes to war, I'll be standing in the front rank of the Athenian army. But right now, what we're debating in Athens is what's in our city's best interest. I've always thought Macedonia was the rising power in Greece and it's in the best interest of Athens to hitch our wagon to the Macedonian Pegasos. And that's exactly what I've been trying to convince my fellow Athenians to do."

"Glad to hear it, Demades. Glad to hear it."

"But money can be more eloquent than the most forceful orator and at the moment there's an awful lot of Persian money rising to address our Assembly."

"Don't worry about the money, my friend. We've got a little money of our own and, more importantly, we've got the better soldiers. The arc of history favors the strong over the rich, so you're on the right side of history."

"I think so too."

"But it never hurts to apply a few hammer blows to the arc of history, just to make sure that it maintains the right curvature." Antipatros laughed. "So, here's what I have in mind."

They spent half the night developing a detailed strategy to keep the seething cauldron of Athenian discontent from boiling over.

"And now you'd better sneak out before people start to wake up. There are spies everywhere, including those employed by the queen mother."

Demades nodded, rose to his feet and attempted – unsuccessfully – to make his way out of the stable with his dignity intact and his footwear unsullied.

On another night, Antipatros entertained one of his leading generals, Zopyrion, in his pungent, private retreat. "I'm going to give you 30,000 men," the regent was saying, "to persuade the Skythians to turn around and go back to whatever hellhole they crawled out of."

"Yes, sire."

"I'd rather take on that horde of nomads where they are now, to the north of the Black Sea, instead of waiting until we have to fight them on our doorstep. Because there's no doubt in my mind; unless we stop them, they're coming for us."

Zopyrion nodded. "I've seen some of the same reports you have, sire. And I think 30,000 men should be a sufficient force."

"Sufficient or not, that's all I can give you. Alexandros, and his mother, are on my ass every day to send more troops to Asia. In fact, the reason we're meeting in my, ahem, 'private' reception hall is because no one is to know about your expedition. We'll put out word that this is a routine military exercise, in anticipation of a march across the Hellespont to join Alexandros's forces. You'll be the only one who'll know your actual destination. Got it?"

"Yes, your majesty."

"I'm just the regent, Zopyrion, not any kind of majesty."

"Yes, sire." The general didn't sound entirely convinced.

And so it went. Ostentatious receptions in the official audience hall, during which nothing of substance was accomplished, and midnight soirees in the stables, during which the de facto king of Macedonia exercised his extensive, albeit unofficial, power. No one, either in Pella or in Tyros, gave the slightest conscious thought to the possibility of a collision between the de jure and de facto kings of Macedonia, although in hindsight such a climax was almost inevitable. No one, that is, with the exception of Antipatros's son Kassandros.

****

When we finally left Tyros and resumed our march to Egypt, every city, port, village, and hamlet on, or anywhere near to, our route hastened to welcome Alexandros and advise him of its submission; every one, that is, except the city of Gaza. This large settlement was more a fortress than a city, located at the edge of the desert and inhabited by a mix of Philistines and Arabs, specializing in either trade or banditry, depending on whom one asked. Strategically situated perhaps a mile from the rocky Mediterranean coast, it controlled the caravan routes between the Levant and Egypt.

Babameses, a corpulent, dark-skinned man of uncertain ethnic extraction and obscure parentage, ruled Gaza as the local representative of the Persian emperor and as principal brigand. Ignoring the recent object lessons of Tyros, Babameses somehow conceived the notion that his desert fastness could withstand a siege by the pan-Hellenic army. In anticipation of Alexandros's arrival, Babameses imported a large number of Arab mercenary marauders, stockpiled provisions and arms, and barred the city gates.

Alexandros, upon being told of Babameses's defiance, was flummoxed. Gaza, even with its imposing walls, was a small city that could be easily surrounded and eventually starved out. What Alexandros didn't realize was that Babameses was a stubborn man who believed that no army could ever storm his stronghold. More importantly, he fully expected the Persian emperor to arrive to his rescue in short order because of Gaza's strategic importance and because of the loss of face entailed in permitting a foreign army to rampage through some of Persia's most important trade routes and holdings. What Babameses didn't realize was that Alexandros was equally stubborn and the Persian emperor was too busy assembling, equipping, and training his largest army yet to have time for rescuing minor provincial outposts.

It should have been easy for us to sack Gaza. It had fewer inhabitants than we had soldiers; its walls were not as tall as many that we'd previously scaled; it had no towers surmounting the walls and no moat surrounding them; and it was compact enough for us to circumvallate, thus precluding any opportunity for resupply. What it did have was sand. It turned out it wasn't possible to undermine Gaza's walls because, as soon as our sappers started to dig a tunnel or a trench, it would immediately cave in. It was also very difficult to clap ladders against its walls because the ladders would invariably sink into the sand and topple. Our siege engines continued to bog down in the shifting dunes. Even building an earthen mound around the walls proved to be challenging because sand is not a great building material.

When we started the siege, it was the end of summer. There was never any rain, there was no shade, and the scorching sun was relentless. If we made any headway with our siege equipment during the day, the defenders would sally forth in the night and destroy whatever we had managed to accomplish. And then there were the periodic sandstorms.

Having wasted the better part of a month with little apparent progress, Alexandros started to lose patience. One night, he decided to lead a small group of our most agile soldiers in an attempt to scale a relatively low segment of the wall on the south side of the fortress using nothing more than ladders. The assault was easily repelled by the defenders, leaving many of our soldiers wounded. One of the most serious injuries was sustained by Alexandros himself. He was shot in the shoulder and then lost a great deal of blood while Philippos the Physician struggled to extract the arrowhead. He was rendered hors de combat for a couple of weeks.

After a month and a half, the incessant pounding of the walls by our catapults began to tell. Sections collapsed and gaps appeared. When our soldiers attempted to clamber across these mounds of rubble, however, they were invariably stymied by the desperate resistance of the besieged. Finally, a substantial breach developed in the eastern wall and Alexandros had recovered sufficiently to lead another assault in person. All was proceeding reasonably well until a large rock rolled off an adjacent wall and pinned Alexandros's leg. It was a miracle all the bones in his foot and ankle didn't shatter but he was once again too badly injured to remain in the field.

Conquest of Persia

Exactly two months after we had arrived at Gaza, our commandos finally succeeded in overrunning the walls. The Gazans defended their city to the last man. Ten thousand male inhabitants were put to the sword. The women and children were sold into slavery. Babameses was captured alive.

Alexandros was resting in his tent, his injured leg immobilized, when Leonnatos and Philotas dragged in the contumacious, cantankerous commander and dumped him at Alexandros's chair. Although evidently injured and bleeding, Babameses rose to his feet and stared defiantly at the Macedonian king. When Alexandros asked him, through an interpreter, whether he had anything to say in his defense, the corpulent condottiere maintained his sullen silence.

Alexandros had had enough. He ordered Babameses tied by his ankles behind a chariot and hauled himself, injured leg and all, into the outmoded conveyance. Then, fancying himself a modern-day Achilleus parading the corpse of Hektor around the walls of Troy, he circled the walls of Gaza. Of course, Hektor had been killed in honorable combat before Achilleus's disgraceful display, while Babameses was still very much alive, at least for the first couple of circuits. Eventually, the abrasive sand stripped him to the bone.

Alexandros normally treated conquered enemy commanders with respect and dignity. He could be a ruthless warrior and a vengeful victor, when it suited his strategic purposes, but that day at Gaza was the first time I'd ever seen him descend into sadism.

Chapter 5 – Pharaoh

After the delay and carnage of Gaza, none of us wished to tarry in the inferno that awaited us. Our entire train – horsemen and foot soldiers, servants, hostages, and camp followers, wagons, carts, and beasts of burden – covered the remaining 130 miles of desert between Gaza and Pelousion, the first Egyptian municipality on our route, in seven days. We reached it in the late fall of 254 Z.E. [15]

We arrived at the ancient port sunburned, dusty, tired, and thirsty. When the sentries in the guard tower sounded the alarm, a jubilant mob rushed out to greet us. We'd thought, when we'd entered some of the Greek cities of Ionia, that we were the recipients of a warm welcome from the inhabitants but, by comparison to the Pelousians, those Greeks were a nonchalant band of ingrates. At this Egyptian port of entry, young girls came running, laughing, squealing, and showering us in flower petals. Weathered old

---

[15] Zoroaster Era, calculated from Zoroaster's purported date of birth

crones, carrying clay bowls on their heads, ambled up and started washing our faces, hands, and feet. Other women brought dates and drinking water. The city fathers, wearing gleaming ankle-length linen skirts, broad necklaces on bare chests, and braided wigs topped by silly-looking cones, buzzed around behind their leader in an arrowhead formation, looking very much like a whirling mass of swarming bees. Finally, their leader located the object of his search, who happened to be our king, and they all sank in unison to their knees and then touched their foreheads to the scorching sand. When Alexandros motioned for them to rise, they regained their sandaled feet but continued to bow like woodpeckers, lacking only the staccato sound of beaks hitting timber. A large litter, carried by a dozen black men wearing nothing but loincloths, materialized in their midst, and their leader insisted that Alexandros mount the ceremonial throne atop the litter. To my surprise, Alexandros complied with this request and was carried into the city, surrounded by an ecstatic throng of overjoyed men, women, and children.

Two hundred years of history lay behind the worshipful welcome. Pelousion, located at the eastern edge of the Nile delta and called the "Gateway to Egypt," had witnessed more than its share of battles. In perhaps the most consequential battle fought under its walls, an Egyptian army commanded by pharaoh Psammetichos was routed by the invading Persians, led by Kambyses son of Kyros, who became, in due course, the first Achaemenid pharaoh of Egypt. In the wake of his coronation came two hundred years of ruthless exploitation, punctuated by repeated rebellions, interludes of independence, bloody suppressions of each revolt, followed by even more repression and despoilment. The final episode of autonomy ended when Nakhthorheb, the last native pharaoh, was defeated at Pelousion by Mentor of Rhodos, fighting on behalf of Artaxerxes Tritos Ochos, only eleven years prior to our arrival. Alexandros led the army that defeated the hated Persians and the citizens of Pelousion worshipped the ground he walked on. Or they would have worshipped it, had they actually permitted him to walk at all, instead of carrying him everywhere he went.

****

There must have been a thousand ships in our armada, ranging in size from small rowboats and fishing vessels, to merchant galleys and military triremes, and up to large, flat-bottomed barges with covered quarters on deck. The barges had no intrinsic means of propulsion and had to be towed upstream – very slowly – by oar-powered tugboats. Some of the barges had huts constructed of reeds and covered with palm fronds on deck and a few contained cabins built of actual wood, affording unparalleled comfort for a riverine excursion. Alexandros had commandeered the biggest of these floating guesthouses, while Parmenion took the next largest one.

Nobody begrudged a little indolent luxury to either Alexandros, who was still recovering from the wounds he sustained at Gaza, or to Parmenion, who had earned a little rest and relaxation by virtue of his rank and seniority. On Alexandros's barge, which could have housed fifty men, there were only two people in residence, Alexandros and Barsine, with a rotating crew of aides, servants, and bodyguards in daily attendance. Parmenion chose to turn the fifteen-day cruise into a rare family frolic, enjoying the company of his three sons, Philotas, Nikanoros, and Hektor, and ignoring, as best he could, the presence of Philotas's petulant paramour Antigone.

We were on our way to claim Memphis, the capital of Egypt. Because the Nile was still swollen by its annual inundation, waterborne transportation was the only practical means of travel. Even with a thousand vessels placed at our disposal by the grateful Egyptians, there were not enough boats for the entire army to make the trip. We had to leave some of our men, most of our animals, and our entire baggage train behind in Pelousion. Almost all the camp followers, including Barsine's children and sister, stayed behind as well.

Of the soldiers who came along, most of the infantrymen sailed on triremes and merchant galleys, crowded on deck like shoaling fish on the first day of school. The cavalry floated on barges, fifty men and fifty horses to a boat. Notwithstanding the congested conditions on the ships, the unrelenting sunshine during the day, and the swarms of implacable insects at night, we were all having a great time. The shores were lined with peasants who stopped their work in the fields to stare and occasionally to wave at us. Naked children ran along, screaming and laughing, until they lost sight of us behind stands of sedges, rushes, and reeds or until some sunning crocodiles brought them to a screeching halt. Using small rowboats, we were able to visit our comrades sailing on other ships in the flotilla during the day and stop by any nearby villages or towns in the evening.

Our trip up the Nile was the opposite of a military campaign. Instead of fighting off ferocious enemy warriors by day, we spent our nights fighting off nubile nymphs showering us with their attentions. (Some of my colleagues lost a lot of those fights.) Instead of marching twenty miles a day in a parching desert, we relaxed while others did the hard work of rowing. Instead of subsisting on limited rations of barley mush and sour wine, we feasted nightly on the bounty of the Nile, washing it down with prodigious quantities of the excellent local beer.

I stayed away from Alexandros's barge during the entire voyage, not wishing to risk violating his injunction against any contact with Barsine. On the other hand, I became a regular visitor to Parmenion's barge.

The old general was sitting on deck, reading, the first time I pulled up for a quick courtesy call. "I haven't read one of these since I was young," he said, looking up from his scroll. He and I had been in attendance at the same staff meetings for years and I'd even served under his command from time to time but I couldn't recall the last time we'd engaged in a social conversation. "Do you read much?"

I laughed. "I used to – when I was young."

"Go ahead, rub it in. If you're no longer young, what's that make me?"

"Experienced," I said. "What are you reading?"

"Herodotos on Egypt."

"And how do you find it?"

"Oh, he's completely full of it. It's like reading children's fairy tales. But he's got some amusing stories and there must be a grain of useful information in there somewhere. Now that we're here, I figure it behooves me to learn something about this country." He paused. "Did you ever expect to find yourself in Egypt?"

"Sometimes circumstances dictate where we end up," I said, more or less truthfully.

"Are you one of those people who believe the Fates determine our actions?"

I shook my head, a skeptical grimace on my face. "No, I don't think so. I believe our actions determine our fates. Oh, it could be that, at some fundamental level, everything we do is predetermined for us but it certainly feels as though we control the choices we make. And even if that's only an illusion, it's a comforting illusion I choose to believe in."

"A philosopher, I see." He smiled. "But if we control the choices we make, doesn't that make us responsible for the consequences of our actions as well? Where's the comfort in that?"

We spent the afternoon in discussion, even though I'd really come to visit with his boys. It turned out Philotas was otherwise occupied. At one point, we could hear the unmistakable sounds of copulation coming from the onboard cabin and not necessarily consensual copulation, either. We continued our discussion, pretending not to hear. Nikanoros, meanwhile, was off, visiting friends on other boats. And Hektor was having the time of his life.

Hektor was Parmenion's youngest child, an unexpected surprise when his father was already fifty-four. He instantly became the old man's favorite offspring. Parmenion hated to leave him behind while off fighting Macedonia's incessant wars. When King Philippos put Parmenion and Attalos in command of the expeditionary corps charged with crossing the Hellespont and preparing the ground for the main-force invasion of Asia, Parmenion decided to take his then ten-year-old son along, even though the boy was obviously too young to be of any use. In the intervening four years, young Hektor proved himself to be an unexpected asset.

Every soldier in the army knew him and considered him a good luck charm. While on the march, he would ride his small pony alongside the infantry troops, always ready to help in case of a mishap or breakdown. Although his proffered assistance didn't have much practical utility, the soldiers appreciated his attitude. When the army was encamped, Hektor would flit from tent to tent, greeting the soldiers by name, listening entranced to stories of military feats and assorted conquests, and accepting the choice morsels of food the soldiers had saved for him. And before each battle, he'd stop by as many battalions as he could to wish the soldiers success, to laugh at their jokes and, if asked, to write down little notes to be delivered to their families in the event they didn't come back.

Now, at the age of fourteen, he was the acknowledged mascot of the army. He stood on deck, waving, laughing, and yelling at the soldiers on the passing ships. Every once in a while, he would dive into the muddy waters of the Nile and swim over to a nearby trireme, much to the consternation of his father and the joy of the passing soldiers, who'd pull him aboard, drink a toast in his honor, tell a few jokes, pat him on the back, and send him back. "There are crocodiles in there," his father would yell when he climbed back on the barge but the youngster would just laugh and run to the other side to see which of his friends might be abreast of the barge over there.

After that first visit, I came to their barge almost every day, as much to see Hektor cavorting as to engage

Parmenion in enjoyable discussions about the merits of various writers and the workings of the Kosmos. I also spent some time with Nikanoros debating the finer points of military tactics but I never did see either Philotas or Antigone, although I heard them screaming at each other quite frequently.

****

I knew it was only a matter of time. I tried not to look at Kleitos, who was standing to my right, because I was sure one look at his face would push me over the edge. I could feel his body vibrating as he fought to suppress his tittering. I glanced to my left instead, where Seleukos was turning red from holding his breath. His coloration betrayed either irrepressible levity or imminent asphyxiation.

Alexandros had spent a good hour inside the inner sanctum of the Temple of Ptah, attended only by a jubilation of priests, while the rest of us stood outdoors, in the hot sun, awaiting his reappearance through the impressive main entrance of the temple. The simple, rectangular opening, which was at least ten feet tall, was dwarfed by the forty-foot-high granite statues of Ramses Deuteros that flanked it. Of course, standing in front of the temple walls, the twin effigies of the great pharaoh didn't seem disproportionately large. The walls on either side of the main entrance were at least sixty feet high and two hundred feet wide. They were plain and primitive by Greek standards, flat and smoothly stuccoed, but they were also at least a thousand years old. It was evident they'd been repaired and repainted innumerable times but the unforgiving climate was once again exacting its inexorable toll on the recently repainted walls. In front of the main entrance stood a large wooden platform on which the public portion of the coronation ceremony would play out.

Finally, Alexandros walked out of the temple and mounted the platform, trailed by dozens of high priests and middling officiants. It was his reappearance that had triggered our involuntary and inadvisable mirth. He'd stripped his armor and was wearing a long, leather apron in front, attached by a wide belt around his waist. His buttocks were al fresco but there was a long bull's tail, hanging from the belt in the back, tickling his crack. His upper torso was bare. The risibility resumed above his neck. His hair was concealed beneath a garish, striped headcloth. Most of his face was hidden behind a fake beard that gave every impression of having been recently sheared off a giant, aging goat. His eyes and eyebrows were heavily outlined with kohl. He was sweating profusely, notwithstanding the vigorous waving of palm fronds by a phalanx of slaves, which was causing the goat's beard and the bull's tail to flutter in the resultant breeze.

He couldn't wipe his brow, not because he was worried about smearing the kohl, but because his hands were otherwise occupied: He was carrying a scepter shaped like a shepherd's crook in one hand and a contraption I guessed to be a fly whip in the other. The funny thing was that he seemed transported by it all, oblivious to the farcicality of the proceedings.

One of the priests was declaiming loudly, in Egyptian, and Alexandros was nodding wisely, although he could not possibly have had the slightest idea of what the man was saying. Two crowns were carried forward ceremoniously. One was a tall, peaked hat, made of gleaming white linen, decorated with gold thread and precious stones, representing the suzerainty of Upper Egypt. The other was a broad, red diadem of the ruler of Lower Egypt. One of the high priests seized the two crowns and, with a prestidigitator's flourish, combined them into one head ornament. A different priest then took the double crown, raised it high in the air, and placed it on Alexandros's head.

It was when Alexandros attempted to acknowledge the moment that I lost it. He raised his hands and shook the shepherd's crook and the fly swatter triumphantly. The motion of his arms caused the striped headcloth to slip backward, taking the double crown with it. Alexandros spun around, trying to catch the falling symbol of his new authority, whipping the bull's tail around and exposing his bare butt. The tip of the tail struck the nearest priest in the crotch, causing the hapless old man to double over in pain.

I'm not sure what happened after that because at that point I fell to my knees, partly to hide behind the backs of the people in front of us and partly because my legs grew weak under me, and I broke into uncontrollable laughter. My merriment proved contagious. Seleukos swayed uncertainly, his body shaking, although no sound escaped his lips, at least not yet. Kleitos, on the other hand, fell to the ground, laughing out loud and pounding the sand with the palm of his hand. Fortunately, the people around us were mostly ordinary Egyptians and they all assumed this was our strange, foreign way of paying obeisance to the new pharaoh. In fact, one or two of them, hesitantly at first, fell to their knees and started to laugh. Before long the entire audience was kneeling or even lying prostrate on the ground, pounding the hot sand with their hands, and guffawing fervently.

Fortunately, Alexandros never noticed our amusement. He stood erect and motionless while a priest restored the headcloth and the double crown to his head. It was impossible to tell whether he was smiling or stern-faced because of the fake goat-hair beard but his forehead was uncreased and his eyes shone brightly, seemingly staring far beyond the present moment.

The priests motioned for him to descend from the platform and start his ceremonial walk around the outer wall of the Ptah precinct. Alexandros was too deeply absorbed in the significance of the occasion to notice. Finally, one of the priests touched him on the arm and he seemed to return to reality with a start.

Conquest of Persia

Somehow Alexandros managed to maintain his dignity during the long walk around the white-washed walls of the sacred precinct, while trailing, like clouds of flatulence, a huge entourage of Egyptian priests, officers of the pan-Hellenic army, and ordinary Egyptians behind his naked rear.

Eventually, the entire procession reached the Temple of Apis, home of the eponymous bull, who simultaneously served the dual role of sacrificial animal and earthly manifestation of Osiris, the god of transition from this life to the next, the god of death, resurrection, and regeneration. The current incarnation of the sacred beast was led out of his temple by a rope attached to a golden nose ring and paraded through the assembled crowd. Many of the natives were clearly affected by their proximity to this august bovinity, falling to their knees, kissing his hide, muttering prayers, and rapturously inhaling the animal's exhalations. Miraculously, no one was trampled during the stately progress of the hulking deity to the large, outdoor altar. Once there, Apis the divine bull was stripped of his jewels and flowers, hammered down to his knees, and slaughtered.

Many long, incomprehensible speeches, prayers, and incantations followed, after which the carcass was reverently lifted by a score of men, placed on a custom-designed cart, and hauled back into the temple for mummification. As soon as the dead Apis disappeared, a new, young bull was produced from somewhere and magically transubstantiated, through prayer and ritual, into the new personification of Osiris. The new Apis was then decorated and led away to replace his recently ascended predecessor in his new abode.

Finally, the coronation ceremony was over, Alexandros was officially deified as the latest son of Ammon, the king of all Egyptian gods and hence Ruler of the World, and we were all free to return to our boats, grateful to whatever god was responsible for our overdue deliverance.

****

In Pella, even the horses were in Olympias's pay. Notwithstanding Antipatros's pungent precautions, the queen mother stayed abreast of all the doings in the Macedonian capital and she did her best to keep her son, campaigning in the field in faraway Asia and Africa, informed about the latest palace intrigues, sending monthly letters detailing Antipatros's latest usurpations of Alexandros's royal prerogatives. Unfortunately, Kassandros, whom his father had put in charge of counterintelligence, became aware of Olympias's epistolary exertions almost before she had finished composing her missives. His agents, the ubiquitous practitioners of the meretricious arts in Pella's dens of iniquity, promptly identified Olympias's couriers, plied them with their favors and other intoxicants, and stripped them of their confidential cargo. While the emissaries lay insensible in the arms of Morpheus,

Conquest of Persia

Antipatros and Kassandros read Olympias's letters and composed, amid much hilarity, clever forgeries, which the sex workers substituted for the genuine article before their customers awoke. Occasionally, if there was not enough time to substitute a counterfeit message or if he was in an ornery mood, Kassandros simply had the couriers killed.

Any incoming messages from Alexandros to Olympias were confiscated by the regent's son in an effort to convince the queen mother that her efforts were for naught and she had been forgotten by her son. However, Olympias caught on soon enough to Kassandros's machinations. Among other things, most of Pella's ladies of the night were followers of Dionysos and Olympias continued to function as the high priestess of the licentious god's cult. At their ecstatic revels and initiation rituals, Kassandros's female agents regularly betrayed their latest assignations to their charismatic officiant.

Kassandros did not idly acquiesce in Olympias's disruption of his spy network. Frequently, soldiers arriving for their regular nocturnal assignations found their favorite means of erotic relief lying in pools of blood, with their throats slashed. Olympias herself was confined to the women's quarter, with guards posted at the entrance. They had strict orders not to admit anyone without written authorization bearing Kassandros's seal. In short order, Olympias found means to suborn the guards. And so the deadly dance continued.

****

Alexandros, still basking in the warm Egyptian sun and the heady afterglow of his recent coronation, was nevertheless frustrated. He wanted to continue our voyage up the Nile, all the way to Thebes, the ancient former capital. "I should've been crowned in the Southern Temple at Thebes. That's where all the pharaohs used to be crowned. Plus, I'm told the Karnak Temple Complex is much larger than anything here in Memphis. And then there's the Valley of the Kings, where all the previous pharaohs are buried. We definitely have to go there."

"The Southern Temple is in disrepair, my lord," a Greek-speaking priest informed him. "Although they still hold the annual Opet Festival there, it's been a long time since they've held an actual coronation ceremony. Most pharaohs, if they're interested in a ceremony at the Southern Temple at all, get crowned by proxy. And we could certainly do that for you, my lord."

"But I like to see things for myself," Alexandros protested.

In the end, it was the added travel time that dissuaded our indefatigable explorer from pressing ahead. Thebes lay another 400 miles farther south and, other than Alexandros's insatiable curiosity (and perhaps his enjoyment of risible rituals), there was no rational justification for expending three more precious months on this detour. Reluctantly, Alexandros bowed to practicality.

He sent a sizeable donation to the priests in charge of the Southern Temple, instructed them to effect all necessary repairs, to crown him by proxy during the next festival, and to erect a monument within the sacred precinct commemorating his donation and coronation. His instructions were in fact carried out to the letter.

And instead of spending three months traveling to Thebes and back, he took one day to visit the monuments at Memphis. For some reason he chose me as his sightseeing companion.

It was a long day. We walked the entire length of the necropolis, four miles there, four miles back, without missing a single pyramid, funerary monument, or sepulcher. And of course, to the extent that some of them had been re-opened to corporeal visitors, as opposed to gods and ghosts, we had to crawl into each one. It was a remarkably eclectic burial ground. There were, according to our guides, mummies of kings and queens but also their spouses, high priests, middling officials, and assorted other people rich enough to afford the cost of being interred in a stone monument, whether large or small. The creepily echoing galleries in which they reposed were highly decorated and came furnished with all the necessities of afterlife, including funerary equipment, death masks, official regalia, weapons, cooking and eating utensils, idols and other objects of worship, boxes and chests, toys and figurines, model boats and chariots, lamps, changes of clothes, jewelry, slaves (mummified), and household pets (also mummified). But the necropolis was not limited to people. There were lots of animal tombs, filled with mummified ibises, baboons, cats, dogs, falcons, and, lest we forget, bulls. Of course, these hadn't been ordinary animals prior to their departure from our mortal coil. They had been temporal incarnations of immortal, albeit bestial, gods, worshipped during their lifetimes and suitably interred after their return to the netherworld.

The oldest tomb at Saqqara, to hear our guides tell it, was the Step Pyramid of Djoser. Strictly speaking, it wasn't a pyramid at all because it had a rectangular base and started out as nothing more than a huge, coffin-shaped box, about 400 feet long, 360 feet wide, and 40 feet high, which was supposed to house old Djoser's sarcophagus. It was, at that time, the largest stone structure built by man. However, according to legend, the architect of the tomb, a man named Imhotep, who was also Djoser's chief minister, high priest, physician, engineer, and all-around factotum, then hit upon the idea of outdoing his own grandiose design by placing a second, somewhat smaller coffin-shaped box on top of the first one. This worked so well that he decided to add another, and another, until there were six rectangular prisms of diminishing size on top of each other, making Djoser's tomb 200 feet tall and giving it its characteristic staircase profile. He then clad the entire structure in gleaming polished white limestone, which still shimmered in our day.

"How old is it?" Alexandros wanted to know. Our guides asserted that it was 3,000 years old. Alexandros turned to me as the font of all historical knowledge for confirmation. I knew from my studies that in my own time it was about 4,800 years old. Since I had traveled back 2,400 years, the correct figure for the age of Djoser's Step Pyramid at that time was 2,400 years. I was struck by the coincidence. *Imagine traveling back in time twice as far as it took me to reach ancient Greece*, I thought. *Old Djoser and his brilliant polymath Imhotep were as long removed from Alexandros's time as he was from my own native era.* So, the priests were a little off in their estimate of the antiquity of Djoser's Step Pyramid but I chose not to quibble with them, simply nodding to confirm their figure. I did, however, marvel at the durability of this simple structure, which had inspired all subsequent Egyptian pyramids.

"It was the first one," one of the priests continued, "but it's far from the largest. The Pyramid of Khufu is the biggest, almost 500 feet high."

"Where is that one?" Alexandros immediately asked. Fortunately, it was too far to walk but the priests assured us that we would see it, along with its companions, when we sailed back down the Nile. "How did you not see it coming upriver to Memphis?"

"I may have been otherwise occupied," Alexandros admitted sheepishly.

"Well, you can't miss it on the way back." It turned out that the priests were right. Standing fifty stories high, its highly polished white limestone casing gleaming in the stark Egyptian sunshine, it tended to attract one's attention.

I noticed, when we started our voyage back to the delta, that Alexandros and Barsine were seated on the deck of their barge, looking portside, making sure they wouldn't miss the great pyramids this time around.

****

Sailing downstream and aided by a favorable breeze, our flotilla reached the apex of the Nile delta in less than two days. After a night at anchor, we headed down the westernmost arm of the mighty river. Alexandros's plan was to visit Naukratis, a port located about half-way down this branch, before making our way to the Mediterranean and returning to Pelousion.

Surprisingly, our reception at Naukratis was less effusive than it had been at our other Egyptian ports of call. Naukratis was inhabited mostly by Greeks. Ordinary Egyptians – after decades of Persian contempt for their religious beliefs, repression of their culture, and exploitation of their labor and natural resources – greeted Alexandros as their liberator, happy to bestow on him whatever earthly and divine honors they could devise. The Greek colonists, by contrast, were somewhat ambivalent in their reactions to Alexandros. He was, on the one hand, the liberator of Ionia but he was also, in the eyes of many Greeks, the conqueror of mainland Greece.

A difference in national character may have been at work as well. Egyptians were used to treating their leaders as gods on Earth and to being treated as slaves in return. Their religious beliefs emphasized the ephemeral nature of life in the present world and stressed the promise of eternal life in the afterworld. The rhythms of their existence were dictated by the vagaries of a river; their welfare and their very lives depended on the whims of unseen forces, unpredictable spirits, and unfathomable gods; like grains of sand in the desert blown about by winds and carried off by floods, they toiled, worshipped, and died, pushed around by the caprice of forces beyond their control or understanding. The Greeks, on the other hand, had an implicit faith in the power of rational thought. Their gods were a lot like ordinary people, except for the minor detail of their immortality. Even the actions of the gods, and hence the forces of nature, could be understood and explained, if only one knew enough, thought hard enough, and was smart enough. Most importantly, people were autonomous actors, responsible for their actions, but also endowed with the dignity that is the birthright of every human being. (Well, the birthright of every free adult male Greek human being.) The Egyptians lavished adulation on Alexandros and his entire army. The Greeks debated amongst themselves how best to respond to this latest twist in the story of their lives.

According to Herodotos, Naukratis had been founded by Greek traders from twelve different places: Ionians from Samos, Miletos, Chios, Teos, Phokaia and Klazomenai; Dorians from Rhodos, Knidos, Halikarnassos and Phaselis; Aiolians from Mytilene on Lesbos and the people of Aigina, the island close to Athens. They wanted to establish a safe, protected emporion (their word for a trading post) for seaborne commerce to and from Egypt. For a long time, it was the only port of entry into Egypt sanctioned by the pharaohs. By the time of our visit, other ports had been established, such as Pelousion, but Naukratis retained its unique, cosmopolitan character, with altars, temples, sanctuaries, and sacred precincts for a constellation of gods, foreign and domestic, sufficient to meet the spiritual needs of traders, merchants, and sailors from all corners of the Mediterranean world. There were also numerous enterprises to cater to their more carnal needs. For example, the brothels of Naukratis were said to employ the most alluring ladies of the night since the last sighting of the sirens.

Naukratis was a thriving commercial hub and a melting pot of cultures and nationalities that had seen many conquerors come and go. Not surprisingly, its inhabitants turned out to be fairly blasé about the arrival of the latest shooting star in the military firmament. Our ships were still straggling into port when Alexandros decided we'd stayed long enough and ordered us to weigh anchor and press ahead to the mouth of the delta.

Conquest of Persia

******

There was a small fishing village called Rhakotis hidden away on a strip of dry land between a shallow, inland lake on one side and the lapping waters of the sea on the other, near the point where the westernmost branch of the Nile emptied into the Mediterranean. It was at this village that Alexandros decided to spend the night after our abortive visit to Naukratis. Although most of our troops stayed aboard their ships, a few of us officers joined our commander-in-chief for what was supposed to be a brief onshore excursion.

Our reception in the village mirrored the welcome extended to Alexandros in all the other villages and towns we'd visited during our Nile sojourn. A banquet was quickly organized, featuring the catch of the day. Although most Egyptians considered fish and other sea creatures low-class fare, I thought the dishes thrown together by the Rhakotian women on short notice were delicious and a nice change of pace from our mostly vegetarian diet. The beer was the typical Egyptian brew. Alexandros seemed quite pleased with it, judging by the quantity he consumed.

It was past midnight by the time the men settled down to sleep in the open air. I had other plans. I knew full well I was being foolish: It was way too early, more than eleven years too early, and yet, I couldn't help myself. While the others snored, I quietly snuck away.

It was a crystal-clear, moonless night, perfect for the celestial observations I had to make. I just hoped I still remembered how. It turned out I had nothing to worry about. I knew, almost subconsciously, what to do. *I guess the homing instinct is stronger in humans than we realize*, I thought as I carried out my observations and made my measurements. When I was done, I marked the spot with a little pyramid of smooth stones. *What are the chances this pile of rocks will still be here eleven years from now? Better yet, what are the chances I will be back here on the appointed day?* And still, I couldn't shake my elation.

I'd arrived at the location where the emergency escape hatch would materialize. When I'd first realized that my scheduled portal had failed to appear, that my extraction team would not be coming, that I was marooned in this ancient era, and that, if I ever hoped to see home again, I would have to make my way from the highlands of Macedonia to the coast of Egypt, through many foreign lands and during a long-ago time, with nothing but my wits to assist me, the probability of success seemed vanishingly small. Yet, here I stood, on the very spot. Now if only I could make the next eleven years magically swoosh by.

Dawn was breaking. I danced a jig, slapped my heels, laughed out loud. I lifted my eyes. The natural beauty of the rocky beach on which I found myself put me in a strange, mythological state of mind. I imagined Eos, the goddess of dawn, stirring from her bed on the far side of the sea. To my right, her brother Helios, his golden chariot groaning under the weight of the Sun, was urging his team of fiery steeds to rise from the cerulean waters of the Mediterranean and begin their diurnal journey across the sky. The bright rays of the emerging sun were transmuted by the perpetual motion of the sea into a myriad facets of shimmering gold. A gentle northerly breeze bathed my face in the cool, fresh, salty air of the new day. The chimes of Poseidon tinkled brightly, in the guise of small, choppy waves that splashed ceaselessly against a rocky promontory straight ahead. Nature, oblivious to my presence, continued its eternal journey through time.

Why am I so happy? I asked myself. *It's so unlike me.* Lyrical flights of fancy were bad enough but a jig? Reaching the site of the portal, even if eleven years too early, was clearly intoxicating. Or perhaps the fact that I still had eleven years to live in this time was at least partly the cause of my exhilaration. I shrugged. Nothing is harder than trying to explore the inscrutable reaches of our own minds.

I was still marveling at the sensory feast that enveloped me when I became aware of the drumbeat of hooves approaching from behind. I refused to turn around, hoping that, by shutting out the sound, I could hang on to this instant of sublimity.

"So that's where you disappeared to," a familiar voice called out. It was Alexandros, aboard Boukephalas, smiling broadly, showing no ill effects from the previous night's festivities. He had ridden up, accompanied by

Hephaistion, Perdikkas, and Aristandros, and was surveying the scene that had enthralled me only moments earlier.

After a good look, he nodded approvingly. "You have a good eye, Ptolemaios. This really looks like a great spot to found a new city. Look at that harbor." There was no harbor yet, only a broad, placid bay, but I could see what he meant. "Now that Tyros is destroyed," he continued, "there's a need for a new port to take over as a hub for all the trade routes in the eastern Mediterranean."

"Our friends in Naukratis won't be pleased," Hephaistion observed.

"Exactly," Alexandros agreed, with a twinkle in his eyes. "This really is a perfect location." He was quiet for a moment. "Just smell the air. And there's plenty of space." He dismounted and started to pace off distances, running around like a delighted child, pointing out where various buildings were going to be.

Hephaistion watched him with an impish smile. "Don't you need permission from the pharaoh before you can found a new port in Egypt?"

Alexandros played along. He stopped dead in his tracks and slapped his head. "By all the gods of Egypt, I think you're right. What are we going to do?"

Hephaistion shrugged. "I don't know, Aniketos. I guess we're out of luck."

Suddenly, Alexandros's face brightened. "Wait a minute," he cried out. "I am the pharaoh."

"And the son of one of the chief Egyptian gods," Hephaistion put in.

"Let me see. I have to think about this." Alexandros hesitated. "Alright, I've thought about it. I hereby grant myself a charter to found a new port on this spot."

We all clapped and laughed. Every now and then, Alexandros's enthusiasm and good cheer could be infectious. Even old Aristandros was applauding.

Alexandros eyed the soothsayer mischievously. "I take it the omens are favorable?"

Aristandros stopped clapping. "As you know, sire, that's not how I operate. I can't possibly give you an answer on the spot. It takes preparations; it takes time; rituals must be carried out; sacrifices made; auspices observed; gods propitiated."

Alexandros raised his hand to stop the hemorrhage of words. "I wasn't asking for an official augury, old man. We're simply chatting. Forget you're a soothsayer for a moment and tell me what you think."

Aristandros hesitated. Finally, he shrugged and delivered his prognostication. "Speaking just as a layman, my guess is that this city will become your greatest, most lasting legacy."

Alexandros's mien clouded and then, without any transition, like a sudden sandstorm, he flew into a rage. "I don't think so," he yelled. "You've got no idea what you're talking about. And you call yourself a seer. My legacy is going to be far greater than founding a mere city – on a whim, mind you – at a place stumbled upon by Ptolemaios, for crying out loud. Get out of my sight. And next time, before flapping your lips, do your work first."

Aristandros said nothing in response. He laboriously mounted his horse and rode away. He really did look old. *Maybe he's sick*, I thought. For reasons I couldn't understand, the soothsayer had been my mortal enemy for years now and I, in self-defense, had resolved to get him off my back. Now, I began to hope my problem might take care of itself, if only I let nature take its course.

Perdikkas waded into the lengthening silence in his usual reckless fashion. "What are you going to call it, sire?"

Alexandros looked at him askance. "Alexandria, of course. But we've got to do something else first.

Chapter 6 – Oasis of Ammon

The 'something else' turned out to be a side trip to the Oasis of Ammon. "How can I found a new city without divine sanction?" Alexandros asked rhetorically. "And, as it happens, there's a famous oracle nearby. Plus, I have a few other questions that have been nagging at me. The oracle of Ammon will give me a chance to get some answers from a reputable deity. So, off we go."

'Nearby' turned out to be more than three hundred miles away, through some of the most inhospitable terrain on the face of the Earth. We left the very next day, a small band of Alexandros's intimates, traveling light. Our group of sixteen included – in addition to Alexandros – Hephaistion, Perdikkas, Philotas, Seleukos, Kleitos, nine ordinary horsemen from Hephaistion's squadron, and me. Pointedly, Alexandros failed to invite Aristandros to join our expedition, thus quite possibly sparing his life.

We rode west, along the Mediterranean, on a desert road, passing no settlements. The only creatures we saw were seagulls, lizards, and scorpions. On the third day, we reached the village of Paraitonion, marking the border between Egypt and Kyrenaike. Surprisingly, while enjoying the hospitality of the local elders, we were told that another Greek-speaking group was already in the village. It turned out to be a delegation from Kyrene, the principal Greek colony on the western coast of Kyrenaike. The envoys were on their way to pay obeisance to the new ruler of Egypt. Alexandros graciously invited them to join us for our modest banquet. They in turn conveyed their city's offer of friendship and submission to Alexandros and handed over a treasure-trove of gifts. Although Alexandros was quite pleased with the expensive offerings, he asked the ambassadors to continue their journey into Egypt and deliver their presents to Parmenion, his second-in-command, because we were on our way to the Ammonion. The Kyrenians, doing their best to conceal their surprise, and perhaps their consternation, wished us a safe journey and retired.

We set off into the heart of the desert very early the next day, having recruited two native Berbers as our guides and having traded in our horses for dromedaries. The Oasis of Ammon was somewhere to our southwest. Our guides assured us we would reach it in a few days. We were still traveling light.

We discovered, almost immediately, that riding a camel is different from riding a horse. On the positive side, camels kneel down to facilitate mounting. On the negative side, it's hard to stay aboard once they decide to stand up because they elevate their rear ends first, pitching the rider forward, and then, when the rider has finally recovered his balance, they extend their front legs, pitching him back. Of course, being thrown off the camel's back might be the luckiest outcome, considering the tortures that await anyone lucky enough to remain mounted.

First of all, because of the hump, there's no level place to sit. Second, the dromedary's hide is extremely bristly and abrasive. Any bare skin that comes in contact with the animal's tough hide gets scraped off in a matter of minutes. Third, camels have a weird, irregular, swaying, jerky gait. Trying to keep from falling off takes a constant, exhausting effort. Fourth, camels are headstrong creatures. Any rider who thinks he has some influence, much less control, over the motion of his beastly conveyance is soon disabused of any such delusion. Camels go where their fancy takes them, at their own pace and in their own good time. We were all walking next to our camels within an hour or two of our departure from Paraitonion. But at least they carried our supplies and provided a tiny bit of shade. They did nothing, however, to keep our feet from getting cooked in our boots.

We'd gotten started well before dawn. In the desert, one travels by night or when the sun is close to the horizon. During the middle of the day, we hid in the shadow of a fortuitous sand dune, if we could find one that was large enough, had a precipitous drop-off, and happened to be oriented correctly to the sun. Otherwise, we erected makeshift lean-tos and did our best not to get roasted on the searing sand. The scorpions, other biting insects, and even occasional snakes were a constant threat.

On our fourth day in the desert, we ran out of water. There were supposed to be water holes on our route but they had either dried up or our guides had failed to find them. We were assured that the Ammonion was close and therefore our lack of water was not necessarily fatal. After two further days without water, it felt as if we were walking on the bottom of a boiling, viscous ocean. Our eyesight was failing because of the glare of the sun; the dunes and small hills around us shimmered, swayed, and receded even as we tried to approach them; if the camels hadn't continued their determined, slow walk, we would've lain down and died. And then, without any warning, the heavens opened up and it rained. We ran around in the downpour, whooping and laughing, trying to catch the life-giving water in our mouths, helmets, hats, water skins, saddlebags, cooking pots, inverted tents, and any other vessels we managed to improvise on short notice. It rained less than half an hour but that was more than enough to keep us alive for days to come.

Our two guides were amazed. "Never in our lives have we seen rain like this, here in the desert."

"That's because you've never crossed the desert with me before," Alexandros told them.

I wasn't sure whether he was joking but laughed all the same because I knew we'd live another day. I tried to convince everybody we should offer some of our water to our camels but the guides told us it'd be a complete waste. "Camels can live a long time without drinking," they assured us. "But when they do drink, they can drink as much water in one go as a man can drink in a year. If we gave them all the water we now have, it wouldn't make the slightest difference to them." I was sure they were wrong but they were Berbers, they'd lived in the desert their entire lives, they knew camels, and my survival depended on them. I chose to hold my tongue, although I found it impossible to suppress my doubts. *We've got as much chance as a spider trying to hang on to his web in a simoom*, I thought.

The next two days were uneventful. We trudged ahead, except when it became too hot; we did our best to ignore the fact that the Oasis of Ammon seemed much farther than our guides had led us to believe; we tried not to calculate how much water we had left; we worked hard to keep various patches of sunburnt skin from getting worse; we tried to squint through the shimmering air for any sign of the elusive oasis; and every once in a while we glimpsed castles in the air, ice-cold waterfalls, and naked maidens frolicking in sun-dappled, verdant meadows. It was these hallucinations that were the worst.

Just before sundown on our eighth day in the desert, we saw a towering mountain in the distance. We all ignored it. As mirages go, it wasn't much to look at. Even when the mountain started to move toward us, it didn't make much of an impression. It was only when the hot wind started to tear the hats off our heads and our camels sank to the ground and refused to get up that we realized there really was a mountain straight ahead of us and it was approaching at a frightening speed.

Within a matter of minutes, we were swallowed by the sandstorm. Day turned to night, as if by the flick of a light switch. It was impossible to breathe, as we lay on the sand, sheltering behind our camels, holding on for dear life. Our mouths, nostrils, eyes, ears, and skin pores filled with sand. We were getting buried alive.

I'm not sure how long the storm lasted. When I finally dug my way out of the newly-formed sand dune on top of me and forced my eyes open, I found myself beneath a celestial dome of breath-taking beauty. The Milky Way was a brightly illuminated swirl of magic dust high in the sky, flanked on either side by thousands of brilliant diamonds, arranged in a dazzling showcase of transcendent, unearthly jewelry. *I guess this is what it looks like after you're dead*, I thought. Then I heard Perdikkas swearing and I knew I was probably still alive.

Even our Berber guides were shaken. Among other things, the sandstorm had buried the landmarks they were using to stay on course. It was news to me that they had relied on any signposts heretofore but they were certainly down to random meandering after the storm. Trying to use celestial navigation at night was useless because they were not sure of the exact direction to Ammonion and even a deviation of a couple of degrees would've caused us to miss the oasis by miles over a distance of several days' march. But we trudged ahead.

The first of our camels to die succumbed to dehydration the next day. Apparently, and contrary to popular belief, camels can only survive for five to ten days without any water, unless the weather is cool and they have access to succulent vegetation in lieu of drinking water, neither of which conditions obtained during our march to the Ammonion.

By the twelfth day, every one of our camels was dead. We ate some of their flesh, both for moisture and nutrition, but in the hot air the meat putrefied almost immediately, so we couldn't take it with us. On day fourteen, we were once again without any water. All our food ran out as well but nobody noticed. We'd started the march into the desert as young men in exceedingly good physical condition but by this point we'd turned into stumbling zombies, with sunken eyes, chalk-white lips, running sores all over our bodies, and no hope of survival. Most of us would've stopped walking, had it not been for Alexandros's relentless belief that the gods would come to our rescue. As for me personally, the emotion that kept me moving was anger. I couldn't believe that, having successfully negotiated the long journey to the terminus of my escape hatch, I was condemned to die on a pointless, but suicidal, excursion into hell.

I happened to be lying next to Alexandros when we settled down for our midday siesta on day fifteen. We were sheltering in the shade of a canvas sheet stretched between two poles but for some reason I imagined I was reclining in the maw of a giant furnace. It had gotten to the point where the heat didn't even bother me. I noticed I'd stopped sweating and now found it difficult to speak. Alexandros, by contrast, couldn't stop talking. His speech was slurred and he was obviously delirious but his mouth never stopped. He was working out the exact phraseology of the questions he was planning to ask the god via the oracle. Curiously, he wanted to discover whether all the murderers of his father had been punished. He also needed to know the identity of the deities to whom he should be making sacrifices in order to assure victory over Dareios. Finally, he had to find out whether the site he had chosen for Alexandria was a propitious one.

"Do you realize the god whom the Egyptians call Ammon is actually the same as the god we call Zeus?" he suddenly asked.

I decided to play along. Evidently, my brain was still functional, even if nothing else was. "How could the same god preside at Mount Olympos and simultaneously be the king of all the Egyptian gods?" In my delirium, I was actually interested to hear how Alexandros would resolve this theological dilemma.

Alexandros was surprised. "What do you mean? It happens all the time, even among humans. After all, I'm here, presiding over the pan-Hellenic army and yet, at the same time, I'm also the king of Macedonia. You, my friend, have a very parochial view of gods and a very limited understanding of their powers. It's child's play for the king of all kings to be in charge of two places at once. The Egyptians rightly call Ammon the Ruler of the World. Doesn't the world include Greece? The Greeks call Zeus King of Gods, who in turn are in charge of the entire universe. Doesn't that include Egypt? In fact, if you think about it, Ammon and Zeus have to be the same god."

The logic of his argument seemed unassailable, at least in my weakened mental state. "I see your point," I tried to say but my mouth was too dry to work properly.

"What's even better, this new understanding I've reached helps to clear up a point that's been bothering me for a very long time."

"What's that?"

"I'm sure you've heard rumors that my parentage is in doubt, haven't you?"

"Never, sire," I lied. In fact, everyone at court had heard the story that Olympias had been impregnated by

Zeus himself, rather than her husband Philippos, the god having taken on the guise of a snake for the occasion. Needless to say, I didn't put much stock in the story, even if Olympias did like to cavort with her snakes.

"Well, in that case you're the only one. Even my mother hinted about it to me, although of course she could never say anything about it openly without jeopardizing my standing as the heir apparent to Philippos."

"Frankly, I think such rumors are ridiculous. I knew your father pretty well and there was never any doubt in his mind that he was your father."

"You know, the cuckold is always the last to know."

"Do you have a candidate for your paternity?"

"I do but that's one of the questions I want to ask the oracle."

I was drifting off to sleep or possibly losing consciousness. Either way, I stopped listening. I was startled back to attention by a shout from Alexandros. "Look!" He pointed to the sky.

I assumed he was hallucinating once again but I looked anyway, having little else to do. I saw two fuzzy, dark specks. I blinked to help my eyes focus. The two specks resolved into two crows, except these crows looked different from any I'd seen before. Instead of being all black, which would have been the appropriate attire for our funeral attendants, these two crows wore white aprons over their black feathers. There was a stripe of white extending from behind their necks, across their shoulders, and covering their breasts and bellies. They circled our camp and then resumed their leisurely flight in the direction of the sun.

"We have to follow the birds," one of our guides yelled. "They must be headed toward the oasis. Crows can't survive for long in the middle of the desert."

"They're Ammon's messengers," Alexandros agreed. "He sent them to guide us to his shrine." There was neither surprise nor doubt in his voice.

The crows quickly disappeared from sight but their sighting energized our entire group and we resumed our march in the direction of the point on the horizon where they had disappeared from sight. We reached the oasis by nightfall.

****

Upon arrival, we were greeted by a scrum of shouting children, quickly followed by a small group of priests in flowing robes. They headed straight for Alexandros. *I've sold these people short*, I thought. *Somehow they've divined who this bedraggled beggar must be.*

"Welcome, Son of Ammon, Lord of the Two Lands," the leader of the priests greeted Alexandros, translating the traditional pharaonic titles into passable Greek.

Alexandros beamed. "That's one question answered already," he called out for everyone to hear. Then, speaking more quietly, he turned to the chief priest. "I have a few more questions I need to pose to your oracle."

"All in due course, your divine highness. You look like you could use some water, food, and perhaps a bath first."

The oasis was much larger than I'd expected. It extended for miles in every direction and it was indeed a paradise on Earth. Exuberant, luxuriant vegetation, including olive trees, date palms, and flowering bushes, filled all available space not covered by ponds full of water or occupied by clean, white adobe huts. Energetic sounds of happy children chasing chickens, goats, and a few cows, filled the air. And presiding above it all was the magnificent shrine of Ammon, within whose walls the god himself answered questions, mediated by the priests, of course.

We ate fresh fruit dripping with juice, various cheeses and breads, poached eggs and vegetables, and drank cool, delicious water. We bathed in the warm ponds and we slept. Most of us would've been happy to remain at this oasis for the rest of our lives, particularly if the alternative was another trek across the trackless desert.

Alexandros, on the other hand, was a man in a hurry. By the time the rest of us finished enjoying our feast, he'd already eaten, bathed, changed into a sparkling white outfit provided by the priests, and was off to consult the oracle. No one, other than the priests, was allowed to accompany him into the shrine. When he emerged, two hours later, a remarkable transformation had taken place. He was once again young and bright and vigorous. All traces of our recent ordeal had been wiped away. He was loud and happy and somehow taller than when he'd gone inside. But it was the radiance of his mien and the blaze in his eyes that struck me the most. *Here is a man who's seen a vision.*

He was smiling, clapping shoulders, squeezing arms, as we gathered around him. "Listen up, men! I have my answers and they're all good. So, we're leaving early tomorrow. Take anything of value you still possess and give it to the priests. We're donating it all to my father. I'll reimburse you when we get back. And get some rest. We want to leave shortly after midnight, so we can make good progress before the sun gets too hot. The priests will give us some camels and some better guides."

Hephaistion articulated the question on all of our minds. "What did you learn, Aniketos?"

"Son of Ammon," Alexandros muttered. "Call me Son of Ammon. I'll tell you on our way back."

Perdikkas, practical and blunt as ever, brought us back to earth. "Which way will we go?"

"Same as we came."

There was a collective groan. "Gotta give the desert another shot to kill us, I guess," Kleitos observed.

Alexandros turned on him, as if waking from a dream. "The desert will do us no harm. You'll be marching under my protection and I am the son of the Ruler of the World, which includes all the deserts on Earth."

The desert has already fried his brains, I thought but held my tongue.

Philotas didn't exercise as much discretion. "Oh great. It was bad enough when we had to obey the orders of a young hothead but now we're going to be commanded by a demigod."

I think he'd meant it as a joke but apparently, in the process of acquiring his divinity, Alexandros had lost his sense of humor. "You can stay up tonight and get the camels ready," he told Philotas. "The rest of you'd better get some sleep."

The trip back was in fact much faster and much less onerous. We had plenty of food and water and didn't lose our way even once. After repeated prodding from Hephaistion, Alexandros gave us a brief summary of what he'd heard from the oracle. His first question, about the murderers of his father, was not even put to the oracle, he told us, since his father Zeus-Ammon, being an immortal god, was self-evidently still alive. As far as the identity of his colleagues to whom he should be making sacrifices in order to assure victory over Dareios was concerned, Alexandros smiled knowingly. "Have no worries, my friends," he said with a wink, "the fix is in." Finally, he told us that Zeus-Ammon had approved of the site chosen by Alexandros for his eponymous city. "He thought it was a very good choice."

We were back to Paraitonion in seven short days, none the worse for wear, except for the permanent mental derangement suffered by Alexandros. He never quite managed to shake the apotheosis delusions implanted in his brain by the various and sundry priests at Memphis and Ammonion and seared in by the hot Saharan sun.

Chapter 7 – The Runup

Alexandria almost didn't happen. No sooner had we returned to Rhakotis from our harrowing excursion to the Oasis at Ammon than Alexandros, armed with Ammon's endorsement of his proposed new city, decided to take on the additional role of city architect. Toting a basket filled with powdered chalk, he started by pacing off the location of the western wall of the city, trailed by his usual entourage of aides, advisors, and bodyguards. Some of the soldiers were carrying additional baskets of chalk because Alexandros had a large city in mind. He was dumping handfuls of chalk onto the sandy soil as he went along to indicate the course of the wall as well as the location of the western gate that would pierce the wall in the middle. He finished his first basket of chalk before reaching the point where the southwestern corner of the battlements would be built but there were plenty more baskets to go.

After he finished demarcating the walls and the three principal city gates, he proceeded to designate the location of the harbor, the future royal palace, the various temples, municipal buildings, residential quarters, and so on. As his excitement grew, so did his pace. Soon, he was practically running, leaving winded assistants and squalls of chalk powder in his wake. Inspired by the example of Ephesos, he wanted a rectilinear street grid, with a broad avenue connecting the harbor to the southern gate, bisected at right angles by another broad avenue running between the western and eastern gates. He had many more streets and buildings to outline when the powder ran out. Alexandros was incredulous. "I'm just getting started," he yelled, "and a lack of chalk is going to stop me?"

A quick-thinking soldier grabbed a basket of barley grain intended for next day's breakfast and handed it to Alexandros. The king's visage lit up like the face of a child given a brand-new toy and he resumed his mad dash, leaving lines of barley behind as he ran. The flocks of seagulls that had mostly stayed clear of our rapidly moving knot of gasping men took an abrupt new interest in our activities. Taking flight, as if by a single command, the birds descended on the newly laid out streets and avenues and ate them.

Alexandros, enthralled by divine inspiration and oblivious to his surroundings, kept running and pouring out baskets' worth of barley until, upon turning a corner of one of his would-be temples, he finally noticed that his carefully laid plans were being consumed as quickly as he made them. He was brought up short, stricken by a sudden horror. "The gods are rejecting my city! These birds are their messengers." The child enjoying his new toy turned, in the blink of an eye, into an old man mourning over the corpse of his dearest companion. Those of us who had managed to keep up with him during his run stood around – panting, mute, and unable to offer any consolation.

Aristandros finally caught up to us. "It's a good omen, sire," he said when he had regained his breath. "This shows your city will become the emporion that will feed the world, both intellectually and literally."

It didn't make much sense but it was exactly what Alexandros wanted to hear. His mien brightening once again. "We'd better send for Deinokrates and let him finish the job."

Deinokrates of Rhodos was the architect who had supervised the rebuilding of Ephesos. The venerable master planner did in fact show up in due course and Alexandria was built, more or less as Alexandros had laid it out, but by then Alexandros had long since resumed the pursuit of his destiny.

****

In Pella, it was a dark and stormy night. The weather was fine; all the drama was taking place indoors. By coincidence, three messengers had arrived at the royal palace almost simultaneously that afternoon. The first messenger had been sent by Zopyrion, whom Antipatros had appointed strategos of Thrake and provided with 30,000 badly needed men in order to pacify the belligerent and rebellious tribes of barbarians constantly threatening Macedonia's eastern and northern frontiers. Zopyrion had enlarged his brief and had marched far beyond Thrake into the wilds of Skythike, where he had somehow become embroiled in a conflict with Olbia, an emporion founded by Miletos on the northern coast of the Black Sea. Olbia served as the principal transit point for the export of grain, fish, and slaves from Skythike to the Greek cities around the Aegean and the import of Greek manufactured goods to the vast, untamed territories of Central Eurasia. While Zopyrion's army was besieging Olbia, their trading partners – the fierce, nomadic Skythians – were in turn harrying Zopyrion's army. Zopyrion was asking for more men.

The second messenger had come from Korrhagos, Antipatros's strategos in the Peloponnese. He reported that the uprising ignited by King Agis was spreading. The Spartan army was on the march, reinforced by contingents of Elians, Arkadians, and Achaians. Korrhagos had withdrawn, with his 10,000 troops, to Megalopolis, which had remained loyal to the Hellenic League and hence to Macedonia, but which lacked the means to defend itself against the combined forces of the rebels led by Agis. Korrhagos did not believe he could hold them off either and urgently requested reinforcements.

The third messenger had brought a letter from Alexandros. Antipatros tossed it aside without reading it. He already knew what Alexandros wanted.

"Do they all think we plant dragons' teeth in the spring and harvest fully-armed warriors by summertime?" Antipatros asked. "Where am I supposed to come up with more soldiers? If the Epirotes decided to invade right now, we wouldn't be able to hold them off."

Kassandros smirked. "For that matter, if Olympias decided to invade right now, we couldn't keep her out."

"It's not funny, son," the old regent fumed. "While our ostensible king is gallivanting Zeus only knows where, our country is at risk of disintegrating. And I'm supposed to keep it together somehow against the day when he might decide to come back and resume his duties as king."

"No, you're keeping it together for us."

"Stop saying stupid stuff," Antipatros yelled at his son. "You have no idea who's listening on the other side of that door."

"Well, in that case, perhaps you should lower your voice. Besides, I've got Olympias confined to the women's quarter."

"I repeat – you have no idea who you're dealing with. That woman is a witch. She can slither through cracks you can't even see. Besides, I think you should be a little more circumspect in how you treat her. Her son happens to be the king of Macedonia and her brother and son-in-law happens to be the king of Epiros. And, last I heard, they were both pretty good soldiers with large armies at their disposal."

This last observation reminded Antipatros of the cause for his fury. "That son-of-a-snake has taken away 47,000 of our best soldiers and he continues to kill them off. And for what?"

Kassandros knew better than to answer.

"While our country is assailed on every side. What am I supposed to do?"

"It does sound like both Zopyrion and Korrhagos are in trouble."

"I'm not entrusting whatever troops we have left to another commander."

"So, what's your alternative?"

"What else," Antipatros shrugged. "I'm going lead them myself."

"That's a trick I'll be interested to see."

"What's that?"

"Watch you split yourself in two, so half of you can march to Zopyrion's aid and the other half to Korrhagos's. Are you thinking of slicing yourself vertically, from head down to your crotch, or horizontally, across the waist?"

Antipatros only glared at his son, who continued undaunted. "If you do it vertically, you'll have half a brain for each expedition but if you do it horizontally, then you can have your head leading in one direction and your balls in the other."

"Oh, shut up," his father finally exploded. "This is no time for jokes."

"I could lead one of the armies for you," Kassandros suggested quietly.

Now, it was the regent's turn to laugh. "You could do what? You talk a good game, and you sure are a nasty piece of work, but you couldn't lead a hunting party trying to capture a rabbit."

Kassandros rose to his feet, ready to pounce on his father, but then he thought better of it. He realized the old man could probably still take him. "Asshole," he muttered under his breath and sat down again.

Antipatros pretended not have noticed his son's uprising. "You're right. I can't be in two places at the same time. Unfortunately, that means I can't do anything for Zopyrion. He got himself into this trouble and he'll just have to dig himself out."

"Even if it means losing 30,000 of our men?"

"What in Haides do you want me to do? I've got to deal with that prick Agis first. Meantime, I'm going to leave you here, as regent in my stead. Can I trust you not to do anything stupid while I'm gone?"

"You can trust me, dad." And, for once, Kassandros meant it.

******

Barsine couldn't wait for Alexandros to wake up. "I have some news, my liege," she said by way of greeting when he finally emerged from his cabin.

"Yes, what is it?" Alexandros was clearly not paying attention. He was busy trying to determine how much progress the barge had made overnight. Because most of the vessels in our flotilla weren't deemed seaworthy, the decision had been made to return to Pelousion by sailing all of our vessels back up the Nile to the apex of the delta and then down to Pelousion, rather than taking the more direct route from Rhakotis to Pelousion via the Mediterranean Sea. Alexandros wasn't happy about the resultant delay.

"I think I'm pregnant, my liege." She touched his arm in an effort to bring his gaze back to her beaming face.

Alexandros finally looked away from the shore. "We should be making the turn for the Pelousion branch of the delta soon but I can't be sure. The river has really changed since the flood receded." Then, realizing from her expression that he must have missed something, "What d'you say?"

"I'm pregnant," she repeated, unable to suppress the happiness in her voice.

"Really?" Alexandros smiled. "Well, I'm not surprised. I never believed you were barren, even if your previous husband never managed to sire a child. Still, Memnon couldn't have been much of a man."

Barsine's eyes filled with tears and she bit her lip to keep it from trembling. She really missed her children. She hadn't seen them for months and could only hope they were safe and healthy. For an instant she wanted to spit the truth into Alexandros's face. *The father of my four children was more of a man than you'll ever be*, she wanted to say but she put on a smile instead. "No one can compare to you, my liege. It'll be the happiest day of my life when I give you a son." *Because it'll be the day when I secure the future of all my kids.*

Alexandros was oblivious to the storm of emotions that had blazed across Barsine's countenance. "He'll be one-quarter-divine, you know." His smile grew wider.

Barsine couldn't tell whether he was joking or serious. "He'll be completely divine because he'll be our son."

"I guess you're right." Alexandros was beginning to warm to the idea of a scion. "But how do you know it'll be a boy?"

"I can feel it." She wormed her way into his arms, as if to let him feel her baby too, although there was nothing to feel as yet.

Alexandros didn't push her away. She was, in fact, more beautiful than ever. Soon, they made their way back into his cabin, delaying their breakfast by fifteen minutes or so.

"You have to wait for this one to come out before you can make another one," she chided him playfully when they were done.

"I don't like to wait." He grinned.

She kissed him, almost fondly. "Don't I know it."

For a moment, each of them was happy with the world.

****

The moment didn't last. There was a sudden commotion, with soldiers yelling from the shore and nearby galleys, with rowboats being launched from every direction, with men stripping off their clothes and diving into the brown, crocodile-infested waters of the Nile.

"What's going on?" Alexandros yelled.

"Young Hektor's missing," somebody yelled back.

There was no need to explain who young Hektor was. Although there were lots of Hektors in the army, there was only one "young Hektor" – Parmenion's fourteen-year-old son, the one who loved to swim between the boats, visiting his friends, the soldiers.

Alexandros stripped off his tunic and dove in as well, joining the churning melee of swimmers in the middle of the stream. As soon as Hephaistion saw what had happened, he, along with a few of his men, boarded a small boat and rowed over. When the boat pulled alongside the king, Hephaistion, with the help of his men, grabbed Alexandros and pulled him into the boat. "Have you lost your mind?" he screamed at his sovereign. It was the only time I've ever heard Hephaistion raise his voice to Alexandros.

Alexandros was beside himself. "The kid's in there somewhere. We've got to save him."

"There are plenty of men trying to save him already. We don't need to lose you to a crocodile as well."

Alexandros looked at his friend as if he were insane. "How could a crocodile hurt me?"

"You're right, Aniketos. It's a ridiculous idea." Hephaistion turned his head to hide a smirk and made sure his men maintained a firm grip on the struggling king.

The search continued until well past nightfall. The entire army came to a halt. Hardened soldiers, some of whom had killed dozens of men and had watched hundreds of their own comrades die, sat in their boats and cried. The body of young Hektor was never found.

****

Finally, more than five months after we had left, we returned to Pelousion. It was hard to tell who was more excited to see us, the Pelousian natives, who appeared more enamored of Alexandros than ever, now that he was officially their pharaoh, or the soldiers and camp followers whom we had left behind. Evidently, life had been quite boring at the camp. The soldiers who had not come along on our trip up the Nile were happy to see their returning comrades, who in turn were happy to see their favorite strumpets, who in turn were pleased with the increased custom. The hostages, who had been biding their time with nothing to do, were once again hopeful of an early release. The servants, slaves, peddlers, fortune-tellers, and assorted swindlers welcomed the return to normalcy. Even our pack animals and dogs seemed pleased to have us back.

While the camp was a cauldron of joyful reunions and pent-up releases, I took advantage of the chaos to look in on Barsine's children. I found them living in utter squalor with all the other Persian captives. However, unlike Dareios's family, they seemed perfectly content with their lot. I was astonished at how much the kids had grown since the last time I'd seen them. The oldest girl was now nine and the baby boy had become a three-year-old toddler. They had enough food to eat, plenty of sand in which to play, a tent secure from nasty adults in which to sleep, and two mommies and an auntie to take care of them.

After distributing some gifts to the kids and the two "mommy" serving girls, I finally had a moment to take a good look at "auntie" Artakama. And when I say "take a good look," I mean gape open-mouthed long enough for a pair of humming birds to build a nest and raise their hatchlings on my tongue. Barsine's younger sister was sixteen now and, overnight, in two short years, she'd turned from an attractive girl into a seductive siren.

"You've grown," I muttered after I'd managed to close my mouth, handing over a bracelet I'd found for her.

"Well, you've gotten thinner. I don't think they're feeding you enough. And thank you for the present."

Before I could think of a witty riposte to those acute observations, a fat eunuch burst into the tent and grabbed me by my breastplate. "My mistress must see you. You must come with me now!"

I gave Artakama an apologetic glance and followed the fat eunuch into an adjoining tent, even more crowded and fetid than the one I'd just left. In the dim interior, lying on a straw pallet that took up half the tent, I saw an elderly woman who bore a passing resemblance to Dareios's number one wife, Queen Stateira.

"Her Majesty is very ill," the eunuch informed me. I looked at the other people in the tent for confirmation of both the identity and the state of health of the elderly woman. They were all there, in the one small tent: Sisygambis, the queen mother; Little Stateira, at fourteen no longer little; Drypetis, twelve and showing the first signs of puberty, and Ochos, ten years old and no longer rambunctious. None of them was paying any attention to the sick woman on the pallet or to me, for that matter.

I turned to the eunuch. "What's the matter with her?"

"We don't know. Nobody is willing to come and take a look at her. They all think she's just faking it."

"Either that or they all simply hate her," Stateira's mother-in-law chimed in.

The stench was getting unbearable. "I'll get a physician to come and examine her." I sprinted out of the tent.

In my hurry to get away, I almost bowled over a young man heading in the opposite direction. "Kallisthenes! When did you get back?"

"I literally just arrived. I'm trying to find Alexandros's tent."

"C'mon, I'll show you."

When we had first entered Pelousion to begin our "conquest" of Egypt, and once it had become clear we wouldn't be encountering much opposition, Alexandros had decided that Kallisthenes should don his "scientific cloak" and embark on a voyage of discovery to find the source of the Nile and to collect any exotic specimens he might encounter along the way. Although Alexandros detailed a small band of soldiers to accompany Kallisthenes, it struck me at the time as a suicide mission, the kind of assignment I used to get when Aristandros was still trying to get me killed. I was therefore pleased to see that Kallisthenes had made it back alive. "So, what did you discover?"

"I can't tell you, Metoikos." He struggled to contain his excitement. "Our king must be the first to hear."

"He's the pharaoh now."

"Not the king?"

"Well, both. And the son of Ammon, too."

Kallisthenes gave me a puzzled look but, before I could explain, we reached Alexandros's tent, putting an end to our conversation.

Alexandros was in the midst of making his dispositions for Egypt. He gave a slight nod in our direction to acknowledge our entrance but then resumed the business at hand. It was soon evident he was following his usual blueprint for the governance of conquered territories. He retained as much of the local bureaucracy as possible, while making sure all tribute and tax revenue would be diverted to his own coffers and superimposing a layer of his own designees to oversee the administration of the province. In light of Egypt's long history of rebellion against outside rulers, he was more meticulous than usual in leaving behind an adequate military force to discourage any uprisings. He stationed large garrisons in Pelousion and Memphis and deployed a naval squadron to patrol the Nile delta. In a departure from his previous custom, he ordered the garrison and fleet commanders to report directly to him, rather than to a provincial satrap. And in recognition of the seductive riches of Egypt, which had a tendency to corrupt even the most upright governors, he split up civil administrative responsibilities among several individuals. The entire machinery of tax collection remained in Egyptian hands, up to and including the chief tax collectors for Upper and Lower Egypt. These chief tax collectors were again directed to report directly to Alexandros, although they were supposed to deliver their collections to a Naukratian Greek named Kleomenes, who was expected to act as the receiver, and transmitter, of taxes. Other than being told to make sure all the taxes were duly collected and see to it that none of the revenue stuck to his hands in the process of transmission, Kleomenes was given very little authority over the civil affairs in Egypt and no authority at all over any military forces. Two other Macedonian generals were appointed to oversee the civil government of the province and to report, once again directly, to Alexandros. No single individual was designated as satrap of Egypt. In theory, all these autonomous commanders and bureaucrats were supposed to keep an eye on each other and to inform Alexandros immediately if any of their colleagues were plotting to seize control of the people, wealth, or resources of the province.

While Alexandros was talking, Kallisthenes kept fidgeting. I could tell he was barely able to contain himself. Once or twice, I was sure he was on the verge of interrupting the pharaoh. Finally, Alexandros dismissed the assembled dignitaries, leaving only the usual commanders, aides, and bodyguards in the tent. Kallisthenes edged forward, his right hand rising, his mouth half open, but Alexandros ignored him, engaging in some light-hearted banter with his entourage instead. It soon became clear, at least to me, that Alexandros, having noticed Kallisthenes's eagerness, was planning to torment his young scribe for as long as possible. Hephaistion, attuned as usual to the vagaries of his friend's whims, suddenly remembered that the two of them were expected at that very instant at a pomegranate-seed-spitting contest on a nearby wharf. Upon hearing the reminder, Alexandros rose briskly to his feet and, nodding solemnly to the soldiers around him, headed for the exit.

"But sire!" Kallisthenes's desperation was stamped on his face. Alexandros pretended not to have heard and continued to walk. Kallisthenes lunged forward. If I had not grabbed him, he might have tackled his king.

When Alexandros reached the tent flap, he spun on his heels and laughed. "So, did you discover the source of the Nile?"

"Me?" Kallisthenes was momentarily discomposed, unsure whether the question was addressed to him. His response provoked fresh gales of laughter among the men in the tent.

"No, I was asking the crocodile that is sneaking up behind your butt. Of course, you. Didn't I send you to find the source of the Nile?"

"Yes you did, sire."

"Well, did you find it?"

"I found out about it, yes, although I didn't see it myself. Or should I say, I didn't see them myself."

Alexandros paused in his laughter. "What do you mean, them?"

"Well, sire, as you ordered me, I sailed upstream with my men. We reached Memphis in four days ..."

"That's good speed."

"... then Thebes, eight days later. The farther south we sailed, the swifter the current became and the weaker and less frequent the breezes from the north that had helped drive us at the outset. After Thebes, our sail was useless and the men had to row hard to make any progress at all against the ever-strengthening current. It was seven long days of unremitting labor to get to the southern border of Upper Egypt. The farthest reach of Egyptian authority is marked by a city called Syene. Unfortunately, its inhabitants seemed less than friendly; we thought it prudent to refrain from docking. Instead, we stopped at a long, skinny island in the middle of the river, called Elephantine. I couldn't find out whether it had gotten its name because of the brisk ivory trade that was conducted on the island or because its shape resembles an elephant's tusk. We rested at the trading post on the island for two days. I'd never seen a more diverse collection of rough characters assembled in one place in my entire life. Men of every shade and size, speaking languages none of our native rowers understood, rushed up to us, eager to buy whatever goods we had. They even accepted our coins in payment for the provisions we bought. And, in exchange for a couple of swords, I was able to hire a local guide who proved invaluable to us the rest of the way.[16]

"The day after we set out from Elephantine, we found out why Upper Egypt ends at that point in the Nile. As we sailed that morning, the current became stronger and stronger, the water turned white, and a low thunder up ahead grew louder and louder. And then we

---

[16] See Map 10 at AlexanderGeiger.com to trace the route traveled by Kallisthenes on his voyage of discovery.

reached a bend in the river and found ourselves confronted by the first of the Nile cataracts. That's what the locals call portions of the river where the granite mountains on either side close in, leaving nothing but a narrow gorge chocked with boulders and stone ledges over which the water tumbles with tremendous power and noise. It's an awesome sight but there's no way to sail across a cataract. I thought our journey was finished. Before we could turn around, though, our guide rushed over and pointed to a path on one of the banks. He insisted that, if we wanted to continue, we could. All we had to do is haul our boat beyond the cataract using this path.

"We unloaded the boat and carried all our provisions first, leaving a couple of men to guard the empty boat. It took us two days simply to trudge, weighted down as we were, to the next stretch of navigable water. More than once during our trek I was sure we'd lose some men down the precipitous cliffs.

"When we reached the landing site on the far side of the cataract, we put down our cargo, slept on a rocky ledge, and then made our way back to the empty boat. How we managed to half drag, half carry the boat across that vertiginous trail, I still don't understand.

"After sailing another two days against the swift, cool waters of the river, we reached the second cataract. This one was nine miles long, with the water cascading over successive ledges of black granite, but the overland portage was easier this time.

"The land on the other side of the cataracts, and continuing all the way to the southern edge of the continent, is called Aithiopia. Except for a couple of cities, it's relatively sparsely populated. After two more large cataracts and innumerable smaller ones, the Nile took a sharp turn to the left. After a while we were actually rowing in the opposite direction, back north. The men were not pleased with this turn of events.

"Fortunately, not long after the sharp left turn, we reached a major port, called Napata. It's inhabited by dark-skinned people, some brown, some completely black, and the rest every shade in between. Many of the inhabitants are giants, much taller than any soldier in our army. Even the women were taller than my men. And all of them were running around naked, wearing nothing more than a loincloth. However, they were healthy, well-fed, and they smiled a great deal. They had brilliant white teeth. They welcomed us with good humor, fed us, sheltered us for a night, and sent us on our way.

"Right after Napata, we hit another major cataract. And we were still traveling back north. After an arduous portage, followed by days and days of hard rowing, we reached another turn and resumed our journey in a mostly southerly direction. For some reason this made us feel better.

163

"The sun was getting higher and higher in the sky. It seemed directly overhead most of the time. Surprisingly, the temperature was still bearable, probably because we were constantly gaining altitude. And, I should mention, there was another major cataract and many more small ones.

"After three more weeks, we reached the capital city of that region, which is called Meroe. At one time, the Egyptian pharaohs must have extended their rule that far because we saw pyramids in Meroe just like the pyramids near Memphis and Thebes. According to our guide, the locals believe it wasn't Egyptian pharaohs who'd once overrun this land but Merovian kings who'd traveled downriver and conquered and ruled Egypt. We had no way to tell which of those stories was actually true because we had no time to investigate. Instead, we pressed on in our search for the source of the Nile.

"After ten more days of sailing, we came to a fork in the road. More accurately, we came to the confluence of two rivers, both about the same size, in terms of width, strength of current, and volume of water delivered. I couldn't tell which was the Nile and which was a tributary.

"We disembarked at this point and spent a day searching for someone who could enlighten us. After sunset, we spotted a campfire and found a lone hunter roasting some animal on a spit. Fortunately, our guide was able to converse with this man. Unfortunately, the information he obtained wasn't very useful.

"The man told us that both rivers are called Nile. The one toward the east is called the Blue Nile; the one continuing more or less in a southerly direction is called the White Nile. He said the Blue Nile originates in a great lake in some tall mountains many days' sail to the southeast of the spot we had reached. The White Nile, he said, originates in a great lake far, far to the south. He'd never been that far in his travels but he thought the confluence of the two Niles was at the halfway point between the source of the White Nile and the point where the combined Nile empties into the sea.

"By then, we'd been sailing, rowing, portaging, and struggling for more than three months. Reluctantly, I decided we could go no farther. So, we turned around and came back. And I reached your camp, sire, a little more than an hour ago."

The men in the tent, including Alexandros, had long since stopped laughing and were listening in rapt attention. When Kallisthenes finished his narrative, there was a long moment of silence. Finally, Alexandros cleared his throat and asked: "Did you collect any interesting specimens?"

"We brought back some elephant tusks and a couple of exotic pelts but mostly we couldn't capture or purchase the animals we saw. I wish we could've brought some back. Alas, they were too large and too fast for us.

"You wouldn't believe all the animals we saw. First, we saw huge herds of elephants, some numbering in the hundreds of animals. And each herd was led by a few enormously large males. We saw elephants that were as tall as three men standing on one another's shoulders. The average adult elephant was as big as two men standing atop each other. Of course, there were many juveniles as well, but even these were much bigger than a horse.

"At least we knew what elephants were. A lot of the other animals we'd never seen before, not even in pictures, and had no name for. We saw a camel-like animal with a very long neck, its head even higher up than an elephant's. It ran briskly and gracefully, had a spotted hide, and ate leaves of tall trees, using a dark blue tongue that was as big and long as a man's arm.

"There were uncountable herds of wild horses, each one striped with black and white horizontal stripes. As they ran, we couldn't tell where one horse ended and the next one began. All we saw was a streaking black-and-white ribbon whirling by, without beginning or end.

"We observed some truly ugly canine creatures with a hideous, barking laugh, that seemed to favor carrion. We glimpsed an incredibly swift, large, spotted cat that covered distances faster than an eagle could fly and that could bring down one those equine creatures before it knew what had hit it. We saw so many other creatures. I wish we had managed to bring some of them back, alive or dead. Best we could do was bring back some pelts."

Alexandros had many questions and Kallisthenes answered them as best he could. It was almost dawn when the king finally clapped his hands. "You did surprising well, Kallisthenes. Who would've thought a mere scribe could do more than misunderstand my dictation?"

Kallisthenes turned beet red. "Thank you, sire."

"Now go get some rest. We'll have a little banquet tonight and then start our march back to Tyros tomorrow."

****

"Sometimes I wish I could believe in metempsychosis," Seleukos said. "Tonight's one of those times."

We were seated next to each other at Alexandros's farewell banquet to Pelousion. It was a massive, open-air affair, illuminated by a full moon, dozens of cooking fires, and a thousand torches. The attendees were spread out from the bottom to the top of a gently rising, barren hill, located about a mile to the east of the city. Everyone was invited, the native Pelousians as well as their soon-to-be-departing visitors. Even the hostages and the camp followers were allowed to participate. However, there was a hierarchy to the seating arrangements. Lounging on a couple of large couches set at the top of the hill were two triads: On one couch reclined Alexandros, flanked by his most fawning flatterers, Hephaistion and Perdikkas; on the adjoining couch sat Parmenion with his two surviving sons, Philotas and Nikanoros. The arrangements reflected the dual purpose of the feast, as a celebration of Alexandros's accomplishments in Egypt and a farewell to Parmenion's youngest son, Hektor. Arrayed in a semicircle below the peak of the hill were Alexandros's top commanders and aides. Farther down the hillside were our honored guests, the Pelousians, mixed in with lower-ranking commanders and ordinary troops. At the very bottom was the Persian royal family, the other hostages, the ladies of the night, and various slaves, servants, tradesmen, eunuchs, and hangers-on.

The idea of combining the adulation of Alexandros with the obsequies for Hektor proved to be an unfortunate choice. The contrast between the evident happiness of the king and the suffering etched into the face of the bereaved father was painful to see.

"What is metempsychosis?" Kleitos, seated on the other side of Seleukos, asked. Seleukos, apparently lost in thought, ignored the question.

Conquest of Persia

People were beginning to form two lines, one leading to Alexandros, the other snaking its way toward Parmenion. Protocol and good sense suggested a brief visit with the king, pharaoh, and son of Ammon first, before stopping by to express condolences to the senior general, but the queue waiting to speak to Alexandros was long and, what was worse, it was full of Pelousians who insisted on prostrating themselves when they reached his exalted highness, taking much too long to spit out their heartfelt gratitude and perform their individual acts of adoration. The soldiers interspersed among the Pelousians, mostly weathered Macedonian veterans, contented themselves with clapping Alexandros on the shoulder and making a few bawdy wisecracks about his upcoming fatherhood. (It was remarkable how quickly word of Barsine's pregnancy had spread throughout the camp.) But for most of the soldiers, the Alexandros line was moving way too slowly and they opted to join the much longer, wider river of men waiting to share their own personal reminiscences of Hektor with his father and brothers. Through it all, Parmenion said almost nothing, nodding occasionally, tears coursing silently down his cheeks.

Seleukos shifted his gaze from Parmenion to Kleitos, as if he had just heard his question. "Metempsychosis is the theory, advanced by various philosophers, including Pythagoras and Platon, that the soul, or psyche, is immortal and that, when a human being dies, his psyche migrates, perhaps after a little delay, into the body of a newly-born child," he explained. "And, looking at those two men above us, I wish I could believe that such a thing could happen."

****

After all the well-wishers, worshipers, and condolers had returned to their seats, Alexandros turned to his loyal, grieving second-in-command. "Your son had more friends than any soldier in this army. He will live on in the memory of all these people."

"Thank you, sire. I'm sure that thought will comfort me in the coming days but right now I just miss him so. Our excursion on the Nile with my boys on board was the highpoint of my life. I suppose the gods were envious and wouldn't let us finish it together."

"He'll live on in the hearts of all these men," Alexandros repeated.

"You are very kind, sire, and your words of solace mean a lot to me. And by the way, I'm so happy to hear Barsine is with child. Please accept my congratulations and best wishes."

"Thank you but I'm trying not to get ahead of myself. As you say, the gods can be so capricious, generous one minute and cruel the next."

Parmenion smiled ruefully. "You have no idea, sire, what a child will mean to you. You're in for the ride of your life. Your entire outlook will change. It's not all happiness, as I can attest, but it's the most precious thing you can have."

Alexandros nodded but Parmenion knew that only a parent could understand. "You'll know what I mean the minute you hold that tiny person in your hands."

The young king and the old general sat silently, side by side, each lost in his own world.

Eventually, Parmenion broke the silence. "Sire, please forgive me. I've considered bringing this up before but it was only the death of my precious youngster that has truly opened my eyes and given me the courage to tell you what must be said. You should marry Barsine. Your kingdom needs a legitimate heir."

"Are you kidding? She's war booty and Memnon's widow to boot. How could I marry her?"

"She's beautiful and intelligent and she's carrying your child. And you can do anything you want. You can marry more than one woman. Your father married seven of them and occasionally he was married to more than one at the same time. But he made sure that, in you, the realm had a legitimate heir."

Alexandros snorted. "Well, he was not really my father. But I take your point." He was beginning to lose interest in the conversation.

"Think about it," Parmenion urged.

Alexandros promised he would but never did.

****

Mazaios and Bessos were fighting, as usual. They were standing at opposite sides of the Great Hall in the Babylon Palace, separated by two dozen distinguished men, and they were yelling at each other. If the emperor didn't make his entrance soon, there was every possibility of a physical altercation. The other men in the cavernous space stood around idly, in groups of two or three, or leaned against the numerous columns supporting the coffered ceiling and enjoyed the show. Ever since Bessos and his twelve thousand savage Baktrians appeared at the Ishtar Gate, some three weeks earlier, and were met there by the Babylonia homeguard, under the command of Mazaios, who ordered them to turn around and make camp outside the walls of the city, there was little love lost between the two satraps.

Mazaios, the satrap of Mesopotamia and Babylonia, considered himself to be second only to Dareios in the Persian firmament. At forty-nine, he was exactly the same age as Dareios but he'd been a satrap (of Kilikia) when Dareios was nothing more than a common

172

soldier in Artaxerxes Tritos Ochos's imperial bodyguard. And, unlike Dareios, Mazaios was actually a scion of one of the great noble families of Persia. He was urbane, cultured, and politically adroit. When, five years earlier, this obscure captain of the imperial bodyguard, named Kodomannos, somehow became Emperor Dareios Tritos, Mazaios wasted no time in placing his bet on the new strong horse. He was rewarded by being assigned to increasingly more significant commands, culminating in his current position as governor of perhaps the two most important satrapies in the Persian Empire. He also managed somehow not to be present at either the Battle of Granikos or the Battle of Issos, thus maintaining his reputation as an accomplished military commander. Such was Dareios's trust in Mazaios that he promised to give him his eldest daughter Stateira in marriage, as soon as Stateira could be liberated from the clutches of Alexandros, whose captive she currently was.

Bessos was the polar opposite of Mazaios. At twenty-eight, he was almost as young as Alexandros. He was uncouth, uneducated, and violent. He was also the satrap of Baktria and thus the commander of the most feared, most savage, most effective mounted warriors of the Central Asian steppes. Unlike Mazaios, he didn't consider himself as second to Dareios in the Persian pecking order. He saw himself as the only man in the empire capable of saving Dareios's crown against the Greek invaders … if he chose to do so.

He was busy expostulating to Mazaios – loudly, coarsely, and profanely – on the relative merits of his fighters, as compared to Mazaios's ineffectual, cowardly, degenerate troops, when Dareios finally swept into the audience hall, flanked by his bodyguards. Mazaios immediately threw himself to the granite floor. Bessos, after some hesitation and with evident reluctance, eventually sank to his knees.

After mounting the throne, Dareios surveyed the assembled luminaries. These were the great nobles of Persia, the leading commanders, the most important satraps. Each of them was a potential usurper, yet he depended on all of them to save the empire. His only guaranty of incumbency was success on the battlefield. In order to remain emperor, he had to destroy Alexandros and his entire army. The pest from across the Aegean had become a menace to the empire but this time Dareios would be ready for him.

Following his ignominious flight from the field at Issos while fighting still raged all around him, Dareios had spent several days regaining his emotional equilibrium. When he'd managed to recover from his embarrassment, he spent two weeks, with the help of Mazaios and Nabarzanes, unblinkingly dissecting every aspect of the battle. They were forced to face certain inescapable conclusions, foremost among them the inability of Persian infantry to stand up against the Greeks. On the other hand, the Persian cavalry had more than held its own and might well have carried the day had their commander-in-chief not prematurely abandoned the field. The necessary tactical correction was blindingly obvious to Dareios. For the next battle against Alexandros, he'd put all his Persian infantrymen on horseback.

Although the idea, once Dareios explained it, was self-evident, its execution was not. The first challenge was to find at least fifty thousand suitable war-horses. Fortunately, huge herds of wild horses still roamed the steppes of Baktria and Sogdiana. The order went out to capture the horses, tame them, and bring them to Babylon. The next challenge was to produce sufficient armor for fifty thousand men and for their horses, in order to turn them into the formidable knights of Persian heavy cavalry. Finally, there was the matter of training infantrymen to fight aboard these unruly, recently-captured beasts. Dareios, who was, among other things, a superb administrator managed to carry out this entire program during the six months that Alexandros had spent in Egypt.

The defeat at Issos taught Dareios other lessons as well. For example, the battlefield would have to be carefully chosen and the tactics adapted to the composition of the new army. The next battle would take place on terrain dictated by Dareios and it would unfold in accordance with his tactical plans. In fact, as Dareios now proceeded to explain to his commanders, he already knew where and how the next battle would be fought. He explained to them that a great battle, involving Persian cavalry and Greek hoplites, had been fought, a mere seventy years earlier, on the doorstep of Babylon. In that battle, the Greeks were neutralized and the Persian cavalry carried the day. Dareios had read all about the Battle of Kounaxa in a book written by a Greek general named Xenophon, who had been there. Kounaxa was located on the western bank of the Euphrates River, about thirty miles north of Babylon, and it lay athwart the logical invasion route for any army seeking to attack Babylon. It was Dareios's intention to await the approach of the pan-Hellenic army in Babylon, then deploy his newly-reconstituted forces, comprised almost exclusively of heavy Persian and light Baktrian cavalry, at nearby Kounaxa. His plan was simple. He would reprise the successful tactics deployed by his predecessor, Emperor Artaxerxes Deuteros, and kill Alexandros – just as Artaxerxes had killed Kyros, the dashing, charismatic leader of the invading army seventy years earlier. Somehow, it hadn't occurred to Dareios that Alexandros might've read Xenophon's classic as well.

Dareios issued detailed orders to the assembled commanders. Mazaios was told to take 3,000 of his best cavalry troops to the last reported location of Alexandros's army and, once he had located them, to harass them as best he could but mostly to shadow their movements and report back to Dareios on their progress. Other commanders were assigned to oversee the equipping and training of the new army. Bessos was told to work with other cavalry commanders to make sure there was proper coordination between his lightly-armed, more mobile horsemen and the heavily-armored, more ponderous squadrons of traditional Persian knights. Dareios even ordered the construction of two hundred scythed chariots, which had long since become obsolete as a weapon of war, simply because Artaxerxes Deuteros had deployed two hundred scythed chariots at the Battle of Kounaxa.

"The days of the pest from across the Aegean are numbered," a smiling Dareios told his commanders as he sent them off to carry out his orders.

******

The pan-Hellenic army returned to Tyros in late spring, enjoying warm Mediterranean breezes and cedar-scented mountain paths en route. The navy, which had accompanied us back from Egypt, was dispatched by Alexandros to the Peloponnese to assist Antipatros in his fight against Agis. We set up a long-term camp atop the ruins of what had been Old Tyros for those who would be staying behind: the halt and lame, the sick and infirm, camp followers and hostages, and all the women whom we had captured during our campaigns or who had joined us voluntarily along the way, including Barsine, Antigone, Artakama, and all the other consorts, courtesans, concubines, companions, and close personal friends of the female persuasion. The rest of us set off for the

Mesopotamian plain just before the arrival of the first hot days of summer.

We marched northeast, through Assyria, all the way to Thapsakos on the western bank of the Euphrates. Assyria, which stretches from a narrow strip of fertile land on the Mediterranean, known as Lowland Assyria, to an even narrower strip of land made fertile by irrigation canals on the Euphrates, is almost entirely desert in between. It took us more than a month to cross the desert. For long stretches, one lasting four days, we saw nothing but sand. We carried as much water with us as we could and Arimmas, the satrap of Lowland Assyria, was supposed to have set up food and water dumps for us along our route. Not seeing many prepositioned supplies, I was beginning to believe we were on another march to the Oasis of Ammon. Finally, we spotted, through hazy, shimmering waves of heat, the first verdant harbingers of the Euphrates, one of the two great rivers that gave Mesopotamia its name. By the time we arrived at Thapsakos, it was the height of summer. Marching through the Assyrian desert, in the middle of summer, with very little water, weighted down by armor and gear, is not conducive to human survival, unless one happens to be a Bedouin. And even the Bedouins, whose nomadic outposts we passed from time to time, took one look at our dust-covered, bedraggled, ghostly columns and ran the other way.

Conquest of Persia

As we approached Thapsakos, however, we noticed that we'd acquired a shadow – a large unit of Persian cavalry, perhaps 3,000 in number, which stayed well to the south of us, while matching our speed and maintaining visual contact. Alexandros watched them for a while and laughed. "Dareios has sent an advance guard to keep track of us. He must be worried the desert will swallow us before he's had a chance to execute our destruction himself."

In fact, making a right turn and marching an additional four hundred miles south, along the west bank of the Euphrates, was the obvious route to take for an army intent on sacking Babylon. Dareios was certain Alexandros was headed for Babylon because he'd threatened repeatedly to engage Dareios in a set piece battle. The Persian emperor wanted to make sure that, when the decisive showdown occurred, he'd emerge victorious. A capable and methodical soldier, Dareios left nothing to chance. Not only was Mazaios charged with the responsibility of shadowing Alexandros's army and reporting our progress back to Babylon, he was also told to destroy every village, farm, hut, silo, and grain of barley between Thapsakos and Babylon, in order to ensure that, by the time Alexandros's army arrived at Kounaxa, just thirty miles north of Babylon, it would be exhausted, starved, and burnt to a crisp. At that moment, Dareios could unleash his well-rested, much larger army and finally destroy these pests from across the Aegean who'd begun to resemble a plague of locusts.

Mazaios carried out his instructions to the letter. Nothing of military value, and very little of civilian use, remained on either bank of the Euphrates. Unfortunately for Dareios, Alexandros decided not to march down the Euphrates toward Babylon. Instead, we crossed the river at Thapsakos and continued our march northeast, toward the other great river of Mesopotamia, the Tigris. Beyond Tigris lay Ekbatana and the eastern provinces.

****

Olympias smiled ruefully, watching the frolicking children. She had absorbed quite a few blows lately, the most recent being the death of her brother (and son-in-law), Alexandros of Epiros, but seeing her grandchildren at play never failed to gladden her heart. The twins, Kadmeia and Neoptolemos, were four. *A perfect age*, Olympias reflected. *Old enough to entertain themselves, as well as their elders, but too young to appreciate the gravity of their situation.*

The children's mother, Kleopatra, brought them to Pella for a short visit with their grandmother, while her husband, the king of Epiros, was off on another one of his military adventures in Italy. That was seven months earlier. They had arrived within days after Antipatros's departure for the Peloponnese and had never been permitted to leave.

In the absence of the regent, his son Kassandros was taking full advantage of his temporary autonomy. At age twenty-seven, he believed himself entitled to a kingship or two somewhere in the world but as long as Alexandros (who was two years younger than Kassandros) was still alive, the throne of Macedonia remained out of reach. And even though Alexandros hadn't returned to Pella in more than three years, he'd left Antipatros, not Kassandros, in charge. Kassandros's status as the regent's son brought many privileges but no actual power.

Even after Antipatros had marched out with an army of almost 20,000 men to deal with the revolt led by King Agis, he left behind precise instructions carefully circumscribing Kassandros's discretion. He also maintained constant epistolary contact with his son, staying abreast of all developments and giving detailed directives on the most mundane matters. Finally, he also salted a number of trusted agents among the servants in the palace to keep an eye on his son and to notify him immediately of any deviation from orders. Antipatros loved and spoiled his youngest son but he also knew him better than anyone.

The one realm in which Kassandros deemed himself absolute ruler was the women's quarter of the palace. Antipatros had agreed that Olympias should be kept confined and incommunicado, to the extent possible, and he had given Kassandros broad discretion in effectuating this objective. There was, of course, a profound difference between father and son as to the permissible means and methods to be employed in connection with the queen mother – Antipatros believed she had to be treated with kid gloves, if only out of deference to King Alexandros – but he'd failed to communicate these views to his son in writing and now that Antipatros was gone, Kassandros felt free to implement his own procedures.

The arrival of Kleopatra, with her two little children and her enormous retinue, was the first operational challenge with which Kassandros had to deal on his own. His preference would've been to deny Kleopatra entry and send her home to Epiros but even he realized that such a course of action might have unfortunate ramifications. Not only was Olympias's son and Kleopatra's brother the king of Macedonia but Kleopatra's husband was also the king of Epiros. (To complicate matters even further, Alexandros of Epiros was also Olympias's brother. Yes, Kleopatra's father Philippos had married her off to her uncle –it had made military and diplomatic sense at the time.)

After much deliberation, Kassandros decided to admit Kleopatra and her children to the women's quarter in the palace but to deny entry to any of her servants. He explained that her mother already had plenty of servants and there was limited room in the gynaikonitis. He didn't mention that he was keeping the queen mother under house arrest. Perforce, he had to place Kleopatra and her children under house arrest as well.

"Your brother has never seen his niece and nephew," Olympias mused. "I wish he'd get back already."

Kleopatra tried to sound cheerful. "Well, at least we're together."

The two women were preparing, side-by-side, for the rare treat – or was it tribulation – of a visit by their jailer Kassandros.

"Maybe a letter has come," Olympias continued hopefully, while trying to adjust the belt of her chiton. *There was a time when I had serving girls for these tasks*, she reflected.

Kleopatra shook her head. "If a letter came, he'd never show it to us." She was the more pragmatic and, in this case at least, the more acute observer of the two. "On the other hand, if he did come in with a letter, it would undoubtedly be a forged fabrication." She continued to peer into the small, scratched mirror they were now forced to share. No matter how deplorable the conditions of their incarceration became, both women were united in their determination to put on an upbeat appearance whenever their tormentor deigned to stop in for a visit.

It had been a steady stream of hammer blows. First, after one of the serving girls was caught trying to smuggle out a letter from Kleopatra to her husband, the callow vice-regent was tempted to remove all serving girls from the gynaikonitis but in the end decided to settle for replacing all the soldiers guarding the staircase leading to the women's apartments with his own men and prohibiting anyone, not just Olympias or Kleopatra, from either entering or leaving the premises. Olympias had no doubt she could suborn these greenhorns as well, just as she had all their predecessors, but it would take time. For the present, though, the two women were effectively cut off from contact with the outside the world.

Kassandros's first visit came about a month later. He strutted in, unannounced, brimming with the pleasure of knowing he'd made the women's lives miserable. He failed to take into account Olympias's fierce pride. While he was chatting with Kleopatra in the ladies' reception room, Olympias came charging from her private chamber, armed with a dagger she had somehow managed to secrete under her pallet. If it hadn't been for the startled widening of Kleopatra's eyes, her mother might well have killed Kassandros then and there. As it was, he managed to turn just in time, escaping with nothing worse than a nick on his left shoulder. He never came alone, or unannounced, again.

Although there was no doubt in anyone's mind as to Kassandros's ultimate intentions, he still felt somewhat constrained by the possibility, however remote, that word of his antagonism against the women might somehow reach either Olympias's son or Kleopatra's husband.

Accordingly, he had to content himself with gradually, almost imperceptibly, tightening the screws.

His next visit came when news of Zopyrion's defeat reached Pella. Even from their upstairs quarters, the women could tell something was afoot in the palace. At first, they noticed an increase in activity, with soldiers running across the courtyard. Then, they overheard hurried, whispered conversations between the soldiers and servants, followed by open weeping and lamentation by various women who had evidently learned of the loss of their sons, husbands, or brothers. Eventually, the courtyard erupted in a general uproar when Kassandros attempted to address the rapidly increasing crowd. No one was in a mood to listen.

The only people who didn't know what was going on were the women in the gynaikonitis. In desperation, Olympias sent a couple of the serving girls to beguile the guards and bring back some news. The girls must've exceeded their brief because neither one returned until the next morning. And when they did stagger in, there were indications that their fraternization efforts must have been intimate indeed. Olympias didn't discipline them, however, because by then she had found out what the news was and she thought the dedication to the cause demonstrated by the girls might prove useful in the future.

Kassandros had come in, late the previous evening, accompanied by three guards (and after first sending word he was coming) and explained that a transport vessel carrying Zopyrion and his soldiers had foundered in the Thermaic Gulf, with the loss of all aboard.

Olympias laughed in his face. "Must have been a very large vessel if it was capable of carrying 30,000 soldiers. You may have locked us in here but we're not deaf. And we're not stupid, either. So, how about telling us what really happened?"

Eventually, she had successfully wormed the entire story out of Kassandros. Zopyrion's unnecessary and self-appointed siege of Olbia proved to be a disaster. The Olbians, known heretofore primarily as shrewd businessmen, proved to be resourceful defenders of their city as well. They extended citizenship to all residents and visitors willing to fight on the walls; they manumitted all slaves and put arms in their hands; they forgave business debts and promised future considerations; they did whatever was necessary to prevent Zopyrion's troops from sacking their city. They also persuaded their trading partners, primarily the fierce, savage Skythians, to come to their aid. Eventually, Zopyrion had no choice but to lift the siege and retreat. However, the Skythians, having tasted blood, refused to let the invaders go. They harried the hapless Macedonians all the way back to Thrake, attacking when and where they could, destroying supplies under the cover of night, forcing the retreating army off course.

Zopyrion's soldiers suffered casualties not only as a result of the Skythians' guerrilla raids but also because they lacked adequate food, contracted diseases in the unhealthy climate, and drowned in the many hidden bogs and marshes. Their destruction was completed when the Getai, a hostile Thrakian tribe which controlled the northern bank of the Danube River and which was still smarting from a defeat that Alexandros had inflicted on them some four years earlier, decided to join in the fun, crossed the great river, and delivered the coup de grace to Zopyrion's demoralized, diminished army. As far as Kassandros knew, the Macedonian expeditionary corps had been killed to the last man.

Afterward, Kassandros could only gnash his teeth at the thought of having been somehow induced by Olympias to reveal far more of the story than he'd intended. He retaliated by removing most of the serving girls from the women's quarter and restricting deliveries of food and other necessities.

By the time the lugubrious letter from Epiros arrived, they had no servants at all and were subsisting on a beggar's diet. For once, Kassandros practically flew up the steps and sauntered in, smiling broadly, unable to conceal his glee. He handed the scroll, with its broken seal and numerous wine stains, to Kleopatra.

She glanced at it and, without reading it, handed it back, smiling just as broadly. "You don't really expect me to believe this, do you?"

"Oh, believe it – it's genuine. Came in an hour ago. And I'm really, really sorry." He tried hard not to laugh.

"Let me have it," Olympias commanded. Kassandros obeyed. Olympias read the letter slowly. Then she read it a second time. "Get out!" she screamed and Kassandros scrammed, followed by his three bodyguards.

"I'm afraid it has the ring of truth to it, sweetheart," she said when they were alone.

"What's it say? I didn't want to give him the satisfaction of reading it in front of him. And I assumed it was a forgery in any case."

"It says that your husband's dead."

"Yeah, I got that from the first line but what else does it say? And how do you know it's genuine?"

"It's a pretty complete description of his activities this past year. I've had other reports about him and this letter matches what I'd already heard."

Kleopatra was stunned. "You knew he was dead?"

"No, that I hadn't known until this letter came," Olympias assured her.

"So, how do you know that part isn't made up?"

"Because I wasn't shocked when I read it. Deep down, I think I was expecting something like this. The risks he took, the engagements he accepted. It was almost as if he had a death wish."

"My husband didn't have a death wish!" Kleopatra stomped her foot for emphasis. "He had two wonderful children. He was a king. He had everything a man could wish. Why would he want to die?" She was sobbing by the time she'd finished.

Olympias hugged her daughter. "I put it wrong, my dear. Your husband didn't want to die. What he wanted was to compete with your brother. He wanted to accomplish in the west what your brother is achieving in the east. But it amounted to the same thing. There's never been a military leader like my son. For anybody, even your husband, to try to equal his feats was inevitably going to be fatal."

They spent the night discussing the Epirote Alexandros's many campaigns in Italy, his final stand, as described in the letter, his drives and motivations, his effervescent personality and his fateful ambition.

By the morning, when the children awoke and Kassandros dropped by to gloat, they had dried their tears, arranged their hair, and pasted smiles on their faces. They wouldn't let anyone see them crying.

Not long after they'd learned of Alexandros's death, the women heard another commotion in the courtyard. It was almost a mirror image of the day when word of Zopyrion's defeat had arrived. It started with the energetic hoofbeats of a messenger on a mission, followed by an exclamation, then more shouting. Soon, there was a deafening uproar in the courtyard. But this time, when the messenger rode in, the clippety-clop of his trotting horse beat out a joyful ode to victory, instead of a funereal march. When Kassandros first read the letter, his shout was triumphant; when the crowd learned the news, their joy unconstrained.

The women barred the entrance door to their jail. They had no wish to hear whatever it was that Kassandros wanted to tell them. After the vice-regent tried, unsuccessfully, to gain entrance, he shrugged and went away. Instead, he sent back the serving girls, carrying enough food and wine for an extended feast.

Olympias arched an eyebrow when she saw the serving girls come in, laden with provisions. "What's going on?"

"We've won, we've won!" They were all shouting at once, too excited to tell a coherent tale. The only thing clear was that the Macedonian army, led by Antipatros, had prevailed and the hated King Agis was dead.

"Well, now I understand why Kassandros has suddenly become so solicitous of our welfare," Olympias said. "His father is on his way back."

And in fact, Antipatros himself, trailing a large entourage, including his son, paid them a visit several days later. "I'm pleased to see my son took good care of you ladies in my absence."

"Oh, that he did, that he did," Olympias concurred. "And we're pleased to see you back, safe and sound. I trust the enemy didn't trouble you greatly."

Antipatros made himself comfortable in the only decent chair in the room. He was pleasant and genial, especially compared to his son. "You have no idea, queen mother. Our kingdom came within a hair of losing its independence. The Spartan revolt was joined by every city in the Peloponnese, except Megalopolis. And Megalopolis only remained on our side because it was held by our garrison of 10,000 troops, commanded by Korrhagos. The Spartan King Agis, with his 30,000 troops, was besieging them, and on the verge of taking the city, when I received Korrhagos's urgent plea for help.

"I marched immediately, at the head of 20,000 troops, which was all that was left in Macedonia, after we had sent our best soldiers to your son and after we dispatched Zopyrion to deal with the Thrakian revolt. Fortunately, there were still some members of the Hellenic League, outside of the Peloponnese, who remained loyal to me, if not to Macedonia, and who answered my urgent call for assistance. By the time we arrived at Megalopolis, I had 40,000 men.

"Most importantly, my friend Demades, whom I have been cultivating for years, did his job in Athens and kept them from joining the rebellion. If they had allied themselves with Sparta, your son would've had no kingdom to return to.

"Tragically, we arrived at Megalopolis a couple of days too late. Apparently, Korrhagos, who had no idea that deliverance was only a javelin throw away, despaired of withstanding the siege much longer. Rather than watching his troops die of starvation, he decided to give them the honor of dying as heroes. He sallied out of the city with his 10,000 men and met Agis's army in the open field. Our boys didn't have a chance, starved and outnumbered as they were. All we found, by the time we arrived, were their bodies. Korrhagos himself died fighting. A neat circle of enemy dead marked the place of his last stand."

Olympias opened her mouth to interject but thought better of it.

Antipatros resumed his account. "At that point, we found ourselves in a difficult strategic position.

Although Agis's forces hadn't yet succeeded in sacking Megalopolis, they did hold the high ground between us and the city. And they'd had plenty of time to get used to Agis's leadership style, whereas half of my troops were still trying to learn who I was.

"Nevertheless, there was nothing for it but to attack and trust in the favor of the gods, which is what we did the morning after our arrival. The enemy, especially the Spartans, fought exceptionally well. Soon enough, my men – mostly troops supplied by our allies – were running back down the hill, in disordered flight, with the enemy in hot pursuit.

"It was all I could do to stem the stampede. In truth, it was the example of my wonderful Macedonian troopers, more than my words, that stiffened their resolve. But we did get them to stop running, to turn, and to start fighting back. We actually had a slight numerical advantage but it was to little avail because the field at the point of the encounter was quite narrow.

"The tussle went on all day, with both sides taking heavy casualties and with neither side making any headway. It became clear that, as long as Agis was on the field, we had no chance of victory. He fought like a man possessed, catching our missiles on his shield, or ducking them, and then rising again to snuff the life out of another of my men. And his men, inspired by their leader, followed his example.

"Finally, I got my Agrianian friends to start chucking lance after lance directly at him. Eventually, one lance got through and pierced his legs. His men, seeing their leader down, immediately broke off the shaft and pulled what remained of the lance through the wound but Agis was bleeding heavily. They put him on a shield and ran off, carrying him on their shoulders. I ordered my men to chase them down.

"The Spartans were beginning to tire and we were closing the gap. Agis, realizing we would soon catch up, instructed his men to put him down and continue retreating without him. They, being Spartans, obeyed his order. Agis tried to regain his feet but his legs wouldn't hold him. He sank to his knees, covered himself with his shield, and started to brandish his spear wildly. My men surrounded him but no one was willing to come within striking distance of his spear. Instead, they started throwing their own spears at him, until one managed to penetrate his chest. Agis violently yanked the spear out, creating a jet of bright red blood spurting from his breast. He gazed at his chest, a look of puzzlement on his face, and collapsed onto his shield. Soon, his bleeding slowed to a trickle and his breathing stopped."

"Well, he might have been a Spartan, but he died a soldier's death." Olympias's tone was remarkably cold considering the arresting tale she'd just heard. "And what did you do to capitalize on their leader's death?"

"We pursued the Spartans and their allies as far as we could, killing perhaps 5,000 of them. We lost 3,500, including a thousand Macedonians. But the good news is that my boys have saved our kingdom."

"Well, that is good news indeed. Although my son would have managed it without losing so many of *our* boys, I'm sure."

Antipatros shrugged, rose to his feet, and left, without saying another word.

"I don't think he remembers he's still only the regent," Olympias observed after the visitors had left.

Antipatros eventually sent a letter to Alexandros, telling him that Zopyrion, Alexandros of Epiros, and Agis of Sparta were all dead. He assured the king that he, Antipatros, was now firmly in control of Greece. He closed by mentioning that Olympias and Kleopatra were doing well. Whether this was meant as reassurance or blackmail was not immediately clear.

It took several months for Antipatros's message to catch up to Alexandros.

****

Dareios was conducting routine business in the Great Hall of the Babylon Palace when a disheveled Mazaios stumbled in and prostrated himself in front of the throne. It was hard to tell whether he fell on his face as a sign of respect or as a result of exhaustion, having ridden 450 miles in four days.

"He's not coming to Babylon," Mazaios cried from the floor, too tired to rise to his feet.

"What are you talking about?" Dareios motioned to the guards to restore his second-in-command to an upright position. Someone handed Mazaios a cup of wine.

"He's crossed the Euphrates, your celestial eminence, and he's continuing on, toward the Tigris. He's not turning toward Babylon."

"You mean, he's splitting his forces?"

"No, your divine potency. The entire pan-Hellenic army is marching toward the Tigris. They're not coming down the Euphrates. I think they mean to cross the Tigris somewhere around Arbela and then continue on and take Ekbatana."

Hearing this, Bessos perked up. "They're headed for Baktria!"

Dareios had no patience for the young satrap. "Nobody gives a crap about Baktria. At least Ekbatana is one of my imperial capitals but even so he doesn't care about territory and capitals. He wants me."

"I give a crap about Baktria," Bessos protested indignantly. "And besides, the entire eastern half of your empire is lying supine, wide open to him, waiting to be ravished like a helpless virgin, while you've gathered the best of our troops to sit around uselessly outside the walls of Babylon."

This was the point at which Dareios was supposed to signal to his guards to seize the uncouth hothead from Baktria, drag him out of the hall, and execute him, but the emperor was too preoccupied by the news brought back by Mazaios. He ignored Bessos's outburst and silently pondered his next move.

"We'll find another Kounaxa and squash the pest there," Dareios said quietly after a few minutes, almost as if he were speaking to himself. "It's mostly flat country on both sides of the Tigris around Arbela. We simply have to find the right spot, array our forces, and wait until he marches into our trap."

"Why would he do that?" an exasperated Bessos called out. "He's not a fool. He'll cross the Tigris, just as he has crossed the Euphrates, and lay waste to the eastern provinces. He's never going to engage your much larger army."

"He's done it twice already." Dareios, still not looking up, continued to keep his voice low. "We've made some mistakes, allowing him to escape both times, but there'll be no mistakes this time."

Finally, he raised his eyes and his voice, speaking directly to Bessos. "Only a fool would attempt to rampage through the eastern provinces. That would be like a bear deciding to rampage through an endless marsh. With every step, he'd sink deeper into the mire. The more vigorously he thrashed about, the faster he'd sink. Even if he tried to turn around, he could never emerge from the bog. His army would be swallowed without a trace.

"I only wish he were fool enough to attack the eastern provinces. No, he knows his only chance of surviving this idiotic, suicidal attack against our empire is to kill me and usurp my throne. Don't you understand, his objective is to kill me." Dareios was screaming by now. "And your assignment is to keep me alive. Otherwise, our empire is lost."

There was a stunned silence in the audience hall. Even Bessos, although looking somewhat skeptical, kept his mouth shut.

Dareios continued to ponder. "In fact, this move by Alexandros is a gift to us from Ahura Mazda. On further thought, here's what we'll do: We'll march up the eastern bank of the Tigris and await their arrival at the usual crossing point near Arbela. When they try to cross the river, we'll be waiting on the opposite bank and we'll slaughter them as they try to clamber out. We almost succeeded in doing that at the Granikos. We had them stopped when they first tried to ford that river but then, for some reason, my commanders decided to permit them to cross the next morning unopposed. From what I heard afterward, it was their belief that, if Alexandros's entire army gathered on our side of the river, our cavalry forces could envelop it and destroy it in detail. Had their plan succeeded, that would've been not only the end of Alexandros and his army but also the end of any thought by the Greeks that they could resist the might of the Persian Empire. Unfortunately, Alexandros somehow managed to break out of the trap prepared by my satraps, so now I have to deal with him myself."

"Had you been personally in command at Granikos it would have been a different outcome," one of the sycophants in the hall called out.

"You bet your life," Dareios agreed. "And this time, I'll be there in person. At the Tigris, we'll do to the pest from across the Aegean what we should have done at the Granikos."

Nobody brought up the Battle of Issos.

"Here is the plan," Dareios continued, speaking with renewed confidence. "Bessos, detach some of your fastest horsemen to ride down the western bank of the Tigris to find the exact location of Alexandros's army and report back to us on their progress. There's no need for them to engage in any fighting. All they have to do is keep track of them and report back. But we need some fast and elusive riders. Do you have men who can do that, Bessos?"

"Yes, emperor, we have men who can do that."

"Good. Mazaios, you get back on your horse and rejoin your troops as fast as you can. In fact, take another 3,000 cavalrymen with you. Your job is still the same. Do what you can to slow them down. Harass them, destroy their ability to forage, buy us a little time. Then cross the river and join us on the other side.

"In the meantime, I'll lead our main force up the eastern bank of the Tigris. We'll be there, waiting for them when they arrive, and we'll squash them like a bunch of slimy little frogs when they try to emerge from the river."

"It will be our pleasure to serve you, emperor." For the first time, there was a hint of enthusiasm in Bessos's voice.

"Aye, aye, your imperial highness." Mazaios seemed much less enthusiastic. Dareios failed to notice the doubt in his voice.

"And now, men, we all have a lot of work to do. So, let's get to it!"

******

Conquest of Persia

Almost by accident, an epic race developed between us and the massed hordes of the Persian army. Dareios was intent on arriving at the crossing near Arbela before we reached the other bank. Alexandros didn't realize he was in a speed contest. He was simply proceeding with his customary celerity. He was also not aiming for the Arbela ford.

There were several possible points where we could attempt to cross the Tigris. The ford near Arbela was the obvious and most commonly utilized shallows, precisely because caravans heading from the eastern provinces to Babylon or Thapsakos, or returning back, usually stopped at Arbela, which was the largest town in the area, to rest and replenish their supplies. However, Arbela meant nothing to Alexandros, to the extent he was aware of its existence at all. He merely wanted to get across Mesopotamia in order to attack Dareios from an unexpected direction. As a result, he chose the most northerly route possible because the climate was cooler farther to the north, because the desert gave way to arable land in the northern reaches of Mesopotamia, and because it was easier to forage for grain and fodder this far up, beyond the point where Mazaios had laid waste to all the native farming communities.

One incidental by-product of the track chosen by Alexandros was to shorten the distance we had to march to reach the Tigris, which flows in a southeasterly direction from its headwaters in the Anatolian highlands, before turning southward after reaching the Mesopotamian plain and coming very close to the Euphrates in the vicinity of Babylon. By the same token, the farther north we marched, the longer the distance that Dareios's army had to cover in order to intercept us before we crossed the Tigris. Had Alexandros decided to cross the river near Arbela, we would've had to march almost 400 miles to reach the ford, while Dareios's army would've only needed to go about 350 miles. But, because we marched toward the Nineveh ford, located some 60 miles to the north of the Arbela ford, our travel distance was reduced to less than 350 miles, while theirs increased to more than 400 miles. Plus, we'd already been marching for four days by the time Dareios even received word that we hadn't turned south toward Babylon after all. In short, Dareios's plan to intercept us before we crossed the Tigris was doomed to failure.

All this was obvious in hindsight. At the time, as we were marching across Mesopotamia, we didn't even know we were in a race. Instead, we could see that our progress was being tracked by enemy scouts, who were careful to stay beyond capture range but who were undoubtedly reporting our position to Dareios day after day. And we suspected that the scouts were but harbingers of larger enemy forces to come.

We were almost within sight of the Nineveh shallows when rising columns of dust on the horizon announced the arrival of Mazaios's cavalry forces. Unsure of the strength of the enemy, Alexandros dispatched our entire contingent of Paionian light cavalry to confront them. I suppose Alexandros considered them expendable. The Paionians, eager to prove they were as good as the Companion Cavalry, promptly rode out, waving their spears and swords and shouting loudly.

It turned out that what we had seen was only a small vanguard of Mazaios's forces. The Paionians outnumbered them three to one. When they approached, the heavily armored Persian knights turned around and tried to make a run toward the rest of their brigade. They never had a chance. The Paionians, unencumbered by armor, rode them down from behind, killed as many as they could, and returned triumphantly to Alexandros, laying three dozen severed heads at his feet. We didn't see any further Persian knights before reaching the Tigris. Contrary to expectations, we had arrived without losing any men to thirst, hunger, heatstroke, or enemy attack. But then, the river crossing awaited.

****

Through absolute miracles of organizational virtuosity, logistical proficiency, and the sheer efficacy of terror, Dareios had managed to march his entire army, numbering well over 100,000 men, all the way to Arbela by the time he received word that they were too late to stop Alexandros from crossing the river some 60 miles north of the Persians' camp. Undaunted, he assembled his high command in the magnificent imperial command tent.

"I wish somebody had told me there was a series of fords up here." His tone was surprisingly mild. Mazaios was tempted to note that any ruler of Persia should've known as much but thought better of it. "It's perhaps for the best that we can't prevent these pests from crossing the river," Dareios continued. Bessos harrumphed but then decided to keep his mouth shut as well. "This will give us a chance to recreate Kounaxa right here, on the eastern bank of the Tigris River." A barely audible groan issued from the throats of some of the assembled commanders, who'd hoped they'd heard the last of Dareios's historical lectures about the Battle of Kounaxa. "My scouts have already located a suitable plain a few miles to the north of here, between us and the enemy forces. We'll march up there, prepare the field, and await their attack."

"What makes you think they'll attack, your celestial brilliance?" Bessos asked.

"Trust me, young man, they'll attack." Dareios's equanimity was remarkable. All the assembled commanders were sure a cataclysmic outburst was about to erupt and were making mental wagers on whose head would be the first to roll when a guard climbed up to Dareios's throne and whispered something in his ear. The emperor blanched and quickly descended from the raised platform. "We'll reconvene soon." He practically ran to his private tent.

A fat eunuch, who'd been waiting in the tent, threw himself face first onto the plush carpeting when he heard the emperor's approach and refused to get up, despite Dareios's urging. When he finally rose to his knees, there were tears coursing down his cheeks. He cleared his throat, made several unsuccessful attempts at speech, before managing to croak out a single sentence: "Queen Stateira is dead." Then he waited for the inevitable execution order.

Dareios said nothing. He didn't order the eunuch to be taken out and torn to pieces. He didn't shout and scream. He didn't descend into paroxysms of grief. He simply sat heavily on his chair, shoulders slumped, hands in his lap, head bowed, and thought. Eventually, he shook his head, looked up, and asked the eunuch to explain what had happened. The eunuch provided a brief description of Stateira's gradual descent into physical perdition, of her final, losing struggle against death, and of his own narrow escape from the camp near Tyros and the long, harrowing ride to Babylon and then on to Arbela. Dareios listened quietly, thanked the eunuch, and then dismissed him.

****

Once upon a time, three hundred years before our arrival, Nineveh, on the eastern bank of the Tigris, was the largest city in the world. As a result, the Nineveh ford was, at that time, the most heavily trafficked crossing point across the river. Then, a combined army of Babylonians and Khaldaians sacked and destroyed the Assyrian capital, already weakened by a calamitous civil war. The ruins of Nineveh were deemed cursed by the gods, avoided by the natives, buried under accumulating layers of sand and soil, and gradually forgotten. Almost no one used the Nineveh ford any more. But it was supposed to be a shallow, safe, easy crossing point. Perhaps it was, most of the time, but not the day we reached it.

The river seemed tranquil enough when the first infantry units waded in. But, as they trudged across, the water level was rising imperceptibly. Soon, the water midstream was up to their waists and exerting a noticeable tug against their legs. Our cavalry units rode in, downstream from the foot soldiers. Although it was not exactly an easy stroll for our steeds, because the riverbed was rocky and slippery, they experienced very little trouble at first. But the level and the force of the water continued to rise. Soon, the infantrymen were immersed up to their chests and had to link arms to avoid being swept downstream. The horses, water lapping at their bellies, were starting to get edgy.

There must've been a tremendous deluge somewhere over the Anatolian highlands because soon we were caught in the middle of a turbulent torrent. The soldiers abandoned all encumbrances – their sacks, bundles, swords, shields, clothes – in an effort to escape from their would-be watery tomb. The horses were shying, whinnying, and drowning. I dove off Pandaros's back, while clutching his reins, and we took turns pulling each other as we struggled to reach the distant shore.

The men and the horses kept coming, even as the sun sank toward the horizon. The raging river gradually subsided overnight but, as the exhausted, sodden men mustered for the morning roll call, we still had no idea how many we'd lost. It turned out that, miraculously, all of our men and animals had made it across. We spent the rest of the day catching our breaths, fishing out the gear and the provisions we'd lost, and attempting to resume the semblance of an army. Alexandros presided over a service of thanksgiving to the local river goddess, who saved our lives but whose name I didn't catch. He also dispatched foraging parties and small teams of scouts to ascertain the location of the enemy because the one thing about which Dareios was incontrovertibly correct was his belief that Alexandros had become obsessed with the idea of killing Dareios and thus wresting the Persian Empire from his grasp.

On the other hand, Alexandros was in no hurry to engage the Persian army after the ordeal of our march across upper Mesopotamia and our harrowing crossing of the Tigris River. When we'd finished building our camp and surrounding it with a protective palisade, he announced a big feast for the next day, to be followed by four days of rest. The troops greeted his announcement with understandable enthusiasm.

****

Dareios had a curious reaction to the news of his queen's death. He didn't display any overt signs of mourning. Such histrionics were, in his view, unmanly, especially with regard to the loss of a wife, when one had so many replacements ready at hand. His affect, however, was clearly subdued. He undoubtedly missed his number one wife, even though he hadn't seen her in two years, but what enraged him was his inability to rescue her, or his mother, or his children, or all the other inmates of his harem who continued to languish in captivity. Even more depressing was the thought that perhaps he'd lost the favor of the gods.

It was in this precarious state of mind that he resolved to take decisive action: He brought in his scribe and dictated one final peace offer. The offer was stunning in its generosity. He increased the proffered ransom payment to 30,000 talents, a cache of riches that may have exceeded the combined movable wealth of all the Greek cities of the Greek mainland, Ionia, and all the islands of the Aegean in between. He also offered to cede to Alexandros the entire western half of the Persian Empire, from the Mediterranean to the Euphrates River; to give him his daughter Stateira in marriage and to leave his son and heir Ochos in Alexandros's hands as a permanent hostage, in effect making Alexandros the de facto heir to the Persian throne.

When the scribe was done with his work, Dareios handed the message to two of his most trusted ambassadors and smuggled them out of the Persian camp. He neglected to confer with his command staff prior to sending his peace offer to Alexandros or to inform them of it afterward.

****

The next morning, Aristandros discretely informed Alexandros that there would be a total eclipse of the moon that evening and tactfully suggested that the king might wish to address his soldiers ahead of the celestial display in order to forestall any potential panic in the ranks. Alexandros made the most of this intelligence. He rose to his feet, during the height of the promised feast, and made a stirring speech to the reveling troops, promising they would soon devour the entire Persian army, just as his celestial colleagues were planning to devour the moon that very evening.

What the troops made of this unusual simile was hard to tell but there was no mistaking their reaction when, approximately two hours after sunset, a crescent shadow began to creep across the face of the full moon. A mighty roar rose in the camp, which continued to swell in volume and intensity, reaching a crescendo when, almost an hour later, the entire moon was swallowed by the shadow, turning the lunar disk a deep sanguinary shade of maroon. Any remaining doubts his soldiers might've entertained about the divine favor enjoyed by their commander were dispelled in that instant.

The mighty Persians knights and their multitudinous local levies observed the same heavenly display in stunned and silent awe, wondering what this apocalyptic, otherworldly omen foretold about the outcome of their imminent encounter with the pan-Hellenic army. Dareios, who was not normally a superstitious man, trembled at this confirmation of his forebodings.

******

I made a beeline to Aristandros's tent shortly after the eclipse began. "How did you know?" I demanded as soon as I burst in.

The great seer was lying on a straw pallet. He looked surprisingly frail. He really was aging at a precipitous pace. "It's about time," he cawed, then cleared his throat. "It's about time you stopped by to look in on me." His attempt at a grin resulted in a cross between a grimace and a glare.

The transformation was stunning. *What's happened to the guy who's been trying to kill me?* I wondered. "You look well," I lied.

His laugh was short, harsh, and phlegmy. "You're an awful liar, you know. And it doesn't suit you. You've got many faults but habitual dishonesty isn't one of them."

"Well, thank you for that. I wanted to ask you a question, though. How were you able to predict this lunar eclipse?"

"It was obvious, if you knew where to look. The flight patterns of the birds, the coruscations of heavenly bodies, the convolutions of entrails ..."

"Don't give me that crap," I interrupted. "Unlike some other people around here, I've never been taken in by your chicanery."

"You may call it chicanery but I did manage to predict the lunar eclipse right on the nose. So maybe my chicanery actually works."

"No, it doesn't," I said firmly. "There may be ways to predict lunar eclipses but divination isn't one of them."

He looked at me curiously. "You're an educated man, Ptolemaios, even though you do your best to hide it. So you know as well as I do that there are clay tablets at the ziggurat of Marduk in Babylon that list the daily motions of the sun and the moon."

"I've never been to Babylon."

"That's not the point. As it happens, Marduk's ziggurat is quite dilapidated by now because the Persian occupiers of Babylon aren't followers of that particular god and nobody looks at the ephemerides any more. The point is that the knowledge contained on those tablets has spread quite widely, even to the Greek world. And everybody knows there's an observable periodicity to the motions of the sun and the moon. Once you have written down the daily motions for a number of years and discovered that periodicity and then perhaps confirmed your findings by observations recorded through a couple of more periods, you're in a position to predict the daily motions of the sun and the moon for any date in the future." His effusion was cut short by a coughing spell. After regaining his breath, he picked up just where he'd left off. "What's more, when you know the daily motions, it's equally easy to compute when these two heavenly bodies will be in conjunction or opposition. And when they're in conjunction, you can expect a solar eclipse; when in opposition, a lunar one. There's nothing to it. But don't tell anyone. I've got to preserve my mystique."

I was unpersuaded. "Let's let that one go. How about some of your other predictions? You've got an uncanny knack for getting stuff right. How do you do that?"

"Haven't you ever known that something was going to happen before it actually did?"

Little do you know, I thought. Before it all went off the charts at Granikos, there were lots of events I knew were going to happen before they did. But that was because I was a time traveler and had read about those events in history books, before making my trip back to this era. "There've been times when I've had a hunch," I admitted. "Although I seem to have lost my knack for hunches lately."

"Well, there you have it. The only difference between you and me is that you've lost your ability to have accurate hunches and I haven't. Now, if you don't mind, I'm getting awfully tired." He coughed again, as if to emphasize his point.

"May I ask one more question before I go?"

"Well, alright. What is it?"

"Do you ever worry that, by making a prediction, you're actually altering the outcome?"

Another long pause. "If one accurately predicts what was going to happen anyway, how is the prediction changing anything? I'm not a god, you know. I don't make things happen or keep things from happening. I just read the will of the gods and convey it to others."

"We're not talking about gods." My tone was sharper than I'd intended. "It just seems to me that by predicting victory, for example, you give the fighters confidence, so they prevail where otherwise they might have faltered."

"Well, that's where you're wrong. You've got the sequence backward. I know they're going to win before I make my prediction of victory. Then, when they go ahead and do it, as I knew they would, nothing's been altered by my prediction." And then he added something that froze me midthought. "Unlike some people, I have scrupulously refrained from interfering in any way. On the contrary, I've tried to obviate the interference of others. So no, I've never altered the outcome of a battle. And now, I really must insist. Please leave me alone."

I stumbled out of his tent. *Could this old charlatan have figured me out?* No, that was inconceivable.

Chapter 8 – Gaugamela

Dareios did not assume that his peace offer, breathtakingly generous as it was, would be accepted by Alexandros. On the contrary, he continued to make his preparations for battle, just in case.

His scouts had located a suitable battlefield near the village of Gaugamela. It was a broad, level, recently harvested plain, with nary a stream or hillock to hinder the free play of his cavalry. There would be no Gulf of Issos against which Alexandros could anchor the end of his line nor any foothills of the Amanos Mountains. No, this time the ends of the enemy line would simply dangle in the open plain, unanchored and unprotected. There would be nothing that Alexandros could do to prevent Dareios's knights from riding around the ends of the Greek line, enveloping it, and destroying the pan-Hellenic army to the last man. Dareios smiled at the thought.

He sent out swarms of sappers to remove every last tree and brush from his chosen theater of history. He even had them raze every slight bump in the terrain and fill in every tiny gully. The stage for the great Persian victory would be as smooth and level as the granite floor of the Great Hall in the Babylon Palace.

There were a few hills to the north of the battlefield but Dareios ignored them. The fight would take place in the plain, well short of those hills. Alexandros's scouts, on the other hand, swarmed all over them. They provided excellent vantage points from which to observe Dareios's meticulous preparations.

******

Alexandros was in his command tent, receiving the reports of his scouts, when the arrival of the Persian ambassadors was announced.

"Let them wait. And keep them cooped up in a tent far from here. I don't need Dareios's agents spying on us and eavesdropping on our conversations."

Our commander wasn't in a good mood. He was sick and tired of listening to the exaggerations and fantastic tales of his scouts. The numbers they were reporting for the enemy strength were absurd: More than a hundred thousand foot soldiers, perhaps two hundred thousand; plus, at least fifty thousand mounted warriors. And the descriptions of Dareios's preparations were just as risible. Battles were not fought on polished stages.

There were always local quirks and contours to notice and exploit.

Finally, he sent an aide to retrieve whatever letter the ambassadors had brought. "There's no need for them to enter. I can read the Persian coward's insults for myself."

After a brief glance, he read the letter out loud, for all of us to hear. It made no difference what Dareios had to say, as far as Alexandros was concerned. He'd been dreaming about this pivotal battle since he was a child listening to Homeros's tales of rollicking exploits by ancient heroes. No peace offer was going to deprive him of his glory now.

To the rest of us in the tent, however, Alexandros's adamant refusal to negotiate with Dareios amounted to a rejection of spectacular victory in order to achieve total defeat. When Philippos first conceived the notion of attacking the Persian Empire, the most he expected to gain was control of the Greek cities of Ionia. When Alexandros inherited his father's cause, he enlarged the mission to encompass the conquest of the Persian maritime provinces. No one, not even Alexandros, expected to gain half the Persian Empire, with the possibility of inheriting the other half upon Dareios's death, when we'd crossed the Hellespont three and a half years earlier. The idea of small, poor, backward

Macedonia ruling over the greatest, strongest, most advanced empire on Earth was dizzying.

We were all thinking exactly the same thing but no one wanted to be the first to speak. Finally, Parmenion cleared his throat. "If I were Alexandros," he said, "I would accept this offer."

"So would I, if I were Parmenion," was the lighthearted response.

And with that, we were dismissed to begin preparations for battle.

****

We marched to within eight miles of the Persian camp the following day, stopping just short of the chain of hills that marked the northern extreme of Dareios's chosen battlefield. We couldn't see or hear the enemy but old veterans swore they could smell them. Alexandros ordered us to make a fortified camp and then gave the men two more days of rest. "The Persians aren't going anywhere," he informed us. "Let them stew in their own terrified sweat for a while longer."

On our second rest day, Alexandros rode out to the prospective battleground, accompanied only by a small contingent of his cavalry commanders. Prancing back and forth on his magnificent Boukephalas, almost within javelin range of the enemy, wearing his finest armor and helmet, with its distinctive white plume streaming in the breeze, he left little doubt as to his identity in the minds of the astonished Persian commanders who carefully observed his every step. However, his insolent insouciance was only a cover for the real purpose of his jaunt. While appearing to meander aimlessly across Dareios's manicured martial stage, he carefully examined every inch of the terrain. And the Persians simply watched, either too stunned or too scared to intervene.

That evening, Alexandros staged another magnificent feast. All the requisite rituals were observed, of course, all the deities propitiated, prayers recited, and paeans sung. A stooped and languorous Aristandros, dressed in sparkling white as usual, a sacred bough in his hand, his head covered and veiled, read the entrails and announced, in a weak but self-assured voice, that the pan-Hellenic army would achieve a signal and historic victory. Alexandros then concluded the ceremonies by telling his men that no mere Persians could withstand the might of their arms; that they stood on the threshold of immortality; that their deeds would be celebrated in the songs of bards. And then he told them to get a good night's sleep. He retired to his command tent, signaling to his officers to follow.

"We must attack tonight," Parmenion urged him as soon as everyone was inside. "The enemy has overwhelming numerical advantage and they have chosen the perfect location to deploy it. If we attack under cover of darkness and surprise them, we might have a chance."

Alexandros had no patience for the old general. "We're not going to surprise anybody. There are Persian spies all around us. Plus, anything can happen in the chaos of a nighttime battle. In fact, the cover of darkness would simply neutralize the superiority of our soldiers and the composure of our commanders, giving the enemy the edge, precisely because there are more of them. In any event, I wouldn't have it said that I stole victory like a thief in the night."

Parmenion was reduced to silence by this outburst.

"But you've given me an idea, old man." Alexandros's tone grew more cheerful. "Let's make the Persians think we're going to attack tonight. Organize enough of a feint by your men to send all those Persian spies running to their emperor."

And so it was that, while our men slept, dreaming of victory, Dareios's serried soldiers, weighed down by their armor, spent the night standing on the battlefield, awaiting an attack that never materialized.

Alexandros didn't sleep, either. He made his way, alone, to the top of the tallest hill overlooking the battlefield and studied the disposition of the enemy forces. Although it was a cloudless night, under a bright, gibbous moon, Alexandros had a difficult time crediting the evidence of his own eyes. The reports he'd received from his scouts weren't an exaggeration. On the contrary, the actual numbers arrayed below him far exceeded even the most extravagant estimates of his scouts.

Most striking was the size of the Persian cavalry. The Immortals had been transformed from foot soldiers into mounted knights. The 11,000-member Persian heavy infantry had become part of an incredible body of 34,000 cavalrymen, each resplendent in chain mail that dazzled even in the moonlight, astride steeds that were themselves clad in armor, each knight equipped with javelins, swords, and long daggers. They occupied the middle of the Persian formation, with Dareios clearly visible in his oversized chariot, standing precisely in the center of his enormous host, a little behind the front of the line. The Persian heavy cavalry was further augmented by the fierce mounted warriors of Baktria, Parthia, Sousiana, Arachosia, and Skythia. Dareios had at his disposal more horsemen than Alexandros had soldiers in all branches of his army combined.

But Dareios's army didn't end with the cavalry. There were, of course, the two hundred scythed chariots, idling at the moment in front of the line, a little to the left of center. Alexandros smiled at the effort and expense wasted on the construction and outfitting of these antiquated fighting vehicles. He was confident his veteran soldiers would be able to deal with them. Dareios, on the other hand, must have placed great hopes in their efficacy because he stationed elements of the Persian heavy cavalry as well as squadrons of allied light cavalry directly behind the chariots. Presumably, the plan was to launch the chariots and then send in the cavalry to exploit any gaps in the Greek line that resulted.

Arrayed behind the seemingly endless line of cavalry, a second line, comprised of foot soldiers, stood through the night, in their massed units, under arms. Although Alexandros held these conscripted infantrymen in low regard, he couldn't ignore the fact that there must have been close to 200,000 of them. His effort to survey their formations was hampered by the cavalry shield massed in front of them but he was fairly confident, nevertheless, that he could identify, on the left end of this second line, a few squadrons of Karian infantry, led by their deposed king Orontobates. There were also a few Persian levies, under the command of Ariobarzanes, supported by two battalions of Mardians and Sogdians. He also saw, in the center of this second line, behind the formidable Persian cavalry and behind Dareios's chariot, a brigade of Greek mercenaries. They were flanked, on either side, by hordes of Indians in their colorful outfits. Farther from the center stood the so-called "lesser" Armenians, Babylonians, Medes, Phrygians, and Parthians, each nationality led by its own native commanders. The right side of the infantry formation consisted of conscripted levies of "greater" Armenians, Kadusians, Syrians, more Medes, Kappadokians, and other nationalities that Alexandros couldn't identify. The double Persian line stretched some three miles across the battlefield.

Alexandros's army numbered some 47,000 soldiers, including 7,500 horsemen, 29,500 heavy infantrymen and 10,000 light auxiliaries. His infantry line would be hard-pressed to stretch to a mile, even if he thinned their ranks and cut their files to a minimum. It was obvious that, no matter what he did, he couldn't prevent his line from being outflanked. Somehow, his 7,500 horsemen were supposed to prevent the elite heavy Persian knights, supported by countless savage horsemen of the steppes, from riding around the ends of his line and attacking his infantry from the rear, while the front of his line would be attacked by the 200 chariots and the remaining mounted warriors, followed by an onslaught of 200,000 infantrymen. Obviously, the plan was to outflank his army, pin it down, disrupt its cohesion, envelop it, and then destroy it in detail. It would've been obvious to any other commander that there was no conceivable way for his troops to prevail in the coming contest but the thought never crossed Alexandros's mind.

Alexandros remained on the hill, staring at the enemy, until he came up with a battle plan. By the time he stumbled back into his private tent and fell asleep, the first streamers of dawn were beginning to unfurl in the eastern sky. He slept soundly, dreamlessly, and restfully, notwithstanding the clamor and tumult of the camp awakening around him.

All the soldiers knew this was the day of decision. They awoke early and consumed a hearty breakfast, washed down with copious amounts of wine. It was a measure of their sang-froid that they were able to keep their food down but they were all chattering excitedly, polishing their armor, sharpening their swords, getting themselves organized in their units, champing at the bit. All they were missing was the order to move out.

Their commander was still asleep. We had spent half the morning peering into his tent but nothing would disturb the young man's untroubled slumber. Finally, Parmenion could wait no longer and gently shook Alexandros awake.

"Your troops are ready, sire."

"So am I, Parmenion, so am I. Get everybody organized while I grab a quick breakfast. Then, as we're marching out, I'll explain how we'll annihilate these barbarians."

******

When Alexandros explained his battle plan to us, his commanders, it seemed, at first blush, insane. His plan was to invite the Persians to outflank our line.

"There's no way we can stop him from outflanking us on that polished plane of his." He seemed awfully cheerful about it. "First of all, their line is three times longer than ours will be and there's nothing we can do about it. Trust me, they've been standing there all night, so I know exactly how long their line is. I also know how far we can lengthen our line and it isn't going to stretch to three miles. You can only stretch a catgut so far before it snaps.

"Second, there are no natural barriers we can use to anchor the ends of our line, no mountains or shorelines, no woods or defiles.

"Third, they've got seven or eight times as many mounted warriors as we do, most of them of the heavily armored variety. I know you guys are ten times better than they are but it'd be a tough slog if we tried to take them head on. So realistically, we can't stop them in their tracks, which means we can't stop them from riding around the ends of our line.

"Now, when it comes to infantry, they only outnumber us about six to one and we all know their infantry is mostly worthless. Unfortunately, Dareios is hiding his infantry behind his cavalry and behind those stupid chariots of his, so there's no easy way for our infantry to engage theirs.

"So, here's what we'll do. We'll invite that huge cavalry swarm to attack our infantry. That's right boys.

The infantry is just going to have to stand there and take it. In fact, the more of their knights who decide to ride around the ends of our line and attack our infantry from the sides and from the rear, the better.

"After their knights are all engaged trying to cut our infantry to ribbons, our cavalry will ride out through the middle and kill Dareios. And that'll be the end of the fight," he concluded matter-of-factly.

The battle plan made no sense. It fell to Parmenion, as usual, to give voice to what we were all thinking. "But sire." He spoke as deferentially as he could manage given his evident concern that our commander-in-chief had taken leave of his senses. "Sire, he's got enough cavalry to shred our infantry to mincemeat and still keep more than enough of his knights around his person to prevent our cavalry from ever getting close enough to ruffle his hair."

"And that's exactly why we're going to make our infantry units look so weak and vulnerable and isolated and engulfed that the Persian heavy cavalry won't be able to resist the temptation to pile into the attack. And guess what, Parmenion. You'll get to command the left wing of our infantry while they're getting turned into mincemeat, as you so colorfully put it."

Parmenion was speechless.

Alexandros continued undeterred. "Don't look so doubtful, old man. It's a good plan and it will work. Trust me; this is the son of Ammon speaking.

"Now, let me give you the detailed dispositions."

****

At first glance, Alexandros's order of battle didn't strike us as particularly unusual. He assigned half of our heavy infantry, including all the allied hoplites and all the Greek mercenaries, to the left wing of the line, placing them under Krateros's command. (This would've been quite a plum assignment for the young, recently arrived commander, had he been tasked with something other than serving as bait on this particular day.) He also assigned most of the allied cavalry, including the veteran Thessalians, to the left wing, plus the Kretan archers and some light-armed Illirians and Thrakians. Parmenion was placed in overall command of the left wing, as usual.

The right wing consisted of three phalanxes of veteran Macedonian heavy infantry, commanded by Polyperchon, Melenger, and Koinos, respectively. The elite Silver Shields, under the command of Parmenion's son Nikanoros, were also assigned to the right wing, as were the remaining archers and the light-armed Agrianians. In additional, several squadrons of allied cavalry, including the splendid Paionians, were also placed on the right. Perdikkas was named the overall commander of the right wing.

The Companion Cavalry, with squadrons commanded by Alexandros, Philotas, me, Seleukos, Kleitos, and Kleandros were to be stationed on the right, behind the infantry line, ready to pounce at Alexandros's command.

Up to this point, the dispositions were quite conventional. The surprising element was Alexandros's instruction to Parmenion and Perdikkas to change the alignment of the phalanxes. Instead of standing in a straight line, he wanted the outside units to be sharply echeloned backward, facing almost sideways, rather than straight ahead. As a result of this slight positional change, our line would appear to the Persians across the field even shorter than it actually was, while at the same time greatly enhancing the ability of our infantry to withstand a flanking attack. He also placed strong reserve units of infantry behind the front line and instructed them to face backward, thus protecting the phalanxes against an attack from the rear.

To conceal this changed alignment from the enemy, Alexandros instructed the various cavalry units, other than the Companion Cavalry, to form a moving screen in front of the line. Once the battle started, he wanted them to do what they could to assist the infantry in standing up against the overwhelming power of the enemy cavalry. The archers and the light-armed troops were also to spread out among the heavy infantry and to help where they could, especially when Dareios initiated his expected onslaught of the chariots.

The Companion Cavalry was to hide behind the right wing and await its opportunity. The success of the plan hinged on the assumption that the enemy horsemen, including the lightly-armored savage scrappers of the steppes and the dazzling, elite, heavily-armored knights of the Persian Cavalry wouldn't be able to resist launching flanking attacks against both ends of our line, which would appear extremely vulnerable. As more and more of the enemy cavalry was drawn into these flanking attacks, the center of the Persian line, where some of these units would be stationed at the start of the battle, would become progressively weaker. Then, at just the right moment, the Companion Cavalry would emerge through a gap in our line and hurl itself against the thinned-out center, where Dareios would still be stationed in his large, gaudy chariot. "If we hit them hard enough," Alexandros assured us, "they'll crumble, especially because the numbers of Persian cavalry and infantry protecting Dareios will've been diminished as they all rush off to join in the destruction of our infantry."

The only problem with this plan was that the assault of the Companion Cavalry couldn't begin too early, before the enemy cavalry had vacated their center, because otherwise they'd simply stay where they were, protecting Dareios, and we'd have no chance of punching through an elite force that outnumbered us at least ten to one. On the other hand, if we waited too long to begin our decisive thrust, the enemy forces would have ample time to surround and annihilate our allied cavalry and our infantry because even our wonderful troops could only resist the weight of the enemy's overwhelming numbers for a very short stretch of time, after which all the enemy cavalry could turn against the Companion Cavalry and destroy us at their convenience.

If anyone other than Alexandros had proposed this plan, it would've been obvious to all that this was nothing more than a desperate gamble, which had no chance of success. To launch an attack with split-second precision in the maelstrom and tumult of battle seemed less than likely. On top of that, even if all our movements were carried out with the requisite timing, improbable as this was, it wouldn't change the balance of forces on the battlefield. Sooner or later, the inexorable logic of numbers was bound to tell.

But no one questioned Alexandros's plan. On the contrary, after he had issued his orders to the commanders, he rode alongside the marching squadrons and battalions and briefly addressed each unit, repeating the same message over and over again. "What a great day for a battle," he would call out. "I can't wait to gut those bastards. Makes no difference how many bastards they've got, 'cause you'll kill 'em all before they can touch you. Remember, with me in the lead, we can't lose. There's a reason they call us Aniketoi. All the gods are on our side.

Trust me, I know. Now, go out there and kill the bastards!" The funny thing was that, even though they had all heard this stuff before and even though the odds against them were demonstrably insuperable, they believed him. They couldn't wait to secure their place in history.

In addition to energizing the troops, as Alexandros passed by each company, he quietly mentioned one tactical adjustment to his phalanx commanders. "When the chariots come, just make a lane and let them through. And as they're flying by, target the horses, not the charioteers. After you get the horses, you can dispose of the charioteers at your leisure."

Before we knew it, we were all lined up on Dareios's manicured battlefield, facing the largest army his empire had ever assembled.

****

Dareios, resplendent in his finest armor, breathed a sigh of relief upon observing the emergence of the vanguard of the pan-Hellenic army from among the hills. He was beginning to worry that Alexandros might've decided to decline the set piece battle prepared for him.

The emperor alighted from his gilt chariot, mounted his silver-covered steed, and rode out, accompanied by a large entourage of commanders, advisors, spear-carriers, and toadies, to address his soldiers. The troops were beginning to sag after standing in the field, under arms, through the night and the following morning. As Dareios made the rounds, addressing the huge contingents supplied by the various nations that comprised the Persian Empire, he spoke in a strong, confident voice. He called upon the divine favor of Mithra, the one deity worshipped, in one form or another, by Persians, Indians, and Parthians, by Zoroastrians, Hindus, and Pagans, by almost all the constituents of his vast host. He reminded his warriors that they were embarked upon a holy war to exterminate these godless invaders who were motivated by nothing more than greed for plunder and who were led by a madman so preoccupied by his lust for power that he was, even at that moment, rushing headlong into the trap set for him by the Persian emperor. He assured them that the gods were on their side and that, before the night fell, they would write another chapter in the glorious history of the Persian Empire.

When Dareios delivered this inspirational address to his Persian knights, they cheered wildly. When speaking, through a translator, to some of the other national contingents, the reception was somewhat more subdued, either because the soldiers were already tired after their nocturnal vigil or because the soaring eloquence of Dareios's words lost some of its vigor in translation or because they simply hated being vassals of this strutting peacock.

After addressing the last of the steppe horsemen, Dareios returned to his chariot and the two armies began a slow, cautious dance toward each other.

****

Neither commander wanted to be the first to sound the trumpets, Dareios because of his innate circumspection and Alexandros because his plan depended on the Persians' attacking first. Soon, it was high noon and the phalanxes were still maneuvering gingerly, moving more sideways than forward, with the light-armed horsemen riding pell-mell between the lines, defying the enemy to hit them. Eventually, the lines had crept crabwise close to the edge of the area which Dareios's sappers had cleared in anticipation of battle and the Persian commander could wait no longer, lest he lose the benefit of his carefully leveled ground.

I sat aboard Pandaros and watched as Dareios launched a well-coordinated, three-pronged attack.[17] The Baktrian cavalry, commanded by Bessos, set off at a breakneck gallop toward the right end of our line. At the same moment, Mazaios, leading his elite Persian cavalry squadrons, attacked our left flank. And straight up the middle came the onslaught of the chariots, followed closely by many more squadrons of Persian cavalry.

---

[17] For an animated depiction of the Battle of Gaugamela, visit AlexanderGeiger.com

A sense of unreality enveloped the scene. The noise was deafening, with men yelling, singing, and beating their swords against their shields, with trumpets blaring and drums pounding, with horses neighing and priests praying, with boots stamping and hooves trampling, and yet, I thought I could clearly hear, and understand, the orders of the commanders, even those issued in languages I didn't know. Forests of pikes swayed across my field of view, mounted men floated hypnotically hither and yon, clouds of dust shrouded the battlescape, and yet, I could discern and follow the action clearly. I was sure that I, and thousands of my comrades, would die in the next few minutes, and yet, I felt serenely grounded. For the first time in a long while, I could foretell, with a high degree of confidence, what would happen next. *Hell of a way to cure a bad case of chronotosis,* I thought with wry bemusement.

Just ahead and to my right, I watched as the Baktrian horsemen attacked and quickly sliced through the light screen of our Paionian and Greek mercenary cavalry, which was supposed to shield from view, but not necessarily protect, our right flank. As they galloped toward our men, the Baktrians unloosed a hailstorm of arrows. Our lightly armored cavalry had no effective defense against this aerial assault. There were way too many arrows to dodge, they carried no shields, and their horses were completely unprotected. And, unlike their Asian counterparts, our horsemen didn't carry bows and arrows. Therefore, they did the only thing they could, which was to get out of the way of the irresistible tidal wave thundering their way. The Baktrians ignored them, the way a charging bull ignores a swarm of flies.

As they closed in on Koinos's phalanx, which constituted the apparent right end of our infantry line, the onrushing Baktrians spread out into a broad fan, while continuing to fire salvos of arrows into the massed foot soldiers. Unlike our cavalry, our infantry carried shields, which they used to protect themselves from the incoming arrows. Also, scattered among them stood a company of Kretan archers who did their best to loft answering volleys of missiles. However, the Baktrians carried composite bows, shaped like figure eights sliced vertically down the middle. These bows easily outranged the Kretan's conventional bows and just as easily penetrated the shields of our infantry.

After the arrows did their damage, a couple of thousand Baktrians stopped just short of the shield wall of the phalanx and hurled their javelins into the Macedonian ranks, hoping to finish the job started with their bow barrage. And then, with a loud yell, they urged their steeds against the bristling points of the Macedonian sarissas protruding beyond the shield wall. Seemingly heedless of the injuries being absorbed by their horses, the steppe warriors continued ahead, using the weight of their animals to push back the Macedonian pikes and the Macedonian shields and the Macedonian men wielding them.

However, the great majority of the Baktrians continued to gallop beyond the end of our line, clearly hoping to outflank our phalanx and hit our men from the side and from behind. It was at this point that they discovered there was another phalanx, this time the elite Silver Shields under Nikanoros's command, stationed almost at a right angle to Koinos's phalanx, waiting for precisely that type of flanking attack.

If the Baktrians were surprised by this unexpected alignment, they forged ahead undaunted. They fired their arrows, followed by javelins, and then unleashed the sheer, brutal mass of ten thousand mounted, screaming, sword-wielding savages.

Charging into the front ranks of our phalanx, the Baktrians certainly appeared savage. They wore no armor and very little clothing, aside from their characteristic leather leggings. They were larger than the Macedonians – taller, thicker, heavier – and they were sitting on horses, each one of which seemed as big as Boukephalas. They were unkempt, with long scraggly beards and wild flying hair, yet their horsemanship was superb and their aggression murderous. Undoubtedly, their cries and looks alone had sent many an opponent fleeing from the battlefield but, at least for the moment, our Macedonian veterans were holding their ground.

I turned my attention to our left wing, to see how Parmenion's men were faring. Their situation appeared to be a mirror image of the charge I was observing in front of me, except that Parmenion had at his disposal all of the Thessalian cavalry, as well as a number of other allied Greek cavalry squadrons. As a result, the opposing cavalry forces were slightly more evenly matched and Mazaios's Persian cavalry had a much tougher time slicing through than the Baktrians were experiencing. On the other hand, once they did get through, the infantry phalanxes confronting them were not quite as accomplished as the Silver Shields. The pan-Hellenic phalangists comprised a mixture of Macedonian raw recruits and Achaian, Boiotian, Phokian, and other Greek mercenaries but they resisted the Persian assault with a resolve befitting men fighting for their lives.

A sudden uproar erupted in the middle of the field. Chariots were flying toward the center of our line. Notwithstanding Alexandros's earlier disdain, these were still fearsome engines of war. Each chariot was pulled by a team of two horses and manned by a charioteer and an archer. They crossed the no man's land between the opposing lines in a blink of an eye. In theory, our infantry troops were adept, as a result of endless drills, at opening up lanes and getting out of the way of these mobile firing platforms. The trouble was that these chariots had been rendered more lethal by the addition of long, sharp blades to the spokes of their wheels, extending about two feet beyond the sides of the vehicles. Once in motion, the blades whirled around madly, slicing, chopping, and mincing anything that came within their reach. Still, our men would have been agile enough to get out of the way of one of these chariots with a minimum of damage or injury. It was a different matter trying to get out of the way of two hundred of them, approaching at breakneck speed, spread out across a front stretching perhaps a third of a mile.

Everybody sprang into action: The heavily armored phalangists, moving in unison and as quickly as their heavy shields and pikes permitted; the light-armed auxiliaries, who were much more lithe but also much more defenseless against the churning blades and the flying arrows; our archers, salted among the heavy infantry; and the thin line of allied cavalry that had been stationed in front of our line, mostly to screen our infantry maneuvers from the enemy's view.

The Persian archers, enjoying the relatively stable platform of a chariot and relieved of any responsibility except to shoot as rapidly as possible, showered our men with their missiles. Our men, in turn, did their best to injure the horses, heeding their commanders' advice that the horses were easier to hit than the men sheltering behind the raised sides of the chariots. Our cavalry men rode as close as they dared in order to thrust and throw their javelins. They often miscalculated, as a result of which the legs of their horses were chopped asunder, precipitating the men to the ground and into the teeth of the lethal blades. New, distinctive, sickening grace notes started to punch through the general cacophony surrounding us – the sound of shrieks being cut short as men were decapitated midscream.

Our lightly armed Agrianians ran, with incredible bravery, among the moving chariots, stabbing the horses in their bellies, and then trying to jump out of the way of the whirling blades. Sometimes they succeeded and sometimes they didn't. And even when they survived their encounters with the chariots, they were confronted by heavily armed men on horses because the Persian cavalry came rushing in hard on the heels of the charging chariots. I don't believe many of these heroic, semi-barbarian allies of ours survived their encounters with the chariots and the ensuing mounted warriors.

But the efforts of our allied cavalry and our lightly armed auxiliaries bought a bit of precious time for the heavy infantry, long enough to enable them to overlap their shields and brace themselves against the impact of the horses pulling the chariots. They were also able to open a wide gap in the middle of the line. Most importantly, they didn't panic. Horses yoked to a chariot were unlikely to leap over a line of infantrymen and tended to shy when driven against a solid wall of shields and sarissas. However, it required courage, discipline, and physical strength to stand up to a line of charging half-ton animals.

Some of the horses pulling the Persian chariots were in fact sustaining wounds and going to the ground.

Better yet, some became uncontrollable and swerved into the paths of other chariots, causing havoc. Most of the casualties were occurring on the outside fringes of the advancing chariots, with the result that the remaining teams of horses, with their attached vehicles, tended to veer toward the middle. With the assistance of the steadfast infantry lines, the chariots were gradually channeled into the gauntlet created by the phalanxes, where they continued to sustain casualties as they thundered through. The Persian cavalry simply followed behind the chariots and thus ended up being funneled into the gap as well.

A loud shout to my right caused me to return my attention to the struggle between the Baktrian horsemen and our Silver Shields. Apparently, one of our archers had managed to down a Baktrian squadron commander, to the audible outrage of the enemy and joy of our men. In general, the fighting around the right end of our line was spreading and becoming even more vicious. As Bessos discovered that the end of the line was much stronger than he had anticipated and that any flanking maneuver would be tougher to execute, he kept sending in more and more reinforcements. And after he had committed the entire 12,000-man Baktrian Cavalry to the attack, he requested from Dareios, and received, further reinforcements of steppe cavalry and eventually Persian heavy cavalry as well. I watched in horror as a few thousand of our infantrymen struggled to stand up against a vicious assault of at least 20,000 cavalry.

In the meantime, on our left wing, the situation was even worse. The Persian cavalry had overwhelmed our Thessalian and allied Greek horsemen and were now charging our heavy infantry. These Persian knights, many of whom used to be infantry as well, were not intimidated by the prospect of taking on a shieldwall. On the contrary, clad in chainmail from head to toe and riding their large, armored horses, they relished the opportunity to take on foot soldiers in one-on-one combat and demonstrate their bravery. Except, of course, there were several Persian knights against each one of our hoplites.

Our men had the advantage of their long pikes, which they could poke against the necks, chests, and shoulders of the beasts, but, unless they were particularly lucky, their pikes tended to slide off or break against the equine armor, without inflicting any injury. It was heavy work trying to dislodge the Persian warriors and even after our men successfully unhorsed them, their reward was a confrontation with an armored, well-armed, experienced warrior.

The prospects for our phalanxes appeared grim. *And this is before their 200,000-strong infantry has even entered the fray*, I realized grimly.

The only prong of Darcios's attack that didn't go quite according to plan was the chariot attack up the middle of the field. After being channeled into the gap between the phalanxes, the teams of tethered horses continued to bolt forward, spooked by the noise and spurred on by the missiles hitting them from both sides. The few chariots that had managed to clear the last of our infantry soldiers continued to race straight ahead, instead of pivoting and hitting our line from behind. And the Persian cavalry continued to charge right behind them, ignoring the Companion Cavalry stationed a short distance to their left, immediately behind the infantry phalanxes. Perhaps they didn't see us, sitting there on our steeds, waiting to attack, or perhaps they preferred to gallop where there was no enemy for them to engage, having just survived the gauntlet of our phalanxes. In the event, the entire thrust of the remaining chariots and attendant Persian cavalry continued unabated until they reached our baggage train, left among the hills several miles behind us. At that point they stopped, killed the few guards, and looted our possessions.

But the baggage train was well beyond my line of sight and far below my level of conscious concern. As I sat at the head of my squadron and next to all the other squadrons of the Companion Cavalry, I was barely aware of chariots and enemy cavalry roaring by. I was trying to follow the battlefield action but it was becoming more and more difficult. The sounds of fighting, and dying, reached deafening levels. Clouds of dust plunged the midday scene into an eerie twilight. It was impossible to tell who was holding which shield, who was attacking whom, which man was wielding a pike and which one absorbing a blow. It was all just a huge, swirling mass of tens of thousands of screaming, fighting, and dying men. Except, I had stopped hearing all the noise.

As my eyes flitted from one sanguinary tableau to the next, they alighted on the still, serene, singular figure of Alexandros. He sat aboard Boukephalas, in a little pocket of space, utterly relaxed, while his stallion munched contentedly on a stray tuft of grass. If it hadn't been for the slight movements of his head and the steady chomping of his steed, I might've thought I was watching an equestrian sculpture. There was even a shaft of light which, through some trick of entropy, rent through the haze of dust and illuminated his gleaming, white-crested helmet. *Maybe he is a demigod after all.* I broke into laughter.

Fortunately, no one noticed my misplaced mirth amid the bedlam. Even though I was beginning to doubt my own sanity, I didn't want my comrades to think I was becoming deranged. A strange contentment, even happiness, washed over me, almost like a warm, cleansing rain. I'd regained my sense of certainty, at least with respect to the timing and manner of my demise, which was clearly imminent. And I no longer cared about any inadvertent violations of the Prime Directive. In fact, I was looking forward to killing as many of the enemy as I could before they managed to kill me.

I looked more closely at the men around me. *These are the fellows with whom I'm going to die.* There was a certain sense of camaraderie in that. *Hey, all I had to do to stop being an outsider was to get killed alongside these guys.* It was all I could do to keep from slapping my forehead with my palm. Luckily, I resisted the impulse because I was holding, at that moment, a javelin in one hand and a sword in the other.

It was at this juncture, with the hoofbeats of the Persian cavalry receding toward the hills and with the infantry and allied cavalry on our flanks resisting, at least for the moment, the ever-increasing pressure of the combined forces of the Persian knights and the savage scrappers of the steppes, that Alexandros raised his sword, let out an unearthly yell, and heeled Boukephalas into action. The transformation from serene stillness to precipitate plunge was instantaneous. But we'd all seen this particular trick before. Our fearless leader wouldn't be leaving us in the dust this time.

Moving as one, the entire Companion Cavalry charged through the gap recently vacated by the enemy cavalry and headed for the center of the Persian line, the unmistakable figure of Dareios standing in his oversized chariot serving as our beacon. Several thousand elite Persian knights were still stationed in front of the emperor's chariot but not as many as there'd been at the start of the battle because squadron after squadron had been drawn off to support what were supposed to have been easy flanking maneuvers against the outlying prongs of our formation.

Conquest of Persia

As we galloped across no-man's land between the opposing lines, the entire Companion Cavalry spread out into one gigantic flying wedge, with Alexandros spearheading the point. During the few moments required to close with the enemy, there was very little sound. Neither side had time to yell or sing or boast or even pray. Each of us was single-mindedly focused on the figure of the first man we were going to kill.

And then the silence was shattered by a thunderbolt of clashing arms, of javelins hitting shields, of swords cleaving helmets, of horses screaming in terror, of men expelling their last, gurgling gasps. Dareios watched with almost disinterested fascination as Alexandros sliced through his elite Persian troops. He found it simply impossible to credit the evidence of his own eyes. No mortal could do what Alexandros was doing. It was almost like watching the dorsal fin of a shark parting the waves, except in this case he could also see all the vicious churning and chomping below the surface.

The rest of us had a tougher time of it. If Alexandros was a shark, we were more like a bloom of jellyfish, tossed back and forth by the ebb and flow of battle. We could only hope that our swords, as we slashed madly at the Persians' armor, carried enough of a sting to keep the enemy from engulfing our leader.

Kleitos, as usual, seemed to be having the most fun. His face was positively glowing as he dealt deathblow after jubilant deathblow, oblivious to the ferocious strokes whistling by his ears. The rest of his squadron, following their commander's example, plowed right in, absorbing almost as many blows as they meted out, but continuing their relentless forward progress.

Philotas, by contrast, spent more time directing traffic than actually engaging the enemy, making sure each squadron kept its shape and contributed to the overall thrust of our wedge. It didn't matter how many men were rendered hors de combat, whether ours or theirs, how many horses went down, how much dust, destruction, and disarray descended on the battlefield. Each of our squadrons had its segment of the sharply echeloned line to defend as part of the overall advance and Philotas saw to it that each squadron did its part. Alexandros may have served as the point of the wedge but Philotas made sure there continued to be a wedge behind him.

Seleukos, while fighting as ferociously as the rest of us, was still the first to notice when a dangerous fissure opened up between Kleitos's and Kleandros's squadrons and rushed in his own men to plug the hole before the enemy even noticed it was there.

I fought as I always did, on autopilot. An adversary would float into view in front of me; I could tell, before he even thought of it, which mode of attack he would employ first; I would parry it, slide and counter, then parry again, and finally, almost gently, push the point of my sword through the small gap above his chainmail breastplate and below the cheekpiece of his helmet, making sure I kept pushing until I heard the crunch of vertebrae being rendered asunder. Then the next adversary would appear in front of me and the process would repeat. And all the while I felt as if I were hovering above the fray, watching myself disposing of one adversary after the next. *I wonder whether this means I'm already dead.*

The Companion Cavalry, to every last man, performed spectacularly. However, this didn't change the fact that, even after Dareios had foolishly thinned the ranks of his own cavalry in the middle of his line in pursuit of the elusive victory on the flanks, there were still more than enough Persian knights left between us and the emperor's chariot to repel our reckless charge. We were killing a lot of them but we were also losing men and it was obvious to me we would run out of fighters before they did.

Dareios finally snapped out of his trance and willed his eyes to look away from the progress of Alexandros's white plume. All around him, the magnificent mounted Persian warriors were laying down their lives to save his. They were bending under the weight of our attack but they weren't breaking. He was a good enough soldier to realize that his cavalry, diminished as it was in its numbers, was still strong enough to withstand our charge. And in any event, they wouldn't have to resist much longer because surely the overwhelming forces under Bessos's and Mazaios's command would wipe out the inferior units opposed to them and then wheel about to take the Companion Cavalry from the rear. He was beginning to savor the sweet taste of victory when, in his anticipatory delight, he permitted himself a quick peek at Alexandros's plume.

This short, sidelong glance proved to be a fatal mistake. The white fin of the shark was still slicing through wave after wave of his elite knights. The brief glimpse became a fixed stare. This time, he was unable to avert his eyes. He realized that, relatively soon, Alexandros would reach his chariot, no matter how many brave men died trying to stop him. Dareios was presented with a dilemma. Should he stand and fight, even if this meant almost certain personal extinction, or should he run away in order to fight again another day?

Dareios chose discretion above valor. He signaled for his horse and abandoned the field. The knights closest to him joined in his flight, if only to provide their emperor with a protective shield. Their comrades, farther forward and therefore closer to the actual hand-to-hand combat decided to follow suit. In an instant, all opposition to our charge melted away.

We – those of us still alive – let out a joyful whoop. Alexandros paused just long enough to organize a pursuit party, led by him, of course. This time the Persian coward wouldn't get away.

We were on the verge of taking off after Dareios, whose progress we could easily follow by the column of dust his troop was raising, when a messenger from Parmenion reached Alexandros. The old general's message was stark: Unless relief arrived immediately, his forces would be wiped out in the next few minutes.

Alexandros didn't hesitate. The pursuit party became a relief regiment. We all turned and rode as fast as our tired mounts would carry us toward the end of the pan-Hellenic line under Parmenion's command, taking Mazaios's forces from the back. Suddenly, the savvy Babylonian satrap found himself beleaguered from all sides. What's more, he quickly ascertained the cause of this unexpected shift of fortune, receiving word that Dareios had once again withdrawn from the field of battle. Mazaios made the only rational choice. Extricating his forces as best he could, he hurriedly departed from the zone of combat and led his cavalry back home to Babylon.

In the meantime, on the opposite end of the line, Bessos watched in disbelief as both Dareios and Mazaios made their escapes. With one shrill whistle he stopped his savage steppe fighters in their tracks. They, too, turned and departed in the direction of their homeland.

Our infantry, finding all opposition abruptly disappearing, roared ahead and engulfed the hapless conscript infantry units, left behind without orders, leaders, or the ability to defend themselves. Some of these poorly-trained and poorly-armed wretched farm boys managed to run away. Most of them were slaughtered on Dareios's carefully polished battlefield.

In the meantime, having routed Mazaios's forces, we were once again preparing to resume our chase after the fleeing Dareios. However, before we could execute our pivot, we were unexpectedly hit in the side by the elements of the Persian cavalry that had finished looting our baggage train and had decided to return to the fray. They, and their animals, were relatively fresh after their uneventful jaunt to the hills and back and they were spoiling for a fight. We, on the other hand, were physically exhausted and mentally drained, not only by the vicious combat but also by the repeated emotional swings between the certainty of defeat and the euphoria of unexpected survival.

It was a silly and pointless encounter, fought after the outcome of the battle had been determined. Nevertheless, my squadron lost more men during this senseless skirmish than we had in all the fighting that had preceded it. Eventually, we defeated these last remnants of the vaunted Persian cavalry and staggered back to our staging point, where Alexandros was waiting, ready to resume his quest to chase down and extirpate the Persian coward.

******

The erstwhile ruler of the Persian Empire, in the meantime, was galloping toward Arbela. His plan, upon reaching this commercial hub, was to utilize the well-trodden caravan route that led out of the city to flee eastward, toward Ekbatana and the remote provinces beyond. He was certain Alexandros wouldn't follow him, not only because an incursion into the eastern provinces by a foreign army would be necessarily suicidal but also because Babylon lay, supine and defenseless, a mere 350 miles to the southwest, down the Tigris. How could any primitive, crude Macedonian invader resist the temptation to ravish the glittering queen city of the Persian Empire, which now lay open to his onslaught?

Dareios and his abject crew of unnerved bodyguards, aboard their half-dead, lathered, steaming steeds, reached Arbela just before midnight. They paused at the market square only long enough to commandeer new mounts and expropriate provisions before heading out of town. But, even during this brief hiatus, they found themselves gradually enveloped by swarms of wretched survivors of the battle, who were starting to stream into the city.

Making virtue out of necessity, Dareios mounted an upturned wagon and addressed the gathering crowd.

He told them that, if they followed him, they had nothing to fear because Alexandros was sure to head southwest, toward Babylon, while he intended to go southeast, to Ekbatana. Furthermore, he promised to raise another army, bigger than the one he had just lost, and to defeat the foreign invaders once and for all. He had some other things to say but no one was listening. The men were milling around, looking for their friends, for food, for a means of salvation. They were certainly not paying any attention to a disheveled madman standing atop an upside-down wagon and shouting in a language many of them didn't understand.

More and more men kept arriving at the market square. The survivors of Dareios's Greek mercenary unit marched in, still organized and disciplined, looking for leadership. They were followed by the Baktrian horsemen, who rode in as a unit, led by Bessos. Unlike most of the survivors, they appeared to be in good shape, antsy for more fighting, dismayed they were somehow deprived of certain victory.

Dareios was pleased to see the arrival of the Baktrians. He concluded his speech and beckoned Bessos to approach. The young satrap ignored him, throwing himself into preparations for the long trip home. Eventually, the emperor gave up, descended from the wagon, mounted his new horse, and rode over to Bessos. The two of them jointly led the troops out of Arbela. It was hard to tell which one was in charge.

Conquest of Persia

****

We rode through the night, bloodied and exhausted, from Gaugamela to Arbela. We reached the town shortly after daybreak. Dareios and his crew were long gone. Alexandros took one look at us in the dawning light of the new day and decided to call off the chase. "We'll catch him soon enough," he assured us. "Now, let's go back to the troops and get some rest."

A striking change in Alexandros's attitude had taken place. The raging, death-dealing, irresistible daemon of battle and the eager, snorting, determined bloodhound of the chase was replaced by a serene, glowing, contented victor of Gaugamela. Dareios may have gotten away but Alexandros, unlike Dareios himself, realized that the nominal emperor of Persia would never again command his empire because he couldn't regain the respect, or even the fear, of his subjects.

Much work remained. We had yet to conquer a single one of the empire's four capitals. Two thirds of the satrapies and more than three quarters of the landmass remained beyond our control. The putative emperor was still out there somewhere, recruiting a new army, and, if he failed, there would be another emperor to take his place. But none of that changed the fact that, against all odds, we had defeated the strongest army the Persian Empire could field, on the ground of its own choosing, in a pitched battle fought for all the marbles.

And in all fairness, the differences between the two commanders had something to do with the ultimate outcome. It was simply inconceivable that Alexandros would've ever withdrawn in order to fight another day. As far as he was concerned, running away from a fight was infinitely worse than dying in the course of battle. Like his idol Achilleus, Alexandros believed implicitly that dying gloriously in combat was a fate much to be preferred to living a long, dull, forgettable life.

Dareios, notwithstanding his superficial religiosity, believed that personal demise was the end of everything, that there was no glory in death, only oblivion. It was better to survive and keep hope alive. He thought he could always regroup and try again. In the end, it was this attitude that killed him.

It helped, in the case of Alexandros, that he'd persuaded himself of his own divine paternity. And, to give him his due, even as he descended into derangement, he never lost his military brilliance. He had great strategic vision, was a superb tactician, an inspirational leader, a cool battlefield commander, and a superlative and ruthless combatant. His belief in himself and in his destiny was infectious. On that particular day, the troops would have followed him into the gates of hell. At Gaugamela, Alexandros proved himself, once again, invincible.

****

Conquest of Persia

It was past noon of the day after, when we returned to Gaugamela – barely twenty-four hours since the battle. We knew we were getting close when we saw the birds. From a distance, they looked like a dark billowing veil in the sky. As we approached, the veil resolved into individual dots, mostly black, of circling, swooping, shrieking vultures, crows, ravens, hawks, and a few eagles. By the time I could make out the birds, I could also smell the carrion that had attracted them. And then we topped a small rise and my breath caught in my throat.

It was a beautiful, sunny day, with nary a cloud in the sky, a warm, gentle breeze bathing our faces. But the tranquility of the scene was belied by the stench of death in our nostrils and the horrendous carnage assaulting our eyes. I'd seen the aftermath of many a battle; I'd seen barley fields strewn with corpses; I'd supervised the removal and cremation of hundreds, perhaps thousands, of dead soldiers; but I'd never seen anything remotely close to what confronted our senses as we returned to the scene of Alexandros's greatest victory.

Dareios's carefully polished battlefield was carpeted by the dead. There were dead soldiers still standing on their feet because there was no room for them to fall. An area of three or four square miles was completely covered in a comforter of corpses, the grisly duvet several bodies thick in many places. Normally, one would expect to see human scavengers among the dead, stripping the enemy soldiers of their gear, armor, and valuables, but the only movement I could see were the feasting vultures, dogs, and jackals. Perhaps the surviving men were finding it too difficult to force their way through the mass of the dead or perhaps the ratio of the dead to the living was too high or perhaps the survivors were too shocked to move.

Led by Alexandros, our small group carefully skirted the field of carnage. Eventually, back among the hills, we found our camp. Parmenion had assumed command in Alexandros's absence and was working hard to organize squads to locate and bring back our own casualties, in order to tend to the wounded and to administer final rites for the dead. Alexandros quickly took in the scene, approved of Parmenion's arrangements, and summoned Kallisthenes into the command tent. He spent the rest of the day dictating reports of his victory to Antigonos in Phrygia, Antipatros in Pella, Demades in Athens, to all his satraps and to leaders of all the cities of Ionia and mainland Greece who had supplied aid to the pan-Hellenic army, and of course to his mother.

He guessed that the enemy dead numbered sixty thousand or more, a figure a subsequent census determined to have been fairly accurate. He also claimed that the pan-Hellenic army had lost fewer than a thousand men. This estimate proved to be a wild understatement. The Battle of Gaugamela turned out to be Alexandros's greatest victory but also his most costly one.

Chapter 9 – Babylon

For once, Dareios had been accurate in his surmise of Alexandros's next move. After burying the pan-Hellenic dead (there were too many dead and too few trees in Mesopotamia for mass cremations), after making sacrifices and giving thanks to all the pertinent deities, after distributing the captured booty, after another celebratory banquet and pro forma victory speech, after he'd had a chance to catch his breath, Alexandros saw no immediate need to chase Dareios to Ekbatana. As far as he was concerned, Dareios had forfeited his claim to the Persian throne on the buffed, bloody battlefield of Gaugamela. What was needed right then was some morale-boosting rest and relaxation for the troops and some prestige-enhancing strutting for their leader. Alexandros chose to march on Babylon.

Mazaios, who had successfully executed his getaway to Babylon, was informed of our impending arrival almost before we'd set off. He immediately launched the necessary preparations: He ordered

Dareios's elite royal cavalry squadrons, which had managed to extricate themselves from the generalized rout at Gaugamela with minimal casualties and had followed Mazaios to Babylon, to polish their armor; he patiently stood through numerous fittings while his splendid new ceremonial robe and suit of armor were rushed to completion; and he summoned several of his remaining Greek mercenaries to the royal palace and immersed himself in the assiduous study of Greek, with a particular emphasis on the Macedonian dialect.

We were still a half-day's march from Babylon when our scouts reported that a massive column of natives had sallied forth from the city and was making its way toward us. Uncertain as to their intentions, Alexandros immediately halted our own column and ordered us to deploy in a defensive formation, with the Companion Cavalry arrayed, squadron by squadron, in the front, followed by the infantry in a hollow phalanx, with the baggage train and camp followers in the middle. And then we waited.

First, we saw the approaching cloud of dust. Then we heard the noise. It was difficult to tell, at least at first, whether the cacophony was supposed to pass for music but eventually the din resolved into loud drumming, cymbal crashing, trumpet blaring, and human shrieking that we interpreted as Babylonian singing. By then, we could make out the figures on the road. The procession was led by a large lacquered litter, carried by a dozen broad-shouldered, dark-skinned, magnificently attired porters. They were followed by squadrons of Dareios's royal cavalry, their gleaming armor coruscating in the blazing Mesopotamian sun. Then came the priests in their flowing white robes and elaborate felt hats. And finally, the bulk of the column, made up of thousands upon thousands of ordinary citizens in gay, colorful costumes, advancing with a peculiar, prancing strut, accompanied by the god-awful noise that had announced their initial approach. It was obvious this wasn't a belligerent sortie and we all relaxed our vigilance.

When the van of the procession reached us, the porters lowered the palanquin and a beautifully accoutered, lavishly bejeweled, meticulously coiffed elderly aristocrat tumbled out. Alexandros recognized the man as Mazaios and rode up to him. Seeing our leader, the satrap of Babylonia and Mesopotamia dropped once again into the dust, landing just short of Boukephalas's forelegs.

"You may rise," Alexandros called out, clearly pleased by the show. Mazaios understood, without the need of translation. He laboriously regained his feet and addressed the Macedonian king and would-be Persian emperor in halting but serviceable Greek.

"Welcome to your new capital, your celestial majesty. The citizens of Babylon have come out to extend a warm welcome to their liberator. I am here to serve as your guide as you take up your new quarters in the royal palace. And of course, your men are more than welcome in our city as our honored guests."

Alexandros listened and smiled. Mazaios had evidently spent his time not only learning Greek but also getting to know the predilections of his erstwhile adversary. He'd had many opportunities to observe Alexandros throughout the past four years, both directly and through eyewitness reports, and he'd judged his man to a fare-thee-well. This intelligence, when combined with the ingrained sycophancy of a Persian courtier, made for a heady mixture that Alexandros found hard to resist.

"Would your majesty like to join me in my litter?" Mazaios inquired. "It's extremely comfortable, I assure you."

A fleeting grimace crossed Alexandros's countenance. "Perhaps a touch too comfortable. Why don't we fetch a horse for you so you can ride like a man?"

By the time the two of them arrived at the Ishtar Gate, Mazaios had been reappointed satrap of Babylonia and Mesopotamia.

******

Barsine was panting. Her labor pains had arrived two weeks before she had expected them. For an ostensible primigravida, she seemed remarkably calm about her imminent parturition. She concentrated on her breathing to take her mind off her contractions. "Fetch some hot water and a couple of clean linen sheets, and then tell Artakama that I'm about to deliver," she told her serving girl between labor pangs. "And be quick about it. I don't think this will take too long."

She tried hard not to cry out as the cramps became more frequent and more intense but it wouldn't have mattered if she had. The hostage camp at Old Tyros was in an uproar. A small squad of Macedonian horsemen had ridden in, more or less simultaneously with the onset of her labor, bringing word of Alexandros's victory at Gaugamela. They also brought orders to the commander of the small garrison guarding the encampment to strike the tents and convey, with all possible dispatch, all the hostages, the previously captured loot, the recuperating soldiers, the camp followers, and all the women whom we'd left behind, to Babylon. Alexandros assumed, possibly incorrectly, that his men were anxious to see their consorts, courtesans, and captive companions after all these months of separation. Perhaps he was projecting his own desire to see Barsine onto his men.

"Take a peek, Arta, and see how large the opening has become." Acting as her own midwife was a novel experience for Barsine but, after four previous deliveries, she knew the process inside out. *It's like an out-of-body experience*, she reflected, *except for the fact it still hurts like hell.*

"Can you see the crown of the head?" she asked after the next wave of agony had passed and was relieved to hear an affirmative answer. She wasn't sure how she would've coped with a breech birth, attended only by three teenage girls, none of whom had seen a delivery before. The urge to push came soon thereafter and she embraced it with all her might. The baby popped out moments later and Artakama, conscientiously following her sister's screamed instructions, managed to catch it before it landed on the dirt floor of the tent.

The lack of sound scared Barsine. "Turn it upside down and slap it!" But, before Artakama had a chance to administer the requisite blow, the tent was filled with the loud, healthy cry of the baby.

"It's going to be a smart kid," Barsine laughed, falling back onto her pallet in relief. "It knows enough to start crying before it gets slapped. What is it, by the way?"

She was told that it was a boy.

****

In Ekbatana, all appeared normal at first blush. Dareios was ensconced in the magnificent royal palace, busily issuing orders and writing letters. There were still some courtiers around and they bowed and scraped because that was the only way they knew how to behave but the orders were generally ignored and the letters mostly not delivered.

A huge tent city had sprung up overnight on the parade grounds surrounding the Ekbatana palace, occupied by the 12,000 savage steppe scrappers from Baktria. The largest, most elaborate tent belonged to Bessos, the satrap of that province and putative vassal of Emperor Dareios.

Dareios continued to hold his usual, daily audiences, which were attended by richly attired aristocrats, who knelt when he entered and who kissed him on the cheek when he bid them to rise. "Did Bessos receive my summons?" Dareios would ask each morning and he would be assured the order to attend had been duly delivered. "He sends his regrets," he would be told.

Each time, Dareios would consider sending an armed guard to escort the recalcitrant satrap to the next reception and each time he would think better of it. He would content himself with sending a brief missive instead, advising Bessos of his intentions and asking him to get the troops ready. There was never any reply.

Dareios also sent countless letters to all the other satraps who remained under his nominal authority, asking for fresh troops. Amazingly enough, every now and then a battalion of raw recruits would show up but none of the satraps came with their troops. They were busy back home lubricating their weathervanes, better to track the shifting winds of change.

****

"Why don't you hang back a little and let the others go in first?" Hephaistion suggested sotto voce.

Alexandros laughed. "The day I hang back a little is the day I stop being the leader of these men."

"This isn't a battle, Aniketos. We're entering a city that's already surrendered. They're welcoming us with garlands, songs, and open arms. No one will think any the less of you if you let some of your men have first dibs on the spoils."

Alexandros's eyes crinkled at the corners. "Don't think I don't know what you're up to. What exactly are you worried about?"

"Just take a look at that gateway." A touch of frustration crept into Hephaistion's tone. "I've never seen a more perfect killing zone."

Mazaios rejoined them. "Beautiful, isn't it?" It was impossible to tell how much of the conversation he'd overheard. "Would you like me to give you a tour? I've become something of an antiquary since taking up my post here."

"How are you as a hostage, is what we really want to know." Perdikkas, who was riding immediately behind Alexandros and Hephaistion, inserted himself into the conversation with his usual tact and aplomb.

Mazaios took no umbrage. "Those six young men standing next to the tower over there are my sons. Standing behind them are many of their wives and most of my grandchildren. If you'll permit me, I'd like to introduce my sons to you."

"I'd be pleased to meet them," Alexandros flashed a reproachful look at Perdikkas. "We're not here as conquerors but as liberators."

"Precisely." Mazaios beckoned to his male offspring. The men, preening like peacocks while, at the same time, more anxious to please than neutered puppies, fell to their knees and started crawling toward us. The women and children lay down in the dust and stayed there.

Alexandros opened his mouth to tell them to rise but thought better of it. He sat patiently on his horse, while the six noble youths traversed the thirty yards or so on their hands and knees. "A handsome crew," he said to a beaming Mazaios.

"Thank you, your celestial highness. I'm very proud of them."

Finally, the scions of the newly-reappointed satrap of Babylonia and Mesopotamia made it to within spitting distance of our horses and collapsed onto their bellies and faces, awaiting the command to rise.

Conquest of Persia

Alexandros let them wait, perhaps a beat too long.

****

Ishtar Gate, named in honor of the Babylonian goddess of sex and fertility, was the ceremonial entry point into the city. It was also the most elaborate of the eight gates that pierced the inner walls of Babylon.[18] (We had already passed the outer wall.) It was more a complex of defensive fortifications than a gateway in any conventional sense. First, greeting the approaching traveler, was the Northern Fortress. Its walls and towers, built of fired brick and clad with blue enameled tiles, flanked the roadway. The two tallest towers were connected by a bridge above the road. A crenelated parapet ran all around shooting platforms at the top of the towers. All the edges of the towers, the parapet, and the connecting bridge were outlined with contrasting enameled bricks. We couldn't see any soldiers inside or atop the towers but that didn't mean they weren't there.

Beyond the towers rose the Sothern Fortress, a huge, rectangular building, perhaps seventy feet tall and a hundred and fifty feet wide. The formidable defensive walls of Babylon adjoined this massive edifice on either side. Despite its enormous size, however, this building looked, at least from our perspective, like an exquisite jewel box. The broad expanse of the wall was covered

---

[18] See Map 11 at AlexanderGeiger.com for a sketch of Babylon.

with more of the gleaming, glazed tiles but these were three-dimensional, sculptural tiles, forming large, naturalistically colored mosaics of sacred animals, projecting from the surface of the wall in bas-relief. There were alternating rows of bulls and dragons, running all the way to the top. In addition, all the edges of the building, including the crenellations at the top and the large, arched opening at the bottom, were once again delineated using bands of colorful bricks, assembled into intricate, repeating, geometric patterns.

At ground level, in the center of the front wall, stood a tall, elegant, arched entrance that gave onto a passageway from one side of the building to the other. We could see a bright patch of light at the far end, which was presumably the arched exit orifice of the vaulted corridor, but from where we stood, it was difficult to tell how deep the building and hence how long the tunnel through it might be.

Flanking the opening at the proximate end of the gateway were two gigantic wooden doors that, when closed, matched precisely the shape and size of the arched doorway. The doors were painted blue and decorated with copious quantities of gold leaf and lapis lazuli. Presumably, a similar set of doors was installed at the far end of the passageway as well. Various apertures suitable for raining down missiles, boiling tar, and stinking excrement on the heads of invaders trapped in the corridor below were undoubtedly incorporated into the sides and ceiling of the structure but these remained invisible to us.

Almost lost between the Northern and Southern Fortresses was a deep, wide moat, more canal than ditch, which channeled water from the Euphrates all around the inner walls and then back into the river. A wooden bridge, supported by massive chains, carried the roadway across the moat, unless of course the bridge had been raised, using some kind of windlass mechanisms hidden within the bowels of the Southern Fortress.

****

"Beautiful, isn't it?" Mazaios repeated. "Shall we proceed through the tunnel?"

Alexandros remained rooted to the spot. "Yes, it's beautiful. How many soldiers are required to man the two fortresses?"

"These are functional fortifications, your majesty, in addition to being a splendid point of entry. They can accommodate hundreds of armed men but naturally they are empty right now. We have no need of defenses against our liberators."

Alexandros gave him a cynical smile. "That's where we disagree, my man. Fortifications should never be left vacant." He turned back to Perdikkas. "Take a battalion of infantry and occupy these buildings to make sure no harm comes to them."

Perdikkas beamed with evident satisfaction. "Yes, sire!" In a few minutes his men set off on the double toward the two fortresses.

Only when he could see the heads of our men peeking above the parapets and out of the myriad shooting portals did Alexandros turn back to Mazaios. "We're ready to start the tour you mentioned, satrap."

"What about the rest of the walls?" Hephaistion asked. "Shouldn't we occupy those as well?"

"Sire, you don't have enough men to occupy the walls of Babylon." Mazaios fought hard to hide his irritation.

Hephaistion was unrestrained by any similar compunction. "You don't say."

Alexandros stepped in before a dispute could develop. "How big are the walls?"

"That's a complicated question, your imperial majesty, because there are a couple of walls. You previously passed through the outer wall. As you undoubtedly noticed, it's a pretty imposing structure. It encloses a three-square-mile area on the eastern side of the Euphrates, is almost five miles long, and rises to a height of seventy-five feet. It's more than thirty feet thick at the base and twenty feet wide at the top. As our citizens like to brag, the outer wall is wide enough at the top to permit two chariots to pass each other without slowing down.

"The outer wall was originally intended to protect not only the city but also the plantations that served, at that time, as its breadbasket. By now, irrigated farm areas have spread far beyond the outer wall, on both sides of the river. In the meantime, numerous slums and shantytowns have sprung up within the outer wall, as you saw during our ride to the Ishtar Gate. They are a real eyesore but, unfortunately, there's nothing we can do about it. The city is growing and the new arrivals have to live somewhere.

"Are we ready to proceed?"

Alexandros checked to see whether our men had occupied both fortresses. "You were going to tell us about the inner wall as well. Let's do that before we enter this tunnel through the Southern Fortress."

"Certainly, your majesty. We're about to enter Babylon proper. Please keep in mind that the city straddles the Euphrates. The Old City is on the east bank and the so-called New City is on the west bank. The Old City is slightly larger and includes the royal palace, most of the temples, and many municipal buildings. The so-called New City, which, despite its name, is more than a thousand years old, is mostly residential apartment buildings and commercial establishments. Together, the two parts make a rectangle about a mile and a half wide and a mile long. The inner walls run all the way around this inner city, or Babylon proper, as we call it.

"There's also a moat around the Old City. The banks of the moat are lined with fired brick and waterproofed with bitumen to make sure neither water nor enemy sappers can get through. The walls are built on top of this solid base. They're just as tall as the outer wall, only a little more slender."

"I don't see any stones. What are these walls made of?"

"Unfortunately, your highness, both stone and timber are rare commodities in all of Babylonia, so most construction has to be done with bricks. The best, most expensive bricks are the enameled bricks you see here at the Ishtar Gate. The next best building material are the fired bricks, which are quite durable. Both the outer and inner walls were built of fired brick, with bitumen used as both mortar and sealant.

"The cheapest, most abundant material are mud bricks, baked in the Sun, as opposed to a kiln." Mazaios laughed. "Most of Babylon is made of mud bricks. But I digress. At the top of the inner walls, there's a crenelated parapet that runs all the way along both the outside and inside edges of the top surface. Every two hundred feet or so, there's a watch tower that straddles the top of the wall. So, as you can see, you could easily station tens of thousands of men on just the inner walls alone.

"Finally, at the north and south sides of the walls, where the walls abut the river, huge iron grates completely fill the gap. Iron bars, driven into the riverbed and embedded into the opposing ends of the wall, keep anything bigger than a rat from getting through.

"Babylon really is impregnable, unless we choose to invite people in. But today, there are no soldiers on the walls. All the inhabitants are lining the streets on the other side of this gate, ready to greet you and pay homage to you, your imperial highness," Mazaios concluded.

Alexandros, seeing our men in position, was ready to proceed. "Well, in that case, we shouldn't keep them waiting."

****

It turned out the tunnel through Southern Fortress was about a hundred feet long. As we made our way through the passageway and into the city itself, Mazaios provided a brief history lesson.

"There's always been a Babylon," he said. "It sits at the point where the Euphrates and Tigris Rivers make their closest approach to each other. It's the natural crossover point for men and merchandise sailing on one and needing to get to the other.

"As far as I know, it was part of the Akkadian Empire, perhaps two thousand years ago, although this place has been inhabited much longer than that."

"Almost as old as some of the pyramids in Egypt," Alexandros whispered to me. I nodded my concurrence with Mazaios's chronology.

"Eventually, the Babylonians overthrew the Akkadians and installed a native ruler. This has been a recurring theme in the history of the city. They keep rebelling but can't keep their independence for long."

"Perhaps we can restore their independence," Alexandros offered.

Mazaios didn't know what to make of the comment. The notion of an independent Babylonia was, at that stage, an absurdity. "They'd like that very much, your divine majesty," he finally ventured.

Alexandros smiled. "Of course, their independence will have to be under our leadership."

"That goes without saying, your majesty," Mazaios quickly agreed. "But to resume my story. At some point, maybe fifteen hundred years ago, a capable native leader named Hammurabi came into power and expanded the reach of the city over the entire area we now call Babylonia, and perhaps even beyond. He left a code of laws behind, chiseled into a large stone stele."

"Really? That's something I'd like to see."

"Well, unfortunately, after Hammurabi died, Babylon once again lost its independence. It was overrun by various invaders, including Assyrians, Kassites, and Elamites. The Elamites dragged the stele off to their capital Sousa, so you'll have to go there to see it."

"It's our next stop."

"In the meantime, we do have some clay tablets with Hammurabi's laws incised on them but only the priests can read those tablets. We can certainly ask the priests to show them to us.

"To continue, about three hundred years ago some primitive sea people made their way here and occupied Babylon. I think they called themselves Kaldu or Kashdu or something like that. We call them Khaldaians now. They have disappeared. Or more correctly, they were absorbed by the native Babylonians, so when you talk to ordinary Babylonians now, they think they're descended from the original inhabitants of this region, when in fact they're just as likely to be Babylonianized Khaldaians. So really, in a way, each group took over the other. But interestingly enough, this cross-pollination yielded what was arguably the golden age of Babylon."

"Well, maybe the previous golden age," interjected Hephaistion, "until the even more golden age that our new emperor is about to inaugurate, starting right now."

"Naturally, that goes without saying," Mazaios readily agreed. "Anyway, these Khaldaians gave rise to a king who called himself Naboukhodonosor, after a much older Akkadian king of the same name, to whom he was totally unrelated."

"A lot like your former emperor Dareios," Alexandros observed.

Mazaios tried, and failed, to suppress a malicious little laugh. "Yes, your celestial highness, much like our former emperor Dareios.

"This second Naboukhodonosor, however, who lived maybe three hundred years ago, was a ruthless and successful military leader who greatly enlarged the kingdom he'd inherited. His rule encompassed Egypt, the Levant, Assyria, Arabia, Mesopotamia, and of course Babylonia. He attributed his long and successful reign to the favor of the gods, especially Marduk, who's the patron deity of Babylon. To thank the gods for past favors bestowed and to propitiate them with an eye to future endeavors, he spent lavishly on the temples and monuments of Babylon. In fact, he's credited with building this Ishtar Gate through which we are riding right now."

"This is supposed to be a temple?" Kleitos asked skeptically. "Looks more like a heavily fortified gateway to me."

"It's a dual-purpose facility," Mazaios explained smoothly. "It's a beautiful monument that serves to glorify and exalt the goddess, while at the same time protecting the city. To the Babylonian way of thinking, there's no contradiction between the sacred and the practical."

Alexandros nodded. "I can see that." By then, we had emerged from the imposing, vaulted, decorated corridor of the Southern Fortress and found ourselves on a broad, limestone-paved boulevard.

"We call this the Processional Way," Mazaios announced grandly.

The entire wide, straight avenue was covered, as far as the eye could see, with a carpet of flowers. Set up at regular intervals on the margins of the road were silver altars, heaped with frankincense and other aromatic resins and spices. It was a visual and olfactory feast.

Beyond the altars, lining both sides of the street ten or twelve people deep were the inhabitants of

Babylon. Upon glimpsing our emergence from the Ishtar Gate, they all fell to their knees, touching the ground with their foreheads.

At that point, our way forward was barred by the prostrate body of a balding man, his arms stretched out, palms against the pavement, legs splayed at a forty-five-degree angle, his body arrayed in beautiful, billowing, colorful, silken robes.

"Who's that man?" Alexandros asked.

"Oh, he's just the eunuch responsible for the treasury, your majesty. I put him in charge of decorating the Processional Way and I guess he couldn't stop himself from attempting to claim credit by obstructing our way forward. His name is Bagophanes. Let me know if you want him punished."

Alexandros was incredulous. "That's a eunuch?"

"Yes, indeed, your majesty. Most of the administrative jobs in the palace are held by eunuchs. We find they tend to be more docile and less ambitious than intact men."

"But he's bald. My teacher Aristoteles taught me that eunuchs were never bald."

Mazaios shrugged.

"Maybe we should check his balls," Kleitos suggested helpfully.

Our entire group dissolved into laughter and Alexandros commanded the eunuch to rise. Bagophanes remained motionless, not understanding the Macedonian command. Mazaios didn't come to his treasurer's aid. Finally, somebody in the crowd said something and the poor man struggled to his knees, looking up fearfully, flower petals fluttering softly from his robes back to the ground.

"He probably thinks we're laughing at him," Seleukos suggested.

"Well, we are, aren't we?" This from Hephaistion.

Alexandros motioned for the treasurer to stand up. Bagophanes gratefully regained his feet and ran up to Boukephalas, kissing the horse on both cheeks, provoking fresh gales of laughter among us liberators.

"I'd tell you to give him some coins," Alexandros said to Hephaistion, "but he's the treasurer, after all, so he's hardly in need of our largess." We started moving again, leaving the flustered eunuch standing in the road.

"Please raise your gaze to your right, your highness," Mazaios urged. "That's one of the seven wonders of the world."

We were surrounded on both sides by monumental buildings. As far as I could tell, every house in the entire city was at least four stories high but the buildings on our immediate left and right were much taller than that. The specific structure to which Mazaios was pointing had a colonnade on the bottom, the roof of which was supported by massive stone arches. In fact, the support columns were almost as wide as the empty spaces between them. *Not very impressive engineering*, I thought. Then I looked above the arches and changed my mind.

Above us, perhaps forty feet above street level, loomed a forest of exotic trees and flowering bushes.

"The Hanging Gardens of Babylon," Mazaios announced in what was apparently his usual theatrical fashion.

"They're not hanging," Perdikkas objected. "They're just sitting there. I thought they'd be suspended from the heavens by chains."

"They've built a luscious, flowering forest, forty feet in the air, in this climate," Seleukos chided him. "It takes your breath away."

"You've hit upon the key aspect, sire." Mazaios gave Seleukos a quick nod, grateful for the assist. "Hidden behind those massive arches are ingenuous machines, mostly endless chains of buckets, turned by mules, that raise a continuous supply of water to the top.

And incidentally, the gardens above us are terraced, rising higher and higher, giving the impression of a mountainside. Running streams cascade down through lush meadows, irrigating all sorts of exotic plants and trees. And all that weight, an entire mountainside, with meadows, trees, and streams, must be kept up in the air. And it all has to be watertight." He paused for a moment, as if he himself were awed by this wonder. "It wouldn't do if all that water, which is laboriously raised all the way to the top, simply poured or seeped back to the ground. It has to be kept up there, so the trees and plants can gradually absorb it. The bottom floors, which house not only the irrigation mechanisms but also chambers for provisions, reception halls, housing for the gardeners, and numerous rooms stocked with booty brought here from various conquered peoples, are completely dry.

"I'll take you up there after you've settled in at the palace, your majesty. It's the most peaceful spot in the world."

"Yes, I'd like that. But why would anybody want to build that?"

"Well, here's the story: Naboukhodonosor's favorite wife, who was a princess from the highlands of Media, didn't much like the flat, arid plains of Babylonia. So Naboukhodonosor built an artificial mountain for her, covered it with all the exotic trees and plants he could import, supplied it with babbling brooks that never ran dry, and recreated for her a small, verdant slice of her homeland."

"He must've had a lot of loot, this Naboukhodonosor," Kleitos observed.

"That he did; that he did. Keep in mind he controlled at least half of what's now the Persian Empire – the more populous, prosperous half, I might add. Plus, all the caravans from the East to the West and back again had to pass through his territory and pay customs duties to his officials. But most importantly, he conquered all the greatest and riches cities of his time, bringing home huge amounts of treasure and an endless supply of slave labor. It took more than money to build these edifices."

We were riding along the Processional Way while he was talking. The wall of prostrate people continued to line both sides of the road.

"How many people live in Babylon?" Seleukos asked.

"Perhaps as many as two hundred thousand," Mazaios said. "It's the most populous city in the world."

At that moment, a small boy, no more than eight, broke away from his mother, stood up, and ran into the road in front of us, waving and shouting excitedly. A mortified silence fell over the crowd. Everyone held their breaths, awaiting the swift, inevitable, merciless punishment that was sure to befall the impudent youngster. The only person moving was the small child, who continued to hop up and down and wave his hand.

Mazaios finally broke the silence. "I'm terribly sorry, your divine majesty. I'll see to it he's promptly put to death. Does your majesty have any particular method of execution in mind?"

Alexandros stared at him. "What are you talking about? He's a kid."

"This kind of serious breach of protocol can't be tolerated, your majesty. Unless he's promptly and publicly punished, who knows what the next person might decide to do. It could lead to a complete breakdown of order and authority."

Alexandros rode up to the boy, leaned over and lifted him high in the air, depositing him on Boukephalas's withers. The youngster was delighted, waving excitedly to his mother, who was too frightened to look up. "I think I'll punish him by making him one of my pages. Have someone notify the parents and secure their permission."

We moved on, leaving Mazaios temporarily at a loss for words. On our left, we were passing fortified barracks, temples, and large apartment houses. On the right, beyond a tall wall, we suddenly glimpsed a huge, phallus-shaped, dun-colored, dilapidated pillar of fired brick, thrusting into the sky. We had to crane our necks to see its top, some three hundred feet above us.

"What's that?" Alexandros asked.

Mazaios, recovering his power of speech, launched into another expostulation. "That's Etemenanki, the famous ziggurat of Babylon. The tallest man-made structure in the world." He was beaming with pride.

Alexandros seemed doubtful. "I don't know. It *seems* taller than the Pyramid of Khufu but maybe that's because we're standing much closer to it. We only saw the great pyramids from a barge as we sailed by on the Nile, so they didn't seem quite as tall. What do you think, Ptolemaios?"

"The great pyramids are indeed taller, sire," I said. "But you're right that this ziggurat gives a more overwhelming impression of height because of our proximity to it."

"So there you have it," Mazaios jumped in triumphantly. "Would you like to take a closer look?"

All of us riding with Alexandros smiled. Asking our leader whether he wanted to take a closer look at a famous sight was like asking a randy sailor whether he would like a free shot at a hetaira. "Of course. Let's go in."

Conquest of Persia

Mazaios led us to a large opening in the wall just ahead. When we reached it, we could see there'd once been an ornamental pair of huge doors separating the Processional Way from a broad promenade that led to the ziggurat. Now, evidently as a result of neglect, the doors had fallen down and only a few broken scraps of wood remained by the side of the road.

We left our horses with the cavalry squadrons which had accompanied us up to that point. Hephaistion instructed the commanders to hold their position on the Processional Way and to maintain their vigilance, notwithstanding the Babylonians' fawning welcome. "Their allegiance seems quite flexible. Let's keep an eye on them."

Negotiating our way through the debris blocking the opening in the wall, we found ourselves on an ancient, stately concourse, now filled with potholes. Our progress proved particularly treacherous because, instead watching our step, kept looking skyward, to a sight that was simultaneously breathtaking, awe-inspiring, and a little dispiriting. Enough remained of the towering monument to give an inkling of its former grandeur. It was constructed of seven cubes (really seven right frusta, because their sides tapered slightly inward), placed on top of each other, each cube smaller than the one below. Atop the highest, smallest cube, way up in the sky, sat a squat temple, looking small at such a remove. And on the side of the frusta facing the promenade was flight after flight of a vertiginous staircase leading all the way to the summit.

Even during the heyday of the ziggurat, it must've been a daunting challenge to climb the staircase all the way up. I counted five hundred steps before the remoteness of the stairs made them too indistinct to count. And there were no handrails to aid in the ascent or arrest a fall or simply fend off the inevitable disequilibrium and lightheadedness.

But the best days of the ziggurat were far in the past. Many of the steps were broken. Entire sections of the staircase had collapsed. Several corners of the cubes had broken off. The surfaces of the cubes looked like the skin of a decomposing corpse: A few smooth patches, still shining in the sun; many more dull, greenish-gray expanses; and then, the predominant expanse of crumbling, pitted, pitiful, dun-colored dirt that had once been fired brick.

The large plaza around the tower, bisected by the promenade, was dotted with dusty piles of bricks, broken building blocks, crumbling beams, and the ordinary, wind-blown detritus of a once-great achievement of human vanity.

Along the boulevard and scattered among the piles of debris were the hovels of the priests, as well as vendors' stalls offering newly-arrived pilgrims food, drink, sexual release, ready-made votive offerings, live poultry suitable for either consumption or sacrifice, counterfeit souvenirs, games of chance, and many other vehicles for separating the pilgrims from their assets.

We saw relatively few people about, however, perhaps because everyone had rushed to the Processional Way to witness our arrival or because the pilgrim business was in general decline.

"I don't think we're going to be climbing up there, Aniketos," Hephaistion said, following his friend's gaze. "It looks rather unsafe."

"What happened?" Alexandros demanded to know.

Mazaios shrugged. "The Etemenanki is built mostly of fired brick. It requires constant maintenance. In fact, it's been rebuilt many times. According to Babylonian legend, Marduk himself built the first ziggurat in this place to mark the center of the world, the axis around which the cosmos revolves."

"Well, that can't be right," I interjected, possessed by some malicious daimon. "We all know the cosmos revolves around the Athenian agora."

Alexandros laughed and the others followed his lead. Mazaios looked baffled.

"Anyway," the once and future satrap continued, "a ziggurat has stood on this spot for millennia. The version you're looking at now was rebuilt by the same Naboukhodonosor responsible for the Ishtar Gate and so many other temples and monuments in Babylon. He reigned for forty-three years and was fortunate to have lived long enough to see the renovation of the Etemenanki completed.

"In his day, all of the fired bricks on the surface of the tower were clad in copper. It must've been something, seeing this huge tower reaching for the sky, emitting vivid flashes of reflected sunlight. The staircase was built of stone and hundreds of people climbed it daily to the Old Temple of Marduk at the summit, bringing food and other offerings to the god. The temple was furnished with an extremely large couch and, according to the priests, each night the god himself would descend, consume all the food and drink left for him, sleep on his couch, and then ascend back to the heavens in the morning. The story must have been true because, when the next wave of pilgrims clambered up the staircase the following morning, the food and offerings were always gone."

"Did anybody ever stay up there overnight, just to see what the god looked like?" Kleitos inquired.

"No, it is forbidden for anyone to stay in the temple after dark. The priests make sure everyone is gone before they themselves climb down for the night."

"So why has the tower fallen into disrepair?" Seleukos asked.

"It's a long story, sire. It starts with the fact that Naboukhodonosor, who was a great ruler, wasn't fortunate in his successors. His son ruled for two years and was murdered by his brother-in-law who in turn ruled for four years before meeting his own untimely death. Six different rulers attempted to hold power during the twenty-two years following Naboukhodonosor's death and not one of them died in bed.

"The dynasty of the Khaldaian kings was finally put out of its misery by our own Kyros the Elder, the real founder of the Achaimenid dynasty. He defeated the Babylonian army and took possession of Babylon for the Persian Empire.

"As it happened, Kyros was a great believer in propitiating all local deities. He spent lavishly on maintaining and repairing the Etemenanki. Some of his successors – without wishing to name any names – have been less faithful and less generous. Now, as we all know, they've paid the price."

"Well, I'm going to see to it that the Etemenanki is rebuilt and made bigger and better than ever,"

Alexandros promised and undoubtedly meant it. "Now, what's next?"

****

The woman looked to be perhaps forty, slightly fat, obviously well-to-do, judging by her attire. She also appeared to be homeless. She lay, sprawled on a soiled cloak, spread out on the bare pavement of the courtyard. Her long, embroidered chiton had ridden up her legs, exposing both thighs. Her body was surrounded by perfume bottles and containers of food and drink, sufficient for that day's consumption, as well as containers of waste presumably excreted during the previous day. Her hair was disheveled, the gaze vacant. The scent of the perfume bottles waged a losing struggle against the other odors hovering above her supine body. I guessed she hadn't bathed in several days.

She'd secured a prime spot, next to the walkway, just beyond the wall that separated the Etemenanki precinct from the courtyard of the "New" Temple of Marduk. (As with most things in Babylon, "new" was a relative term.) She was the first person we saw as we made our way along the walkway connecting the two sacred enclosures. When she saw us pass through the gap in the wall, her gaze focused momentarily on Alexandros, who was leading our group. She stretched an open palm toward him. Taking her for a beggar, he looked over his shoulder to Hephaistion, who promptly handed over a coin. "Here you are," Alexandros said kindly and flipped the coin to her.

The coin never reached the woman's palm. Even as the silver piece was arcing through the air, picking up speed as it went, and while the first glimmering of a smile started to light up her face, Mazaios, moving with amazing speed and agility, sprang forward and snatched the coin out of the air. "You don't want to do that, your imperial highness." He handed the coin back to Alexandros. "Just look around."

Sitting next to the intended object of Alexandros's generosity was another woman, younger, less opulently dressed, but also less fragrant, looking curiously at our group. Beyond her sat another young woman, this one clearly a farmer's daughter, her tunic hiked indecently up to her hips, the deep bronze hue of her skin attesting to a lifetime of outdoor work.

As we took in the scene, we realized there were scores of women scattered throughout the outer courtyard of the temple, ranging in age from barely pubescent teenagers to mature matrons, some modestly covered up and others leaving nothing to the imagination. They all perked up when they grasped the full extent of our group.

"It's not a problem, Mazaios. We have sufficient coins for all of them."

"That's not it, your majesty. By handing a coin to one of them, you would enter into a binding pledge from which it would be sacrilegious to back out. I'm sure you wouldn't want to do that."

"What do you mean?"

"Let's just keep moving. I'll explain as we go along."

We resumed our walk. "These women are here to fulfill a religious obligation," Mazaios explained. "Every Babylonian woman must, once in her lifetime, come to the Temple of Marduk and demonstrate her submission to the god by copulating, within the inner sanctum of the temple, with the first man who pays her for the privilege. There used to be a huge, golden statue of Marduk inside and the act was supposed to be performed within his sight, but Xerxes carted off the effigy when he conquered Babylon, so now it's sufficient for the couples to perform their devotions inside the naos, where the sculpture used to stand.

"The women must accept the first stranger who hands them a coin, regardless of who it is or how much he has paid. And the man, having made the payment, must follow through with the act on pain of divine retribution."

"Must be a lot of pressure to get it up," Kleitos observed in his usual trenchant fashion but this time we were all too shocked to laugh.

"It's no joking matter," Mazaios chastised him. "The women are supposed to stay here until someone pays them. The young and pretty ones show up at dawn and are on their way back to their husbands in time to make breakfast. But some of the older or uglier ones can stay here for days or weeks. There've been instances of husbands paying men to come to the temple and release their wives from their bondage but that sort of venality is frowned upon and may well incur Marduk's wrath."

"Maybe I'll come back at dawn tomorrow and help one of these ladies out," Kleitos offered, oblivious to the tenor of the conversation.

Alexandros turned on him and snapped sharply. "You'll do no such thing. We don't profane other people's religious customs. Now, let's get out of here."

****

Our tour ended at the palace grounds, where one more surprise awaited. As we rode, surrounded by a cordon of worried cavalrymen, through the teeming crowds of worshipful natives, we were heartened by the sight of the huge royal palace at the far end of the plaza. If only we could reach those massive walls protecting the palace, perhaps we could finally escape all this adulation and get some rest. The sun had already disappeared behind Babylon's imposing skyline, daylight was beginning to fail, and we were all exhausted. Although Babylon had thrown open its gates, it felt as though we had fought every step of the way to the palace.

"Can we get through the palace gate?" Hephaistion asked Mazaios.

"Of course, sire. My men are on the other side, awaiting my signal. They're keeping it barred to keep all these well-wishers from pouring in."

"How many men?" Alexandros asked.

"Perhaps a thousand of my knights are in the inner courtyard, plus all the noblemen, courtiers, palace eunuchs, attendants, servants, and slaves. The entire palace staff awaits your arrival."

Alexandros and Hephaistion exchanged a quick look. We didn't have nearly enough cavalrymen to cope with a thousand knights, particularly knights occupying an easily defensible position behind massive walls and a narrow gateway.

Alexandros shook his head. "They wouldn't dare. Not with most of my army already inside the city walls and Mazaios's family in our custody." He urged Boukephalas forward and the rest of us followed in a tight formation behind him.

The gate opened. A dozen men ran out, with their spears extended, and fanned out to keep the crowd at bay. In truth, the ordinary citizens packed into the palace grounds were far too overawed to move an inch. They were content to fall to their knees, bow their heads, and peer surreptitiously at their new rulers, led by the invincible King Alexandros, as we rode by.

The surprise was on the far side of the gate. The inner courtyard was filled with squadron after squadron of Mazaios's knights, fully armored, but on foot. Their mounts were nowhere to be seen. As soon as Alexandros entered, a command rang out and they all fell to their knees as one, touched their foreheads to the ground, and remained motionless. Mazaios looked expectantly at Alexandros, who nodded slightly. Mazaios raised his arm, there was another shouted command, and the knights rose in unison, maintaining their orderly ranks. Then they pivoted smartly, opening a wide corridor in the middle for us to pass through.

"Not bad for a bunch of cavalrymen," Seleukos observed.

"They've had a lot of practice surrendering, I guess," Kleitos put in. "Maybe they should've spent more time learning how to fight."

"Quiet!" Alexandros ordered. "They fought bravely," he added quietly after a moment, "until Dareios fled the field."

Beyond the dismounted phalanxes of Persian knights stood the Babylonian priests in their serried plagues. There were almost as many holy men as there were soldiers, all in spotless white robes, only the length of their beards and the design of their headgear differentiating sect from sect. They bowed their heads respectfully, regardless of the identity of the god whom they served. However, they also all remained defiantly on their feet.

All around the clutch of standing priests lay the entire palace staff, from the highest-ranking noblemen to the lowliest slaves, all prostrate on the ground and motionless. Alexandros was about to let them rise when he noticed the menagerie positioned on either side of the palace portico.

A dozen lions, several leopards, and a number of other exotic animals, all in their respective cages, awaited us. Pacing restlessly next to the cages were two elephants. In between the cages, strutting free as birds, roamed flocks of peacocks and a few ostriches. And then we noticed the wooden caskets, presumably containing untold treasure, sitting on the ground and guarded by a variety of pure-bred dogs and cats, all thankfully collared and leashed.

But Alexandros only had eyes for the elephants. He finally waved distractedly for everyone to rise as he rushed over to the enormous animals. "I've never seen one of these in the flesh," he told Mazaios, "although I've certainly heard of them and I've seen them depicted on coins and carved in stone. Are they liable to charge?"

"Oh no, your majesty. Their mahouts have them under complete control. Plus, just in case, you'll notice there are shackles and chains on their hind legs.

"All this and more is our welcome present from Babylon to you," Mazaios added grandly.

It was completely dark before Alexandros could be persuaded to enter the palace and settle down to the lavish repast getting cold in the kitchens.

****

Less than three weeks after our grand entrance into Babylon, the baggage train, the hostages, and the camp followers arrived from Tyros. Most of the consorts, courtesans, concubines, and close personal friends, who had assumed that their men would be starved for their companionship after months of enforced celibacy, were sorely disappointed. It turned out that, after a couple of short weeks in this cauldron of carnal concupiscence, the lascivious appetites of even the most libidinous of our men were fully sated.

There was no place in the world better suited to beguile, besot, and bewitch a bunch of victorious, virile parvenus than Babylon. They were the new masters of the world, strutting with confidence and laden with booty. Alas, under the veneer of hardened warriors, there lurked the naiveté of Macedonian farm boys. They were easy prey for the professional strumpets of Babylon, of whom the city boasted a generous supply. Nevertheless, the pros couldn't keep up with the demand. Fortunately, their ranks were augmented by bevies of eager amateur volunteers, sent out by husbands looking to make a quick killing (mostly in the figurative sense) or simply wishing to ingratiate themselves with the new ruling class.

Among the most eager procurers were the palace courtiers and Persian aristocrats who unexpectedly found themselves stranded in an occupied capital. They competed with each other in presenting lavish entertainments, complete with food, wine, and the company of their own wives. Since they had many wives and concubines, they could afford to share them with abandon.

Unlike many of the new arrivals from Tyros, Barsine wasn't one of the disappointed paramours. Alexandros attended many of the banquets, resplendent in Dareios's downsized robes, ate and especially drank to excess, but he didn't partake of the pudenda on offer. Somehow, he found the Persians' mores, at least in this respect, offensive. He was therefore eager to visit Barsine as soon as she was settled in the familiar quarters of the Babylonian harem.

"Your son," she said, in lieu of a greeting, when Alexandros entered her chamber. The tiny newborn, tightly swaddled in a soft woolen shawl, was peacefully asleep. "You can hold him, if you'd like."

Alexandros reached out for the proffered bundle but then changed his mind. He had held many things in his hands before but never a baby. "I don't know how to hold him," he confessed.

"Don't worry, my liege. The only trick is to make sure to support his head."

The baby started screaming as soon as it found itself in the crook of Alexandros's arm. He hurriedly handed it back. "He's got a good set of lungs on him," he said, once the baby was safely back in its mother's arms.

"He's going to be a great warrior, my lord. I knew it, even before he popped out of my belly. He eats ravenously, is full of energy, and look at him – he's prettier than Adonis. Takes after you." She gave him a coquettish smile, which he missed, his attention focused on the baby. "If you'll get a little closer, he'll look right into your eyes."

"But he's so tiny. Shouldn't he be bigger by now?"

"He's only three weeks old, my love. He's actually quite big for his age. Trust me, I know. I'm the one who had to give birth to him."

"I forgot to ask. What's his name?"

"He has no name yet, my liege. He's your son; you get to name him."

Alexandros thought for a while. "Let's call him Herakles. He was one of my ancestors, you know."

"Yes, you've told me. It's a wonderful name. We should have a naming ceremony and ask the gods to make sure he grows up as great and powerful as his namesake."

"We'll certainly do that as soon as I can arrange it. Now, let's put him back in his crib. It's been a long time, you know."

It turned out that, while Alexandros may have refrained from indulging his carnal desires at the banquets, all those salacious sights and sounds had stoked his lust well beyond the bursting point. Barsine, who was still healing from her delivery, had her hands full and, when that proved to be insufficient, did what it took to satisfy her man.

******

Conquest of Persia

I had accompanied Alexandros on his trip to visit Barsine in my capacity as one of his bodyguards, remaining on duty outside their chamber. After a while, I decided that, in the interest of discretion, I ought to find a more remote location in which to wait, in order to escape beyond earshot of the sounds emanating from the happy couple. Searching for a suitable guard post, I stumbled onto a large, carpeted room, filled with soft cushions, pillows, and simple toys. It was occupied by Barsine's four other children, their two servant girls, and Barsine's sister. The three young women failed to notice my approach, preoccupied as they were with their eavesdropping and giggling. Finally, Artakama lifted her gaze and saw me in the doorway. She turned beet red. "M-my liege," she stuttered, in imitation of her sister's usual form of address to Alexandros, "what a surprise to see you."

She spoke very loudly, presumably to cover the ambient noise. I was too stunned to respond. It had been more than six months since last I saw her at Pelousion. That brief meeting had caused me to studiously avoid any further encounters, even though the army had traveled in close proximity to the baggage train all the way from Pelousion to Tyros. On the other hand, I thought of her almost daily and, every time I did so, the Prime Directive would raise its ugly head and alarm bells would go off in my brain. I didn't want a repetition of my experience with Lanike.

"You're looking better than ever," she continued, ignoring my failure to answer. Her Greek was fluent and charmingly accented. "Campaigning must agree with you." There was a merry twinkle in her eyes.

"I survived, which is as agreeable as it gets."

A loud, high-pitched, surprisingly musical squeal pierced the wall between the adjoining chambers.

"Would you like to see the grounds?" Artakama asked, before the treble trill had even died down. Not waiting for an answer, she took my hand and led me out.

The gardens of the Babylonian harem weren't suspended from the sky. They were at ground level but spectacular nonetheless. And I'm referring not only to the vegetation. After all, these grounds were supposed to be the women's private preserve, cloistered from male intrusion. Unfortunately, all that pulchritude was lost on me as I had eyes only for my escort.

Artakama was still a couple of months shy of her seventeenth birthday but girls matured faster under the hot Mediterranean sun. Her luscious, shimmering, jet-black hair framed a copper-hued, oval face, much given to fleeting, flirty smiles. Her lips, usually parted, were like plush pillows after a long day's ride, begging to be scrunched, squeezed, and plumped. Of course, if her lips were like pillows, then the rest of her body was like a regal bed, a firm, ripe, curvaceous bed. I worked hard, albeit unsuccessfully, at keeping my gaze above her neck.

We sat on a shaded bench and talked. She wanted to know about my adventures, especially our great victory at Gaugamela. I wanted to know when she had become so beautiful but made self-deprecating jokes about my part in the battle instead. She found reasons to touch my hands, arms, even my face. It was a fairly cool, late autumn afternoon; I was perspiring profusely nevertheless.

"Perhaps I could offer you a drink?" She started to walk back inside.

Having lost all volition, I rose to my feet and followed. She led me to a small, windowless cell, furnished with nothing but a straw pallet. "Have a seat." She pointed to the low bed. "I'll be right back."

She returned in minutes, carrying a pitcher of sweet wine and two silver cups. "Here, hold onto these while I pour." I noticed she'd changed her chiton. This one was thinner, clingier, and seemingly suffused with pheromones.

I carefully placed the two cups on the floor, rose to my feet, and, without a further word, sprinted out of the room. I nearly collided with Alexandros who, having concluded his congress with Barsine, was now anxious to leave and quite put out at my having deserted my post.

"Where have you been? You're supposed to be guarding me, not sampling the merchandise." His reproof was belied by his exceedingly good cheer. "You've got to keep me in one piece, you know, now that I'm a father."

I'd never seen him in a better mood.

****

"I could get used to this, you know." Alexandros was stretched out on the ground, shielding his eyes against the sun, when Hephaistion walked up. "It's amazing what these people were able to create in the middle of a desert. Here, have a seat."

Hephaistion searched for a spot not covered with ferns, flowers, herbs, and grasses but, seeing none, plopped down next to his friend, crushing some gorgeous purple phlox in the process. "It's not exactly a desert, Aniketos. It's more like a huge oasis, watered by two great rivers and crisscrossed by thousands of canals."

"Well, except for the rivers and canals, it'd be a desert." Alexandros laughed. "But I meant this garden, rising above the roofs of a metropolis. A Greek-speaking gardener came by, sent by Mazaios I think, and gave me a tour.

"Did you know you could be stranded here for years and never go hungry? Besides the huge cypress trees and various pines, they've got olives, dates, figs, almonds, walnuts, terebinths, pomegranates, pears, apples, and who knows what else. And lots of streams with pure, clean water. And if you climb a little higher, you'll see sturdy oaks, cedars, rosewood, mahogany, ebony. And flowering, aromatic shrubs and plants of all kinds. Just smell that air."

Hephaistion was amused. "Who knew you were a farmer at heart?"

"Not a farmer." Alexandros feigned hurt feelings. "More like a forester. Anyway, where is everybody? We have business to conduct."

"I think they're afraid to come up here. The Babylonians believe this place is reserved for the emperor and his invited guests, presumably of the female persuasion."

Alexandros stretched his arms and yawned. "Well, now that you mention it, maybe that's not such a bad idea. Why are you here?" He was wearing a silk tunic and linen loincloth, under one of Dareios's luxurious plush robes, which was picking up clover stains every time he moved. He had dispensed with any armor or weapons.

"If that's what you want." Hephaistion started to rise.

"I'm just kidding, for crying out loud. Sit down. But I do wish Kallisthenes would show up already. I have letters to dictate."

"He's cloistered with the priests, day and night, reading those ancient tablets. He says they have astronomical records going back two thousand years."

"Actually, that sounds pretty interesting. Have him prepare a summary for me. In the meantime, would you mind going back down and dispatching an escort to fetch him as soon as possible. I really do need to get some work done. And while you're down there, have them send up some food and wine."

"Yes, your highness." Hephaistion rose to his feet. "Anything else you want me to do?"

"Yes, I want you to come back up here. I'm not going to eat by myself." As Hephaistion was leaving, Alexandros called after him. "Do you really think we can't have a staff meeting up here?"

Hephaistion returned in minutes, bearing a basket of food, a pitcher of diluted wine, and two cups. "I sent a squad to fetch Kallisthenes. He should be here shortly. And yes, I do think that you can't have staff meetings up here. That's what the palace audience hall is for."

"I guess you're right. Imposing a certain formality on the proceedings is probably a good idea. It's kind of fun watching while they all fall on their faces."

"I thought you wanted a meeting with your command staff."

"I do. But I also need to deal with the local administrators. And we do have to begin to incorporate some Persians into my command staff, people like my new satrap Mazaios. So, if I'm going to have a meeting in the audience hall, all these folks might as well be present."

"That's fine but be a little careful. There's been some grumbling about too much oriental ritual at the palace audiences."

Alexandros flared up. "Who's grumbling? I won't tolerate dissension in the ranks."

"Calm down, Aniketos. There's no dissension. These are men who've been fighting for you for years, men who worship you and would willingly march to Haides and back for you. They're not dissenting; they're just grumbling, as soldiers are wont to do."

"What the hell are they grumbling about?"

"Part of the problem, I think, is that they're getting used to living in Babylon. They're becoming soft and losing their discipline. They're spending their bonuses on prostitutes and getting into fights with each other. The longer we stay here, the more they succumb to the allure of this decadent city."

"I thought spending a little time in Babylon was a reward for their victories."

"It is. Of course, it is. And they're enjoying themselves hugely. But at the same time, they're peeved at seeing their bonuses disappearing into the treasure chests of pimps. Deep down, these are good, upright, old-fashioned farm boys. They realize they've won spectacular and unexpected victories and garnered unimaginable riches. Now, they want to go home to their wives and their farms, while they're still young enough and healthy enough to enjoy the fruits of their military success."

"What do you mean 'unexpected victories'? There's nothing unexpected about them. I knew we were going to win every time."

"I misspoke, Aniketos. Naturally, the victories were not unexpected; they were inevitable. Why else does everybody call you Aniketos? You can't be invincible if there's any possibility of defeat."

"You've got that right."

"I apologize. I misspoke. All I wanted to say is that some of the old veterans want to go home. Please forgive me."

"Come here, you fool." Alexandros opened his arms. "You're my closest friend. You never have to ask for my forgiveness, no matter what." He leaned over and embraced the embarrassed Hephaistion, crushing dozens of pink pussytoes in the process.

****

Try as I might, I couldn't get Artakama out of my mind. It had been hours since I'd fled her seductive cell but my heart was still racing. My loins, despite several attempts at self-relief, remained acutely exigent. The physical discomfort, though, was minor compared to my mental torment.

I'd fallen in love twice before in my life and neither time did it end well. Arguably, the Prime Directive was to blame in both instances. I'd left my first love behind in my former life, before my ill-fated trip to this era, without so much as a goodbye. The mission was classified, of course, and I expected to be back in Paloma's arms in a few days, none the worse for wear. Still, I should've left some word behind. A spasm of pain and regret still seized me every time I thought of my unintended, but cruel, breach of faith. And it was too late now.

Although I knew exactly where and when my end of the escape hatch would appear (in Egypt, ten years hence), I had only a hazy idea where the distal terminus was supposed to disgorge me. All I could remember was that it would be more than four years, not some hours or days, from the date of my original departure. Even if I could find Paloma again, after successfully negotiating my way back through the escape hatch, what would be the point? Having neither seen nor heard from me for eons, she would've undoubtedly moved on. She'd be older, wiser, probably married, and undoubtedly pissed off. Worse yet, I would turn up, out of the blue, after missing for some four years, a grizzled old man, twenty-three years older than the last time she saw me. Where once we had been contemporaries, I would suddenly sashay in more than twice her age. Even the legendary Penelope would have kicked Odysseus out under those circumstances. And the worst part was that the failure of the departure portal to materialize, and therefore my failure to return as scheduled, was attributable to my unwitting violation of the Prime Directive, as I now realized.

My second romance started shortly after I'd found myself marooned in this ancient time and place. On that occasion, I couldn't even blame the eventual breakdown of my relationship with Lanike on some time travel glitch. If anything, the fact I couldn't go back home anytime soon should've helped matters along. However, every time Lanike and I moved closer to each other, there would be the Prime Directive lurking between us, forcing me to pull back. Eventually, with great regret and hating myself for being unable even to provide an explanation, I complied with the dictates of the time travelers' paramount commandment and ran away from her. I told myself my departure had freed her to pursue a more suitable match but the passage of time had yet to heal the aching void left by her absence or the guilt I felt over the way I'd broken off our affair.

And now, despite my best intentions, I was well on my way to another hopeless relationship with another lovely, bewitching, irresistible woman who deserved better. More importantly, I could see that the situation would never change, no matter how long I stayed in this time and how many other desirable women I met, because the strictures against doing anything that might disrupt the inexorable flow of time would always get in the way. Even subtle changes in the time traveler's destination era could have far-reaching consequences back in the time of his origin. And creating and leaving behind a new human life, however inadvertently, would certainly not be a subtle change. Alas, the only sure way of avoiding such a drastic violation of the Prime Directive was total abstinence. By the same token, committed celibacy wasn't conducive to lasting relationships with members of the opposite sex.

It was thoughts such as these that kept me awake. Finally, I decided to go see Aristandros. He'd said something the last time we had spoken that kept nagging at me. I'd asked him whether he ever worried his oracular pronouncements might alter the course of events whose outcome he was asked to divine, thus turning his predictions into self-fulfilling prophesies. He denied any such possibility and added, somewhat beside the point, that: "Unlike some people, I have scrupulously refrained from interfering in any way."

At the time, I'd considered his comment a random observation that, simply by accident, happened to hit a nerve with me. I had in fact interfered, albeit inadvertently. But neither Aristandros or anyone else, for that matter, could've possibly known that. As I lay sleepless in my bed, a new thought struck me. *What if his comment wasn't an accident? Is it possible he really does have some special powers that enable him to read minds and see the future?*

I rejected the thought immediately. Nobody had any such supernatural powers. Yet, I decided to go see him. Perhaps he might say something else that might help me navigate around the constraints of the Prime Directive without causing any permanent damage. After being hamstrung for the past thirteen years, I was ready to try anything, even consulting a soothsayer whose hobby was plotting my demise.

The house in which Aristandros was lodged, really a palace, was owned by one of Mazaios's sons. Penetrating behind its walls required a considerable amount of suasion. The guards didn't recognize me, didn't speak Greek, and had strict orders not to admit any uninvited visitors. I, on the other hand, was determined not to create a scene. I tried using the few words of

Aramaic I had picked up but to no avail. The corrupt version of Akkadian spoken by the common folk was completely out of my reach. Finally, I resorted to the lingua franca of the Persian empire – money. I offered the guards a few local coins, which they flatly refused, brandishing their swords to dispel my insulting presumption that they might be corruptible. I escalated to silver sigloi, which met a less hostile reception but still failed to do the trick. Finally, I pressed a newly minted gold daric into the palm of each guard. They nodded and let me through the gate, smiling and clapping me on the shoulder, undoubtedly to indicate they were accepting the coins not as a bribe but as proof of my importance.

One of the guards escorted me through a deserted reception room and into a paved, shaded, fountained courtyard. Under a portico to our left, an elderly bald man was evidently conducting a class for a group of small children. The guard led me to him and said a few words in a language I didn't understand.

The elderly man turned from his charges and addressed me in four languages in quick succession. I chose to reply in Greek. When I told him I was there to visit Aristandros, he hesitated for a moment.

"Aristandros will want to receive me," I assured the old man. "In fact, I'm surprised he didn't foresee my visit and greet me upon my arrival."

"I'm afraid my master's honored guest is not receiving any visitors these days. He's not well."

"But I must see him. I'm sure my visit will cheer him up."

Eventually, I was allowed into Aristandros's chamber. It was dark, dank, and fetid. My erstwhile mortal enemy lay on a straw pallet, motionless. He failed to respond when I called out his name. I looked in vain for a window or some artificial source of light. When I knelt next to him and shook his shoulder, he stirred ever so slightly but failed to regain consciousness.

"Help!" I hollered. It was the one word I knew in many languages. Eventually, a burly eunuch appeared. I was gratified to see a brightly burning lamp in his hand.

"He's been asleep for days now," he informed me apologetically. "We try to feed him, wash him, and remove his waste but we can't get him to wake up."

In the flickering light of the lamp, I could see that Aristandros's face was whiter than the dirty, tattered sheet that covered him. Much of his flesh had melted away, leaving behind only skin, sinew, bones, and a rigid, pained grimace.

"Thank you." I dismissed the eunuch with a wave. He turned but, before he could leave, I snatched the lamp from his hand. He shrugged and walked out.

When he was gone, I put the question I'd come to ask to Aristandros. "How are you able to do as you please without interfering with the natural course of events?"

Aristandros kept his counsel. The oppressive silence of his cubicle was disrupted only by the labored, rasping sound of his breathing.

Notwithstanding my lack of medical expertise, I decide to remove his cover to see whether I could determine what was wrong. He wore nothing but a soiled diaper underneath. Palpating his neck, I detected a slow, regular pulse, as strong and steady as a tolling bell. His skin felt cold and clammy. I didn't see any wounds, sores, boils, or other obvious indicia of illness or injury. Moving down to his emaciated abdomen, I failed to detect any lumps, swelling, or inelasticity. As I ran my fingers toward the top of his diaper, I felt a thin, almost invisible scar in the area between his navel and right hip. *Either a hernia or an appendectomy*, I thought.

And then I jumped away from him, as though hit by a surge of electromagnetic energy. *It's a surgical scar,* I kept repeating to myself. *A straight, neat, thin, nearly invisible surgical scar. People don't have such scars in this era.*

I ran out of the chamber, almost bowling over the eunuch standing in the hallway. I handed the lamp back. "Take care of him!"

****

I couldn't shake the implications of the scar from my mind. Several possible explanations occurred to me, each more farfetched than the last. There might've been some unknown virtuoso surgeon somewhere in this ancient world who'd left the telltale incision on Aristandros's abdomen. Reluctantly, I was forced to abandon that hypothesis. Not only had I never heard of such a surgeon, either during my studies about this era prior to my trip or during the thirteen years I'd spent actually living in this time but the infrastructure needed to accomplish the task was also missing. The requisite scalpels, retractors, forceps, suction tubes, needles, sutures, antibiotics, and anesthesia didn't exist.

I considered the possibility that the scar I'd felt and examined was not a scar at all but some kind of a fluke disfigurement or birthmark. Random chance and genetic mutation can produce all sorts of fantastic chimeras but, alas, a straight, neat, thin, nearly invisible surgical scar is far less likely to occur by random chance than a frog with two heads.

After considering, and discarding, all the extremely improbable scenarios, I was left with only one explanation, which was not only possible but actually quite likely. It was simply difficult to accept psychologically. *Aristandros was a fellow time traveler and had acquired his scar prior to his departure from his native era.*

Once I had forced myself to consider this theory, not only did it explain the existence of the scar, it explained a great many other things about Aristandros. It certainly accounted for his ability to predict future events, since for him those events were history. It could also explain his antipathy toward me. If he'd somehow divined that I was a time traveler long before the same thought had crossed my mind about him, he might well have concluded that two time travelers in one place and time were one too many. With two time travelers, the possibility of interference multiplied geometrically. Plus, on a more mundane level, I was the one person in this world who might well unmask him. Sooner or later, even someone as obtuse and oblivious as me was bound to stumble on the obvious thought that, if one person could travel back in time, so could others.

Strangely, I was pleased with my discovery. Not only did everything about Aristandros suddenly make sense but I realized at the same time that he too had somehow become stranded in this era, just as I had. Notwithstanding his protestations to the contrary, he must have violated the Prime Directive as well. For some reason, the thought made me smile.

But then another thought wiped the smirk off my face. *What if it was my violation that stranded not only me but him as well?* Before I could start feeling too guilty about what I may have done to him, however, I decided that my violation of the Prime Directive was unlikely to be the cause of Aristandros's marooning. He had arrived years before I did. His time hop couldn't possibly have been intended to last for years. *Nah, he'd managed to get himself stranded all by himself.*

I was drifting happily off to sleep, when another thought jarred me wide awake: *How come he, unlike me, hadn't lost his predictive ability when I changed the course of events?*

****

The Audience Hall was packed but there was no mixing between the two groups. The walls were lined by Macedonian bodyguards, armed to the teeth. Spread amidst the massive columns on the right side of the spacious hall were the Macedonian officers, in armor and carrying swords and daggers. On the left side, caught between the bodyguards and the officers, were the Persian and Babylonian nobility, courtiers, and high-ranking administrators. They were all dressed to the nines, in luxurious, colorful costumes of linen, felt, leather, wool, and the occasional scrap of silk. They were all unarmed, having been carefully searched before being admitted into the hall. The noise of conversations, laughter, and occasional verbal combat echoed from the marble walls but there was no fraternization. I didn't observe a single interaction between a Macedonian soldier and one of the gaudily attired dandies.

The din subsided abruptly when Alexandros appeared at the rear door of the Audience Hall. The

Conquest of Persia

Persians and Babylonians fell to their knees and touched their foreheads to the granite paving stones. The lower ranking officials flattened themselves on the floor, arms outstretched to the side, palms down. The Macedonian soldiers mostly stopped talking and gaped.

It wasn't the locals' proskynesis that amazed us; we'd seen them abase themselves many times before. The truly astonishing sight was Alexandros's getup. He wore one of Dareios's shimmering robes, heavily larded with gold and precious stones. Someone had attempted to cut down the lavish garment to fit Alexandros's smaller frame but the job had been botched, resulting in jagged edges and lopsided folds. On his head, instead of the customary simple diadem, he sported a tall, gold-bedecked, felt hat.

As Alexandros struggled to mount the throne, which was much too big for him, a hem of his robe caught on a step, causing him to lose his balance and crash-land into his seat. The natives gasped, while the Macedonians broke into hearty laughter. By the time he'd managed to position his buttocks in the middle of the seat, with his feet dangling in thin air, and his hat tumbling slowly, step by step, to the bottom of the small ziggurat that formed the platform for his throne, all the attendees had regained their former composure – stern, stone-faced, and trying not to titter. One of the bodyguards snatched up the rolling hat and attempted to hand it up to Alexandros but the would-be emperor waved him aside.

"Mazaios," he said, "you may start the coronation ceremony."

The satrap of Babylonia and Mesopotamia, still on his knees, placed his palms on the pavement, bowed again deeply, and beckoned to the chief magos of Ahura Mazda. He had been specifically imported to Babylon for this occasion. Neither the local Babylonian clergy nor some run-of-the-mill Persian magos would do. Only Ahura Mazda's chief priest was authorized to officiate at an emperor's investiture.

The wizened old man and his fellow magoi were the only non-Macedonians in the room to have remained standing while Alexandros had made his entrance. At Mazaios's signal, the chief magos stepped forward to where we could all see him. He was enfolded from head to toe in a shimmering white sheet, a portion of which had been fashioned into a cowl covering his head. His sheet was cinched at the waist by a hempen rope and bronze brooches deployed strategically at the throat and shoulders kept the garment in shape. His face was concealed in the shadow of his hood, with only the burning coals of his deep-set eyes and the trembling points of his forked beard clearly visible.

The shaman raised his palms toward the ceiling, causing his robe to fall away from his arms, revealing withered muscles and puckered skin. He started chanting a keening prayer to his god. After hitting a particularly long and shrill note, he stopped abruptly and clapped his hands above his head. When his palms came apart, there was a large golden medallion in his right hand. How it got there was anybody's guess. We were all too stunned by this feat of prestidigitation to utter a sound.

The magos bowed curtly to Alexandros and threw the medallion on the pavement in front of him, where it promptly burst into flames. I could see in Alexandros's eyes that he was dazzled by the show. He clearly believed the old man had a direct channel to his god. The priest made an embracing motion with his arms, as though ingathering the spirit of Ahura Mazda as it arose from the flaming coin. His fellow magoi interpreted the gesture as an invitation to join the sacred circle and crowded around the guttering flame, dousing it with some powder, which caused the flame to flare up once again.

"This guy's quite a magician," I whispered to Kleitos but my friend was as astonished by what he was seeing as everyone else in the hall. He simply ignored my comment.

Mazaios, in the meantime, still on his knees, was expectantly looking toward Alexandros for permission to rise. When the signal was slow in coming, he started nodding meaningfully toward the great, elaborate, heavy scepter lying on the pavement next to his left knee. Unfortunately for Mazaios, the chief magos had resumed his chanting. I fully expected to see him pull a dove from under his robe at any moment and evidently so did Alexandros because his eyes remained fixed on the old man.

Alas, there were no further acts of legerdemain, only endless chanting, singing, and sprinkling of flammable incense on the sacred fire. Eventually, the shaman completed this performance and Mazaios was permitted to rise and present the imperial scepter to Alexandros, which only provoked renewed gales of incomprehensible incantations.

Eventually, even Alexandros grew tired of the protracted proceeding and asked for the imperial crown to be placed on his head. His request was met by an embarrassed silence.

"It's the imperial tiara, your celestial highness," Mazaios finally said.

"Alright, so give me the imperial tiara, then."

"We can't, your most merciful magnificence." Mazaios's voice was barely audible. "The imperial tiara has disappeared. Presumably Dareios took it with him when we marched to Gaugamela. But it makes no difference, I assure you, your mystical majesty. You are the new Persian emperor as far as everyone in this hall is concerned."

Alexandros motioned to Seleukos to approach the throne. "Is he right?"

Seleukos shrugged. "Traditionally, there are three requirements for ascension to the throne: The would-be successor must possess the imperial tiara; he must hold the imperial scepter; and the previous incumbent must be dead. But as long as the people and the troops accept you as the new emperor, you can always commission a new tiara and declare that Dareios is as good as dead."

Alexandros was unpersuaded. "Alright, everybody out," he finally bellowed. "We'll resume when the tiara turns up."

****

The tiara didn't turn up and Alexandros left Babylon in pursuit of the elusive emperorship of Persia shortly after the abortive coronation ceremony. Before leaving, he saw to the usual administrative provisions. This time, though, he took a more expansive view of the territory to be administered. He appointed satraps not only for Babylonia but also for a number of other satrapies, some of which were at the moment well outside his ability to control.

Mazaios, as promised, was confirmed as satrap of Babylonia and Mesopotamia. His authority, however, proved to be severely circumscribed. First, Babylon itself was to be controlled by a permanent garrison of a thousand soldiers, composed of Macedonian veterans and Greek mercenaries, commanded by a Macedonian general. Second, while Mazaios would continue to be the highest civilian authority in the two satrapies, all his military and taxing powers were reassigned to loyal Macedonians.

Alexandros made similar arrangements for all the satrapies not previously placed under Alexandros-appointed administrators and commanders between Egypt and Phrygia and from the Mediterranean to the Caspian. Some of these assignments were aspirational. For example, showing his sense of humor, he assigned the satrapy of Lesser Armenia to the old traitor Mithrines as payment for services rendered.[19] Unfortunately, no Macedonian (or Greek for that matter) had ever set foot in Lesser Armenia.

When Mithrines appeared somewhat skeptical about his new position, Alexandros sought to reassured him. "It's part of the Persian Empire, isn't it? And I'm the emperor of Persia, right? So, what's to stop me from naming you satrap of Lesser Armenia?"

"Nothing, your celestial highness." But it would be some time before Mithrines assumed his new post.

---

[19] Mithrines had been the Persian garrison commander of Sardeis when our army approached that city. He had not only turned over the city and its treasures to us but continued to tag along and assist in our campaigns ever since.

Conquest of Persia

Having seen to his administrative dispositions, Alexandros ordered the army, except for the garrison he was leaving behind, to prepare to move out on two days' notice. The baggage train, including all the treasures seized in Babylon, as well as the priests, soothsayers, eunuchs, women, children, and assorted hangers-on would follow a few days later. Unfortunately, and much to Alexandros's regret, his newly acquired menagerie of elephants, lions, leopards, and scores of other exotic animals would have to be left behind.

Our next objective: Sousa, the second of the four great capitals of the Persian Empire.

Chapter 10 – On the March Again

It proved unexpectedly difficult to persuade the Macedonian veterans to leave the fleshpots of Babylon behind and resume the struggle. The soldiers were perfectly content with the loot they'd amassed and believed, with some justification, that they'd achieved all the original goals of the pan-Hellenic expedition and then some. If the time had come to leave Babylon behind, the place they wanted to go was home.

Alexandros, on the other hand, still had unfinished business to attend to. After being acclaimed as the pharaoh of Egypt and a demigod, he'd become obsessed with achieving universal recognition as emperor of Persia and keeper of Ahura Mazda's flame on Earth. He wasn't going to let some Persian clerics deny him with their incantations the position he'd won on the battlefield against the massed forces of the Persian Empire.

In the end, Alexandros's charisma and new-found wealth carried the day. Relying on his dwindling yet still unparalleled rapport with his soldiers, he spent days chatting, haranguing, and imploring them to complete the mission. And he did his best to bribe them. Not only were the troops paid in full for their services up to that point and not only did they get to keep all the spoils previously captured by them but Alexandros also ordered Harpalos, his chief treasurer, to pay, on the spot, a bonus equal to their respective annual salaries to each commander, cavalryman, infantryman, mercenary, auxiliary, and supernumerary. By the time he was done, Alexandros had distributed most of the coin seized from Dareios's Babylonian treasury. Eventually, the battle-hardened veterans of the pan-Hellenic army agreed to resume the campaign.

As we marched out of Babylon, in mid-October 255 Z.E., the soldiers sang of victory, homeland, and pretty women. Alexandros dreamt of the royal tiara, a dead Dareios, and complaisant magoi. And I, riding at the head of my squadron, hoped for answers I'd failed to obtain from the comatose Aristandros.

******

In Pella, Antipatros slammed his fist on the rough-hewn tabletop, making the scattered scrolls jump. "Is this what he needed our best soldiers for?"

Kassandros shrugged. "I've been telling you to ignore his requests for a long time."

Behind the closed and barred doors of the armory of the royal palace, Antipatros continued to rage. "If I'd had some reserves to spare, Zopyrion and his 30,000 men wouldn't have been lost!"

For once, Kassandros was the calming influence. "I know, father. I know."

"Thirty thousand fine young Macedonian soldiers – lost."

"You could say the same about Korrhagos and his 10,000 men."

"Yes, I could. In fact, I was about to. That's 40,000 warriors lost unnecessarily. Worse than that, we came within a hairsbreadth of losing our entire kingdom. And why? Because Alexandros keeps demanding more and more troops."

"He's been winning, though."

"What good does that do us? And what's he doing with our soldiers now? He's feasting, guzzling uncut wine, and screwing anything that moves in that whore city of Babylon, turning our men into effete degenerates. He'll never come home. He's happy being an Asian despot."

"We don't know that, father. It takes months for the messages from our embedded friends to get to us. For all we know, he's on his way back right now."

"In that case, what did he need that last batch of reinforcements for? While we're besieged on every side."

Kassandros held up a newly-arrived letter from Alexandros. "Are we going to show this to his mother? It is addressed to her."

"No, we'll summarize it for her. No point swelling her head even further. She's hard enough to control as it is."

"I've got an idea, dad. Why don't we tell her he's debauching and drinking himself to death in Babylon? Maybe she can think of some way to get him to come back even if we can't."

Antipatros laughed. "Why not? It does have the additional advantage of being true."

"On the other hand, do we really want him to come back? What's wrong with simply remaining in charge here and refusing to send any more reinforcements?"

The regent of Macedonia stopped laughing. "As long as he's king, he'll call the tune, here as well as there. Whether we like it or not. And even if he never comes back, his troops are coming back. So stop talking nonsense."

"It's not nonsense, dad. Just think about it."

"It is nonsense and I don't want to hear you say it again. Remember, even the walls have ears. Now, let's go see his mother."

****

Our column soon stretched for many miles along the royal road from Babylon to Sousa. At our normal speed, it should've taken us about three weeks to cover the 375 miles between the two capitals. But we weren't making anywhere near our normal speed. The army had grown large, fat, and complacent. And then there were the frequent stops and interruptions.

We were barely two days out when one of the veterans assigned to the rearguard came galloping up, yelling as he approached. A large army was catching up fast. His report seemed puzzling at first since the only force in our rear should've been the garrison we'd left behind in Babylon.

Taking no chances, Alexandros ordered us into defensive formation and set off at breakneck speed to investigate. Those of us assigned to guard him were left in the dust, as usual, struggling desperately to catch up.

Conquest of Persia

By the time Alexandros, trailed by his personal bodyguard, reached our tail end, the advance elements of the approaching force were already there. They'd alighted from their mounts and were engaged in amicable conversation with our rearguard veterans.

We recognized the massive figure of Amyntas son of Andromenes exchanging backslaps with everyone within reach of his long arms. Alexandros vaulted off Boukephalas and submitted to one of Amyntas's bearhugs. "Man oh man, you sure took your time."

Amyntas released the king, a hurt expression on his face. "We came as fast as we could, sire. When we heard upon arrival in Babylon that we'd barely missed you, we continued our pursuit without stopping."

"The whores of Babylon must've been disappointed."

"Not as much as the men, sire, I assure you."

"Well, serves you right. While you were gallivanting in Greece, we conquered Egypt and half the Persian Empire.[20] But I'm glad to see you all anyway. Now, give me a headcount of what you've brought us."

---

[20] Alexandros had dispatched Amyntas to recruit reinforcements immediately after the sack of Tyros, some sixteen months earlier, to make up for the thousands of soldiers lost during the siege.

It took Amyntas a while to list all the new contingents: Seven squadrons of cavalry, 1,500 horsemen in all, mostly from Thessaly; 13,500 infantry, 4,000 of them good old Macedonian farm boys looking for their share of the fabled riches that their neighbors were said to have amassed, the rest mercenaries from throughout Greece; and finally, a battalion of light infantry sent by our barbarian allies, mostly Agrianians.

In addition, and somewhat surprisingly, fifty new royal pages had come along. These were the sons of Macedonian noble houses, sent by their fathers in order to ingratiate their families with the king. Alexandros winked at me when he heard about their arrival. "They'll make fine hostages," he whispered.

Lastly, Amyntas brought a wagonful of letters. He personally retrieved and handed over the ones intended for Alexandros. Interestingly, the king read his mother's missives (forged though they might have been) before getting to the dispatches sent by his regent. Antipatros's reports were uniformly dour, complaining of threats against the Macedonian homeland from every direction. Having read them carefully, Alexandros merely shrugged. "The old man is prone to exaggeration," he assured us. "I'm sure he's cleaned up all those messes by now. After all, it took these guys months to get here so anything they tell us is way out of date."

Conquest of Persia

Needless to say, our march to Sousa came to a halt. The mail had to be distributed and then painstakingly read to the soldiers, almost all of whom were illiterate. Friends, neighbors, and acquaintances from the old country had to be welcomed and debriefed. Clearly, a service of thanksgiving was mandatory, followed by a sumptuous feast.

It took a day and a half of foraging by our troops to round up the necessary provisions. Finally, the time had arrived for the start of the celebrations. But first, there had to be an invocation. This created a small problem. Normally, Aristandros the Seer was charged with supervising all religious performances. Alas, Aristandros had been in no shape to accompany us when we marched out of Babylon. Two contenders immediately stepped forward to fill his ceremonial robes.

On the one hand, from among the swarm of Khaldaian shamans who had accompanied us since we left Babylon, Niqarqusu, the high priest of Marduk, rushed in to slaughter the sacrificial victims. On the other hand, a multitude of Persian magoi, led by Ardumanish, Ahura Mazda's principal magician, surrounded the makeshift altar and refused to budge. Next thing we knew, the shamans were brandishing ceremonial mallets and very real butcher knives, threatening to cut the throats of the magoi. The Persian divines, in the meantime, were busy casting spells against their rivals and setting their peaked miters on fire. The garlanded bulls munched contentedly on whatever grass they could find underfoot.

Our soldiers, who were used to boxing, wrestling, and pankration contests, readily embraced this new sport. They formed a large circle around the contending teams and cheered them on. Small sums of money changed hands as bets were proposed and accepted. When a mallet blow landed smartly on the felt hat of a magos, stunning the man momentarily, a loud ovation rose from among the supporters of the Khaldaian contingent. The swipe of a blazing torch, igniting the back of a shaman's robe and singeing his hairy buttocks, brought loud plaudits and much laughter.

Alexandros was right there, among his men, enjoying the unexpected variation on the usual religious rituals. After a while, Hephaistion elbowed his way through to him and tried to whisper in his ear. Just then, the largest of the Khaldaians lifted the smallest Persian above his head and tossed him amidst the bulls. The placid animals made room for the new arrival, welcoming him to their own feast. Alexandros looked quizzically at his friend, unable to hear above the shouts of the crowd.

Hephaistion gave up on trying to be discrete and yelled as loudly as he could. "You have to put an end to this, Aniketos, before they kill each other." By chance, there was a sudden lull in the roar, causing Hephaistion's advice to rise above the crowd like a battle cry.

"No," one of the soldiers yelled back, "let them sort it out." His sentiment met with universal approval.

Alexandros shrugged. "What's the name of our new soothsayer? Go and find him. See which side is favored by the signs."

Hephaistion cast an incredulous glance at his commander but said nothing. Instead, he set off in search of Aristandros's understudy. Seleukos, taking pity on our leader, slid into the space vacated by Hephaistion. "You'll need the magoi, sire, to ratify your donning of the Persian tiara. You'd better put them in charge of this ceremony."

The advice made sense and, besides, the contestants were tiring. Several shamans were bouncing up and down on their haunches, trying to put the flames out, while a couple of magoi crawled about on their hands and knees looking for lost teeth. When Alexandros raised his hand, the contestants were more than ready to stop. Order was quickly restored and the festivities proceeded with a minimum of discord. Everybody was anxious to get on to the food and wine.

After the men slept off the effects of the feast, we received word the baggage train and camp followers had managed to catch up to us during our unexpected delay. Naturally, the men couldn't resist a brief visit with their favorite ladies. Even Alexandros spent some time with Barsine and their baby boy. He was, once again, in a remarkably good mood when he rejoined us.

Unfortunately, I didn't get a chance to see either Barsine or Artakama, having been put in charge of maintaining security while our soldiers and commanders frolicked. We lost five days before resuming our march to Sousa.

******

In a breach of the usual protocol, Antipatros and Kassandros mounted the stairs to the gynaikonitis unannounced. Olympias and Kleopatra, not having had any visitors in several weeks, didn't raise a fuss.

The queen mother was her usual charming self when she saw the two men at their door. "Must be something mighty important to drag your carcasses all the way up those rickety steps."

"A missive, madam, from your son." Antipatros handed over the scroll, broken seal, wine stains, erasures, and all.

Olympias frowned. "How long have you had this?"

"Just got here today, your royal highness. We ran over here as soon as it arrived." Kassandros couldn't help himself. Or perhaps his studied insolence was a calculated ploy.

Olympias rose to the bait, as always. "It's so old the papyrus is all frayed, you smart ass. The seal's broken; it's covered with dirt; somebody's obviously tampered with it."

"It's had a long journey, queen mother." Antipatros tried to smooth her ruffled feathers. "Just read it. It brings good news."

For once, Olympias did as she was told. Her exclamations grew louder and more triumphant as she read. "I've told you." Her tone was emphatic. "I've always told you."

"You did, madam. That you did."

"He's the ruler of the world now, isn't he?"

"Not quite, your highness. The world is a big place. Right now, he's the ruler of Babylon. And very little else."

"Nonsense. He marches from victory to victory." She shrugged. "He's invincible, that's all. My only concern is that the world isn't big enough." She handed the letter to her daughter. "Put this with the others and bring us some wine. We have to celebrate."

"There were other letters we received along with this one, queen mother. You can read them if you'd like." Antipatros held out several more tightly wound rolls.

Olympias read them quickly, without exclamations and without any change in her expression. When she finished reading, she rounded on the two men with a fury. "You expect me to believe this? After all the lies you've told me and all the forgeries you've sent me? Don't act so surprised! I know exactly what you two 've been up to."

"This is no forgery, queen mother," Antipatros said quietly. "And it's not the half of it, either. He's whoring and drinking himself to death in Babylon while demanding more and more troops from us. He's stripped his homeland of its defense while all of Greece is preparing to rise up against us. He's killing our troops, and himself, in far off Persia, while leaving us to the mercy of our enemies here at home."

"Stop that right now!" Olympias screamed. "Or I'll have you, and your son, executed here on the spot."

Kassandros sneered. "You can't have a chicken executed unless we say so, you old crone. Haven't you noticed you're a prisoner? If we don't feed you, you'll starve to death."

"How dare you? Wait 'til my son hears about this."

Kassandros scoffed.

"And he will hear, trust me."

Antipatros stepped between them before they could come to blows. "Yes, queen mother, you're right. He will hear from you. And perhaps he'll listen. That's why we're here. That why I showed all those other letters to you. We need your help. Please, help us save our kingdom, save our people, and save your son. Before it's too late."

"What are you talking about? He's marching from victory to triumph to endless conquest. He's invincible. He's practically ruler of the world already."

"The only correct word in what you just said is 'endless,' your royal highness. You have to help us talk some sense into him. Please write him a letter, congratulate him on his victories, and ask him to come home. We've tried and failed. You're our last hope. If he continues this march from victory to triumph to debauchery, none of us will live through it. None of our men over there in Persia and none of us back here in Macedonia."

Olympias was silent for a moment. "You're wrong. My son is invincible and headed for immortality. I don't believe a word of what you say. And besides, what do you need me for? You can go ahead and forge any letter you want."

Kassandros barked a short, malicious laugh. "Yeah, we just might have to do that."

"Keep quiet, son. Like it or not, the only person in this world who can change our king's mind is standing in front of you. Now, queen mother, won't you please write that letter?"

He turned back to Olympias but she was already walking away. "Kleopatra, please tell those two dimwits to get out of our home. And bar the door behind them."

****

This time, we managed three uninterrupted, albeit leisurely, days of marching before another messenger arrived. We saw him galloping toward us from a fair distance away; evidently, he was alone. Nevertheless, and despite the fact that at least two hours of daylight remained, Alexandros ordered a halt for the day and told the men to make camp while we awaited the messenger's arrival.

He sprang off Boukephalas and stretched his limbs. "Looks like a Persian messenger to me. What do you think he's up to?"

Hephaistion jumped in immediately with the first guess. "He's bringing a letter of surrender from Dareios." He managed to deliver his prediction with a straight face.

When several of the other commanders scoffed, he fished out a handful of coins and threw them in the dirt. "Five gold darics says it's a letter of surrender."

Perdikkas rose to the bait, as usual. "You're on!" He threw his coins on the pile.

Hephaistion looked around. "Anybody else?"

Another commander stepped up. "I'll put in another five, if you're willing."

"The more, the merrier." Hephaistion pulled out five more gold coins.

Pretty soon Hephaistion's purse was empty while commanders continued to walk up, eager to get a piece of the action. The king's favorite sycophant put an arm around my shoulder. "Ptolemaios, lend me your purse."

With a shrug, I handed it over. "If you win, I expect to participate in the winnings."

"Of course."

"And if you lose, I expect my loan to be repaid in full."

Hephaistion laughed. "Always said you were the smartest guy here. Don't worry about the loan. I'm sure you've got more money stashed away than the rest of us put together."

By the time we had managed to retrieve all the coins from among all the cracks and crevices in the road and place them into an empty pot, the messenger was upon us. Hephaistion handed the pot to Alexandros. "Here, Aniketos. You'd better hold this. As far as I can tell, you're the only one here who didn't make a bet."

"It wouldn't be fair now, would it? I already know the answer."

"You do? How?"

"It's my business to know."

Kleitos leaned in to me. "Do you think he really knows?"

Before I could answer, the messenger, surrounded by our sentries, walked up to Alexandros and handed over the wrapped and sealed scroll. Our commander-in-chief broke the seal. He read the letter slowly and carefully. His face betrayed nothing. When he finished, he went back to the beginning and read it again.

Hephaistion could stand it no longer. "Well, what's it say?"

"It's an offer of surrender …"

Hephaistion let loose with a joyous shout.

"… but it's not from Dareios. It's from Abodetes, satrap of Sousiana. He's offering to turn over Sousa to us."

"A surrender is a surrender." Hephaistion reached for the pot resting at Alexandros's feet. "I win."

"No, you don't," somebody shouted. "You said it was a letter of surrender from Dareios."

"I may have said that but, when it came to the bet, my five gold darics said it was a letter of surrender. They said nothing about the identity of the sender."

"That's ridiculous."

"You're a cheater."

"Hand over the money."

Swords were drawn.

"Gentlemen, gentlemen! Calm down!" Alexandros's voice rose effortlessly above the commotion. "I'm holding the pot and I will resolve this dispute. Now put those swords away and listen up."

The men instantly obeyed.

"Ptolemaios, you can back me up on this." I nodded. "Hephaistion did say that it was a letter of surrender from Dareios, isn't that right?"

"Yes, sire, he did say that."

The tight clutch of men around us voiced their approval.

"But – hold on a minute – when Hephaistion actually proposed the bet and threw his darics down, there was no mention of any sender. Is your recollection the same, Ptolemaios? And before you answer, remember that half the money in that pot is probably yours."

Two dozen pairs of angry eyes pivoted toward my face.

"We-e-ell, the two sentences came hard upon each other, sire. And the darics didn't speak. I only heard Hephaistion's voice. So, ..." My voice trailed off.

Alexandros slapped me on the back. "You're an honest man, Ptolemaios. And you men – let this be a lesson to you. You should never gamble." He laughed at his own wit. "It only leads to disputes and fights. Nobody ever wins. Am I right?"

For once, nobody agreed with him. He continued undaunted. "The bet was ambiguous. I can't tell at this point whether the surrender had to come from Dareios or if any old surrender would do. So, nobody wins."

This time, people actually raised their voices to our commander-in-chief. He simply shouted them down. "Listen, men, there is something you seem to have forgotten."

"What's that?"

"That the satrap of Sousiana just offered to turn Sousa, one of Persia's capitals, over to us. Do you have any idea how much treasure there is in Sousa waiting for us? And you're squabbling over a few golds darics?"

An uncertain silence took hold as the import of Alexandros's words sunk in.

"So, here is what I'm going to do. I'll hold on to the money in this pot. Kallisthenes will make me a nice list of the amount contributed by each of you. When we get to Sousa and get our hands on the imperial treasury, I promise to pay you ten darics for each daric you put in. How's that sound?"

"Sounds good, sire."

"OK, then. Now who wants to ride ahead to Sousa as fast as possible to take Aboaletes up on his offer before he changes his mind?"

There was no shortage of volunteers. Next morning, before dawn, a mobile contingent of cavalry, unencumbered by infantry or baggage, set off for Sousa, led by one of our gambling commanders, Philoxenos. The rest of us were still only half way to Sousa when Alexandros received Philoxenos's report that his contingent had secured the surrender of Sousa and seized the imperial treasury.

Alexandros halted our march once again to celebrate the good news. He also used the occasion to reorganize the army, ostensibly to integrate the new arrivals with the veterans. In fact, he did away with the previous regional divisions. From that point forward, men from all corners of Macedonia and mercenaries from around the Greek world were all assigned to geographically diverse infantry units.

The units then elected their own commanders, based on demonstrated battlefield valor. Alexandros nominated the candidates and supervised the voting. The new commanders, coming from all strata of Macedonian and Greek society, shared one unifying characteristic. They all owed their promotions to Alexandros.

The Companion Cavalry was not reorganized quite as thoroughgoing as the infantry units but the squadrons were enlarged and then split in two, with each new half-squadron receiving a new commander appointed by Alexandros. The new commanders then reported to the preexisting squadron leaders. Thus, at least for the time being, I retained my position at the head if my squadron while gaining two subcommanders charged with implementing my orders.

The newly-reorganized pan-Hellenic army was said to be a more efficient fighting machine. While that proposition might have been debatable, there was no doubt the new command structure was far more loyal to Alexandros personally than the previous regime had been.

It was almost the end of November when we resumed our march to Sousa, the capital of Sousiana and one of the four great capitals of the Persian Empire.

****

At last, we crossed a spur of the long and imposing Zagros mountain chain and emerged into the Garden of Eden. At least that's what our local guide called it.

Seleukos was immediately interested. "Where did that name come from?"

Our guide shrugged. "Many stories to explain the name. I've been told the Elamites, who came to this area thousands of years ago, called it Edinnu, meaning 'fertile or well-watered.' When the Assyrians conquered the region, they shortened the name to Edin. And when the Assyrians were in turn displaced by the Persians, they liked they name and kept it. No idea whether any of these stories are true. Only thing I know for sure, this valley really is the most wonderful natural garden, or paradeisos as the Persians call it, on Earth."

"How so?" I wanted to know.

"It's really a bowl, nestled in the palm of the Zagros mountains. If you followed the fingertips all the way down, you'd find yourself in a marshy region not far from the northern end of the Persian Gulf, where the Euphrates and Tigris empty into the sea. But we won't be going that far; we'll be staying right here in this valley, where nature has contrived to create a perfect growing environment for trees and plants and flowers and vegetation of all kinds." He spread his arms, seeking to embrace his country's bounty. "The soil is deep, rich, and fertile. There are rivers and streams and, during the rainy season, daily, life-giving, drenching downpours. When the showers end, the sun returns, bright, intense, and nourishing. The farmers bring in three bumper crops per year, year after year." He pointed to both sides of the road. "Just look around. Have you ever seen such voluptuous abundance?"

Seleukos smiled, catching some of our guide's enthusiasm. "Must be a great place to live."

The guide nodded vigorously. "It is, sire, it is. Except in the summertime, of course. Then it's hell on Earth."

Seleukos's smile dissolved into a skeptical, sidelong frown. "What do you mean?"

"It gets awful hot here, sire. Those same mountain ridges around us that wring out, for our benefit, all the moisture from passing clouds during the rainy season also turn our valley into a searing furnace in the summertime."

"Must get pretty hot, I bet."

"Hot doesn't begin to describe it. All sentient beings endowed with the power of locomotion hide during the midday hours. Except for the lizards, that is."

It was my turn to raise a querying eyebrow. "The lizards don't mind the heat?"

"Oh, they do, they do. Most of them have sense enough to find shelter during the hottest part of the day. But a foolish few think they're swift and nimble enough to get across the road before succumbing to the scorching sun. They never make it half way over. We find them, when we emerge from our darkened dwellings at dusk, broiled to a crisp in the middle of the road. Believe me, sire, it gets hot in Sousa in the summertime."

"Some Garden of Eden," Seleukos observed.

"Sure is, sire, sure is. Most of the time. Your leader was very clever to get here right at the start of December. Couldn't have picked a better time."

"Yes, our leader has a knack for that sort of thing."

****

A small troop of riders crested a hill and materialized without warning less than a mile in front of us. Their steeds, clad in chainmail, glistened in the fading sunlight. The riders wore the familiar armor of Persian knights. A few Sousian banners fluttered above their heads.

Alexandros took one look and prodded Boukephalas into motion. "They look harmless enough. Let's go meet them."

"Wait, Aniketos! They might be assassins."

Alexandros laughed. "C'mon, Hephaistion, ride with me." He swept his hands in our direction. "You guys come along as well."

As we approached, the Persian knights dismounted. They appeared unarmed, except for their leader, who had a scabbard lashed to his left hip. He walked up to Alexandros and unsheathed a large, curved sword. Instantly, the unmistakable rasp of two dozen swords emerging simultaneously from their scabbards hissed through the air. Alexandros didn't even flinch, his eyes locked on the eyes of his adversary.

The young man smiled, bowed his head, and handed his sword to Alexandros, hilt first. "I am Oxathres son of Abouletes." Alexandros accepted the proffered weapon and motioned to us to sheathe our swords. Oxathres, evidently having exhausted his store of

Greek, looked over his shoulder and beckoned to an elderly man in civilian garb standing at the back of the Persian group.

The old man shuffled hesitantly forward and prostrated himself within kicking distance of Boukephalas's forelegs. Oxathres, who was still standing, looked expectantly up to Alexandros. Our king remained motionless on his mount, patiently awaiting the next installment of the surrender ceremony. Finally, growing impatient, he leaned over in the direction of the old man. "Speak!" he boomed.

The old man cringed and, still lying prostrate in the road, starting speaking into the dirt. "Your celestial majesty. Welcome to Sousiana."

"You may stand up, old man. Do you have a name?"

"I do, your majesty, but I'm only the interpreter." The man struggled back to his feet. "My name is of no consequence. I'm the voice of my master, Oxathres." He looked over at the young man standing next to him, who continued to grin like an idiot. "He wishes to welcome you and your men to Sousiana."

Oxathres, hearing a word he recognized, started to speak. I knew enough to recognize it as Persian. When he paused, the old man translated: "My father Abouletes, satrap of Sousiana, apologizes for not coming to meet you in person but he's still engaged in making preparations for your majesty's arrival in Sousa. He will be coming to meet us shortly. In the meantime, he asked me and these men to escort you the rest of the way."

Alexandros hesitated momentarily, trying to decide whether he should be offended that neither Oxathres nor the men accompanying him were groveling in the usual Persian fashion.

Oxathres, as if reading his mind, started to speak again, through his interpreter. "Forgive us, your majesty, for remaining on our feet but we're soldiers, here to serve you. We can't do that effectively on our knees and bellies."

Alexandros turned to Hephaistion, speaking under his breath to stay out of earshot of the interpreter. "What do you think? Mazaios had the good grace to learn some Greek."

"Yes, he did. And he came out to greet us in person, along with all his sons."

"Who, in the accepted fashion, crawled through the dust. Naturally, I held them in contempt as a result but still, you have to go by the local mores. I kind of like this fellow but I'm worried he's not paying sufficient respect."

Before Hephaistion could respond, Perdikkas rode up to join them, holding his spear at the ready, speaking even more loudly than usual. "I recognize this man, sire. He led the Sousiana contingent at Gaugamela. He killed our men. Request permission to run him through."

The interpreter stopped breathing.

"Permission denied." Alexandros reached for the spear. "I killed a lot of their men, too, and look how nicely they're treating me."

"Well, that's because you won, sire. And they lost."

For once, Hephaistion came to Perdikkas's aid. "He's right, Aniketos. This man's head is way too big for his felt hat. We should cut him down to size."

The interpreter started to twitch but said nothing.

Alexandros spun Boukephalas around and started to trot away. Hephaistion and Perdikkas followed on either side. "Look, guys, he's also an ambassador of sorts. I can't harm him. Put them all discreetly under guard and let's get going. We'll decide what to do when we get to Sousa."

Chapter 11 – Sousa

Like all the Persian satraps we'd met before, Abouletes was cunning, well-informed, and flexible in his allegiance. Receiving word of his son's less than successful reception, he rushed out to meet us in person. He was there, camped out at the Choaspes river crossing, awaiting our arrival. He tried hard to match the welcome extended to us by his fellow satrap Mazaios in every particular. To the extent he fell somewhat short, blame could be assigned to his personal failings, to differences between Babylon and Sousa, and – ultimately – to changes in Alexandros himself.

As we approached the river, at midmorning, two days after the encounter with Oxathres, we spotted a lone figure standing astride the royal road, in front of the bridge across the Choaspes, arms akimbo, head held high, wearing a suit of shimmering gold armor and a magnificent ceremonial cloak of crimson silk with fur trimming. Alexandros, as usual, rode out to inspect this curious creature, accompanied only by his bodyguard.

When our little group got within shouting distance, the lone figure sank to his knees, raised his arms, and collapsed to the road. There he lay as we pulled up short, face down, fingers clawing the ground as far overhead as he could reach, as if trying to approach us by pulling himself forward by his fingertips.

Alexandros winked at Hephaistion. "Now that's better."

Bending over the prone figure, he clapped his hands. "You may rise, Abouletes."

The man sprang to his feet. He was younger and more athletic than Mazaios, less oleaginous, and less smooth. "Vacome to Sousa, your cerestial maggotsy."

Alexandros couldn't stop laughing, forcing Seleukos to step in. "You'd better call your interpreter, before you get yourself into even more trouble," he said in Persian.

Abouletes's shoulders sank with relief. He turned and signaled to the far bank, where a colorfully clad throng stood watch. They all started to move as one, causing the satrap to shout and wave his arms frantically. Finally, they understood, stopped, and retreated from the bridge, while a single young man continued to stride forward. Although dressed in a simple white tunic, his bearing gave him away as a soldier.

When he reached the satrap, they consulted briefly. The young man nodded, knelt, touched his forehead to the road, and rose once again – unbidden – to his feet. "Your celestial majesty, welcome to Sousiana. The gates of our capital are open and await your entrance." He spoke better Greek than any of us.

"Where're you from, soldier?" Alexandros's tone was mild, unthreatening. We all recognized trouble brewing.

"I was born in Sousa, your celestial majesty. My mother and father are from Athens. They came here when my father was offered the position of court physician by one of Abouletes's predecessors."

"Did you fight at Gaugamela?"

The young man hesitated. He looked uncertainly at Abouletes. The satrap, not understanding a word, continued to smile benevolently. Finally, the young man set his jaw and nodded. "Yes, your worship, I was there."

"Did you fight?"

"Yes, I did."

"For which side?"

"I was conscripted into the Sousiana contingent, like everyone else of fighting age."

"That's what I thought." Alexandros reared up in his seat. "Let's get across this bridge and I'll address the rabble on the other side."

By the time we crossed the bridge – Abouletes and the young interpreter doing their best to jog alongside our horses – the crowd on the far bank of the Choaspes was lying respectfully on their bellies. "Tell them to rise," Alexandros said to the interpreter. "I have a few words I wish to say."

Seleukos leaned into my ear. "This should be interesting. I want to hear how he'll explain to these Persians, living in the heart of Persia, that we're here to liberate them from foreign oppression."

Alexandros surprised us. "Citizens of Sousa, listen up! Most of you standing here in your colorful costumes took up arms and fought against the pan-Hellenic army two short months ago. You were defeated, along with your former emperor and the rest of the Persian army." He leaned down to the interpreter. "Go ahead, translate!" Then, turning to Seleukos, "and you make sure he gets it right."

When the interpreter stopped speaking, Alexandros continued. "My troops are in control of your city, of its fortress, and the royal palace right now. Greek arms have prevailed over the might of the Persian Empire. 'How could that have happened?' you're probably asking yourselves. Well, I'll tell you." The crowd listened sullenly to the voice of the interpreter. "It happened because Ahura Mazda willed it so." A murmur rose from the crowd. "That's right. Your god is a just god and your emperors have ignored his wishes and have violated his commandments for many generations now. They invaded our homeland, without provocation, not once but twice. They burned and looted our cities, killed our people, desecrated our temples. No just god was going to tolerate such unprovoked aggression forever."

The folks, most of whom probably had no idea what he was talking about, listened in silence. "I, and my soldiers, are but the instruments of the gods. The reason our arms have prevailed over yours, time and time again, is because we carry the swords of justice, the spears of freedom, the message of liberation. A new day has dawned in the Persian Empire, a new order, and a new emperor. Now, get on your knees and stay there until my entire army has passed."

They did as they were told.

****

Once we were inside the city walls, Alexandros paused. "I need a guide to tell me the history of this place. Where is Abouletes and that interpreter?"

Abouletes and the interpreter came running in short order. "We have gifts, your celestial majesty, we have gifts. Please wait."

358

Alexandros condescended to wait. "Tell me about Sousa while we wait. When was it founded and by whom?"

"Your highness, I have just the man for you. He's a Greek-speaking scholar who's lived with us for most of his life. He can answer all your questions. Just don't arrest him, please."

Alexandros drew himself up on his mount. "Why should I arrest him? I just want to get some information."

"Here he is, sire. His name is Indabibi." A bearded, stooped old man was thrust toward us. He fell to his knees and touched his forehead to the ground.

"Put him on a horse so he can ride along."

By the time this little by-play was finished, Abouletes's welcoming ceremonies were ready to proceed. There was a cast of thousands. Dancers twirled, singers trilled, acrobats tumbled, magoi chanted, and firefighters put out the resulting flames.

Alexandros paid no attention. He was busy chatting with his new best friend Indabibi. "So, tell me about this place. Who founded it and when?"

"Nobody knows, sire. People have lived in this sun-kissed, god-favored valley since time out of mind. Perhaps four thousand years ago, the Elamites came and built a fortress here. It still stands. We can visit it later, if you wish."

Hephaistion stuck his head in. "He always wishes. You can count on it."

"A city grew up around the fortress and the Elamites made it their capital. For reasons I can't explain, they called it Sousa, which is why this region is called Sousiana nowadays. Eventually, the fortunes of Elam waned and the might of Assyria waxed. An Assyrian king named Ashurbanipal conquered and destroyed Sousa some three hundred years ago."

Alexandros nodded but said nothing.

"After the fires burned themselves out and after the conquering soldiers went away, the people came back and rebuilt the city. They lived in peace, as subjects of the Assyrian Empire, for another hundred years. By then, the Assyrians had undermined the might of their realm through incessant civil wars and a new empire arose to fill the vacuum – the Persian Empire. Kyros, the founder of the empire, came along and occupied Sousa on his way to greater conquests elsewhere. He, however, didn't destroy the city, believing that a living, breathing, productive city was worth more than a burnt-out, smoking hulk. Several of his successors, liking the climate in the wintertime, enlarged the royal quarter and made the city one of their capitals."

Indabibi's narrative was interrupted by Abouletes. "Animals, your worship, we have animals for you."

Alexandros's ears pricked up at the word 'animals.' He liked his beasts. And Abouletes, learning from the experiences of his colleague Mazaios, did his best to indulge his new overlord's foibles. We were treated to a parade of trained camels, racing dromedaries, and a dozen Indian elephants. "All for you, your celestial highness." Abouletes was beaming. "All for you."

It started to pour. We followed the animals to the royal quarter, dodging heaven's raindrops and the animals' ordure as we went.

****

Babylon was a great city, which included a royal palace. Sousa was a royal palace, around which a city had grown. The walls of Sousa were relatively flimsy by comparison to Babylon's formidable fortifications. The rulers of Sousa were apparently always too secure in their hold on power to fear an attack – until it was too late to do anything about it. The only defensible position in the city was the fortress built atop the one rather mild hill in the area. Unfortunately, the fortress was too ancient and primitive to afford the creature comforts demanded by the emperors of Persia. So, they decided to build for themselves a sumptuous palace.

The palace was designed to overawe any would-be attackers, rather than repel them. It was built on a man-made platform, rising some fifty feet above the surrounding terrain. The buildings themselves were monumental in scale; they towered over everything in sight, even the ancient fortress.

To reach the elevated platform, one had to climb a long, steep, paved causeway. The entrance onto the platform itself was guarded by an impressive gatehouse, which we now approached through the pelting rain.

"I sure hope they open those great big gates for us," Kleitos fretted. "I'm tired of getting soaked. And what happened to that nice warm climate?"

In fact, the gates did swing wide open just as we approached. And the man in charge of swinging them open was none other than our own Philoxenos, grinning broadly, pleased as punch with his joke.

"Sire, I'm pleased to report the city of Sousa, the royal palace, and the treasury are all secured. Your soldiers are patrolling all these areas as we speak. Welcome to your latest acquisitions, sire."

Alexandros jumped off Boukephalas and embraced Philoxenos. "Man, am I glad to see you. I was getting worried we'd have to break down those huge doors."

"All the doors are open to you, sire. What would you like to inspect first?"

"Well, we've got this old man with us, giving us a tour. A guess we'll let him show us around the palace."

Hearing this, Indabibi rode forward. "At your service, celestial highness."

"On through the gates we go," Alexandros ordered.

Once we entered the gatehouse, the roadway became a level, paved, enclosed promenade, some sixty feet long. The high, coffered ceiling above the roadway was supported by four huge columns, two on each side. Beyond the columns, extending the length of the covered roadway, were twin galleries, furnished with marble benches. On the walls of the galleries, keeping a wary eye on our transit, were two tightly-packed files of Immortals, forty-eight soldiers on each side, executed in high relief. Made of colorful, glazed bricks, the soldiers were exactly the same size, each one depicted in profile, facing the entrance of the gatehouse, one foot in front of the other (couldn't tell whether right or left; all the feet looked the same), each soldier gripping with both fists the traditional eight-foot-long spear, held vertically, the "apple" butt resting on the toes of his forward foot, the leaf-shaped spear tip pointing to the ceiling. On their backs, they carried their wicker shields, depicted in three-quarter view so as to fit within the narrow vertical space allocated to each soldier. There was no evidence of any swords, daggers, quivers, or arrows and only one end of their curved bows peeked out above their heads.

Alexandros couldn't resist dismounting once again to take a closer look at the serried files of Immortals. "Hey, guys, look at this. They look identical but each one is dressed differently. Same faces, same beards, same hats and headbands, but each one wears a different robe. What does that mean, Indabibi?"

"I have no idea, your perspicacious majesty. Maybe the individualized patterns of the robe fabrics served as a signature of sorts for the artisans who created these soldiers."

"That's not the only thing that's individualized, either. Look here! They each wear different bracelets on their wrists and different earrings."

"Well, I know what that means," Kleitos called out.

Alexandros fell for the joke. "What's it mean, Kleitos?"

"That they're all pussies, sire." He tried to add something but it got lost in his guffaws. Everyone else, including Alexandros, joined in.

"Alright, let's move on," Alexandros ordered when he'd finally caught his breath.

We emerged from the far end of the gatehouse and found ourselves in a large open space, facing the eastern facade of the palace. The rain had slowed to a drizzle while we admired the glazed Immortals but the top of the palace wall was still shrouded in a cloudy mist.

"How tall is that wall, Indabibi?"

"More than sixty feet, your celestial highness. Would you like to go inside? The entrance is a little way to our right."

It took us a few moments to ride across the open space to the enormous, ornamental front portal of the palace. Indabibi used the time for a brief history lesson. "This palace was built by the original Dareios, your celestial majesty, not the current ... err, recently deposed Emperor Dareios."

"Yes, I know which one you mean. The one who led the first Persian invasion of Greece."

Indabibi nodded nervously. "Yes, that's the one. May I continue, sire?"

"Sure. Go ahead."

"It's said Sousa was the first Dareios's favorite capital. He died before the work on the palace was completed. Construction continued under Dareios's son, Xerxes, and was finished during the reign of his grandson, Artaxerxes, about a hundred years ago.

"No sooner was the construction finished than the whole place burned down. It stayed in ruins for fifty years until it was restored by Dareios Deuteros and was brought to its current level of splendor by Artaxerxes Deuteros, who also added the Apadana. That addition was finished only thirty-five years ago."

Alexandros interrupted. "So, how big is this platform we're riding on?"

"It's hard to measure because it's irregularly shaped. But when the original Dareios decided to build this palace, he first conscripted the entire local populace to dig up all of the surrounding countryside until they reached solid bedrock. Around here, that means going down through some twenty feet of soil. After they were done, they heaped up and compacted all that soil to create this platform. If it were square-shaped, it would make a square more than half a mile on each side."

A set of four wide granite steps led up to the ceremonial doors, now flung open in anticipation of our arrival. Although the steps were clearly meant for human feet, Alexandros urged Boukephalas to leap to the top. Miraculously, the great stallion accomplished the feat without breaking any bones, either its own or its rider's. The rest of us dismounted and led our horses to the top.

Indabibi ran after Alexandros. "Your celestial majesty, perhaps you'd like to tie up your mount on the outside. You'll get a better view of the interior of this magnificent palace, which is now yours, if you walk on foot."

Alexandros raised a querying eyebrow in the direction of Hephaistion, who looked to Seleukos in turn. Seleukos nodded. "No point desecrating the place." Hephaistion signaled his concurrence. Alexandros alighted and left his horse outside.

The scope of the palace complex was gigantic. After walking through a few large rooms, we found ourselves in a grass-covered, colonnaded courtyard. "This is big enough for military maneuvers," Alexandros observed to no one in particular.

"You're so right, your sagacious majesty, "Indabibi jumped in. "We often use it to review and drill our troops. But not cavalry, of course," he quickly added.

Alexandros turned to Philoxenos, "Which reminds me. Where are your troops?"

"They're around, sire. They're discretely out of sight but they're in control. Trust me."

Alexandros seemed doubtful. "Alright, Philoxenos, I'll trust you. But if we run into trouble, it's your neck on the line."

Philoxenos leaned in. "All these Elamites and Persians and Sousians or whatever they are," he whispered, "have shat their fancy leather pants. They won't give us any trouble."

Alexandros rewarded him with a grin and turned around. "Alright, Indabibi, let's continue the tour."

The palace was endless. The sun set, torches were lit, snacks and wineskins were passed around, and still we continued to march on. There were two more courtyards, not quite as large as the first one but each bigger than the entire royal palace in Pella. There were rooms without number, small, large, and everything in between. The ceilings in the larger rooms were supported by huge, fluted columns. The bases of the columns were decorated with bas-reliefs of scenes of battle, subjugation, tribute-paying and obeisance, emperor worship and adoration. The tops of the columns were sculpted into a fantastic variety of animals, both real and imaginary, from cows to lions, from eagles to sphinxes, from griffins to three-headed monsters. On top of the columns rested huge wooden beams of oak or cedar which in turn supported the elaborately decorated, coffered ceilings. The walls were stuccoed throughout and, in many rooms, covered with colorful mosaics composed of vivid, glazed tiles. These mosaics depicted a wide variety of subjects. There were pictures of beings divine and mortal, royal and merely human, soldiers and civilians, Persians and conquered people, men and more men. (Persians didn't go for female figures in their art.) All kinds of animals and monsters menaced the viewer in their stylized stolidity. Occasionally, even the natural beauty of the many lands comprising the Persian Empire found its way to the palace walls, with gorgeous depictions of mountains, plains, and rivers, majestic trees, fertile fields, and colorful flowers.

Taking my eyes off the walls for a moment, I caught a glimpse of Indabibi. The old man was ready to collapse. "Perhaps we should resume in the morning, sire," I suggested.

"What, are you getting tired, Ptolemaios?"

"No, Aniketos, but he is." I pointed to our guide, who was barely able to speak by now.

Alexandros shrugged. "You're right. Let's take a break. We can bed down right here and resume at first light."

Indabibi was visibly relieved. "I know just the place, your celestial majesty." He led us to a complex of rooms we had not seen before. The floors were covered in deep, luxurious carpets, with plum pillows and animal skins scattered everywhere. Little tables, stools, and trunks stood in corners and a strange aroma filled the air.

Alexandros looked around curiously. "What is this place?"

"The harem, your highness."

"Perfect," Alexandros laughed. "Except for the missing women, of course. But I suppose Abouletes couldn't think of everything. Make sure a filling breakfast is waiting by the time we awake."

He was asleep before his body hit the plush, carpeted floor.

****

If there was one thing Alexandros pursued more indefatigably than victory, it was sightseeing. And the Sousa royal palace gave him a chance to combine the two. On the one hand, his sheer presence, a twenty-six-year-old upstart striding the granite floors built by the greatest emperors of Persia, was tangible evidence of spectacular military triumph. On the other hand, there was so much great stuff to see here. Alexandros was in his element.

"Wait until you see this, your celestial majesty."

"Where're you taking us now, Indabibi?"

"This is the Apadana, the audience or reception hall, as you might call it. I'm told it's the second largest indoor space in the world."

We all rushed in, stopped, and gaped. It didn't have the soaring elegance of the Parthenon or the chiseled beauty of the Mausoleion or the effortless lightness of the Artemision but it was big. Indabibi gave us the dimensions: "It's three-hundred-twenty by three-hundred feet. Ninety columns support the seventy-foot-high ceiling. It can hold twenty thousand people."

"Or ten thousand, if you want them to breathe." Kleitos was irrepressible.

Alexandros, on the other hand, was voracious in his curiosity. "Where is the largest indoor space in the world?"

"That, your inquisitive majesty, would be the Apadana in Persepolis. But I've never seen that one, so I'm only going by what I've been told."

"We'll be checking it out soon enough. I'll send you a note to let you know for sure." Alexandros's bold promise met with appreciative laughter by all in attendance, with the possible exception of the handful of Persian officials who accompanied us. "Now, what else have you got to show us?"

"We've seen just about everything, your majesty, except the Throne Room and the adjoining Treasury Suite, which your men have locked up and are keeping under guard."

Alexandros turned to Philoxenos. "I assume he's talking about your men?"

"Yes, sire. As soon as we located the Treasury Suite, I had it locked and barred and posted guards. I didn't let anyone so much as take a peek inside. Don't want any of that loot disappearing."

"Not even you?"

"Well, I did take a quick look, just to make sure what was in there. But I didn't linger."

"And? What did you see?"

"It was pretty disappointing, sire, at a quick glance, to tell you the truth. Nothing like what we saw in Sardeis or Babylon or some other places. More like petty cash for everyday needs than a treasury. A couple of thousand talents at most, I'd guess."

"That's impossible. They must've hidden it somewhere. What about the fortress?"

"The fortress, sire, is sealed off. Walled up. Impossible to enter without breaking down some masonry. I posted guards but we didn't try to enter."

Alexandros turned back to Indabibi. "What about the fortress? Isn't that on our itinerary?"

"I was saving that for last, your majesty. But I must warn you, there isn't much to see. It's just an ancient, crumbling fortress, not nearly as impressive as this palace. And you can't get inside anyway. Some previous king or satrap sealed it off, probably for safety reasons. Wouldn't want those ancient walls collapsing on our heads."

"We'll definitely want to check that out. And we're going to go inside as well." He laughed. "In fact, we're going to send you in first, to make sure it's safe."

Indabibi failed to appreciate Alexandros's sense of humor. "Yes, sire. But let's go see the Throne Room first."

When we reached the Throne Room, we were greeted by a double surprise. First, the hall, although quite a bit smaller than the Apadana, was absolutely spectacular. The beauty of the decorations, the quality of the materials, and the level of workmanship rivaled anything we had seen in the Greek world or during our journeys in the Persian Empire. Second, the hall was full of people.

"Who are these folks?" Alexandros asked Philoxenos.

"I rounded up all the soldiers, courtiers, eunuchs, priests, and assorted riff-raff we found in the palace prior to your arrival, sire. This morning, the satrap Abouletes suggested we should assemble them all in the Throne Room so they could properly welcome you to the palace. It seemed like a decent suggestion, so here they are. Under the watchful eyes of my soldiers, of course. I hope that meets with your approval, sire. If not, we can clear the room in short order."

"No, that won't be necessary. Let them stay. Just make sure they pay me the proper respect."

That last admonition proved to be entirely superfluous. As soon as the milling crowd noticed the arrival of the would-be emperor, they fell to the floor as one. Before Alexandros could stride toward the throne, however, Indabibi tugged at his sleeve. "There's one more thing I'd like to show you, celestial highness." He walked over to a large granite plaque set into the back wall, covered in writing.

"What's it say?" Alexandros wanted to know.

"I'll translate it for you, your inquisitive majesty, if you'll permit me: 'King Dareios says: A great god is Ahura Mazda, who created this Earth, who created man, who created happiness for man, who made me king, king of kings, lord of many.

"'By the favor of Ahura Mazda, I, king of kings, lord of many, Ahura Mazda's representative on Earth and keeper of his flame, built this palace. At my command, downward the earth was dug, until I reached rock in the earth. When the excavation had been made, the rubble was packed down, some 40 cubits in depth. On that rubble the palace was constructed.

""The sides of the platform were secured with sun-dried brick. This work was done by my Babylonian vassals.

""The cedar timber was brought from a mountain named Lebanon. My Assyrian vassals brought it to Babylon; from Babylon the Karians and the Ionians brought it to Sousa.

""The gold was brought from Sardeis and from Baktria and wrought here at Sousa. The precious stones, including lapis lazuli and carnelian and turquois, were brought from Sogdiana and Khorasmia and cut and polished here at Sousa.

""The silver and the ebony were brought from Egypt. The ornamentation with which the walls are adorned was brought here from Ionia. The ivory was brought from Aithiopia and from Sindh and from Arakhosia and carved here at Sousa.

""The stone for the columns was brought here from a village named Abiradu, in Elam, and chiseled here. The stonecutters who chiseled the stone were Ionians and Sardians.

""The goldsmiths who wrought the gold were Medes and Egyptians. The men who carved the wood were Sardians and Egyptians. The men who molded the baked brick were Babylonians. The men who adorned the walls were Medes and Egyptians.

"'King Dareios says: At Sousa a very excellent work was ordered, a very excellent work was brought to completion. May Ahura Mazda protect me, my father Hystaspes, and my country.' That's all it says, your celestial majesty."[21]

"He was a modest fellow, that Dareios. Let's get going."

Alexandros strode down the narrow path left vacant down the middle of the room. The Macedonian contingent followed behind, trying hard not to step on the prostrate bodies. Finally, stopping just short of the throne, Alexandros turned and benevolently signaled to the assembled multitude to rise. Then he attempted to climb up to the throne, beneath its billowing golden canopy.

The throne was an elaborate, intricately-carved affair, seemingly designed for someone at least seven feet tall. Four steps led up to it, with a footstool on the top one, but a normal person would still have to leap up to get his buttocks onto the seat.

"No, celestial majesty, don't!" Indabibi cried out as Alexandros mounted the first step. "Sitting on this throne means instant death for anyone other than the legitimate emperor of Persia."

---

[21] For the location of Persian satrapies mentioned in Dareios's inscription, see Map 12 at AlexanderGeiger.com.

"So I've been told." Alexandros continued his climb. With considerable agility, he deposited himself in the ridiculously high and wide chair and smiled. Lightning didn't strike.

On the other hand, his feet didn't come close to touching the footstool, dangling risibly in the air instead. Philoxenos, wishing to show initiative, leapt up, snatched a nearby small table, and placed it under Alexandros's feet. It was the perfect height.

Seeing the table beneath Alexandros's feet provoked a collective, horrified intake of breath by all the natives present in the room. Several men were a beat too slow in suppressing their looks of consternation. Silent tears rolled down the plump cheeks of one eunuch.

Alexandros rounded on the crowd. "What's the matter? What's got into you?"

There was no response, the Persian men in attendance struggling to maintain blank stares. Alexandros looked directly at the weeping eunuch. "You, fat-face, what's the matter with you?"

The eunuch evidently knew some Greek. In a strangled voice and in broken Greek, he managed to explain that the table currently supporting Alexandros's feet used to be Dareios's favorite eating table. To put one's feet where the emperor's food used to rest amounted to sacrilege.

It was now Alexandros's turn to be horrified, all his efforts to ingratiate himself with the local Persians undone in an instant. With a peremptory wave of his hand, he ordered the table removed.

Before Philoxenos could move, however, Fast Philotas leapt up. "Leave it where it is, sire. You couldn't possibly have given offense either to the gods or to these craven Persians. Having no knowledge that this used to be Dareios's eating table, your placing your feet on the table is the opposite of sacrilege; it's a divinely inspired symbol of your supplanting of Dareios."

Alexandros's countenance brightened instantly. "You're right, Philotas!" He stamped his feet on the table. "Take that, Dareios."

Kleitos, enthusiastically following the lead of his commander-in-chief, stamped on the toes of the nearest Persian, who happened to be Abouletes. "Take that, old man."

The satrap let out a loud yelp and seemed on the verge of punching Kleitos in the nose.

"Alright, everybody," Alexandros called out. "That's the end of the ceremony. Clear the room."

****

After everybody but the staff was gone, Alexandros turned to Philoxenos. "Alright, let's see that Treasury Suite."

"It's right next door, sire, but, as I said, it's pretty bare."

A quick inspection confirmed Alexandros's worst fears. A few boxes of silver coins, one large pile of silver bars, two bags of gold darics. Enough to make one man rich; not enough to run the pan-Hellenic army for more than a day.

"There's got to be more, somewhere. Get Indabibi back here!"

"We haven't explored the fortress yet, sire."

Indabibi appeared at the door. "There you are, my good man. Let's resume the tour. I believe the old fortress is next."

"There are two ways to get there, your celestial majesty. We can go back to the eastern portal through which we entered, retrieve our horses, take the causeway back down, and then ride around the palace platform to the bottom of fortress hill and clamber up to the fortress. Shouldn't take more than an hour.

"Or we could walk out the western portal, which is not far from here, walk to the postern gate at the edge of the platform, scramble down as best we can and then climb back up to the fortress. If we were birds, it would be but a short flight. Or, if we were mountain goats, it would be an easy jaunt. For us humans, it's a short but perilous scramble."

"Let's take the western route. We're all eagles here." Alexandros laughed. "With the possible exception of you and Abouletes there."

"We'll need some picks and shovels, sire," Philoxenos reminded us.

Although the palace platform and the fortress hill adjoined each other, originally there'd been a steep precipice between them. The sides of the platform had been especially vertiginous. However, over the centuries, people looking for a shortcut managed to fashion some steps down the almost vertical side of the platform and to fill in the bottom of the chasm with dirt and debris. As a result, Alexandros and his coterie of young men reached the foot of the fortress wall in minutes, without even getting winded. It was another story for the two old Persian gentlemen, who struggled long and hard to catch up.

"So, where is the entrance?" Alexandros asked the sentries that had been posted by Philoxenos.

"There's no entrance, sire. It's been walled up."

Conquest of Persia

Alexandros grabbed a pick and started to pound away at the temporary seal. The rest of us joined in with whatever implements we could grab. It took less than an hour to break through.

We found a courtyard on the far side of the entrance, from which a single doorway led into a tall stone tower. That entrance had been sealed as well but our men made quick work of the flimsy wall. After two or three steps into the bottom room of the tower, we froze in our tracks. Among other things, it was hard to find a path to get through. Everywhere, there were glittering piles of gold and silver ingots, ceramic and wooden containers overflowing with coins, shimmering fabrics and random heaps of assorted articles fashioned from rare woods, ivory, and gold.

"Alright, there's no room in here. Everybody, get out! Hephaistion, you stay here with me. And Ptolemaios, you make sure nobody enters."

Hephaistion was put in charge of sorting and counting the loot. Eventually, he had scores of soldiers working in the tower and an additional crew deployed outside to make sure none of the treasure left the premises.

It took eleven days to finish the job. After a while, we started to discern the true character of this hoard. It became clear that, since the founding of the Persian Empire, more than enough revenue had flowed into the imperial treasuries from the tribute-paying subject nations to cover the current funding requirements of the empire. Therefore, there was no need for all the booty seized by the successive emperors in their never-ending round of conquests. For almost three hundred years, all the spoils of war from the farthest edges of the empire were simply bundled up and sent off to the Sousa fortress, where they were stored and forgotten.

After eleven days, Hephaistion handed Alexandros a partial list: 45,000 talents of gold and silver ingots; 9,000 talents of gold darics; 3,500 talents of purple-dyed cloth, still bright as new after two hundred years; and all the loot sent back by Xerxes from Greece. The list went on and on.

The amount of gold and silver beggared the imagination, far exceeding all the gold and silver possessed by all the Greek-speaking cities of the world combined. The one find that pleased Alexandros more than any other was the double statue of the tyrannicides, Harmodios and Aristogeiton, which had been carted off by Xerxes during his sack of Athens. Once upon a time, as a visiting teenager to the violet-wreathed city, Alexandros promised to find the beloved sculpture and return it to Athens. The leading citizens of Athens, who heard the pledge, laughed at him. Now, he had the larger-than-life bronze tableau carefully packed, crated, and shipped back to Athens.

The one item that didn't turn up was the missing imperial tiara.

****

Alexandros was understandably ebullient. He called in his new best friend Indabibi and handed him ten shiny new gold darics. "Now you're a rich man, Indabibi."

"Yes, I am, your bountiful highness. Thank you."

"I need your help with one more matter."

"Anything you wish, your magnanimous majesty."

"I need you to organize a splendid banquet in the palace. I want to do it in the Persian manner and I want it to outshine anything Dareios might have done here in the past."

"Your heavenly brilliance, I have no expertise in such matters."

"Yes, but you do speak Persian and you strike me as a sensible and honest man. And from now on, you carry the authority of my command. Assemble all the experts and helpers you need and agree to pay whatever is required. I'll make sure all debts you incur are paid in full."

"When would you like to have this banquet?"

"As soon as possible. How about tomorrow night?"

"That will be difficult but I'll do my best. How many nights do you wish the banquet to last?"

"What? What are you talking about? It can go on until the last man has passed out. If we serve good, lightly-diluted wine, that should happen well before dawn."

"Yes, yes. But after they wake up, they'll expect the wine to start flowing all over again."

"Is that how it's done in Persia?"

"I've never been to a royal banquet, your majesty, but that's what I understand. The noble guests keep drinking, passing out, waking up, retching and pissing, and then drinking again, for days on end."

"But that's disgusting."

"It's the Persian way, your majesty."

"Well, alright. Let's go for three nights. That should be enough for anybody. I'll decide whom to invite but assume a couple of hundred guests. We'll need plenty of food and wine for all three nights. And lots of entertainment, both girls and boys. Mostly girls for my men but I don't know about your Persian nobles. And I'll need three spectacular Persian outfits to wear. Find

Dareios's three best ensembles and get them altered to fit me."

"Yes, your majesty."

"And one more thing. I want everybody in attendance to address me as Emperor Alexandros, king of kings, lord of many, Ahura Mazda's representative on Earth, and keeper of his flame."

"That may be a bit too long to spit out, Emperor Alexandros, king of kings, lord of many, Ahura Mazda's representative on Earth, and keeper of his flame – especially for a bunch of inebriates."

"Well, they can shorten it, if they have to. Now, off you go. There's much to do and little time."

The festivities proceeded pretty much as badly as one could have expected. The decorations in the king's hall were adequate but not spectacular. There were hangings of white cotton and blue wool, caught up to silver rods and alabaster columns by cords of fine linen and purple wool; and there were couches of gold and silver on a pavement of marble, alabaster, mother-of-pearl, and mosaics. The food was served on silver plates but was generally cold by the time it arrived. The wine was served in golden chalices but was sour and overly diluted. The Macedonian officers in attendance refused to kowtow. Alexandros looked like a little boy playing dress-up in Dareios's outfits. The Persian officers and noblemen found it hard to hide their derision, especially after getting drunk out of their minds. The two groups of guests, forced to mingle with each other, made up for their inability to communicate by conveying their mutual contempt with their fists. Worst of all, the magoi in attendance refused to recognize Alexandros's authority either as emperor or representative of Ahura Mazda, even when threatened with instant extinction. By the end of the third night, the King's Hall looked more like a morgue than a banquet room.

"Well, that went well," Hephaistion observed as he carted Alexandros off to bed after the third night.

****

Bleary-eyed and headachy, Alexandros rose, in both senses of the word, the following dawn. Dispensing with any breakfast or morning ablutions, he decided the time had come to pay a visit on Barsine. Marching out of his tent, he woke me with a peremptory shout. "Ptolemaios, are you still asleep? Daylight's here and we've got things to do."

I struggled to my feet. "What's up, sire?"

"We're going back to the palace. Specifically, to the harem portion thereof." He was already moving, practically skipping down the muddy path leading to the one gate in the palisade. "I've been neglecting Barsine for way too long."

"I can see that."

"Now, let's not get obscene. You know that mostly I want to see my son. But if Barsine were to prove as insistent as usual, I might be unable to resist her."

"I understand, sire."

"And by the way, in case you're getting your – ahem – hopes up, I made sure Artakama is not housed in the harem. So, you have no excuse to desert your station this time. You're the only bodyguard I'm taking; I need you to stay on post. And I don't mean that other post."

"I'll do my best, sire. It's hard with all the racket you two make."

He laughed. "Well, if it gets too hard, we'll see whether we can find a suitable concubine for you later on."

"Thank you, sire, but that won't be necessary. If you wanted to help me out, you could find out where Artakama is housed. And don't worry, I'll stay at my post no matter what."

"I know exactly where she is. But if you keep working at your post, you won't be much use to her when you see her."

By the time we reached the harem, I'd managed to inveigle Artakama's whereabouts out of Alexandros and he'd managed to work himself up to the bursting point. We sprinted down the soft, meandering paths of the paradeisos. In his headlong rush, Alexandros ignored the exotic trees, ornamental shrubs, and aromatic plants meant to induce passersby to slow down and indulge their senses.

A beaming Barsine greeted us at the front portal of the largest of the dwellings scattered amidst the gardens. This was really a small, tile-clad, gleaming palace, which normally housed the emperor's favorite wives. Now, most of the sumptuous suites stood empty, except for rooms occupied by Dareios's mother, Sisygambis, and her grandchildren, Stateira, Drypetis, and Ochos, and the lesser but still opulent rooms assigned to Barsine and her son, Herakles.

Someone must have tipped Barsine off to our arrival. She couldn't have had more than a few seconds to prepare, yet she looked ravishing. At age twenty-four, and after five children, her figure retained the sleek, sinuous, seductive allure – and coiled menace – of a prowling puma. And her sparkling white chiton was just dense enough to conceal the olive-tinged flesh underneath yet sheer enough to make it abundantly clear she was as glad to see Alexandros as he was to see her.

"My liege, what a wonderful surprise. Your son is asleep just now but we can certainly wake him, so he can bask in your presence."

"Nah, let him sleep. We can look in on him later." He swept her up in his arms. "Which way to your bedchamber?"

I stood in the doorway, uncertain whether I was supposed to follow. Alexandros nodded in the direction of a small cubicle near the entrance. I got the message and took up my post.

Barsine's room couldn't have been too far off because I could hear every word between them. However, words were few and far between. Instead, the other inmates of the harem and I were treated mostly to outcries of carnal lust, followed by brief intervals of groans and giggles. Trying hard to keep my mind on other things, I lost count of the number of cycles they went through before they subsided into soft, amorous snoring.

Barsine awoke first and started moving around her chambers. I surmised she was primping once again. After a long pause, she spoke. "Ah, my liege, you're awake. Would you like some wine or perhaps something to eat?"

Alexandros, his voice still groggy with sleep, declined. "I just want to eat you, my love."

"Let's save something for your next visit, big boy. Right now, your eyes are bigger than your sword. You get it nicely polished up so you're ready for me next time."

Alexandros laughed. "I'm always ready for you, sweetheart."

"That's what I'm afraid off. Why don't you get dressed and we can go over and check on Herakles. He's probably anxious for his next feeding."

"Why don't you go ahead and get him. I'll wait for you here."

The baby started to cry as soon as Barsine brought him in. "He's hungry," she explained.

"You can go ahead and nurse him. I don't mind."

"Are you planning to watch?"

"Of course. That's the best part."

Alexandros interrupted the ensuing silence after a moment. "There's nothing as tender as a nursing mother and child. I'll treasure this picture as long as I live."

"You could see this picture every day, my liege. Free us from this enameled prison and take us along wherever you go. I'd much rather live in a tent as your wife than in the most luxurious palace as your occasional paramour."

Alexandros leapt to his feet. "That will never happen!" He stormed out of Barsine's suite, almost knocking into me as I stepped out to meet him. "Let's get out of here."

Although none of us knew then, it would be a long time before Alexandros saw Barsine and Herakles again.

****

More repelled than inspired by Alexandros's example, I decided, after much deliberation, to pay my respects to Artakama once again. We hadn't seen each other since our abortive, exceedingly frustrating stroll through the gardens of the Babylonian harem. I managed to persuade myself that a visit would be nothing more than an act of disinterested, platonic charity. Plus, I'd promised Barsine that I'd look after her sister and her four older children, whom she was unable to see herself. *Absolutely nothing romantic will happen*, I told myself. *If I have so much as a prurient thought, I'll cut my balls off.*

I gathered up a few gifts for all involved and was about to leave my barracks when a messenger intercepted me in the doorway. "A note, sir." He gave no indication of urgency or gravity and I had other things on my mind. Without looking at the missive, I nodded, gave him a coin, and rolled up the small leather tube in my sleeve.

After a few wrong turns and a meandering conversation with a pair of loitering soldiers, I finally found the former government building on the south side of the Sousa market square that now housed many of our female camp followers. Some of these ladies of easy virtue had been with us since our march out of Egypt but their ranks seemed to swell with each stop. After Babylon, there were enough of them to form at least two battalions of fighting Amazons. *They'd certainly be fierce enough*, I thought.

Behind the government building huddled the servants' huts, now repurposed as temporary housing for our lower-ranking Persian hostages. Here, in a small, dingy room, I found Artakama, trying to cope with her sister's four elder children, now ranging in age from just under four to almost ten.

Surprised to see her without the two serving girls and in a way glad to have a mundane topic to discuss, I barged in without a greeting. "Where are their two 'mommies'?"

Artakama looked up. Watching her expression go from distracted to startled to surprised to delighted reminded me of a glorious sunrise bursting into a crisp, clear, endless day. "My liege!"

She sprang to her feet and, before I could assume an appropriately asexual slouch, smothered me in a tight embrace, squeezing my good intentions right out. *I wonder how much it'll hurt to cut my balls off.*

I tried to interpose the two large satchels I had brought with me between us. "Here, I've got some food."

"Oh, thank you!"

My reflexes betrayed me once again and I was way too slow to fend off the kiss she firmly planted on my lips. "Please don't. I simply thought you and the children might need some treats to round out your diet." I thrust my satchels at her.

A swift, transparent squall clouded over her countenance. Tears welled up in her eyes.

"I didn't mean it like that, my love." I dropped the satchels and tried to wipe her tears away.

She turned her back on me but couldn't suppress the shaking of her shoulders. "Just leave! Please, leave us alone! And take your lousy treats with you!"

I took her hand and forced her to face me. "Come, let's take a walk. The kids can look after one another for a bit. And I'm sure the serving girls will be back soon."

Our walk lasted a couple of hours. We spent it mostly in silence. There was so much I wanted to explain and so little I could actually say. Somehow, I think she read my thoughts. Without any conversation at all, we parted friends.

I came back twice more during our stay in Sousa, always bearing gifts. She accepted them politely, each time expressing her gratitude and pleasure at seeing me. Her face remained clear, composed, and blank throughout, carefully concealing whatever storms raged inside her heart.

****

As I strode back toward the barracks after my first visit with Artakama, I remembered the little leather tube rolled up in my sleeve. After reading the message, I sat down, unable to continue. As luck would have it, I was passing through the chicken sellers' colonnade at the time but nobody seemed to mind my unexpected presence, least of all the doomed but still very much animated poultry on whose crates I plopped myself down.

The note was from Seleukos, who had some inkling of the complicated, contentious, formerly murderous relationship between our Great Seer and me. The message was terse: "Aristandros is dead. Thought you might want to know. Seleukos."

The news set off a chain reaction in my mind. All the constituent elements necessary to figure out Aristandros's story must have been percolating in there for a long time but evidently it required a catalyst to break through the subconscious barriers. Seleukos's note jarred my mental processes enough to enable even me to see the truth at last.

Conquest of Persia

Aristandros was a time traveler too – that much was obvious. However, now I finally understood why he hadn't lost his ability to foresee events even after I'd changed the course of history by averting Kleitos's impending demise as a fourteen-year-old youngster, which in turn enabled Kleitos to save Alexandros's life during the Battle of Granikos. Aristandros, as I now clearly saw, was a time traveler sent back to this ancient era at some point after I'd embarked on my own ill-starred journey, even though he arrived in Philippos's Macedonia several years before I did. Evidently, he'd traveled back from a different future, one that already reflected the changes I'd wrought by my inadvertent but unwise and far-reaching violation of the Prime Directive. The history he'd learned in school included Alexandros's victory at Granikos. No wonder he remained so uncannily accurate in his predictions even after I'd lost my clairvoyance.

A new, unexpected thought burst into my consciousness. *He must've screwed up, too. Maybe even worse than I did. He, after all, never made it back home at all.* I wondered what he'd done. Perhaps it was when his vanity caused him to make a spectacular dream interpretation to King Philippos of Macedon, which, on the one hand, catapulted him to the foremost ranks of soothsayers in the ancient world but which, on the other hand, may well have also caused him to become marooned in this gullible and superstitious era. I found little solace in my new realization. I wondered, instead, what his original mission had been, what had gone wrong, and how he felt about it all. *Well, it's too late to ask him now.*

It occurred to me that perhaps he'd been sent back specifically to stop me from interfering with the flow of history. I rejected the thought immediately. Aristandros might have known I was a fellow time traveler but he certainly couldn't have been aware of the fateful, culpable act I'd committed by saving Kleitos's life. *Well, he obviously figured it out in the wake of Granikos.* It all started to make sense. His new-found, unexpected antipathy toward me after Kleitos's pivotal role in our victory; his decision to neutralize me before I could do more harm; his gradual loss of resolve as he realized he wouldn't live long enough to make it to the next escape hatch, assuming he even knew about its existence. *We should've been friends and collaborators.*

My reverie was interrupted by a forceful shove against my shoulder. A huge, fleshy man loomed over me, yelling in a tongue I didn't understand. Seeing the confusion on my face, he switched to Aramaic, which I understood well enough to get his meaning. He had a customer for the chickens confined in the crates on which I was sitting and was anxious not to lose the sale. I jumped to my feet and got out of their way, still preoccupied with thoughts of what might have been.

******

Alexandros stayed in Sousa until mid-January. At that point, we all knew that our next destination would be Persepolis. We also assumed we'd be staying put until spring because the Zagros Mountains lay between Sousa and Persepolis and all the passes were snowbound. As usual, Alexandros decided to defy expectations.

"We're moving out in two days," he announced out of the blue. He made the usual arrangements. The local bureaucrats were retained in their prior positions. Abouletes found himself confirmed as satrap of Sousiana, perhaps to his own surprise. On the other hand, Alexandros also left behind the largest garrison to date, comprising 3,000 allied volunteers and mercenaries under a Macedonian commander. He left Philoxenos in charge of sealing up once again and guarding with his life the largest hoard of riches the world had ever seen. Finally, he also named a trusted Greek as the treasurer in charge of collecting taxes. Learning from his Persian predecessors, he decided it made no sense to dip into accumulated wealth if one could make ends meet from current income.

He left behind all the hostages, including the Persian royal family, all the women, including Barsine and their infant son Herakles, all the camp followers, and the bulk of the baggage train. Despite the urging of his most trusted advisors, he hadn't married Barsine prior to his departure.

Chapter 12 – Persepolis

Alexandros was obsessed with gaining recognition as the legitimate emperor of Persia. Perhaps it was the adulation heaped upon him in Egypt that had pushed him over the edge. He'd been crowned pharaoh without any real opposition. The natives, including the priests, welcomed him as their liberator and were happy to worship him not only as their new ruler but also as a demigod. It was heady stuff, especially for a youngster conditioned to believe, practically from birth, that he was destiny's darling. Gradually, with additional impulses provided at Ammon, Gaugamela, Babylon, and all the other intoxicating venues in between, he'd come to believe he'd been chosen by the gods to become ruler of the Persian Empire and maybe one of their colleagues.

The Persian ruling class, especially those who found themselves in territories conquered by Alexandros's army, were willing to acquiesce. Ordinary folks hardly noticed any difference and certainly didn't care. However, for some reason, the Persian magoi refused to go along. And Alexandros was determined to change their minds.

Persepolis, the one capital of the Persian Empire actually situated in ancestral Persis, the home base of the Ahura Mazda religious establishment, and the place where Persian emperors had been traditionally crowned (and buried), seemed as good a place as any to press his claim. Besides, after Sousa, Persepolis was the next stop on the royal road. The only trouble were those snow-bound, impenetrable passes through the Zagros Mountains. But Alexandros was an impatient man who'd always believed in the efficacy of speed and surprise. So what if it was the middle of January? There was an emperorship to be seized.

****

Dareios was obsessed with regaining his empire. He was also completely alone. His predicament illustrated the Achilles heel of Persian governance. When every male relative, every competent military commander, every savvy advisor, and every highly placed eunuch is a potential assassin, it's hard to get reliable counsel. When there is a different woman in your bed every night, and they're all vying with one another for primacy, it seldom leads to the development of close personal ties. When the exercise of authority is predicated on terror and fear, rare is the subordinate willing to risk life and limb in order to provide unvarnished advice. And three battles lost, against all odds, to an upstart youngster from backward Macedonia tend to tarnish the aura of the office.

Dareios's isolation was exacerbated by the fact that he was an outsider at the court, a stranger to power, a latecomer who emerged from nowhere and seized power at a relatively advanced age, without any help from family, friends, colleagues, or collaborators. His only living relatives – his mother and children – were currently out of reach. There was no one he could ask whether, in addition to letting his empire slip through his fingers, he was also losing his mind.

Dareios was convinced of two things: First, the momentum of Alexandros's thrust into the Persian Empire would dissipate over time, even without any overt resistance by Persian forces, as the never-ending rounds of debauchery eroded the invading soldiers' military fitness and as their ever-increasing riches weakened their motivation to fight; second, the unfathomable resources of what was left of the Persian Empire, in terms of manpower, materiel, and disposable wealth, were more than enough to defeat those insolent invaders from the west, provided a competent leader managed to marshal these resources. He fancied himself as that leader.

But he was also struggling with doubts. Could it be that he was kidding himself? Had the strategic acumen and psychological insights, which had served him so well till then, suddenly deserted him? Was it possible that he'd run out of luck? Were those whispers, containing the word 'coward,' real or imagined? Was it true that he'd lost the favor of the gods? He wished he knew.

The reports trickling in from Babylon and Sousa seemed to support Dareios's calculations. Alexandros's soldiers were wallowing in depravity, reveling in loot, and disinclined to forge ahead. On the other hand, the reinforcements and supplies requested by Dareios in countless dispatches were slow to arrive. He told himself there was plenty of time to get ready but he couldn't completely suppress the nagging uncertainty at the back of his mind.

There was one idea about which he was fairly sure: Given Alexandros's extended stay in Babylon, it was reasonable to assume he'd spend a similar amount of time in Sousa. Certainly, he wouldn't be moving until springtime.

****

In Sousa, there was no replay of the protracted haggling and cajoling that had been required in Babylon to get the troops back on the warpath. Alexandros, flush with coin, was generous to a fault. He also promised his veterans and newcomers alike that, after a quick strike against Persepolis, the war against Persia would be over and they could all go home, rich beyond their wildest dreams. The soldiers believed him.

The distance from Sousa to Persepolis was not too daunting, only about 450 miles, on one of Persia's excellent royal roads. The problem was that it was mountainous terrain most of the way, reaching almost 14,000 feet at its highest points. The weather, in the meantime, was ferocious, with temperatures well below freezing, fierce winds, and copious snowfalls. The day after the men left Sousa, they were hit by a blinding blizzard that made any movement impossible. Not that movement was easy even during the lulls between storms. By footwear, attire, and temperament Greek soldiers were ill-prepared for winter campaigning. Despite Alexandros's impatience, progress was slow.

Ariobarzanes, satrap of Persis and Media, the two satrapies covering the Persian plateau, received word of Alexandros's march almost before the pan-Hellenic army had left Sousa. A professional soldier who'd fought well, albeit in vain, at Gaugamela, he'd been anticipating just such a movement. Unlike Dareios, he didn't assume Alexandros would hunker down for the winter in Sousa and he surmised, correctly, that the capital for which he was responsible, Persepolis, would be the next target. He'd spent all his time since making his escape from Gaugamela assembling as large an army of all-Persian soldiers as possible. When word came, he was ready.

Ariobarzanes marched out with 25,000 foot soldiers and 700 cavalry, leaving only a small garrison behind. His destination was the tightest chokepoint along the entire route between the two cities, a narrow, deep defile through one of the highest mountain ranges in the Zagros chain, known as the Sousian Gates. His force reached the famous gorge long before Alexandros's troops got anywhere close. Ariobarzanes set them to work immediately building a tall, stout wall across the entire width of the pass. It wasn't a long job; the chasm was barely wide enough for two chariots to pass abreast at that point. Once the wall was finished, Ariobarzanes drilled his troops and prepared to defend the Gates. He was an educated man and was familiar with the Battle of Thermopylai, where a couple of thousand Greeks, led by 300 Spartans, withstood the might of the entire Persian army for three days. He had a better position, a stronger wall, and ten times as many troops. He rubbed his hands with glee at the prospect of routing the pan-Hellenic army – and also to keep them warm in the numbing cold.

As Ariobarzanes knew, there was a second, longer but easier, route through the mountains. He doubted Alexandros was aware of this alternate route but he had a contingency plan ready, just in case. He posted scouts near the fork between the two roads with instructions to report immediately if Alexandros chose the longer route. In that case, he was ready to withdraw to the outskirts of Persepolis and halt the invaders there. Because of his interior lines, he was sure to get back to Persepolis long before Alexandros reached it. The one possibility Ariobarzanes hadn't considered was Alexandros dividing his forces. To split one's forces was a prescription for defeat.

When Alexandros learned of Ariobarzanes's seizure of the Sousian Gates, he split his forces. He sent Parmenion, with the bulk of the infantry, the Thessalian cavalry, and the baggage train on the more roundabout route, while keeping only the Companion Cavalry and the elite Silver Shields for himself. He ordered these troops to carry minimal gear for maximum speed, leaving their baggage and heavy weapons with Parmenion. And then, against the unanimous advice of his commanders, he decided to attack Ariobarzanes's wall across the Sousian Gates, counting on the element of surprise to compensate for the tactical weakness of his position.

Ariobarzanes wasn't surprised. When Alexandros's crack troops reached the wall, boulders started rolling down on their heads from both sides of the gorge, missiles rained from atop the wall as well as from every cave, crevice, and footpath above. The pale winter sky was blotted out by clouds of plunging arrows. Alexandros's best fighting men were repulsed with heavy losses. The most positive thing they accomplished was capturing one lonesome shepherd who'd somehow found himself in the middle of the fight.

Alexandros withdrew beyond missile range with his tail between his legs. It was a disastrous foray. He wasn't, however, disheartened. Immediately after making sure the dead and wounded were being properly looked after, he started planning his next attack. His first order of business was to interrogate the shepherd. Alexandros was familiar with the history of Thermopylai as well and he'd read the story all the way to the end. As every Greek boy knew, the Persians eventually prevailed at the Hot Gates when a traitor led some Persian troops on a path above and beyond the Greeks' defensive wall, allowing the Persians to take on the Spartans from the back as well as the front.

Eventually, the hapless shepherd was persuaded, by threats and promises of a king's ransom, to show Alexandros a path above and beyond Ariobarzanes's defensive wall. The reason the shepherd was reluctant to show us the path was not because of any compunction about betraying the Persians; he was simply loath to commit suicide. Unlike Alexandros, the shepherd knew that it was impossible to negotiate the path in the middle of January.

******

Dareios was seated on his throne in the Ekbatana royal palace, issuing orders as usual. The assembled commanders pretended to listen while openly snickering at everything he said. Most of the satraps had long since left Ekbatana to look after their own private militias. Bessos, satrap of Baktria, one of the few satraps still left in Ekbatana, was holding his own meeting at the other end of the audience hall, plotting Dareios's overthrow.

Suddenly, there was a commotion at the far end of the hall. A disheveled man, his clothes covered in dirt and face streaked with sweat, tried to enter while the guards posted at the door did their best to keep him out. Dareios's voice, weary with resignation, finally reached the guards. "Let him through, let him through." More out of curiosity to see what would happen next than in response to a direct order from the emperor, the guards let the man through.

The bedraggled man ran up to the throne, forgetting to prostrate himself before mounting the steps. Dareios tensed in his seat, unsure of the man's intentions, but otherwise neither he nor any of his guards made a move to stop him.

The man thrust a large leather tube at Dareios. "A message from Satrap Ariobarzanes, your majesty."

Dareios read the missive slowly and with rising consternation. After reaching the end of the letter, he read it again. He shook his head, his face crimson with anger. "That's impossible! And Ariobarzanes has disobeyed my direct order."

The outburst quieted the men in the room. They drew nearer to the throne, anxious to hear the details of the latest outrage against the dignity of the emperor. "What's he say, your majesty?"

"He says Alexandros is on the move. Supposedly marching on the royal road toward Persepolis. It's absolutely ridiculous. It's the middle of January."

"Well, the man has been known to do ridiculous things before." This from Bessos.

"But that's the least of it." Dareios was beginning to splutter. "Ariobarzanes, on his own initiative, has decided to block the royal road by building a wall across the Sousian Gates and to defend the wall by bringing most of the troops at his disposal into the Zagros Mountains."

"You must admit, your majesty, at least he's doing something to defend his satrapy." Bessos's voice was dripping with sarcasm.

Dareios stood up from his chair, towering over the assembled men, his voice ringing with rage. "He's disobeying orders. There's no chance Alexandros is on the march. And even if he were, Ariobarzanes's orders were to bring his troops here to Ekbatana, surrendering Persepolis if necessary. Instead, most of my troops under his command are going to perish of cold and disease in the Zagros Mountains. In the middle of January – imagine that! I need those troops here, for the great counteroffensive I'm going to launch against the invader this spring."

"What would be the point, your majesty? You'd just run away as soon as battle was joined."

Dareios paused, unsure he'd heard correctly. "What d'you say?"

Bessos walked up to the throne and raised himself to his full height. He was still forced to crane his neck to look at Dareios, who was a tall man, standing at the top of an elevated platform. "You heard me, your cowardly majesty."

"Seize that man!" Dareios's voice reverberated from the rafters. Nobody moved. They all just laughed. And Dareios was trapped, with no way out.

******

The plan was simple in principle. Only the execution was difficult. Alexandros left 5,000 troops, under Krateros's command, encamped in front of the wall. Their orders were to keep as many campfires burning through the night as before, so as to conceal the departure of the majority of our force, and to await Alexandros's signal. When the signal was sounded, they were to attack Ariobarzanes's men on the wall with everything they had. The rest of us set off shortly after nightfall.

Conquest of Persia

The first stage of the so-called trail led straight up a sheer rockface. There was no trail, no path, no steps, no handholds. It's possible some of those things existed in the summertime but in the dead of winter we were confronted by an almost vertical sheet of ice, with no illumination and no obvious way to scale it. We did what we could, inserting fingers into tiny cracks in the ice, trying to gain purchase for our toes on small outcroppings of rock, while hauling heavy swords at our sides and daggers clenched in our teeth.

It took the entire night for our force of 10,000 to get to the top of the cliff. I have no idea how many men we lost in the process. I personally heard several fall but in the darkness it was impossible to see and the men were under orders to maintain strict silence no matter what. Scores of men must have fallen but not one of them yelled out as they descended weightlessly to certain death. Only the occasional dull thud at the bottom of the ravine indicated another man lost. Once we reached the top, our first job was to scramble away from the edge, to increase our margin of safety and to conceal our presence from the enemy. Then we were given an hour of rest. We had no food but we drank snow that we melted in our hands and mouths.

That day we covered ten miles of treacherous, icy, invisible trails, trying not to fall and slide off the edge while also remaining out of sight and utterly silent. When night fell, we could see the campfires of the enemy far below us. We had managed to slip-slide beyond the wall. All we had to do during our second frigid night under the stars, without any food and with very little rest, was to descend close to the enemy camp and lie in wait. Fortunately, the sides of the gorge became less precipitous as we made our way beyond the wall, with an occasional stunted tree or bush to aid in our mountaineering endeavors. One unlucky contingent of our comrades was dispatched by Alexandros to circle far behind the enemy camp and climb up the hill above them on the opposite side of the gorge.

At dawn of the second day, still in total silence, we crept up to the sentries posted by Ariobarzanes and killed them. Two men were assigned to each guard, one to cut his throat and the other to catch the body before it could make a sound in the process of falling. When all the sentries were dead, we silently converged on the enemy camp, except for our reserves. Those men, left behind by Alexandros, continued to lurk in the hills above the camp and the road behind it. Then our trumpets rang out.

At the first sound, with a tremendous roar, we sprinted forward, killing as we ran. Simultaneously, Krateros and his 5,000 men clambered over the wall. The enemy, asleep in their tents, didn't know what hit them. Some tried to grab their weapons and fight back. They died where they stood. Some attempted to scramble up the hillsides, only to be cut down by the reservists we had left behind. Some attempted to surrender but we were too tired, too sleep-deprived, too hungry, too inflamed with bloodlust to take prisoners. Out of Ariobarzanes's 25,000 infantry and 700 cavalry, only eight horsemen, including Ariobarzanes himself, managed to escape the slaughter.

We resumed our march toward Persepolis the next day. We had provisions and some of us had horses but it was a nightmarish march: Howling winds, temperatures cold enough to freeze piss before it hit the ground, snowdrifts taller than a house, blinding blizzards, treacherous cliffsides. It's a miracle any of us got through but Alexandros never slackened his pace.

****

When Ariobarzanes's small group was sighted by the sentries atop the Persepolis city wall, his garrison commander, a man by the name of Tiridates, marched out to greet him, accompanied by some of his soldiers. Tiridates offered food and wine to the tired and bloody Ariobarzanes. He listened sympathetically to the tale of woe recounted by the satrap. When he had ascertained all the facts, Tiridates calmly walked up to Ariobarzanes and stabbed him to death. No one from either Ariobarzanes's small group or Tiridates's squad raised any objection. In Persia the consequences of a military defeat were usually fatal.

As soon as Tiridates returned to his barracks, he dictated a letter to Alexandros, offering to surrender the city and all it contained, without condition. This too was apparently in keeping with Persian conceptions of loyalty.

In his letter, Tiridates urged utmost speed, citing the possibility of a Persian relief force under the command of Dareios arriving in Persepolis before Alexandros could occupy the city. This was a highly unlikely exigency but perhaps Tiridates thought it possible. Certainly, having dispatched an unauthorized letter of surrender, he expected to be safer in the hands of the Macedonians than surrounded by his own soldiers.

Alexandros decided to redouble our already suicidal pace. He left all infantry behind and we, the Companion Cavalry, set off for Persepolis, literally at breakneck speed.

******

We were finally leaving the worst of the mountains behind when our progress was halted by a peculiar delegation. The first oddity were their greetings, which were in Greek. When we halted, we noticed they were all elderly men, dressed in rags, notwithstanding the harsh weather. But they definitely spoke Greek. A couple of them leaned on crutches, each missing a foot. Then we noticed some men shorter than the rest because they were missing both their feet. We realized many of them lacked one of their hands; some were missing both hands. When we took a closer look under their hoods, we saw that almost all of them were horribly disfigured, with brands burnt into their foreheads and their noses and ears hacked off.

Alexandros was shocked. "Who are you? Who did this to you?"

Their story emerged gradually. They had fought as mercenaries on the side of the Persian nobles who had rebelled against the new Emperor Artaxerxes Tritos, known as Ochos. Ochos eventually won and the nobles (including Artabazos, the father of Barsine) fled. Their Greek mercenaries, having chosen the wrong side, were killed or, if they were lucky, merely mutilated and confined to a desolate village in the foothills of the Zagros mountains.

Alexandros, outraged, promised to avenge their torments and offered to send them back to their homes in Greece, laden with gifts. The men asked for time to consider the offer. They met in assembly (there were about 800 of them) and debated. Eventually, their delegation returned and informed us that they had voted to remain where they were. "We've lived here most of our lives; we have wives and children; we've gotten used to our circumstances. If we went home, nobody would know who we were. We'd be objects of curiosity or pity or derision. We prefer to stay and die here."

Alexandros promised to send back clothes and provisions and any other supplies they might need. He also exempted them and their descendants from all taxes in perpetuity. Then, having said his goodbyes, he heeled Boukephalas into a gallop, even more anxious to get to Persepolis than before.

****

We had covered the distance from Sousa to Persepolis in record time – less than three weeks – notwithstanding the slight delay at the Sousian Gates. Tiridates met us just outside the city walls, offering bread and salt. When Alexandros learned of Ariobarzanes's demise, he placed Tiridates under arrest. He didn't approve of traitors, even when their betrayals accrued to our benefit, and he especially didn't like soldiers who murdered their commanding officers. Tiridates was never heard of again.

We entered Persepolis unopposed. The small garrison, finding itself leaderless and outnumbered, melted away. Once the walls, fortifications, and military barracks had been secured, we gathered in the market square, where Alexandros addressed us. I expected the usual admonitions to treat the residents, who had not fought against us, with respect, to pay for what we took, and to refrain from destroying what was already ours.

Alexandros made a different speech. He reminded his soldiers of the outrages inflicted on Greece by Persian troops who invaded the Greek mainland under the original Dareios. He spoke about the burning of Athens and the desecration of Greek temples by Persian troops led by Xerxes. He grew indignant at the treatment of our wounded and defenseless veterans by the current Dareios just before the Battle of Issos. He bemoaned the comrades we'd lost at the Sousian Gates. And he raged as he recalled the elderly Greek soldiers we'd encountered a few days earlier.

"These people are savage barbarians who have mutilated our soldiers, outraged our women and children, and burned down our cities. Do with them as you wish. Take from them what you will. And stay safe. Make sure they can't do any harm to you or your comrades, now or in the future. Just remember, the royal quarter, the palace, treasury, akropolis, and all the temples are mine. Leave those alone."

The soldiers got the message. They'd been kept in check in Egypt, in Babylon, in Sousa. All their pent-up frustrations, avarice, and fury were released. An orgy of killing and looting ensued. Civilians – men, women, and children – were murdered in the streets and in their homes, unless they managed to commit suicide first. Anything of value – statues, carpets, paintings, jewelry, gold, silver, ivory, precious stones – was looted. Anything too heavy to carry off was wantonly destroyed. When rival gangs of soldiers happened to enter a house simultaneously, they smashed priceless works of art into pieces, so each group could add a fragment to its collection of booty. Eventually, the soldiers ran out people to murder and houses to ransack so they turned on each other. They fought and tried to steal each other's spoils. They injured and killed one another. It was the most shameful moment in the long and storied history of the Companion Cavalry. And Alexandros simply stood aside and watched.

The magoi, including Ardumanish, the chief magos, were not harmed. They were simply captured and handed over to Alexandros. The royal palace, the treasury, and the akropolis escaped looting and destruction. The entire royal quarter remained out of reach of our marauding men.

Eventually, the looters ran out of energy, got drunk, and went to sleep. The sacking of Persepolis was finished.

****

A few days after the pillaging of Persepolis, the Silver Shields, who had fought with us at the Sousian Gates, made it to the city, dismayed to discover they'd missed out on all the plunder. Three weeks later, the bulk of our army arrived, along with the baggage train. Parmenion, upon being briefed on developments, bit his tongue.

The entire army bivouacked in tents outside the city walls. Alexandros made daily visits to the royal palace, seeing to his administrative duties and conducting regular business in the Apadana. He dressed in the height of

Persian royal fashion and strictly enforced Persian royal protocol during his audiences.

When told by his Khaldaian shamans that the signs were propitious, he had the Persian magoi brought in. He demanded that they preside over his installation as emperor of Persia. Ardumanish, displaying a good deal of courage in light of the carnage recently visited on his city, flatly refused. He explained to Alexandros that the imperial installation ceremony could only be conducted during the annual New Year's Festival, which occurred shortly after the spring equinox. Alexandros shrugged and told him he would wait. Ardumanish refrained from mentioning that there was no chance the magoi would ever acquiesce in legitimizing Alexandros's seizure of power.

Alexandros spent the rest of his time until the New Year's Festival taking stock of his newly-acquired possessions, tallying the riches in the treasury, touring the sights, and hunting in the mountains around Persepolis. The size of the imperial treasury was astonishing, even after Sousa. The tally of gold and silver alone had reached 120,000 talents when Alexandros decided we'd counted long enough. He was now wealthier than all the Greeks in the world combined. There was so much treasure, it became a logistical problem. Alexandros only wanted to keep enough coin with him to finance his immediate needs. The rest he wanted locked up in a secure location and he didn't believe Persepolis offered such a place.

Therefore, he sent out an order commandeering every available beast of burden from Sousa and Babylon. In due course, a caravan of 20,000 mules and 5,000 camels transported all this treasure to Sousa, where it was inventoried and immured in the fortress, side-by-side with all the treasure already there.

****

Having taken care of business, it was time for some pleasure, starting with the usual round of sightseeing. After much searching, we even managed to find a Greek-speaking guide for Alexandros – no mean feat, considering the small number of civilians left alive in Persepolis. He was no Indabibi, and he was scared out of his mind, but he knew his stuff. It turned out Persepolis was in many ways similar to Sousa. This was no accident. Construction of both royal palaces had been started by the first Dareios, more or less simultaneously. He used the same architects, designers, and craftsmen. The idea in both cases was to build a great royal complex and let the city develop around it. In fact, the civilian population of Persepolis was even smaller than in Sousa because Persepolis didn't exist as a city until Dareios started his building project. Sousa had been inhabited for thousands of years before the arrival of the Persians.

There were other differences between the two cities, beginning with their location. Sousa was situated in a sheltered, humid, warm valley. Persepolis was to be sited in a much colder spot high up on the wind-swept Persian plateau. In both cases, Dareios wished to build his palace on a raised platform but there were no soft, flat expanses where Persepolis was destined to arise. Everything had to be built on terraces laboriously clawed out of mountainsides. Half of the great platform on which the Persepolis palace complex stood was created by quarrying stone out of a mountain; the resulting stone was then used to create the other half of the platform. As a result, the platform backs up against a sheer rockface on one end and stands high above the surrounding terrain on the other. However, the platforms in Sousa and Persepolis cover roughly the same acreage and the buildings on both are quite similar. Another point in common between the two is that first Dareios didn't live long enough to see either one of the palaces completed. They were both finished by his grandson Artaxerxes many years after his death.

Instead of a causeway, the Persepolis platform was approached by a wide staircase clinging to the steep, high, front side of the platform, switching back and forth as it climbed to the ceremonial gatehouse, known as the Gate of All Nations. This was a large hall, built during the reign of Xerxes, whose main purpose was to advertise the extent and power of the Persian Empire. Both sides of the hall were embellished with numerous murals, bas-reliefs, and sculptures, all designed to illustrate the multi-national effort that went into building the palace complex. Above these decorations ran friezes capturing the arrival of ambassadors from all the vassal nations of the empire, each one wearing national dress and bearing gifts, and all closely controlled and supervised by the emperor's Immortals. Finally, occupying a prominent spot right at the entrance was a plaque, in three languages, informing all visitors that, "Xerxes built this," which was only partially true.

There were gates leading out of this hall toward the Apadana and toward the back of the palace. Everything about the Persepolis palace complex, including the Apadana, the Throne Room, the treasury, and king's private quarters, was larger, more lavish, and generally more over the top than even the already excessive analogous spaces at Sousa.

The biggest difference between the two cities, however, was that Persepolis was unquestionably the spiritual center of the Persian Empire. It was the location of the annual New Year's Festival, the place where Persian emperors were installed on the throne and where they were eventually buried, and the home seat of their principal deity Ahura Mazda. The only problem with Persepolis was that it was just too cold to live in during the winter, just as it was too hot to live in Sousa in the summer.

Our guide also took us to the ancient capital of Pasargadai, which was located only twenty-five miles away, and which had been the home base and burial site of Kyros, the founder of the Persian dynasty. For whatever reason, the tomb of Kyros made a deep impression on Alexandros, whereas he seemed totally disinterested in the eight or ten tombs at Persepolis, which included the tombs of the first Dareios, Xerxes, and Artaxerxes.

After all that sightseeing, it was time for some official audiences and a great many banquets. At the audiences, Alexandros continued to put on Persian attire and Persian airs, all to the great irritation of his Macedonian commanders and the covert but unmistakable contempt of the Persian priests and collaborators in attendance.

On the other hand, the never-ending round of banquets was a great success. The food was bountiful and delicious, the wine sweet and mostly undiluted, the ladies (and boys) of the night lascivious and accommodating.

And then, one evening, a truly amazing event occurred. The most famous woman in the Greek world, the Athenian hetaira Thais, showed up. She was the foremost practitioner of that uniquely Athenian profession, a woman of the world who was a great conversationalist, entertaining companion, symposion adornment, and sex worker.

She and Alexandros had met once before. Alexandros was an eighteen-year-old country bumpkin at the time. Thais was young but already famous, sophisticated, and sought-after. Alexandros, callow but preternaturally self-confident, had been sent to Athens by his father Philippos to accompany the ashes of the fallen Athenian soldiers following the decisive victory of the Macedonian army at the Battle of Chaironeia. Thais had been hired by the Athenian demagogue Demosthenes, the foremost opponent of King Philippos in Athens, to seduce the inexperienced Alexandros as part of Demosthenes's plot to co-opt the Macedonian heir apparent and turn him against his father. Thais succeeded brilliantly in her assignment. Alexandros never forgot their one-night stand. (And neither did Hephaistion, who had somehow managed to horn in on the action.) Evidently, Thais must have remembered this particular client as well.

Now, eight years later, here she was. The lapse of time had changed them both. Alexandros had become the most powerful man in the world, conqueror of the Persian Empire, and possessor of unimaginable riches. Thais had become the most successful female entrepreneur in history, the leading lady of Athens, and possessor of an immense fortune, although she was a pauper compared to Alexandros. But then, so was everybody else in the world.

When Thais entered the King's Hall that evening, all conversation stopped. None of the men, except for Alexandros, Hephaistion, and me, recognized her but she commanded instant attention. She was no longer as young and fresh as when Alexandros had first met her but she was still strikingly beautiful. Her bright red, flowing chiton displayed her physical assets to their greatest advantage and her assets were sufficient to arouse every man in the room. But what was most striking was the air of authority she carried. As soon as she stepped across the threshold, it became her room.

She headed straight for the largest couch at the far end of the hall, where Alexandros and Hephaistion reclined, well into their cups. She had eyes only for Alexandros, her smile illuminating his face. "My lord, it's been a long time."

Alexandros sprang to his feet. "Thais, is that really you?"

Hephaistion tried to join in. "I remember it like yesterday."

If Alexandros's eyes had the power to kill, Hephaistion would have been dead. Thais, on the other hand, smiled sweetly. "I'm sorry, have we met before?"

"Yes, yes, don't you remember?" Hephaistion was beside himself. "I've never forgotten. My name is Hephaistion. I'm his best friend."

Thais's smile faded a bit. "Well, it's a pleasure to meet you, Hephaistion. And, if you wouldn't mind, I could really use a favor."

"Anything, madam. Just say the word."

"Thank you, sir. I've just arrived here in Persepolis. My luggage is still sitting in the palace courtyard. Could you possibly see to it?"

Hephaistion looked a little perplexed but Alexandros continued to beam. "Yes, yes, Hephaistion. Take a couple of men and transport all the lady's possessions to the camp. Make sure the tent Dareios's family used to occupy gets erected right next to mine and is ready by the time we get back."

Before Hephaistion could utter another word, Alexandros resumed his seat on the couch and Thais scooted up next to him, taking over the spot recently vacated by the sycophant-in-chief. Soon, the amorous couple were lost to the world.

I couldn't help wondering how she'd managed to get here. The journey from Athens to Persepolis was hazardous under the best of circumstances. Now, at a time of war, traveling for months through the dead of winter, the arrival of this woman, here in a remote corner of the Persian plateau, was nothing short of miraculous. I resolved to ask her how she'd managed it, first time I got a chance to speak with her. *I wonder why she'd come and what she intends to do next.* For obvious reasons, I couldn't help but admire this woman. But, at the same time, there was something about her that set my synapses afire deep within the primal folds of my brain.

Conquest of Persia

******

In Pella, the volcanic struggle between Antipatros and Olympias continued to simmer, creeping inexorably toward its next eruption, as the former pressed repeatedly for a missive asking Alexandros to return home and the latter adamantly dug in her heels.

Sitting at her spinning wheel in the depopulated and deathly quiet gynaikonitis, trying to utilize the last of the day's remaining light, Kleopatra looked pensively at her mother, bent over her sewing. "Maybe you should write that letter to Alexandros after all."

There was no response.

"Do you think what they're saying about him could be true?" Still nothing. "That he's lost his drive; that he's spending his days in debauchery and will never return to us?"

Olympias slammed down the tunic she was mending. "No, it's not true. Don't believe everything those two tell us. They simply enjoy coming up here to torment us from time to time."

"But he hasn't come back, has he? It's been almost four years since he crossed into Asia."

"For crying out loud, he's been winning all that time. Never a loss, never even a setback. Does that sound like somebody lolling about in debauchery?"

"I know, mother, I know. But that's exactly why the country needs him back here. Our enemies are snarling on all sides and our diminished forces are commanded by that old goat, Antipatros. Imagine what we could do if our veterans came back, led by the invincible Alexandros. And besides, you and I need him. Aren't you tired of living in this prison?"

"It's not about you and me, my love." Olympias reached over and took the distaff out of her daughter's hand. "It's getting too dark to work. Go light a lamp while I brew some vegetable broth. If you want to talk about this, let's at least make ourselves a little more comfortable."

As they sipped their hot broth, sitting companionably in the gathering darkness, a strangely subdued Olympias resumed her disquisition. "As I said, it's not about you or me. First of all, it's never about us women. Our job is to support our men, to feed them, screw them, build their self-confidence, and make sure they make their way in the world. And, of course, make babies. We must be content to achieve our ends through our men. I've done it my entire life."

She savored her broth. "My son is king of Macedonia, conqueror of Asia, Phoenicia, Egypt,

Mesopotamia, and who knows what else. My son is Alexandros Aniketos. Do you think all that happened by accident?"

"I don't understand what you're driving at."

"You're right, my darling. You have no idea." Olympias waved her hand dismissively. "Never mind. Let's talk about why I will never write that letter Antipatros keeps badgering me about. The obvious reason is that I never do what some man demands of me."

"But mother, you just said …"

"You misunderstand, my love. We women have to achieve our ends through our men but that doesn't mean we have to let them govern us. On the contrary, it's our job to govern them, to induce, cajole, and inspire them. To show them the way, to get them to do our bidding. Do you see what I'm saying?"

"I think so. But in that case, how come you can't make Antipatros do your bidding and you can't get my brother to come back home to us?"

"It's complicated, my child. As far as Antipatros is concerned, I've got him just where I want him. As far as my son is concerned, I'm still trying to figure it out."

Kleopatra looked up, her countenance brightening. "You mean how best to convince him to come home?"

"No, not that." Olympias was beginning to lose patience. "I'm trying to figure out what the gods have in mind for him."

Now it was Kleopatra's turn to bristle. "How can you possible know what's in the mind of any god. For that matter, you can't even tell what the Fates have in store for either one of us." She hated it when her mother descended into the inscrutable realms of her arcane mysteries.

"How can you tell whether a storm is coming?" It was a rhetorical question; Olympias didn't wait for an answer. "You read the signs. You smell the moisture carried by the freshening wind; you watch the skirmish line of black clouds advancing over the mountain tops; you sense the temperature cooling your skin; you watch the birds swooping into their nests; you pay attention to the insects seeking shelter. You just know a storm is coming.

"Well, in the same way, if you pay attention to the signs, you can dimly discern the threads Fates are busy weaving. And if you work at it, you can communicate with the gods."

Kleopatra scoffed but her mother forged ahead undaunted. "Yeah, you laugh, but I've done it all my life. I've begged and pleaded and bartered and bribed. I've flattered and worshipped and sacrificed and sanctified. But most of all, I've observed the signs."

"And what have you seen, mother?"

"I knew, before I ever met your father, that it was my destiny to accomplish things that changed the world – even as a woman. Or perhaps especially as a woman. With the aid of my guide and protector Dionysos I would become the queen of a great and rising power and, best of all, I would bring into this world an immortal son who would grow up to shape history. And you're asking me to write a letter to that son telling him to set aside his god-given role in order to come back and relieve us of some petty inconveniences?"

Kleopatra was reduced to stunned silence. Finally, she screwed up her courage to ask the one question that had been plaguing her all along. "What does Dionysos tell you about our future, mother? What's in store for you, for Alexandros, for me?"

Olympias smiled ruefully. "I'm tired, my love, and it's getting late. Let's save that discussion for another day."

******

The New Year's Festival did not take place as scheduled two months after Alexandros arrived in Persepolis. After waiting a few days, in case there had been a mistake, Alexandros sent a handful of cavalrymen to invite the chief magos to the Apadana. To avoid any misunderstanding, the soldiers stuck around the priest's official residence while he put on his vestments and then formed a protective cordon around him as he walked to the palace grounds. The possibility of declining the invitation didn't come up.

Alexandros, already seated on the throne when the cleric was dragged into the hall and thrown down on the floor, didn't beat about the bush. "When will the imperial installation ceremony take place?"

Ardumanish rose to his feet. "The current emperor of Persia was installed six years ago. There is no reason to install him again."

"The position is currently vacant." Alexandros's voice was beginning to rise. "I control the Persian Empire by right of conquest and the favor of the gods. I wish to have my rightful position ratified according to the local customs and rituals. Will you and the other magoi organize the festival and preside over the ceremonies?"

"We will not. There is an emperor already; we cannot have two. To elaborate further, you do not control the Persian Empire; you do not possess the imperial tiara; and you have not received the mandate of Ahura Mazda.

430

You cannot command our god to comply with your wishes."

"But I can certainly have you killed and then kill your replacement and keep killing magoi until a more complaisant one turns up."

The old man shook his head. "You cannot command our god," he repeated.

"Take him away and lock him up! Then go back to his house, take away anything of value, kill anything within its walls that moves, and burn it down. I'll figure out what to do with this worm in the meantime."

******

Try as he might, Alexandros couldn't figure out what to do with Ardumanish. Conveniently, the chief magos died shortly after being placed under arrest. A number of other magoi followed in his footsteps. Alexandros considered putting on his own installation ceremony but then opted to stage a memorable banquet instead.

Hundreds of guests were invited, both Macedonian officers and collaborating Persian noblemen. The banquet took place outdoors, on the palace platform, on a warm spring night, under a gorgeous, star-filled sky. There was plenty of food, lots of undiluted wine, and sufficient concupiscent company of both genders. Thais, who was once again the chief attraction of the evening, kept mostly to Alexandros's couch and left with him at some point after midnight.

Everyone else stayed and drank past the point of stupor. They slept where they'd collapsed, on the couches, chairs, throw-rugs, and the hard, stone pavement, alone and in each other's arms. The celebrants began to stir as the stars were extinguished, one by one, at dawn.

I marveled at the fact the attendees were still able to rise after their dissolute night of gluttony, intoxication, and debauchery. *I guess their tolerance of alcohol has reached the point where it has no more effect on them than drinking water has on me.* I looked on, bemused, as they searched for a pot to piss in.

Alexandros rejoined us before noon, accompanied by Thais. The couple looked none the worse for wear. "We'll burn it down," he announced, as affectless as a butcher describing the lamb he slaughtered for last night's meal. "Get together some crews and cart all movable treasure out of here!"

"Out of the Apadana?" someone asked.

"No, out of the palace, the entire royal quarter, the treasury, the temple of Ahura Mazda, out of every building still standing in Persepolis. And do it now!"

The hungover inebriates sprang into action, recruiting assistants as they went. By dusk, all the treasure in Persepolis that hadn't been previously looted and removed and that wasn't fixed to a wall or nailed to a floor had been carted away and stored in tents in our camp. Items that couldn't be moved, such as large sculptures, murals, fancy architectural elements, were at least wrecked beyond recognition.

Alexandros returned as twilight faded into night to confirm that his orders had been carried out. Satisfied with the meticulousness of the vandalism, he beckoned for torches held by a couple of soldiers. "Here, take one and burn it down." He lit a torch and handed it off. "Burn it all down!"

"Sire, you must cast the first torch," someone said.

"Alright, I will." With his highly-trained, accurate arm he threw a torch as far as he could. It described a long, lazy arc, flying in through an open door, skidding along the floor, and coming to rest beneath some tapestries affixed to the side of the Apadana. The dry fabric promptly went up in flames. The others followed his example, tossing lit torches, whooping and hollering as they went. Soon, flames were rising above the walls in every direction.

Soldiers, unaware of the cause of the conflagration, came running up the ceremonial staircase carrying buckets of water. Alexandros stopped them. "Put that down. Here, take some torches and join in the fun."

****

I watched the royal palace burn. Even though our soldiers had removed all portable items of value, innumerable treasures remained. Marvelous marble statues melted in the flames; paintings, murals, bas-reliefs, all destroyed; elaborately carved and decorated wooden ceilings tumbled in flames to the stone floors; tapestries, rugs, priceless furniture went up in smoke. Only the stone columns and the enameled tiles survived, although many of those broke as the walls covered by them collapsed. *These buildings embodied the highest achievements of a great civilization. And now they're irretrievably gone.*

Trying to chase away these melancholy reflections, I thought of Artakama. I missed her. *Shouldn't have walked out on her. But what could I have done?*

Pensively, I stroked my chin. Within the limits imposed by the Prime Directive, I'd tried to help Barsine and her children and her sister Artakama. I told myself I'd done my best but was it really true? And was it simply disinterested compassion? Or was it lust, masquerading as benevolence? They were both extremely attractive young women and I was a young man sentenced to celibacy by the strictures of some capricious edict. Ever since I had met her, in Tyros, when she was only fourteen, I had longed, ached, for Artakama. And, once she had reached

434

womanhood, she was certainly available and more than willing. But, because of the dictates of the Prime Directive and because of the ill-starred course of my previous dalliance with Lanike, I'd scrupulously refrained from evincing any sexual interest in Artakama, causing much pain to both of us.

I thought of Aristandros. What light did his fate shed on the Prime Directive? The more I thought about it, the more certain I was that not only was Aristandros a fellow time-traveler but that he must've violated the Prime Directive as well. After all, he'd never made it back home at all.

My determination to comply with the dictates of the Prime Directive wavered. Perhaps a small, minor deviation might be acceptable, as long as I didn't stray too far beyond the banks of the river of time. *Does the fact that Aristandros didn't kill me in the end mean I didn't commit a major transgression of the Prime Directive after all? That it would be all right for me to relax my vigilance somewhat?* Even as these rationalizations crossed my mind, I knew they were nothing more than wishful thinking.

Still, there were good reasons to allow some little violations of the Prime Directive. Simply as a decent human being, I had an obligation to Artakama, Barsine, Lanike, Kleitos, and all the other people in my orbit. *How could it possibly be right and moral to subordinate the interests of all these people to some abstract injunction, to the point of letting some of them die? Where is the cutoff point for this directive? How many people is it OK to let die for the sake of this principle?*

I was treading a dangerous path, one that I'd scrupulously avoided stepping onto since the day I'd arrived in this era. The fact of the matter was that I had a lot of scientific knowledge and technological know-how that, if shared with this world, would improve the lives of countless people, perhaps an entire civilization. A civilization that had taken me in and given me advancements and important positions and that had, on the whole, treated me pretty well, especially considering I was an interloper and a rank outsider. *Shouldn't I share what I know?*

I shook my head. I knew better than that. How could I voluntarily undertake the risk of altering the entire future course of human history for the sake of what I might consider a benefit to one person in my current orbit or even a bunch of people or even this entire current civilization? Who had appointed me god? And besides, it was obvious I was just kidding myself because I wanted Artakama. I laughed. The power of the libido to subvert rational thinking was truly amazing. I realized with a start that I'd been fondling that other font of motivational thinking located at my groin. I snatched my hand away.

The bottom line was that, to a near certainty, any time traveler was almost bound to violate the Prime

Directive the moment he or she arrived in the past. Of course, if the change was slight, it didn't matter. But that was a cop-out. Even the slightest change could have unforeseen consequences way out in the future. Meantime, this was no way to live. My activities were cramped in so many ways. My military effectiveness had been severely subverted; my love life was screwed up; my ability to be of use to the society in which I lived totally undermined.

I knew I was just venting. I couldn't possibly want to have on my conscience the destruction of my home world with the attendant possibility of millions of lives never coming into existence. But millions of other lives would come instead, possibly better lives. *Should I simply ignore the Prime Directive from now on? No, I cannot play dice with the future.*

I resolved, once again, to adhere to the dictates of the Prime Directive as best I could and hope that any minor violations – ones that I had already committed and ones I was likely to commit in the years to come – would dampen out before causing too much change. One thing I knew for sure: Time travel was too risky; it put an impossible burden on any time traveler; and impermissibly gambled with the future of humanity. The hazards of time travel far outweighed the benefits. I resolved that, if I ever made it back home to my own era, I'd fight to ban time travel once and for all.

******

The fires consuming the palace inflamed the passions of Alexandros. Long before the conflagration had died down, he was ensconced in Thais's arms, enjoying her ministrations. As so often happened, he'd taken me along to stand guard outside the tent and make sure they weren't disturbed.

The sounds escaping through the flaps were different from the last time I had occupied a similar post. Missing were Barsine's endearments and little sighs of pleasure. Missing were Alexandros's forceful grunts and groans of release. Missing was the mutual enjoyment of each other's company.

Thais was the consummate professional. She knew what to touch and how to touch it. She was a master of the suggestive innuendo, the provocative giggle, the teasing flash of flesh, the lewd leer. She was adept at simulating transports of ecstasy and paroxysms of pleasure. She just wasn't able to arouse Alexandros.

The last thing I heard, before stealing quietly into the night, was Alexandros's crestfallen, plaintive protest. "This has never happened to me before."

Author's Note

Ptolemaios, known to English-speaking historians as Ptolemy I, was born circa 364 B.C.E. (the date is disputed) and died circa 282 B.C.E. He accompanied Alexander III of Macedonia, also known as Alexander the Great, on his military campaigns, rising through the ranks to become one of Alexander's leading commanders. Books One and Two of the Ptolemaios Saga covered the period 343 to 333 B.C.E. This volume carries the story forward to 330 B.C.E. It is the author's hope to recount the history of Ptolemy to his death, and beyond, in subsequent volumes.

Ptolemy left behind a memoir describing his experiences during Alexander's campaigns. Unfortunately, Ptolemy's memoir is now lost. However, a distant echo of Ptolemy's history continues to reverberate in our collective memory because it was utilized as original source material by ancient historians writing during Roman imperial times, such as Lucius Flavius Arrianus (Arrian), Quintus Curtius Rufus (Curtius), and possibly Lucius Mestrius Plutarchus (Plutarch), whose works are still extant today. Modern histories of the period covered in this book are in turn based largely on these ancient Roman accounts.

The Ptolemaios Saga is an attempt to reconstruct Ptolemy's lost memoir. Of necessity, some of the narrative, much of the characterization, and almost all of the dialogue were invented by the author. However, all the principal characters mentioned in this book were actual historical figures; the major events really happened; and the minor characters and events interpolated by the author, it is hoped, do no violence to the historical record.

The spelling of the characters' names is an accurate transliteration of their names in Greek. The spelling of place names is inconsistent. Those places that have well-known English names have retained those names. Places less well known in the English-speaking world have been given their Greek names, transliterated into the English alphabet. The author regrets the inconsistency.

Finally, although this is a true story, albeit embellished by the author, there is no historical evidence to suggest that Ptolemy I was a time traveler.

April 15, 2019

Alexander Geiger

Conquest of Persia

Additional Materials

Additional materials, including sources, illustrations, maps, battle depictions, an author's blog, and descriptions of upcoming volumes, are available at AlexanderGeiger.com.

Acknowledgements

The author wishes to express his gratitude to the following individuals who kindly read (and, in some cases, re-read) the manuscript of this novel and offered numerous helpful suggestions and corrections, ranging from fixing typographical errors to pointing out infelicitous phrasing to urging a restructuring of plotlines: Helene Geiger, Kathy McGowan, Alan Unsworth, Aviva Schwarz, David Schwarz, George Rifkin, Ken Krevitz, Joe Mazzetti, and Fran Noble. Special thanks to Scott Schmeer of Prometheus Training, LLC, for the cover design.

Any remaining mistakes are attributable solely to the obduracy of the author.

Alexander Geiger

About the Author

The author is a history buff who has always wished he could travel back in time to visit some of his favorite historical figures, places, and events. The entire Ptolemaios Saga is an account of one such extended trip, intended to witness the dawn of the Hellenistic world. The men and women who lived, strived, fought, and loved during this seminal age didn't know their ideas, exploits, and accomplishments would reverberate all the way to the present day but, boy oh boy, did they leave a mark. Imagine being able to see, through the eyes of Ptolemaios Metoikos – who was actually there – all the adventures, sights, and colorful figures of that vibrant, memorable, and thrilling era. It's the author's hope that you will enjoy the ride.

In real life, the author is a graduate of Princeton University and Cornell Law School and a retired commercial litigator. He lives with his wife in in Bucks County, PA.

Please email all comments, questions, suggestions, or requests for author interviews and appearances to Alex@AlexanderGeiger.com.